Keeper of the Jewel

Book 1 of the Highcliff Guardians

A Soul Forge Universe Story

Keeper of the Jewel by Richard H. Stephens

https://www.richardhstephens.com/

Paperback ISBN: 978-1-989257-48-7

2nd Edition August 2021

Cover design by Paradise Cover Design:

https://paradisecoverdesign.com/

Though I love and appreciate all my book fans, I have been blessed by a few special fans along the way who help carry me through times of self-doubt and inspire me to carry on.

In no particular order, *Keeper of the Jewel* is dedicated to:

Sandy Fosdick: You have supported me from day one. Not only do you order multiple copies of signed books, but you go out of your way to hand out my business cards at an international airport and shout out my name in reader forums. You have even named a dragon.

Georgiana Gheorghe: You have been with me since my debut novella. If there was a prize for liking every social media post I put out, you would win hands down. You also write amazing reviews about my books and mention me in reviews of other authors books. You, too, have named a dragon and had my books shipped to you halfway around the world.

Gary Adams: Receiving fan art doesn't happen very often for me, but you took that to a whole new level when you created a unique picture frame, included an interior picture from *Reecah's Gift*, and mailed it to me. It is hung proudly in my personal library for everyone to see.

John Cabral: I met John and his lovely wife, Angela, at a book event. Since that day, whenever I release a new book, John and Angela drive for a couple of hours to buy a signed copy from my house. I always look forward to your visits.

Lambert Cook: I met Lambert through a local author group. He is usually the first to buy a signed copy of every book I release. One day soon, I hope to be the first to buy your debut novel.

Artwork in the Highcliff Guardians

I include pieces of artwork in all my books as I believe the images provide the reader with a more intimate connection to the characters in my stories.

Interior Art in Order of Appearance

1. Queen of the Elves by Sleepy Fox Studio:

https://www.sleepyfoxstudio.net/

2. Princess Ouderling and Buddy by Covered by Nicole:

https://www.facebook.com/groups/1854783081235835/

3. Balewynd Tayn by Hannah Sternjakob:

www.hannah-sternjakob-design.com

4. Scale and Aelfwynne in Crag's Forge by Richard H. Stephens: www.richardhstephens.com

5. Jyllana Ordalf by BRoseDesignz:

brosedesignz-bookcovers.com

6. Princess Ouderling by:

https://paradisecoverdesign.com/

A little history and acknowledgements

Keeper of the Jewel is book 1 in the Highcliff Guardians Series.

With 2020 and 2021 shut down due to Covid, my research trip to the British Isles has been placed in a holding pattern. As a result, so has the series I had originally set out to write after the completion of the Banebridge Companion Novels.

With that door closed, I decided to open another, and relate the story of the rise of the clandestine society of Windwalkers—a sect of elves who devote their lives to protect a powerful source of magic. A magic so strong that should it fall into the wrong hands, it would spell the end of South March and the lands beyond.

From the foundations of the Highcliff Guardians, you, the reader, will embark upon a fantastical adventure to discover the rich history behind many of your favourite characters in the Soul Forge Universe. Learn about the events that forged the ancestry of memorable characters such as Reecah Draakvriend, Devius Misenthorpe, Sadyra Ors, Tamra Stoneheart, and so many more.

Choose your dragon and hang on tight. The Highcliff Guardians promises to be an epic flight.

None of these stories would be possible without the invaluable input of my incredible beta readers. As always, I would like to express a heartfelt thank you to: Caroline Davidson and Joshua Stephens. Your insightful input conjures the magic in my stories.

A big thank you also goes out to my cover designer, Melony Paradise. The Highcliff Guardians was originally planned as a trilogy, but through the discovery of your amazing cover, *Keeper of the Jewel* came to life. All 600 pages of it. The Highcliff Guardians is now a tetralogy. (Ya, I had to look that word up. ☺)

Lastly, I wish to give credit to the following people for naming dragons in *Keeper of the Jewel*. Thank you for enhancing my story with a touch of you.

In Order of Appearance

Victoria Jadrych, for naming the dragon, Dawnbreaker.
Misty Cummings, for naming the wyvern, Miragan.
Allyson VanDellen, for naming the dragon, Atsila.
Melissa Sharp, for naming the dragon, Zorain.

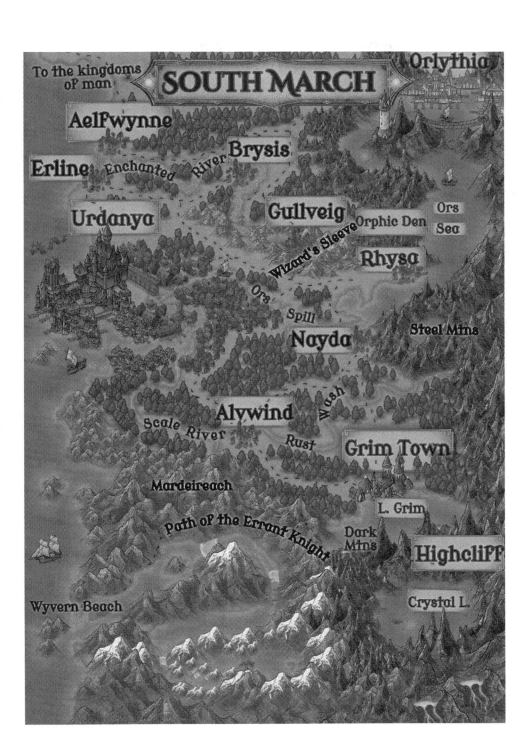

Table of Contents

Keeper of the Jewel

Tremors

"We should just lay siege to his castle and be done with it." Khae Wys held the King of the Elves' stare without blinking. It had been a long day deliberating grievances with the inhabitants of South March. A few involving a certain, rogue duke.

The king raised thin eyebrows. "Really?"

A slow smile dimpled Khae's cheeks, her pale skin and pure white hair marking her as an elf as surely as the pointed ears securing her husband's spun gold tiara in place—a diamond-shaped piece of dragon ivory resting in the centre of his forehead. "No, not really, but some days I find myself wondering how to deal with him."

Disappointment registered on the king's features.

Khae rose from the Willow Throne, cupped his gaunt face in her hands, and kissed him deeply, thinking all the while, *May the faeries keep this elf of mine.* Her precious husband would do anything for her. If she asked him to fall on the rapier hanging from his belt, he would do so without a second thought if it meant her happiness. If only her brother would be so noble and utilize his own sword in the same manner.

For some reason her brother, Orlythe Wys, had always strayed from the norm. Growing up, she never thought much of his strange ways. Named after their father, the original king of South March, Orlythe was older than Khae and her

1

Keeper of the Jewel

twin sister, Odyne, by several years. She had idolized him as
an elfling. Admired how proudly he bore the family name.
But, according to elven law, Orlythe had to be content with
the fact that when their parents' rule came to an end, it was
the eldest female who ascended the throne.

Not that she had wanted it. As far as Khae was concerned,
Orlythe was welcome to the burden of spending the rest of
his life appeasing the masses—a thankless task if ever there
was one.

Khae had been quite content during her parents' reign. As
South March's chief practitioner of nature's essence, her
duty had required her to be in tune with the subtle nuances
and shifts in the environment—seeking out and analyzing
portents that might become problematic. There weren't
many elves adept in the workings of the delicate magics to
call themselves practitioners of the art.

Her brother, on the other hand, was a natural leader. His
skill with the broader magic at his command, and indeed, his
prowess with his rapier, separated him from the regular
fighters of the land. In Khae's estimation, Orlythe's biggest
downfall was his vocal support of those who desired to bring
the dragon community to heel. He had been heard more than
once saying that a dragon rider was worth ten warriors on
horseback.

But as history recalled, that hadn't always been the case.
The attempted assassination of the great, blue dragon known
as Grimclaw had fleshed out that false supposition. Many
dragons had died at the hands of the skilled horse riders from
the north. If the elves weren't careful how they dealt with the
dragons who had remained loyal to South March, Khae
feared the majestic beasts would follow Grimclaw into the
wilderness beyond the cities of man. An act she genuinely
believed would lead to dragonkind's extinction in

2

generations to come. She could feel it in her bones. Something she sensed while communicating with the Fae. But that was a long time ago.

Khae released her husband's face.

His curious frown considered her. "You're up to something."

"Ha!" Khae spat.

Dear old Hammas was too smart for his own good. She placed a delicate finger on the tip of his nose and ran the pointer finger of her opposite hand across his clean-shaven chin.

Deep, green pools of intelligence stared back.

She smiled. That's why her parents had fostered their marriage. Although a valiant swordsman in his own right, Khae's mother had picked up on Hammas' intellect long before he had reached adulthood.

Independent to a fault, Khae had never balked at her parent's intervention. She and Hammas had been friends their whole lives. Her earliest memories as a wee elfling included Hammas and his family.

Court life had been a pleasant occasion back then, growing up oblivious to the concerns of the bigger world. If not for the rift that had developed between certain governing factions in South March regarding their attitude toward dragonkind, her life would have known nothing but happiness.

She cupped Hammas' chin again and lifted it to accept her kiss. "Nothing to trouble you, my sweet. At least not yet. Something's amiss, but I can't put my finger on it."

She smiled and tapped his nose. "Perhaps it's nothing more than a shift in the seasons."

Hammas gave her a skeptical look. "Or perhaps you're not telling me everything, hmm?"

Keeper of the Jewel

She raised her eyebrows twice in quick succession, the corner of her plush lips turning up with the mischievous smirk he loved so much. "Time will tell."

Her hand trailed off his shoulder, down his arm, and lingered for but a moment in his palm before she skipped away, tossing her voluminous hair to one side. She paused to look over the thin shoulder strap of her white dress and winked. "Or perhaps not."

Exiting the throne room, her gaze fell on a life-sized painting of a small elfling sitting on the neck of a green dragonling.

She smiled. Maybe someday.

The polished white marble floor slipped beneath her thin leather boots as Khae made her way through the royal residence of Borreraig Palace in the northern city of Orlythia. Centuries ago, her mother had commissioned dwarfs from a land northeast of South March to erect the new home for the elven monarchy. Once built, they had vacated their original seat in the coastal city of Urdanya—the carnal city ironically named after the sorceress who had nearly prevented Grimclaw's birth. If not for the intervention of the Dragon Witch, South March's skies would never have been graced with the creatures who had brought with them a higher level of consciousness to the realm.

Khae had barely been old enough to walk that fateful day a ghost ship had appeared out of the fog bearing its priceless cargo and those sworn to keep it from the wrong hands. The dragon crystal had been transported high into the virtually unreachable heights of the Dark Mountains and deposited into the Crystal Cavern at Highcliff.

Most of that long ago time was a blur, but she remembered hearing of the titanic battle that had been waged at Highcliff.

Keeper of the Jewel

Somehow, amidst the chaos, Grimclaw had been born, and the world as they had known it was forever changed.

The thought of Grimclaw and many of his followers deserting the elves took the spring out of her step. If only she had acted sooner and informed her mother what her nature's essence had told her, the outcome might have been different. She sighed. What a legacy to leave behind. To be known as the one who had allowed such a travesty to occur. It was almost too much to bear.

She turned off the main hallway and descended a long flight of marble steps that led beneath the shoreline of Ors Sea, dropping into the ground so deep that it ran below the dungeons; the access tunnel built for servants to circumvent the longer, winding route to the eastern wing of the palace above. Not many people cared to venture so deep into the earth only to have to climb up the long stairwell at the passageway's far end, but she enjoyed the cool air and silence the underground route offered.

Faerie lights winked into existence in the darkness ahead—their faint light enough to see by. Not that she needed it. Her dark vision rivalled that of a cat. Besides, she had travelled this way hundreds, if not thousands of times before. She mused that it was a wonder her passage over the years hadn't left a rut in the floor.

Two side tunnels branched off the main corridor at its midpoint, their routes dropping into caverns that delved leagues below the sea bottom. Though the enormous caverns were wondrous to behold, the side tunnels were little more than treacherous chutes formed through ancient volcanic activity. Many elves had gone to explore the deep places and were never heard from again.

A shadow passed in front of the faerie lights floating in the central junction.

Keeper of the Jewel

Khae stopped and gasped, looking around. "Who goes there?"

Muted silence answered her. So complete, it was as if she had gone deaf.

She swallowed. Never in all of her time living in Borreraig Palace had she ever felt threatened. Deep beneath the northern edge of Ors Sea, her mind raced with visions of every possible creature that might be down here with her—real or imaginary. Of things that may have crawled their way up from the bowels of the earth.

The path behind her had gone dark—the faerie lights flitting ahead to light the way. Had she been able to concentrate beyond the misgivings twisting her stomach, she might have communicated with the sprites and asked them to take her back the way she had come, but her irrational fear prevented her from doing so.

Although it was basically a straight run back to the stairwell that had brought her down, something ominous about the darkness prevented her retreat. In her heart, she knew she had to go forward.

A nervous chuckle escaped her. She shook her head. She was being silly. It was like she was an elfling again. Her imagination had gotten the better of her. Some of the faerie lights floating ahead must have winked out of existence. The lively sprites weren't blessed with a long lifespan in the mortal realm—mere moments in the life of an elf.

Swallowing her nerve, she started forward. As silly as it seemed now that she thought about it, it took everything she had to step into the space comprising the intersection of the three tunnels. Inhaling deeply, she dared to look sideways into the black abyss of the two side passageways; their ominous thoroughfares branching off at forty-five-degree angles from each other.

Keeper of the Jewel

Nothing stirred. She shook her head, embarrassed—thankful that no one was there to bear witness to her folly. Unconcerned about being overheard, she said aloud, "You see? Nothing to be worried about, silly. There's no one down here but you."

She had no sooner spoken than the faerie lights flickered and began to disappear. Starting from those farthest away, one by one, they winked out of existence—a wall of inky darkness trailing on the edge of their diminishing light.

Wild-eyed, she looked every which way at once. Heart racing, she thought she had known fear before, but the tremors shaking the floor informed her she hadn't known how absolute that terror could be.

Not easily frightened, the ground lurching beneath her feet instilled a cold dread into the depths of her soul. Oddly, she didn't fear what a physical confrontation with whatever occupied the tunnel with her meant to her own well-being. Her concern lay with the safety of those inhabiting the palace above. Her husband and daughter first and foremost.

Without having to see whatever was responsible for drastically lowering the temperature in the passageway below the sea bottom, her innate ability to sense its intent shook her to the core. Bereft of all light, her eyes were nearly as blind as her mind to what could possibly exude such a malevolent presence.

It brushed up against her—its cold touch eliciting a silent scream. And then it was past her.

She staggered against the wall and slid down its smooth surface to sit on the cold, stone floor, afraid to breathe.

She sensed, rather than saw, the outline of a wispy apparition that appeared to be cloaked in ratty, black robes. Before she could gather her wits, it ducked into one of the side tunnels and drifted away.

Keeper of the Jewel

Just as she thought it had gone, an icy tendril wiggled its way into the darkest recess of her mind—the place where she kept her most sacred fears. The angelic face of her dear, sweet daughter jumped into her thoughts.

The revelation chilled her to the bone.

The phantasm had come for Ouderling!

Keeper of the Jewel

Seventeen

Borreraig Palace was a huge complex of intertwined buildings, seemingly sprawling forever along the north shore of Ors Sea. Exacerbated by her need to find her daughter, Khae cursed the dwarfs who had spent decades erecting the palace of the elf queen. An act of solidarity fostered through the bond her parents had forged with the squat race from the distant land of Sarsen Rest.

Alarmed by her encounter beneath the earth, Khae jumped and started every time she passed a deep shadow clinging to the wondrously carved stonework that lined the myriad of hallways and foyers comprising the east wing.

Startled elves jumped out of her way as she charged headlong up broad stairways of veined white marble. Thankfully, it was still early. The only ones she passed were servants going about their business before the sun crested the Steel Mountains in the east.

If she knew Ouderling, her rambunctious daughter would be dead to the world after a late night of whatever young adults did these days. Other than the times that required them to depart the palace to tour the realm, or attend a wedding or funeral away from home, she doubted Ouderling had seen the best part of a morning in years. If Khae didn't know better, she would have sworn Ouderling were part cat the way she slept the finest part of the day away.

9

Keeper of the Jewel

She smiled inwardly despite her raging emotions. The thought of a cat reminded her of her daughter's striking eyes. Their penchant to vary in colour with her many moods was off-putting to say the least, but it served to give Ouderling away whenever she attempted to stretch the truth if questioned about her daily activities.

Khae and Hammas had been up well before dawn's first light, enjoying a stroll through the lush gardens as the early birds heralded the new day. She so enjoyed their daily ritual. Alone, together, without the incessant attendance of those entrusted with their well-being. Oh, to return to her days as a practitioner of nature's essence.

Bounding up the last flight of stairs to Ouderling's private corridor, Khae nodded absently at the attentive guard posted at the top of the steps, her face reflecting shock at the queen's rapid approach.

The guard pulled her short sword free and ran after Khae. "What is it, my queen? What's happened?"

"Has Ouderling arisen?" Khae answered, not slowing her headlong dash toward the closed, double doors at the end of the polished marble corridor.

"No, my queen. At least she hasn't come out of her room."

The absence of her daughter's handmaidens shouldn't have struck Khae as anything but normal—Ouderling was just like her. She detested anyone waiting on her. But Khae's disturbing encounter with the phantasm had thrown her sensibilities into a dervish of wild suppositions.

Khae's soft-soled boots slid on the glass-like floor as she pulled up and latched onto the knurled oak handle of one of the tall doors. The heavy wood panel flew open, almost hitting the guard who deftly slipped into the spacious chamber beyond.

Keeper of the Jewel

Muted sunlight filtered through wide, bay windows on three sides of Ouderling's vaulted bedchamber. Her room hung over the eastern parapets, affording a magnificent view of the Steel Mountains and an inland sea that stretched past Grim Ward Island—a daunting spike of land dominating the northern reaches of Ors Sea—its crags eternally lost in roiling mist.

Startled awake, the look on Ouderling's face as she sat bolt upright, holding a gossamer sheet over her bare chest, would have made Khae bend over and laugh on another day.

Ouderling's thick mane of white-blonde hair whipped back and forth, taking in the guard and her mother crashing into her bedchamber. "What the…?"

Khae and the guard ignored her, searching behind and under everything in the spacious room.

"What are you doing? He's not here!"

That got Khae's attention. Face darkening, she spun from beside the full-length mirror standing on the edge of Ouderling's private bathing pool. "Who?"

Ouderling's piercing blue eyes widened. "Um, no one."

Khae marched to Ouderling's bedside, hands on hips. "Marris?"

Ouderling's pale skin flushed. She swallowed and said so quietly, Khae barely heard, "No."

Khae's heavy breathing wasn't entirely due to her frenzied flight through the palace. She raised thin eyebrows skeptically, but her aptitude with nature's essence informed her that Ouderling was telling the truth. "It's a good thing he isn't. If I even think he might've made it past the guard at the end of the hallway," she gazed pointedly at the guard who hadn't stopped searching behind curtains and inside the various ante-rooms of Ouderling's chambers. "I'll have him skinned alive."

Keeper of the Jewel

Ouderling gaped and started to protest but Khae cut her short. "Is that understood?"

Ouderling scowled, but to her credit, kept her words to herself. She lowered her gaze to the sheets covering her long legs. "Yes, mother."

Khae's stare lingered on her daughter a while longer for good measure. Features softening, she dismissed the guard.

As soon as the door latched into place, Khae sat on the side of the bed—thankful her legs hadn't collapsed beneath her, she had been so distraught. She wrapped her arms around her reluctant teenager and held her close.

Ouderling didn't return the embrace at first, but noticing her mother's shoulders trembling, she released the sheet and hugged her back. "What is it, mother? Why are you crying?"

Khae's grip tightened.

"Mother. You're choking me," Ouderling grunted, trying to wiggle free. "Is everything okay?"

Khae sat back and held Ouderling by her bare shoulders, nodding through tears. "It is now."

Ouderling wrestled a thin sheet over her nakedness. "You look like you've seen a ghost."

Khae almost choked. "I'm just glad you're okay."

"Why wouldn't I be?"

Khae forced a smile. "I just had a fright is all. I was worried something had happened to you." She wiped at her tears. "Not to worry. Everything will be alright now. I promise."

Ouderling frowned. "Um, you're scaring me."

"Tsk, tsk. You have nothing to fear while I'm around." Khae knew her hysterical intrusion into Ouderling's bedchamber must be confusing for her young daughter. The poor way she had handled the situation had only made things worse.

Keeper of the Jewel

"What is there to fear?" A crazed look replaced Ouderling's frown. She struggled to get out from underneath the covers her mother sat on. "Is daddy okay?"

"Yes, my sweet elfling. Your father's fine."

"Then what? Geez, mother, I've never seen you like this."

"I'm sorry. Just being silly, I guess."

Ouderling's frown returned. "You guess?"

Khae smoothed the bedsheets beside Ouderling, struggling to think how she could explain her experience beneath the palace. There was obviously a logical explanation. There was no need to upset her daughter any further. "I had a premonition that something had happened to you. I had to see for myself that I was wrong."

"Mother, I'm almost twenty. I can look after myself."

Khae spit out a laugh. "Twenty? You turned seventeen less than a fortnight ago."

Ouderling gave her a serious look. "Seventeen is closer to twenty than ten. I'm not an elfling anymore."

New tears welled in Khae's eyes. As far as she was concerned, sweet, little Ouderling would always be an elfling in her eyes, no matter what age she achieved. In an elf's life, seventeen barely marked Ouderling as separated from the womb. She swallowed the fear she would always have when it came to her only living child.

The thought of Hammas scolding her for coddling Ouderling made her smile. He was right, of course, but she didn't care. Nothing could ever take the place of a mother's love for her elflings. She had lost her only son two decades earlier to the sea. She was damned if she'd let anything happen to Ouderling. As long as she drew breath, she would be forever vigilant, whether Ouderling or Hammas liked it or not.

13

Keeper of the Jewel

She could tell by how Ouderling clasped the sheet to her chest that her presence made her uncomfortable. She almost laughed out loud. Ouderling was a late bloomer. She was barely blessed with more chest than her dear husband. It was cute, but she understood. Ouderling was quickly turning into an adult.

Getting to her feet, Khae sighed and gazed longingly at her perturbed daughter. Ouderling might be growing up, but that didn't mean she had to like it.

Keeper of the Jewel

Beware, the Dragonborn Comes

Orlythe Wys brooded on the edge of his lava glass throne, gazing across the dimly lit, royal chamber in the heart of the black castle above Grim Town. Fittingly, he was the Duke of Grim, the leader of a large duchy that consisted of little more than a dirty town built upon the northern shores of Lake Grim. Though he was sure his parents had found it amusing, he failed to see the humour in his southerly appointment. Aside from Highcliff, Grim Town was as far away from the royal palace in Orlythia as one could get.

Long, black hair draped limply over slumped shoulders, his black pigmented eyes stared into the depths of a lava fountain erected next to the public entrance into the throne room. Beyond the molten rock's red glow, silhouettes of the Grim Guard stood watch outside.

The words of the stranger who had demanded an audience earlier in the day troubled him. If there was any semblance to the truth in his message, it would be irresponsible for a prince of the realm not to act on it.

A bubble formed along the slow flowing lava cascade. He waited, anticipating. To his surprise, the bubble almost slipped from view into the channel at the base of the fount, but just as he had expected, it popped and glopped tendrils of fiery liquid into the catch basin at the fount's wide base. He shook his head, marvelling at the engineering that had gone into such a wondrous creation.

Keeper of the Jewel

How his wizard had constructed it was beyond comprehension. He doubted the craftsmanship of those vile dwarfs his parents used to employ could match that of his wizard.

He grunted. His *human* wizard, Afara. Oh, how his parents would have protested had they lived to see the day a human wizard held sway in an elven court. It was a shame they hadn't been as liberal as their son when it came to accepting other races into their fold.

Had he been born human instead of elf, his conniving sister would have been banished to this drafty keep, while he ruled in the palatial comfort in Orlythia. The city ironically named after his father, and by extension, himself.

Just thinking about his self-centred sister raised his dander. Khae wasn't happy with him. Hadn't been for a long time now. Why she treated him the way she did, he had no idea. Probably driven by that weaselly husband of hers.

His mood grew darker. At the end of the day, Khae was responsible for her own attitude. Unfortunately, she was just like their parents. She hadn't approved of Afara Maral any more than they would have. Oh well. Orlythe was nobody's fool. The elven way wasn't necessarily the best way. Afara's command of the arcane was second to none in all of South March. He doubted the Dragon Mage at Highcliff could withstand Afara should they ever come to blows.

He grunted again. Perhaps that scenario would provide him with the impetus he needed to prove to Khae and the spineless king that his ideas on dragon reform should at least be given the consideration they deserved. If the bloodthirsty human population from the unstable lands to the north banded together and marched south, he doubted his people could withstand their might a second time. But, with a dragon between one's legs, the tide of battle would surely flow the other way.

His troubled thoughts reverted to his audience earlier in the day. Under normal circumstances, he would have insisted on knowing the identity of the dark stranger, but something about the man, if that indeed was what he was, had warned him against forcing the issue. The stranger had claimed to possess knowledge of a malign force stirring across the Niad Ocean and coming this way. A force that sought to steal the magic of the dragons. The stranger had warned that if this event were allowed to happen without opposition, the realm of South March would pass into legend beneath a wave of fire.

When asked why he hadn't gone to the Elf Queen, the wraith, for that was the image the visitor's presence instilled in Orlythe, had become visibly upset. Perhaps the most intriguing part of their entire conversation was that the stranger had inferred what Orlythe already knew. Queen Khae's brazen disregard of the other races would spell disaster for South March in the end.

Orlythe clenched his fists. He was tired of rotting in Castle Grim with no prospect of a future in South March. He was certain that King Hammas' soft ways had undermined the fortitude and determination of the Wys' bloodline in his sister. For as long as the simpleton king had his sister's ear, Khae was doomed to be an ineffectual leader. The elven borders would never swell, nor would the queen's hard line on keeping the other races out of South March be swayed.

The elven people deserved more. They were the superior race. As such, they were entitled to venture into the world and spread their influence. The uncivilized realms would be better off for their intervention.

Keeper of the Jewel

The stranger had implied as much, if not in so many words, but it was his parting warning that had shaken Orlythe to the core. "Beware, the Dragonborn comes."

What the wraith had meant, it hadn't bothered to elaborate, but the seriousness in which it had imparted the warning left no doubt that it believed the duke should take the dire pronouncement to heart.

Orlythe heaved a heavy breath, the weight of the circlet binding his thick hair a burden he constantly wrestled with. It was time to honour his namesake and ensure South March became the great nation it was destined to be. His father had made substantial inroads establishing a powerful base from which to set out. If Khae refused to take the elves to the next level, Orlythe Wys, son of Orlythe the Fist, and Nyxa Wys, the first Queen of the united lands of South March, would have to lead the way.

It was time to show the world how much better it would be under elven rule.

He hammered the wide arm of the throne with a fist. "Guards! Send for Afara!"

Keeper of the Jewel

Nature's Essence

Queen Khae had some serious thinking to do. Taking the long way back to the western end of the palace where she and her husband shared a suite of lavishly appointed chambers, she considered her options.

The side corridor that led to the stairwell in question passed by on her right. She shuddered. It would be a long while before she took that route again.

As soon as that thought crossed her mind, she gritted her teeth, mad at herself. It wasn't like her to shy away from a perceived danger. Making matters worse, she considered what Hammas' response would be when she told him what had happened. He'd likely roll his eyes and go on about her overactive imagination getting the best of her. Intentional or not, his reaction would make her feel silly.

And yet, she couldn't ignore what had happened. Though, thinking on it, it did seem ridiculous. In all of the tomes written about Borreraig Palace and the surrounding city of Orlythia, she couldn't recall mention of anything remotely resembling the malign presence the shadow creature had instilled in her. Unless…

She stopped and looked back to the gap in the marble wall where the small hallway ducked in. It would be irresponsible of her as Queen of the Elves to shirk her responsibility to her people should something actually live beneath the palace that might cause them harm.

Keeper of the Jewel

She smiled for the benefit of two noble elves who took the time to stop and bow their heads on their way by.

"My Queen," they said in unison before turning eyes to the ground and continuing on their way.

"Noble elves." Khae returned their nod, barely registering the distraction.

She glanced one last time at the side corridor. It would also be irresponsible to return to the junction by herself on the off chance that something evil really was moving around down there. She was the leader of South March. It wouldn't be prudent to put herself in harm's way. Not to mention how furious Hammas would become when he learned of her folly. He'd never allow her to wander alone again, and *that* was a freedom she had fought so hard to attain in her role as queen.

For some reason, thoughts of the young elf, Marris, came to mind. Ashamed of jumping to the conclusion that Ouderling would consider taking the silly boy into her bed irked her, but neither was she naïve. She only hoped that Ouderling and Marris weren't getting up to half the things she and Hammas had done at their age.

Her cheeks flushed. She had been younger still when she had had her first intimate encounter. Hypocritical as it seemed, she couldn't help herself from wanting to keep Ouderling from making the same, questionable decisions she had made during her own age of discovery.

The noble elves walked past the side corridor and passed through an archway. Watching their receding backsides, she wished, not for the first time, that she hadn't been born into the role of sovereign. She would have been content to be a nature's essence practitioner until the end of her days.

Her eyes widened. That was it. That was how she might discover the truth and alleviate her fears.

Keeper of the Jewel

It took the better part of the morning for the fast skiff she had commissioned to reach the base of the only way to access Grim Ward Island. The waters around the island were much too hazardous to attempt a direct landing. Turbulent currents and the reef infested shoreline meant that access to Grim Ward Island could only be attained by ascending the heights of an inhospitable crag on the northeastern shores of Ors Sea. Halfway up the black spire, the route traversed a suspension bridge strung thousands of feet above the Strait of Nyxa, an unnavigable stretch of water. From there it passed through the summit of the eastern tor on Grim Ward Island, exiting its far side at a higher elevation.

The two peaks comprising Grim Ward Island were known as the Fangs of the Dragon, but the most impressive stone spire was that of Grim Watch Tower—its height surpassing the taller of the fangs.

Khae refused the company of the skiff's captain, making him vow to wait for her. The last thing she wanted was for him to breathe a word of her visit to Grim Ward Island to the people who were entrusted with her well-being—especially the king!

She shrugged into her rucksack and craned her neck to observe the daunting span swaying in the air high overhead. In her youthful days she had looked forward to the challenge the trek ahead of her entailed, but age had curbed that enthusiasm. If not for the events earlier in the morning, she wouldn't dream of making the daylong journey to Grim Watch anymore.

Sighing, she started along the steep trail snaking precariously up the mountain face. Providing the trail remained relatively uncluttered by rockfall, she estimated she should reach Grim Watch before nightfall.

Keeper of the Jewel

She smiled as the seaside dropped away. Hammas would be fit to be tied when the lone guard she had left instructions with back at the palace informed the king as he sat down to the evening feast where his wife had gone.

The trek up the mountain face proved more taxing than she remembered, but her aches and pains were soon forgotten as the weathered slats of the rickety span creaked beneath her feet, two thousand feet above the Strait of Nyxa. Clinging to coarse rope handrails, she gazed at Orlythia sprawled across the water on the northern shoreline beneath the spectacular spires of Borreraig Palace, and thought of her mother.

Nyxa had been an amazing elf—her exploits involving the Dragon Witch, legendary. They had brought together a divided people and formed the kingdom of South March, much to the chagrin of the human kings in the north.

The bridge swayed more than she cared for, but thoughts of her mother gave her the courage she needed to traverse the long span. Before she knew it, she was entering the eastern face of Grim Ward's eastern summit. Calling upon pixie lights to show her the way, she followed the sparkling imps up a steep incline to the interior of the summit.

Exiting the peak's western face, a smaller, more precarious span sagged between the Fangs of the Dragon. Though she knew that a fall from either bridge would be just as fatal, it took everything she had to muster the courage to enter the second span. Broken rock and angry-looking defiles loomed far below, visible through breaks in the ever-present mist clinging to the island. The bridge was barely a quarter of the distance across than the previous one spanning the Strait of Nyxa, but it felt like it took twice as long to cross.

Reaching the western crag, its summit lost in swirling mist, she mused that Grim Ward Island had been aptly named.

Keeper of the Jewel

A steeply descending path led to an entranceway halfway up Grim Watch Tower. Why no one had thought to build a third bridge to span the gap between the top of the tower and the summit she had recently left behind, she had no idea. A sick joke on the weary traveller, perhaps.

It was late afternoon by the time she entered the tower of Grim Watch proper. Summoning faery lights to push aside the darkness within, an interminable stairwell rose into the gloom overhead—the sight sapping the last of her strength. She had a long climb ahead of her before she reached her final destination.

She sighed. If she wanted answers, it was up to her to do what was required to find them. "One step at a time, Khae. You got this."

Her voice echoed in the hollow confines of Grim Watch Tower. Try as she might, she couldn't stop herself from imagining what might lie in wait for her at the top of the tower. It wouldn't surprise her at all if she were to encounter something unworldly on Grim Ward Island. There were reasons the mystical spit of land was avoided by all but the foolish.

The fiery orange glow of sunset filtered through the few thin, rectangular slots in the side of the lofty tower. Khae stopped at one such opening and ate a quick bite. From her vantage point, the lower crags of the Steel Mountains bordered Ors Sea's west coast like a rampart. The town of Brysis, clearly visible, nestled on the southern shore of the Enchanted River where the waterway veered sharply west. Unseen, the river emptied into the Niad Ocean between the twin port cities of Aelfwynne and Erline.

A sadness gripped her. It had been a long while since she had attempted to communicate with the pixie folk. She hadn't set foot on Grim Ward Island since the time she had come seeking answers for her son's death. Ordyl's body had been plucked from the waters off the island's west coast. The faeries had been silent that day, provoking her to lash out at them. It had been a day she would never forget.

During the intervening years, she feared the faeries had abandoned her, but shortly after Ouderling was born, they had come back to her—slowly.

Her biggest worry now was what she would do if they ignored her plea. She knew she wouldn't be able to accept the rejection. It would crush her. She was tempted to turn around to avoid such a scenario.

Shrugging into her rucksack, she swallowed her apprehension and attacked the rest of the stairwell with renewed determination. There was no better place to harness her magic in all the northland. Only Highcliff possessed a stronger binding to the ethereal world around it.

Keeper of the Jewel

From Beyond the Grave

Grim Watch Tower had taken its toll on Khae's endurance by the time she reached the rotunda at the top of the spire—both mentally and physically. If there was someone, or something, waiting for her beyond the door at the head of the stairwell, she doubted she could lift a hand to fend it off.

Taking a deep breath, she pushed down on the handle of an ancient door. Nothing happened at first, but after jiggling the mechanism a couple of times, the latch disengaged and the door swung inward under the press of her weight. The eerie squeal from its hinges made her cringe.

A gust of wind ripped the door from her hands and slammed it shut. She thought about testing it to see if it would open again but decided not to—afraid she might not like what she discovered.

The chamber at the top of the tower was nothing more than a wide space between circular walls. Several stone benches littered the flagstone floor, some upright, while others were broken. Vines crept into the interior through eight evenly spaced bay windows and climbed the inside walls.

Fancy, wrought-iron filigrees had been inlaid in the arched tops of the vaulted window enclosures—their rusted surfaces dull in the muted moonlight basking the land.

Exhausted, Khae shrugged out of her rucksack and sat in the north facing enclosure—the lights of Orlythia visible through roiling mist.

Keeper of the Jewel

Not expecting much, she leaned her head back against the cold stone and closed her eyes. Opening them again, she was surprised to find the symbol of her youth fluttering before her.

Keeper of the Jewel

Holding out a palm, she stared at the beautiful image of a butterfly, unable to contain her excitement as it landed on her hand.

Her breath caught at its touch. With the sensation of being brushed by a cat's whisker, the significant faerie fluttering before her imparted a euphoric impression of the distant past. And yet, it wasn't nature's essence she was experiencing. She would have been surprised if it were because she hadn't had time to gather the strength required to invoke the latent magic. Instinctively, she knew the magical presence was something more substantial than any she could muster.

If what the signs were telling her were true, it was a message from beyond the grave. As incredulous as that notion felt, there was no doubt in her mind that Nyxa Wys was in the chamber with her. Or, at least the spirit of her dear mother—born on the wings of a being nobody in recorded history had ever been privileged to encounter before.

Barely able to find her voice, Khae whispered, "Mother?"

The faerie butterfly's wings slowly beat up and down, a faint trail of sparkling light glinting in their wake, but nothing happened.

"Mother. Why have you sought me out? I seek answers concerning your granddaughter." Khae dared cast a quick look around the open-air chamber and swallowed. "Do something, mother. Give me a sign. Let me know it's really you."

The butterfly's wings lifted and lowered, lifted and lowered. If it had been sent by her mother, it did nothing to indicate that it was anything more than an intricate grouping of faerie light.

Khae pulled her upraised palm closer to her face, trying to see the individual sprites that made up the larger form, but almost touching her nose, she couldn't differentiate the dozens of individual faeries that she knew would be required to create something so exquisite.

She raised the pointer finger of her opposite hand and attempted to touch the image. As soon as her fingertip connected with the light, she pulled her hand back. "Ouch!"

It felt as if she had been pricked by something sharp. The skin appeared untouched, but as she studied the spot that had been affected, her upraised palm began to irritate her. A deep cold gripped the nerves in her hand, causing her fingers to wrap tightly around the butterfly. Pain so intense she screamed; her fingers tightening of their own accord. White light oozed between her fingers as if she were squishing thick mud.

Her hand went so cold, it felt like it was on fire. The light spilling through her fingers increased in brightness, forcing her to look away, cringing and whimpering as the significance of what she held trapped within her fist sank in.

The light in the chamber grew so bright that her closed eyelids weren't enough to protect her from the harmful glare.

One moment she cried out in agony, and the next, it was as if the light exploded inside her head—blossoming into a fiery, white sun.

The sun pulsed three times and detonated.

In the timeless void that followed, everything went black.

Moonlight filtered through the open bay window high atop Grim Watch Tower. A soft breeze rustled small leaves clinging to the ivy-covered walls. Other than the distant crash of waves breaking on reefs far below, nothing disturbed the tranquility of the desolate chamber.

Khae's eyes fluttered open. She frowned, her mind struggling to come to terms with her surroundings. She gasped and sat up, reeling.

Keeper of the Jewel

The moon hung high in the night sky. A wispy cloud muted its brilliance as she absently glanced around the chamber in disbelief. Images and unspoken thoughts that weren't her own flitted upon the periphery of her consciousness.

Whatever the butterfly had been, she knew without a doubt it had been sent to warn her. But of what, she couldn't fathom. The message had been vague. It was like waking from a dream and trying to remember all of its parts. She knew the essence of what had been revealed to her. Its profound meaning had turned the blood in her veins cold. She had no idea what she was supposed to do—her bleary mind trying to wrap itself around who had sent the terrifying message.

Her mother's spirit had been in the chamber with her, of that she was certain, but someone had accompanied Nyxa. Someone powerful enough to transcend the boundaries of death.

The Dragon Witch!

She tried to swallow but her mouth was dry. As impossible as that revelation seemed, she was certain her premonition rang true. There had been a third spirit present. Someone who had never before revealed themselves to the world of the living.

The implication of who had facilitated her session at the top of Grim Watch Tower was staggering, but the portent could only mean one thing. Her family was in danger. Someone, or *something*, sought to destroy the royal household and dispense with the magic of the elves. As she thought on it, the message had gone deeper than that. By harnessing the magic of the elves, someone was trying to capture the magic of the dragons.

For some inexplicable reason, Khae was convinced she knew what that portent had alluded to. The glimmering wisp

Keeper of the Jewel

of a thought coalesced deep within her mind, forming a comprehensive message.

A cold wave of dread threatened to paralyze her.

She had been right to seek the counsel of the Fae.

Her brush with the phantasm had been the harbinger of Ouderling's demise.

Keeper of the Jewel

Dragonborn

𝕺𝖗𝖑𝖞𝖙𝖍𝖎𝖆 was resplendent under the midday sun as a skiff bumped into its berth on the western flank of the palace. Just as she knew he would be, Hammas stood with many of the house guard, her husband looking none too pleased.

Several vessels tied off around them. The Home Guard that had found Khae halfway through the night at the top of Grim Watch Tower appeared tired.

Upon hearing of his wife's folly at last night's supper, the king had dispatched the most capable of the Home Guard to see to her safety.

Khae was certain Hammas had wanted nothing more than to accompany them, but his presence would have been a hindrance and a distraction to those younger and more fleet of foot. Once she won free of his ministrations and lectures, she promised herself that she must see to the release of the guard who had delivered her message last night—Hammas was sure to have had him locked up for not reporting to him sooner.

A warmth drove away the midday chill. Her dear husband meant well. He took her safety seriously.

She smiled up at his handsome face, the worry lines etched there not lost on her. He appeared on the verge of a public display of outrage, but seeing her grim expression, held back and offered a hand to assist her onto the sturdy pier.

Keeper of the Jewel

"Come. Let's get you out of the cold." Hammas' tone brooked no argument. He searched out the nearest Home Guard on the dock. "You there! See that food and hot water await the queen's arrival in the royal chambers."

A hand on the small of her back, Hammas urged her toward the palace gates, issuing further orders as he went.

Khae paused to instruct a female guard standing at attention at the foot of the dock. "Fetch the princess to our chambers."

The guard dipped her head, waited until they passed her position, and scurried through a smaller door into a servant's passageway.

Noble elves approached as they strode with purpose along meandering pathways throughout the lush gardens on the inside of the gates, but stopped and left them alone at a subtle shake of the king's head.

"You know I hate when you do that," Hammas kept his voice low. "What could possibly make you visit Grim Watch at night? Alone!"

"Trust me, I didn't make the decision lightly."

He stopped walking, genuine concern on his face. Hammas was nobody's fool—he knew something grave must have occurred to make her do what she had.

His green eyes darkened. "I should suspect not. You're the queen of South March. There are people you could've appointed to do whatever it was you felt needed to be done. Not to mention people you should've taken with you."

Khae guided him off the pathway and sat him down on a curved, stone bench overlooking a shallow pond—two swans gliding across its glassy surface. She twisted on the bench to face him, unsure how much she wished to reveal. The last thing she wanted was to worry him further.

Keeper of the Jewel

She grabbed his hands. "You know that when I go to Grim Watch, I do so to consult with the essence of nature. If I were to take someone with me, my chance of achieving a good rapport would be compromised."

"Compromised or not, it's your life we're talking about." Hammas shook his head and looked away, visibly upset.

She knew he wanted nothing more than to remind her what had happened to their son all those years ago on Grim Ward Island. How Ordyl's desire to take up his mother's place and become attuned with nature had ultimately led to his death.

Though they had never found out the real reason behind what had happened that stormy night, they assumed it had had something to do with his insistence on visiting the mysterious island. Grim Watch Tower was possessed of earth magic, but that didn't mean summoning such forces could be done with impunity.

Khae and Hammas had both known Ordyl was more than a rogue magic-user. Though he had proven himself as someone to be reckoned with at an early age, his parents suspected that his overzealous ambition to become the greatest practitioner of nature in the history of South March had a direct correlation with his untimely death.

Khae sighed. Hammas deserved to know the truth. On a matter this important, holding back to spare him the worry wouldn't be fair. Ouderling was his pride and joy. He would never recover if something happened to his, 'Little Sprite.'

She put a hand on his thigh. "My sweet. You know I wouldn't have gone if I didn't believe it was important."

He turned on her, about to protest, but she put a finger on his lips. "You must listen for a change, o' mighty king. Once you hear what I have to say, you'll be glad I did what I did. Trust me."

He swallowed, waiting for her to continue.

Keeper of the Jewel

"Do you remember what the Dragon Witch said to my parents that day she disappeared?"

Hammas tilted his head, looking skyward as he searched his memory. His eyes darted back to hold her gaze. "Yes, but—"

"She mentioned a being so sinister that should it ever find the outlet it sought, the world as we know it would be forever scarred."

Hammas' dark look transformed into one of startled revelation, knowing that Khae had unearthed something they had both hoped would never come to pass.

"Aye. Rhysa never did name that creature, but she feared it had come to our side of the Niad in search of something." Khae raised her eyebrows and nodded. "This is going to sound silly at first, but please, hear me out. Yesterday morning, I passed beneath the palace like I often do on my way to the eastern side. While in the servant's passage I saw...sensed, rather, an evil presence. Fortunately, it left me alone, but something about it instilled in me an immediate fear for Ouderling. Anyway, I went straightaway to her chambers. Thankfully, she was okay."

Hammas' frown deepened with what she knew was skepticism.

"Oh, aye. I knew that'd be your reaction. That's why I didn't bother you with it. Even I thought it was silly when I took time to consider it. And yet, I know I hadn't imagined the vileness beneath the palace. Whatever was down there instilled in me a sudden fear for our daughter."

"You're jumping to conclusions, Khae. Whatever it was, I'm sure there's a logical explanation. A troll, perhaps. A creature from the earth that lost its way in the underground warrens. You likely scared it more than it scared you."

Keeper of the Jewel

She gave him a patient smile. "That's what I thought too…Hoped, in fact, but deep down, I knew it was something more. Ensuring Ouderling's safety was worth the risk of Grim Watch."

Hammas shook his head. "And your safety doesn't mean anything?"

"Of course it does, but I had to know. Call it mother's intuition or whatever you like, there's more to my brush with whatever I encountered in the passageway than either of us cares to admit."

Hammas sighed. "Well, what's done is done. I'm almost afraid to ask what you discovered on that vile island."

"That's the weirdest part of the whole thing. Usually, when I connect with nature, I talk, so to speak, with the forces involved, but this time it was different."

"How so?"

"You've seen me speak with the faeries."

Hammas nodded.

"Well, this time I was met by a different type of faerie creature—one I never expected to ever meet." She took a quick breath and said, "The Queen of the Fae, if I have the right of it. She brought with her the essence of Nyxa."

Hammas gasped. "Your mother?"

Khae dipped her chin. "Aye, though she never actually spoke. Her essence insinuated that she had enlisted the aid of the faerie queen to spirit a warning to us. To me, specifically." She paused, still not sure she had interpreted the message properly.

Hammas' incredulous look urged her on.

"Do you remember the Dragon Witch informing us that the only way forward was dependent upon our harmony with dragonkind?"

Hammas swallowed and nodded ever so slightly.

Keeper of the Jewel

"The spirit that I encountered beneath the palace is searching for someone specific."

Hammas stared hard.

Khae struggled to keep her eyes from watering. "There's more. Harmony with the dragons can only be brought about through someone special. One who possesses the ability to wield both elf magic *and* dragon magic."

Hammas' complexion noticeably paled in front of her.

"If I'm to trust the vision, and there's no reason I shouldn't, the creature the Dragon Witch had warned us about, searches for this person. Has found her, in fact."

Hammas appeared as if he were about to faint.

Khae searched their immediate vicinity to make sure they weren't being watched or overheard. She lowered her voice. "If what the essence bespoke is true, the creature is here, below the palace. It's after someone it considers dragonborn."

She swallowed, her voice dropping to a whisper. "It seeks Ouderling."

Keeper of the Jewel

For Your Own Good

Ouderling Wys looked up from where she bent over the outstretched back leg of her chestnut horse, Buddy, picking at clods of dirt impacted in the contours of his hoof. An out of breath Home Guard leaned on the door to Buddy's stall, sweat dripping from her glistening face.

The guard swiped at a long strand of hair hanging in front of her eyes. "There you are princess."

Ouderling straightened and toyed with Buddy's braided mane, arranging them to fall along his neck in perfect unison. "Where else would I be, Ryona?"

The question caught the brown-haired guard by surprise. She swallowed. "I-I wasn't trying to insinuate anything, Your Grace."

Ouderling's striking blue eyes regarded the short-haired guard. If Ryona knew her better, she would realize that blue eyes meant Ouderling was happy. "It's okay. It was a rhetorical question."

Ryona frowned. "Rhetorical, Your Grace?"

"It means...oh, never mind. What is it? You look like my mother yesterday, all worked up in a lather. Are you looking for demons as well?" Ouderling exited the stall and inspected the wide aisle running down the center of the barn. Other than one of the grooms tending to a horse tethered in the common walkway several stalls down, nobody else appeared to be in the large building. Least of which, her mother.

The lack of people in the pungent building gave her pause. Come to think on it, it had been unusually quiet around the yards since she had returned from her morning ride. Judging by the sudden gathering of troops and the boats that had sailed out to sea last night, something big had happened but she didn't know what. She shrugged it off and turned on Ryona. "If you're looking for Marris, he isn't here."

Ryona's brows came together. "No, princess. I've come to fetch you to an audience in Queen Khae's chambers."

"Ah. So, I'm to visit *her* bedchamber this morning, am I?"

"I'm sorry, princess?"

"Nothing." Ouderling smiled with the hope of alleviating the guard's tension. "Okay. Let me clean up. It won't do to appear in front of the Queen of the Elves looking and smelling like this."

Waiting until Ryona took the hint and left her alone, she searched the immediate area for her personal guard, Jyllana. She would be around here somewhere, just out of sight.

Ouderling sighed. Being a princess came with its burdens. She couldn't recall a time when she was ever on her own. There were always eyes watching, making sure nothing happened to her.

Ouderling absently noted that Ryona practically had to jog to keep up with her long strides as she marched through the palace. Where Jyllana was, was as usual, a mystery, but she knew from long experience that her personal protector wouldn't be far away. How Jyllana remained out of sight baffled her more than she cared to admit.

Since there was nothing to be done about them, she ignored both of the Home Guard and decided it best to use the servant's tunnel that dipped beneath the palace to get to her parent's chambers as quickly as possible. The sooner she bore witness to whatever lecture they had planned for her this time, the sooner she could spend time with Marris.

She appreciated the dual benefit the underground passage offered, even if it was a little spooky. It provided an efficient route through the massive palace, avoiding the winding thoroughfares that meandered all over for no apparent reason—something the builders had claimed gave the palace flair. The tunnel also gave the household nobles a way to avoid contact with the many visitors Borreraig hosted on a daily basis.

For some reason, there was more traffic in the halls this morning. Today would be a perfect day to make use of the side tunnel.

She slowed her pace and asked Ryona, "What's going on? Is the Home Guard conducting a training session?"

"No ma'am."

Ouderling almost laughed out loud. *Ma'am*! She was seventeen. Ryona was at least ten years her senior. She shook her head. The way people were expected to treat her as if she were something special never ceased to amaze her. Nor did she care for it. It made her uncomfortable.

If it was up to her, she would rather be left alone to muck the stalls; gladly trading that for her tiara and the increasing responsibility of overseeing the monotony of court life. Tight dresses and bodices cinched so snug that they left her afraid to breathe on the off chance she ripped a seam wasn't something she looked forward to. And the high expectation of manners and decorum! She felt like retching just thinking about it. These things might be fine for older nobles, but to Ouderling, nothing bored her more.

Keeper of the Jewel

She cast a glance behind her, smiling as she managed to espy Jyllana slinking down the corridor behind them, before reverting her attention on her escort. "Why is there so much activity going on?"

Ryona didn't answer right away.

"It's okay. You can tell me."

Ryona kept pace, one step behind. "I'm not at liberty to say, Your Grace."

Ouderling slowed, her stern look informing Ryona it would be in her best interest to answer the question.

"The queen visited Grim Watch Tower last night."

Ouderling stumbled. "She did what?"

Ryona shrugged. "That's all I know. She came back this morning and immediately asked for you."

As they approached the side tunnel leading to the underground shortcut, Ouderling watched guard after fully armed guard slip down the small corridor, their metal shod boots clattering on the stone steps descending into the ground. Something big *was* happening.

Ouderling rolled her eyes. There was no point taking the shortcut today.

"Do you really think that's necessary?" Hammas asked from where he sat in the comfort of a red velvet cushioned, high back chair, tracking his wife's progress back and forth across an expansive area rug in front of a softly burning fire. "And for the love of everything that's elven, would you please sit down. I'm exhausted just watching you."

Khae ignored him. She did her best thinking when her feet were moving. Without looking at him, she replied, "It's for her own good. I don't want her anywhere near Orlythia."

"Come on, Khae. I've got everyone who's anyone with a sword hunting for this thing. If it's anywhere within leagues

Keeper of the Jewel

of the palace, they'll find it. On top of that, elite squads have been dispatched to sweep the catacombs. There's no way it can harm us now."

Khae stopped and gazed out a large bay window overlooking the sea. "What's taking her so long?"

"Who knows? If she's not sleeping, she's likely on her horse."

Khae ripped her gaze from the dark blot of Grim Ward Island and spun to face him. "Oh my! She'll be an easy target on the trails. We need to—"

Hammas' eyes widened, realizing his blunder. He jumped to his feet. "Khae! Stop. You're making a big deal out of nothing. She'll be fine."

The king was a terrible liar. Khae could hear the underlying worry in his tone. He didn't believe a word he said any more than she did.

She walked over and hugged him. "It's for the best if she leaves the palace. At least until we learn more."

"But why there? Surely she'd be better off with your sister in Urdanya."

Khae stiffened in his arms. She broke free, shaking her head. "No! That's the last place I'd send her. I'm trying to protect her, not corrupt her."

Hammas raised skeptical eyebrows. "And that's not a better option than sending her to your brother?"

"Well, not to him exactly."

Hammas shook his head, his face darkening. "Just where exactly *are* you thinking?"

"Highcliff."

"Highcliff? That's still too close to your brother."

Khae shrugged, at a loss as to where else Ouderling might be safe. "Orlythe may consort with strange people from time to time but he'd never harm his niece. Besides, Highcliff might as well be on the other side of the realm from Grim Town. There's no easy route through the Dark Mountains."

"Unless one has the use of a dragon," Hammas muttered, clearly not happy with her reasoning.

"Yes, but you know full well that with Grimclaw's departure, flying dragons isn't likely going to happen anywhere outside of Highcliff anymore, is it?"

Hammas glared. "*He* may still have use of the dragons."

Khae was about to respond, but her words caught in her throat. Hammas had a good point. Orlythe had been a staunch supporter of subverting the dragons to South March's advantage. The winged leviathans travelled great distances in short amounts of time and were capable of raining fiery death from the sky.

She fought the urge to cry. "I don't know what to do, but she can't stay here."

"Why not? There's no safer place in all the world than Orlythia. My warriors are second to none, you *know* that." Hammas sighed, clearly exasperated. "Look. If it makes you feel better, just say the word and I'll give the order to seal the tunnels. We can ship our ore up from Nayda."

Khae glared. She bit back the angry retort she wanted to fling at him. Shouting unwarranted insults wouldn't help the situation no matter how strongly she felt about the danger Ouderling was in.

Hammas was the King of the Elves. When it came to fighting and strategy, he always spoke true. If his warriors couldn't protect Ouderling from harm, no one could. And yet, she knew in her heart that the cryptic message her mother's spirit had imparted intimated that Ouderling's presence must be removed from Orlythia before it was too late.

Keeper of the Jewel

Unfortunately, Hammas hadn't been privy to Nyxa's warning. No matter how she phrased her experience at Grim Watch, he would never be totally sold on her feelings about the gravity of the spirit's plea.

A rap sounded on the exterior door to the royal chambers. Before Khae or Hammas could respond, one of the tall, double doors flew open, admitting their daughter, Ouderling's face intense. Judging by the red tinge in her eyes, she wasn't happy.

"What's going on?" Ouderling stormed past Hammas, not bothering to look at him. She stopped in front of Khae, her slight torso convulsing with heavy breaths. "First you break into my room and scare me half to death, and then you visit Grim Watch?"

Not waiting for her mother to answer, she spun on her father. "And what's with all the activity below the palace? The servant's passage is full of Home Guard. I had to walk across the entire estate to get here."

Khae grabbed Ouderling by her thin wrists and pulled her onto the cushioned ledge of the bay window. "Have a seat. I have something to tell you."

Hammas cleared his throat.

"*We* have something to tell you." Khae forced the biggest smile she could muster given her mood. "Just be warned, you probably aren't going to like what you're about to hear."

Ouderling appeared poised to argue but her mother's words startled her enough to keep her quiet. The red tinge in her eyes faded to brown.

"Do you remember the histories taught to you by the Chronicler?"

Ouderling frowned. "How could I forget? Trapped in a library beneath the ground forever while all my friends were out playing."

43

Keeper of the Jewel

Khae glanced at Hammas for help.

The king walked over and said in his best authoritarian voice, "And it's a good thing you did. One day we'll be gone and you'll be the leader of South March. You'll look back and thank us."

Ouderling stared at the ornate, marble ceiling and the scenes masterfully depicted between vaulting arches, clearly unimpressed. "A lot of good that'll do me. That was centuries ago. Nothing's like that anymore."

Khae shook her head at Hammas. He wasn't helping.

The king shrugged and walked across the room. As tough as he could be with the meanest of the citizens of South March, he was a sap when it came to his 'Little Sprite.'

Frustrated, Khae returned her attention to Ouderling. She felt like slapping her. "Ya, well, you'll see. You think you know everything there is to know and then some, but I assure you, an educated mind is worth a squad of good blades any day. Does that make sense?"

Ouderling kept her attention on the ceiling, a pronounced pout twisting her chin. When Khae said no more, Ouderling sighed and looked her mother in the eye. "Sure. Whatever you say."

Khae fought hard to control her temper. She kept reminding herself Ouderling wasn't the same dear, sweet daughter she had been not too long ago. She had grown up much too fast, possessing her with the headstrong attitude that coming of age inflicted. Khae could only imagine the trouble she had put her own parents through, but that didn't make it easier to deal with Ouderling.

"Do you remember when I came to you yesterday? Afraid that you might not be okay?"

Ouderling rolled her eyes. "How could I forget? You and Jyllana invaded my privacy."

44

Keeper of the Jewel

Right, Khae thought. *That's the guard's name. Why can't I ever remember that?* "We meant well. We didn't do it to upset you. We did it because I...well I..." She struggled to find a way to express what she had experienced in a way that wouldn't shock Ouderling, and set up the next part of their conversation—the tough part.

"Just say it, mother. I'm not an elfling."

Khae bit back the retort, *Oh, you're still an elfling, believe me,* and mustered the sweetest smile she could. "Yesterday morning while walking around the palace, I encountered something, um, unusual. I had a brush with what I can only explain as a phantasm."

Ouderling's face scrunched up. "A phantasm? What the heck is that? A ghost?"

"More or less. I never really saw it."

"How do you know what it was if you never saw it?"

"You sound like your father."

They both looked at Hammas who smiled sheepishly from the other side of the chamber.

"It's hard to explain. You'll have to trust me on that one. I just know. Anyway, I got to thinking about what its appearance might mean. The best way for me to find out these things was to go to..." She raised her eyebrows for Ouderling to finish her statement.

"Grim Watch? After what happened to Ordyl? Are you crazy?"

"Pretty much. I'm sure your father will agree with you on that one."

Hammas nodded but kept silent. It was obvious he struggled with Khae's plan.

Khae chuckled nervously, not relishing the reaction she was sure to receive. "Nothing happened to me, so it's all good, but my visit wasn't wasted. You know my previous

45

role in the kingdom was as a practitioner of nature's essence. That's why I went to the tower. Aside from the Crystal Cavern at Highcliff, there's no better place than Grim Watch to attune oneself with the faerie creatures and the nuances of the ethereal plane."

Ouderling studied her dirt encrusted fingernails, uninterested.

On another day, Khae would have laughed. There was nothing delicate about their sweet, little princess. Stick her feet in knee-high, leather boots, and place a horse between her legs, and she was happy. It saddened Khae to know what lay in Ouderling's future when she and Hammas passed on to the next life. Judging by Ouderling's indifference, she doubted their headstrong daughter heard half of what she was being told.

Khae raised her voice. "I spoke with your grandmother last night."

It took a moment for the words to sink in, but Ouderling's dark eyebrows came together. "Grandma who?"

"Grandma Nyxa."

"That's...interesting," Ouderling said with hesitation.

"You're not kidding. Scared the life out of me when I realized she was in the room with me."

"And how is, grandma?"

Khae didn't miss the sarcasm in her daughter's words. Ouderling was definitely more like her father than Khae cared to admit. "We never really spoke. I know it's tough for you to understand," she included Hammas with a raised eyebrow, "but you'll just have to trust me. Grandma Nyxa came to me in a vision, warning me of an inherent danger we're facing...To be more precise, a danger *you're* facing."

Ouderling leaned back. "Me?"

Keeper of the Jewel

Khae nodded. Grabbing Ouderling's hands and hanging on tight as her daughter attempted to pull away, she swallowed. "Do you remember your lessons concerning Rhysa?"

Ouderling thought for a moment. "Yes mother. I didn't goof off *all* the time. She was the Dragon Witch."

"That's right, she was. Rhysa played an important role in bringing about the age of dragons and stabilizing the elven clans. Without her, your grandparents would never have been able to bring our people together to form the realm of South March as you know it."

Khae paused. The look on Ouderling's face spoke volumes. She was losing her daughter's attention already. She squeezed Ouderling's hands harder. "Please, my sweet elfling. This is important."

Ouderling rolled her eyes and returned a bored stare.

Khae prided herself on her ability to control her temper. It took a lot to rattle her to the point where she lashed out in anger. Her mother, Nyxa, had said on more than one occasion that she had the patience of an eroding mountain. Glaring at Ouderling's insolent face, she had difficulty believing that. She wanted to wrap her hands around Ouderling's neck and throttle her.

Biting back her rising anger, Khae struggled to keep the frustration from her voice. It was time to treat the future queen of South March like the adult she should be. "Alright, Ouderling Wys."

Ouderling frowned. She tried to pull away but it was no use. Whenever Khae spoke Ouderling's full name, it usually meant trouble.

"Aye. I'm serious. It's time you severed your proverbial strings to your father and I, and ventured into the real world on your own."

Ouderling's eyes widened.

Keeper of the Jewel

"I don't say this lightly. You've reached an age where you must put aside your elfling ways and commence the training required to become the future leader of our realm."

"What? You're throwing me out?"

Hammas sighed. "We're not *throwing* you out."

He strolled over and stood over them. "Your mother fears the Home Guard cannot protect you if you remain in Orlythia."

His voice dipped to a whisper. "It's for your own good."

Keeper of the Jewel

Troubled Eyes

Ouderling stormed from the royal chambers, the large exit door hitting the wall hard, startling a pair of guards stationed outside.

Baleful, ruby eyes held the guards speechless, daring them to react. Marble steps flew beneath her feet three at a time. She hit the second landing in a huff and pushed through a pair of noble elves who jumped to either side to avoid being run over. Half-walking and half-running to the head of the next staircase, she descended the curving flight as fast as her feet would carry her, fully aware of Jyllana's presence keeping pace on the level above—the Home Guard's red ponytail bobbing along in her wake.

The gardens behind the palace witnessed her determined march—their expansive green space running the length of the curved fortress' walls.

Ouderling didn't keep to the meandering walkways. She dipped behind an ivy wall and slipped through a tall hedgerow. Pausing on the far side of an elaborate fountain she waited until Jyllana sprinted through the gardens, the redhead turning this way and that, desperately searching where she had gone.

As soon as Jyllana disappeared from view, Ouderling dashed across the garden. Fueled by her angst, she ran all the way to the barnyard where she kept her horse. If her mother wanted to expel her from Orlythia, she may as well save the queen the bother of saying goodbye.

What hurt most of all was her father's reluctance to disagree with the ridiculous notion that she would be safer somewhere else. His elite Home Guard were stationed in Orlythia. And safe from what? A ghost? A phantasm, as her mother had called it? The delusional elf hadn't even seen it! Rounding the corner of the stable, she shook her head. Ungrateful parents.

Lost in her misery, she didn't see the brown-haired groom until he wrapped her in his arms to avoid being trampled. "Hey! Easy, Oud. What's the hurry?"

Ouderling instinctively tried to break free, but as it dawned on her who held her in his arms she stared into his face and shook her head, tears brimming. Without giving him an explanation, she wrapped her arms around his thick chest and buried her face in his neck, breathing in his musky scent. Marris always smelled of sweat and the barn.

A head taller than Ouderling, Marris returned her hug, tangling his fingers in her thick mane of long, white hair. "Shh, shh, shh."

"Why are they doing this to me? Why?"

Marris kissed the top of her head and leaned back, looking around. Cupping her face in dirty hands, he asked, "Who's doing what to you?"

Tears flowing freely, the intensity left her eyes; their colour fading to a dull brown. "Oh, Marris. I can't leave you. It's so unfair."

"Leave me? What're you talking about?" Marris led her around the side of the barn and sat her down against the wall. He crouched in front of her. "Slow down and tell me what's happened. Whoever's after you won't get at you as long as I'm here."

Keeper of the Jewel

Ouderling held his stare, appreciating the genuine concern on his unshaven face. She swallowed. "Come with me."

"Come with you? Where are you going?"

Ouderling looked away, mad at herself for crying in front of the one person in Orlythia who treated her as an ordinary adult. "Highcliff."

Marris' face screwed up. "Isn't that in the Dark Mountains? That's dragon country!"

She returned her attention on him. "Uh huh."

"But why?"

She shrugged. "You tell me. Apparently, mother thinks I'm in danger."

"In danger? From who?"

"Aye." Ouderling nodded. "That's what I'd like to know."

Marris pulled a handkerchief that had seen better days from a pouch on his belt and handed it to her.

She wiped her eyes and blew her nose before trying to hand it back to him.

Marris scrunched up his face in mock disgust. "Keep it."

Ouderling regarded the handkerchief and spit out a short laugh. Marris always knew how to make her feel better. She patted the ground beside her. "Sit with me."

Marris looked around the barnyard and sighed. He settled in beside her, grabbed her near hand, and raised it to his lips before lowering it to his thigh, firmly in his grasp. "What did the queen say to you exactly?"

"It's a long story. You have work to do."

Marris searched the yard again, his warm smile creasing his cheeks. "I'm in the company of the princess. I doubt anyone's going to say anything."

"Fair enough." Ouderling forced a smile. "I just don't want to keep you from your duties. I know how much you have to do."

Keeper of the Jewel

"Come now. You needn't worry about me. I don't mind working all night if it means I get to steal a few moments with you."

Ouderling fought back a new batch of tears. She leaned into him, pressing her cheek against his muscular shoulder. "You're so sweet."

"Of course. You mean the world to me." He put an arm over her shoulder and held her tight. "What did Queen Khae say?"

Ouderling remained quiet for a while, not wanting the moment to end, but a gentle squeeze by Marris prompted an outpouring of bitter words. She didn't bother to stop as Marris' mouth dropped open a bit more with each revelation. "Mother thought she saw a ghost in the palace yesterday. Because of that, she went to Grim Watch to speak with the faerie creatures. She said she was visited in the tower by her dead mother who insisted she heed the words of a long dead witch. Not just any witch, but the Dragon Witch. Apparently, the shade of Rhysa claims that my life is in danger."

She sat up and stared Marris in the eyes. How she loved his rugged complexion. How she loved everything about him. The one true friend she had in all the world. The one person who understood her. The fact that he was several years her senior made no difference. His company gave her an escape from the immature behavior of the noble elflings her age. The same ones her parents encouraged her to hang around. She gazed longingly into Marris' soft eyes. If only he had been born to a family of worth.

Marris' stunned look as he considered her words mirrored exactly how she felt. "I know. Crazy, isn't it?"

He jumped to his feet, pulling her up with him. "We have to get you out of here."

Keeper of the Jewel

His sudden intensity shocked her, but she nodded, remembering what she had set out to do on her way to the stables. She pulled at his hand. "Quick, grab your gear."

Marris frowned. "Huh? I can't come with you. The king would have my head."

A sinking feeling sapped her spirit. "But—?"

"But nothing. If Queen Khae says you're in danger, then you're in danger. Especially if she talked to the faeries. When's your escort leaving?"

"What are you talking about? I'm not waiting for my father's men. I came to grab Buddy and leave on my own."

"With a phantasm after you? No way!" Marris practically shouted. "I would never allow that."

Battered by conflicting emotions, Marris' attitude enraged her. "*You* won't allow it? You're nothing but a lowly groom. You can't tell me what to do. I'm a princess!"

As soon as the words left her mouth, Ouderling regretted them, but there was nothing to do about it. The hurt registered on Marris' face gutted her, preventing her from lashing out further. She stomped a petulant foot and strode toward the distant mountains in the east, her troubled eyes blurred by frustration. Even Marris was against her.

"Ouderling, wait! It's not safe for you to leave the palace grounds."

She spun on Marris who followed on her heels, and pointed a shaky finger in his face. "Don't! By the order of the princess of South March, I command you to remain where you are."

Tromping up the roadway leading out of the stable yard and into the outlying city of Orlythia, Ouderling didn't bother to acknowledge the attendant guards manning the eastern gate.

Keeper of the Jewel

Ouderling's Oasis

Marris led the contingent of Home Guard into the foothills. A vast chain, the lofty, dark peaks of the Steel Mountains stretched the length of South March's eastern border. He tried hard not to meet the livid expression of the king riding beside him. Though this was none of his doing, he felt personally responsible for letting Ouderling go off on her own. If anything were to happen to her, he would never forgive himself.

The roadway narrowed as it exited the city limits and wound into the foothills, its cobblestone surface turning into hardpacked dirt—the mountainside ahead awash in brilliant sunshine. Brooding crags interrupted the passage of wispy clouds drifting amidst their soaring bulk.

The Home Guard craned their necks to study everything in sight, searching for signs of Ouderling's passing, but Marris knew exactly where she would be hiding. Keeping pace behind the king, Jyllana rode with her head hung low.

Marris had overheard the king berate the poor elf for her part in allowing the princess to sneak away from Orlythia without an escort. He felt sorry for the redheaded Home Guard, knowing full well Ouderling was a handful at the best of times. If the headstrong princess decided she was doing something, despite the best efforts of others to dissuade her, there wasn't much Jyllana or anyone else could do to stop her.

Keeper of the Jewel

The palace and the surrounding city of Orlythia looked like an elfling's toy far below their position when Marris nodded toward a narrow cleft, the crack in the rock face on their left barely visible in the shadow of the towering cliff it cut through. "In there, Your Highness."

Marris leapt from his saddle. Holding his reins in one hand, he offered to help King Hammas dismount.

Hammas accepted the assistance, the king's eyes never leaving the fissure. "Are you certain? It doesn't look wide enough to squeeze through."

Marris nodded. "Aye, Your Highness. It's a tight fit for sure, but I've been through it many times."

The king eyed Marris for a long moment, his dark glower unsettling, before indicating that Marris should go first.

Marris handed his reins to Jyllana. "It's probably best if just the king and I go."

The captain leading the accompanying Home Guard hit the ground hard and unsheathed his rapier. He stepped between Marris and the king. "The king doesn't go anywhere without a proper escort."

Marris stepped back and bowed his head. "As you wish, my lord. I didn't mean to imply anything."

"No, captain," the king surprised everyone, "the groom is correct in his thinking. If the princess sees a horde of Home Guard coming for her, she's likely to bolt." He stepped to the edge of the path and nodded for Marris to precede him, giving him a once over as he slipped sideways into the breach. "Besides, I'm sure that this strapping young lad can deal with anything that might befall us."

The captain's face turned red but he had the sense to bow his head in acquiescence. "Of course, Your Highness."

Once through the first section of rib-scraping rock, the space barely wide enough to slip one's head through sideways, the passageway opened wide enough for a person the walk normally, provided they kept their elbows tight to their body or their arms above their head.

"That's a tight squeeze, Marris. You come here often?"

Marris swallowed. He thought of stretching the truth but decided he had better not. It wasn't the wisest idea to lie to a king. "Yes, Your Highness. I've been here many times."

"With my daughter, no doubt."

Happy the king couldn't see his shock, Marris fought to keep his voice steady—the king obviously knew of his relationship with Ouderling. "Yes, Your Highness. Other than being on the back of her horse, there's no other place in the world that Ouderling likes more."

The king harrumphed but said nothing more about it. Instead, as the tight passage rose between two daunting rock walls, he asked, "How much farther?"

"Oh, a short hike yet. We'll have to climb a rockfall to get there."

"How long have you known about this place?"

Marris looked over his shoulder. "Couple of years. This crevice wasn't here before then. The mountain must have settled."

The king's face dripped with perspiration. He glanced at the sheer walls. "I'd hate to be caught in here if it settles again."

Marris laughed nervously. "Indeed."

"And how long have you and Ouderling been an item?"

Marris stumbled. "I'm sorry, Your Highness?"

"Oh, don't be concerned. We've known about you for some time. Not much gets by the queen."

Or her spies, Marris thought. The image of Jyllana came to mind. It made sense. Ouderling's personal guard would be charged with reporting on everything the princess did, especially if it involved a *lowly groom.*

Aware that the king had stopped to rest, Marris turned and waited, uncomfortable at being alone with the monarch of South March. He didn't dare meet the king's eyes. "I'm sure it doesn't, Your Highness."

"Look. It doesn't matter to me who Ouderling chooses to associate with as long they have her best interest at heart, but there is the matter of station to be considered."

Here it comes. "Yes, Your Highness. I understand. If it pleases you, I'll refrain from further contact."

The king studied him for the longest of moments. "You would do that?"

"Aye, my liege. It's only proper."

Hammas nodded. He walked up to Marris and placed a hand on his shoulder. "Between you and me, the political and royal ethics regarding the interaction of the different walks of life is totally misguided. Sure, they have their place, but I'm not naïve. Though I appreciate the subtleties and reasons for these practices, in the grand scheme of life, I struggle to fathom how one elf's existence is fundamentally different from another. Ouderling was born to a king and queen. That makes her a princess, but, at the end of the day, she's no different than Jyllana. Fortunate circumstances…" the king smiled ruefully, "or *unfortunate*, if you listen to Ouderling, have elevated her status above most others."

Marris' brow lifted in agreement. "Aye. If I may speak candidly, Your Highness, you're right about Ouderling's perception of the world."

Hammas nodded. He removed his hand and motioned for Marris to continue toward what appeared to be a blockage in the cleft. "You seem like a good sort, Marris. If it were up to me, I would encourage Ouderling to see more of you."

Keeper of the Jewel

Marris nodded his thanks, wondering for the life of him where that left him. He hoped the king would expand on that thought, but nothing else was forthcoming. With little left to say, he turned and led King Hammas to Ouderling's oasis.

Cresting the precarious height of a thick rockfall blocking the narrow defile they travelled along, Marris reached a hand down to assist the king up the final stretch. He leaned his back against the northern wall to allow Hammas a clear view of the deep blue waters of a small lake surrounded entirely by cliffs. Great slivers of cascading water rippled the water's surface in several places, falling from heights unseen. The rockfall hemmed in the low side of the lake, preventing the waters from flowing through the fissure and down the mountain trail.

As expected, Ouderling's white mane was clearly visible hanging over the water's surface several paces along a ledge to their right.

The princess looked up as Marris came into view, her wet cheeks lifting in a sad smile, but when her eyes fell on her father, her face transformed into the cruelest of looks.

"How dare you bring him here?" Her anger echoed off the lake and the surrounding walls, as if to berate him further. "How could you?"

"Ouderling!" King Hammas rose unsteadily atop the rock pile and carefully made his way along the ledge. "Marris did the responsible thing and reported your actions. Don't blame him for your foolishness."

Marris cringed. He couldn't meet her gaze.

Ouderling didn't wait for her father to reach her. She stood up and stormed past him, almost knocking him from the ledge. She stopped at the top of the rockfall long enough to growl at Marris—eyes fiery red. "Don't ever speak to me again."

With that, she scrambled down the rockfall, slipping several times before she hit the stone path, and marched away.

Marris helped to steady the king's descent, slipping himself more than once, scraping his elbows and legs. Watching the king tromp after the distant form of Princess Ouderling—her white hair bobbing about her shoulders and back as she went—Marris fought back the tears blurring his vision. He had likely just lost the most important person in the world to him.

He swallowed his grief. If he had to do it all over again, he knew he wouldn't change a thing. Ouderling's safety meant more to him than life itself.

Keeper of the Jewel

Princess Grim

Morning couldn't come quick enough for Ouderling Wys. Sitting dejected on the edge of her bed, still wearing the clothes she had on yesterday, she awaited the fateful knock that would signal the end of her time in Orlythia.

She didn't care. Her parents obviously didn't appreciate her view on the subject that had prompted this rash decision. They couldn't wait to get her as far away from Borreraig Palace as possible. She gritted her teeth. After the way Marris had betrayed her, the farther away, the better.

She got up and stormed around her chambers, trying to decide what to wear. The trip south to Grim Town would be full of cool mornings and evenings, but the days should prove warm enough—even for someone who felt the cold as much as she did. Her father had often told her she needed to get more meat on her bones, but what did he know? A king never had to worry about what to wear. He had servants for that.

A soft rap on the chamber doors startled her. She stared at the offending doorway, hoping she could will Jyllana, or whoever stood on its far side, away.

The knock sounded again, sharper this time. A muted voice, the words barely understandable, confirmed it was her personal guard.

"Go away!"

Keeper of the Jewel

To Ouderling's consternation, the latch clicked and Jyllana eased her head into the room. "Your escort awaits at the east stables, Your Highness."

Ouderling bit back a nasty retort. It wasn't the guard's fault. Jyllana was only doing her duty. "Tell them I'll be down when I'm good and ready."

Jyllana's green eyes scanned Ouderling from head to foot. "I'm not to leave you unattended, Your Highness."

"Oh for—" Ouderling refrained from expanding on her frustration. She turned her back on Jyllana, hoping the welling tears weren't obvious. "I'm fine. I don't need someone to hold my hand."

The door closed, but something told Ouderling that Jyllana hadn't left. She looked over her shoulder and sure enough, the redhead smiled back at her with the boldness of someone who followed their orders to the letter. Jyllana had always been one to obey the chain of command, but Ouderling suspected her guard's orders came from a higher rank than even a princess of the realm.

Stripping down to her shift, Ouderling padded to the bay window overlooking the eastern grounds. A large crowd had gathered in front of Buddy's stable. It didn't take much effort to spot the focus of the crowd. Queen Khae and King Hammas conversed with a group of high-ranking nobles. She gritted her teeth. It looked as if everyone who was anyone had turned out to see her off.

Her rising angst toward each and every one of the pompous aristocrats threatened to make her scream. She was about to turn away from the window but caught sight of a wavy-haired groom holding Buddy at bay. Her fury heightened. The sight of Marris confirmed it would be better to leave Orlythia for a while.

Keeper of the Jewel

With newfound determination, she stomped to the wide alcove in the wall between her bed and her washing pool and selected a long-sleeved tunic, ankle-length breeks, and pulled on yesterday's brown riding cloak trimmed with golden filigree around its hems. Not bothering to tuck in the voluminous tunic, she slipped on her mud-covered riding boots and turned to face Jyllana.

She could only imagine how she looked, but to the guard's credit, Jyllana said nothing.

Ouderling raised her eyebrows. "Ready."

"What about your hair?"

The question gave Ouderling pause. Her waist-length hair had been a source of pride over the last decade as she grew it out, vowing never to cut it. She had always been particular at meticulously combing it out every night before going to bed, and again, first thing in the morning.

She briefly considered the large, bone comb lying atop an ornate wooden stand. "What about it? Ain't gonna matter much where I'm going."

She quickly tied a thong around the bulk of her tresses and slid her royal headdress into place to keep her hair from her eyes. Stashing the comb into a pocket in her riding cloak, she nodded.

Jyllana bowed her head and opened the chamber doors. Standing aside, the faithful guard motioned for Ouderling to go first.

Ouderling took a last look around her luxurious chambers. She doubted her uncle's accommodations would offer anything close to what she was used to. Resigning herself to the long journey ahead, she could only imagine the poor conditions that awaited her at Highcliff.

Purposely avoiding eye contact, Ouderling lifted her chin high and exited the princess' wing.

Keeper of the Jewel

"Ah, there you are." Queen Khae did her best to smile but couldn't prevent her eyes from widening as she took in her daughter's appearance. She knew at once her daughter chose to look the way she did to vex her.

Hair past her waist, bound by a simple thong in the middle of her back, Ouderling's impressive mane of white-blonde hair looked as if it hadn't seen a brush in days. At least the silly girl had the presence of mind to wear her delicate tiara of spun, white gold. It served to keep her bangs from falling in front of her red-tinged eyes. The princess' stern look informed all in attendance that she was not a happy person.

Oh well. There was nothing to do about it. Khae would rather bear the brunt of Ouderling's anger than face the reality of what might happen if the princess were allowed to remain at the palace. At least Jyllana would be with her. A friendly face during a troubling time.

Khae nodded at the calming face of the Home Guard standing a pace behind Ouderling, happy that she remembered the elf's name. "Jyllana. I charge you with the princess' safety while travelling. I trust you'll allow nothing to harm the heir to the Willow Throne."

Jyllana bowed at the waist, keeping her eyes low. "Of course, Your Highness. I'll guard her with my life."

King Hammas stepped forward to confront Jyllana. "That's good to hear, for your life will mean nothing if anything untoward should happen to her."

Jyllana stiffened but kept her eyes down. "Of course, Your Highness."

The king stood over Jyllana for a moment longer before turning to hold his arms out to Ouderling. Their daughter, the little imp, lifted her chin, but refused to meet his gaze.

Keeper of the Jewel

Hammas' 'Little Sprite' was in fine form. Khae didn't think Ouderling was going to acknowledge either one of them, but in the end, Ouderling accepted her father's embrace; albeit, with little enthusiasm.

Khae's gaze swept the stable yards, looking for something, or *someone*, out of place. Other than the groom, Marris, everyone else was either part of the Home Guard or the palace nobility.

Why the creature they feared hadn't acted sooner if it knew of Ouderling's presence in the palace, was a mystery. The only thing Khae could think of were the charms invested in the stone itself; a gift from the dwarfs of Sarsen Rest and the one known as Grimlock—the warlock who had built Grim Watch Tower many centuries ago.

Khae studied the shadows. Out here on open ground, they weren't afforded the same security. The sooner they got Ouderling's contingent moving, the better.

Khae smiled for Hammas' sake. The sight of his tear-streaked face left a lump in her throat, threatening to cause a similar reaction in her own eyes. Being the Queen of the Elves, Khae was determined not to allow that to happen. Not in public. She was the face of the nation. She must exude strength no matter what circumstances threatened the peace and prosperity of South March. She hardened her resolve. She was Nyxa's daughter.

Judging by the tears freely flowing down Ouderling's cheeks as she released Hammas, Nyxa's granddaughter wasn't as concerned about her public image—the contempt on her cheeky expression as she turned to face her, clearly evident. Nonetheless, Ouderling accepted Khae's embrace.

It was all Khae could do not to crush the breath from her insolent daughter. Her overpowering love of the person who meant more to her in all the world, with perhaps the exception of Hammas, tempered her urge to choke the life out of the impertinent, ungrateful elfling. Holding Ouderling's slight body tight, Khae hoped that someday Ouderling would realize the sacrifice her parents had made for her. Perhaps when the princess had elflings of her own would she realize how much the decision to exile her this day had broken their hearts.

No matter how hard her mother squeezed, Ouderling refused to give her the satisfaction of grunting. Although she tried hard not to return her parents' affection, she couldn't help patting her mother's back—absently noting how bony her mother had become.

As soon as she felt a lessening of pressure, Ouderling broke the embrace and stood back, not meeting anyone's gaze. Movement on her right made her look up to see Jyllana accept Buddy's reins from a dejected Marris.

Ouderling scowled deeper. He had only himself to blame. The treacherous traitor had done this to himself. Ouderling had been prepared to shirk her duty to the crown and the kingdom in order to be with him, but he obviously hadn't been willing to risk the same for her.

Marris took a step forward but the hatred emanating from her red eyes prevented him from coming any closer. His lips opened as if to say something, but she didn't give him the chance. Snatching Buddy's reins from Jyllana, Ouderling led her mount to where the sizable Home Guard escort waited on the edge of the yards.

With practised ease, Ouderling mounted Buddy in one fluid motion. Taking a moment to straighten her clothing and adjust her place in the saddle, she urged Buddy into a trot.

She didn't bother to look back. If she ever saw Orlythia again, it would be too soon.

Keeper of the Jewel

Jyllana rode her black destrier alongside Ouderling, keeping pace with the two-score mounted brigade surrounding them. Scouts galloped along the fringes whenever the terrain allowed them to spread out.

The first leg of the journey had been by ship. They had berthed in the port city of Rhysa but had remained on board. Ouderling spent the evening hours that second day out of Orlythia staring at a lower ridgeline of mountains to the west. Remembering her history lessons with the Chronicler, she tried to envision the mountain aerie of Orphic Den in the setting sun high atop a treacherous pass that led from the original home of the wizard's guild, Gullveig. Nestled along the western foothills of the Wizard's Sleeve—the old base of elven magic named after the infamous warlock who had lived during the time of the Dragon Witch. If Ouderling recalled correctly, the ancient warlock Gullveig had been referred to as Grimlock.

She snorted her derision. It seemed as if half the places in South March were named such. Grim Town. Grim Ward Island. Grim Watch Tower. Everything was grim. She swallowed. Much like her future.

The following afternoon, they put in at Nayda, the southern most city on the Ors Sea, and disembarked to follow the main roadway into the interior of South March.

The journey thus far had been tiring for all involved— sitting around the ship's deck for days on end, absorbing the monotonous roll of the choppy sea, and then navigating the circuitous forest trail through the heavily wooded interior of South March on horseback. Ouderling was glad she had spent so much time riding Buddy over the last few years. By nightfall of the first day on horseback, it became evident

Keeper of the Jewel

which of the Home Guard weren't accustomed to spending time in a saddle.

The leader of the Home Guard, Captain Gerrant Wood, a grizzled veteran who had made a name for himself while in the employ of Ouderling's grandmother, Nyxa Wys, brought the contingent to a halt on the banks of the Rust Wash and ordered camp to be set up.

In the scant rays of the next day's sunrise, Captain Gerrant's well-drilled troops had the camp fed and their provisions stowed long before the early morning twilight exposed the line of mountains in the east. They crossed the Ors Spill and rode well into the afternoon. Fording the next major river, they set up camp on the southern shore of the Rust Wash as the sun set in the west.

Well into the afternoon the following day, the fast-moving contingent from Borreraig Palace dismounted in the middle of a vast flatland devoid of trees. The short-grassed, Bascule Plains was bordered far to the west by the meandering Rust Wash, while the forested slopes of the Steel Mountains stretched across the distant, eastern horizon.

A junior officer charged with the comfort of Ouderling and her personal protector, Jyllana, walked up to where they nibbled at the scant fare they were given. He waited patiently until Ouderling acknowledged him with a raised eyebrow. Flicking a stray lock of dirty-blonde hair from in front of his eye, he asked, "Is everything to your liking, Your Highness?"

Though he asked Ouderling, his attention was directed at Jyllana.

Jyllana looked to Ouderling, but the princess ignored them both. She nodded. "Yes, Scale. Everything's fine. Thank you."

Keeper of the Jewel

"Very well, Your Highness. If there's anything you need, just ask and I'll do everything in my power to see that you have it."

When Ouderling didn't respond, Jyllana said, "Thank you, Scale. Say, is that Grim Town we can see?"

Scale followed Jyllana's gaze to the south. "Aye. Those are the spires of Castle Grim beyond the city wall."

Ouderling rolled her eyes and muttered in disgust at the fitting name of her uncle's castle, "Grim Keep."

Jyllana joined Scale in looking at her in question. "I'm sorry, Your Highness?"

Ouderling ignored Jyllana. Everything about this whole quest was grim. The world had conspired against her so quickly she hadn't had time to digest what had actually happened. It was like she was trapped in a dream—a nightmare, she corrected herself. One moment she had been lying in bed, happy and content, and within the time it had taken her heart to beat again, her whole life had fallen apart around her.

For reasons she didn't understand, her parents had disowned her—exiled her from the only home she had ever known. To make matters worse, she had fled to her secret mountain oasis to contemplate a future that involved sneaking away with Marris and living happily on their own, only to be betrayed by the horse groom. Perhaps she should refer to herself as the Princess Grim.

A slow smile split her sullen face. She liked the sound of that. The Princess Grim travelled to Grim Keep in Grim Town, to speak with her grim uncle—for truly, that was how the boor of an elf had presented himself the last few times she had seen him at court. A far cry from the cuddly bear she remembered from her youth.

A strange sound grabbed everyone's attention.

Keeper of the Jewel

Ouderling looked to the sky but the continuous thunder rising in volume wasn't coming from above. Discernable tremors shook the ground. Whatever came for them, came from every direction.

Keeper of the Jewel

The Duke of Grim

Afara Maral wasn't well-loved in Grim Town. For that matter, the human wizard wasn't appreciated anywhere in South March as far as Duke Orlythe was concerned. Being a purveyor of the mystical arts set the wizard apart from most. Combined with his heritage, it was a wonder no one had assassinated the cantankerous, pale-skinned diviner yet.

Orlythe raised his eyebrows. For all he knew, perhaps someone *had* tried. He smiled grimly, pitying anyone foolish enough to make that mistake. A horrible death awaited anyone driven to such an end.

The bony-framed wizard shuffled away from his lava fountain, a creation he liked to dote on whenever he made the odd appearance above ground; his shoulders hunched as if he carried the weight of the world upon them.

"She is close, m'lord," Afara said more snakelike than human, his sunken cheeks partially hidden beneath a black cowl.

Orlythe picked at his teeth with the tip of a black-bladed dagger and nodded. "Aye. So you've said."

Afara stared into Orlythe's eyes.

Orlythe held the man's gaze. Not many things caused the Duke of Grim discomfort but it was all he could do not to shudder under the mage's scrutiny. If he didn't know better, he'd swear the conjurer was able to delve into the depths of

Keeper of the Jewel

his mind. Orlythe swallowed despite his fortitude. Perhaps Afara could.

"You play dangerous games," Afara hissed.

Despite his profound respect for the wizard's prowess, Orlythe wasn't one to be cowed easily. It infuriated him that Afara possessed the ability to unsettle him. He gripped the arms of the lava glass throne and rose to his feet, the motion causing Afara to step back lest he get bumped aside by Orlythe's substantial girth. Orlythe's intimidating size, taller than most elves, was comprised of muscle and large bones, bolstered by extra inches that time and recent inactivity had added to his waistline.

"Khae made it clear that the princess is to travel to Highcliff," Duke Orlythe growled. "We're in no position to gainsay her directive."

Afara clasped his ringed fingers together and bowed his head. "Do not lose sight of the greater goal. You must heed the wraith if you're to step free of her shadow."

Orlythe wanted to berate Afara's impertinence, but he couldn't deny the truth of the wizard's words. Highcliff had the potential to become problematic, especially where the wraith was concerned.

"No need to worry, my mystical friend. I've taken measures to ensure that he won't get his hands on her while in my house."

Afara nodded without meeting his gaze, not bothering to ask who *he* was. "Very well, m'lord. You're aware of the consequences. I shall leave you to it."

Orlythe watched the wizard shuffle out of the throne room, the hunched man stopping momentarily to inspect the lava fountain before disappearing from sight.

Orlythe sighed. Afara knew the ways of wraiths better than anyone alive. If his wizard counselled that immediate action

71

must be taken, he would be foolish not to take heed. But there was the small matter of the Queen of the Elves. Until he was ready to seize his rightful place in the palace erected in the city that bore his name, his far-reaching plans must be held in check. Bringing the wrath of his sister down upon him before he had all his pieces in play would not go well for him *or* Afara.

As much as he respected his wizard's abilities, Afara was only one man.

No. He would have to wait.

He thought about sitting down again to resume his habitual brooding, but resisted the urge. The princess of South March would be at the gate before nightfall. There were arrangements to be made and resources to be checked. If he were to trust Afara, and by extension, the wraith, he would have to deal with his niece with the utmost of care.

"Ward the princess!" Captain Gerrant's gruff voice rose above the commotion. "Don't let any through!"

Jyllana and Scale drew their rapiers, the tapered edges of the slim blades sharpened to a gleam, and took up positions on either side of Ouderling.

Ouderling accepted Jyllana's hand. Rising to her toes, she tried to see beyond the heads of those milling around her.

A great cloud of dust billowed above the plain; hanging in the air and expanding as the noise grew louder.

"Easy," Captain Gerrant warned; his thick figure visible as he wandered through the tight circle of Home Guard around Ouderling's position. "They won't hurt you. They just want to see our horses."

Ouderling frowned at Jyllana.

Keeper of the Jewel

Jyllana shrugged and turned her gaze on the captain who came up to them. "What's happening, captain? Are we under attack?"

"Hah! If we were, we'd be dead by now."

Ouderling rolled her eyes. "That's reassuring."

Captain Gerrant straightened. He bowed his head before addressing Ouderling. "Sorry for the inconvenience, Your Highness. I should have mentioned that this might happen."

"Should have?"

The captain's cheeks reddened above his well-manicured goatee. "Aye. My apologies. It seems the Herd of Bascule has taken an interest in our horses."

"Herd of Bascule?" Ouderling pushed past the captain and into the knot of Home Guard who had their backs to her. The troops grunted at being knocked aside but as soon as they realized who was responsible, they stepped back and apologized for being in her way.

Captain Gerrant followed on her heels. "Be careful, Your Highness. The Herd of Bascule is nothing more than a band of wild horses. They wander the forests between the Rust Wash and Lake Grim. They don't normally take to being this close to people but it seems they've made an exception this day."

Ouderling stepped to the front of her ring of protectors and gasped. Wild horses of every colour and size were sniffing and nuzzling the Home Guard horses—both groups appearing like they weren't quite sure what to think of the other. Something the Chronicler had taught her years ago flitted about the periphery of her mind. One of his lessons had been about a nomadic band of horses that frequented South March's interior. The only thing she remembered about that lesson was that the Chronicler had been adamant that no one had ever broken a member of the Bascule.

Keeper of the Jewel

She located Buddy amongst the domesticated horses. Her chestnut quarter horse strained at his tethers, inquiring nostrils flaring as they brushed up against a similar looking Bascule mare.

Delighting at the innocent affection, Ouderling couldn't help but think of Marris and how deeply his actions had hurt her. Softly, she said to herself, "Don't bother, Buddy. You're only asking for heartache."

As she watched, the wild horses seemed to grow bored with their inspection and turned to trot away. Before long, they were galloping toward the eastern foothills, shaking the ground, and raising a cloud of dust in their wake. A sense of envy gripped her. If only she were as free to live her life as the Herd of Bascule.

Horns blared from the parapets announcing the imminent arrival of the second highest-ranking person in all of South March. The fact that Princess Ouderling outranked him, irked Duke Orlythe to no end. According to elven tradition over the last several centuries, the firstborn princess' place in the hierarchy of the realm was only superseded by the queen herself. Not even King Hammas had actual authority over Ouderling Wys. Fortunately for Duke Orlythe, the naïve girl was too young to realize the power at her command, though just the thought of it left a bitter taste in his mouth.

Seldom jealous of anything, Orlythe recognized the fact that he coveted Ouderling's place in the world. Oh, the things he could achieve if only their roles were reversed.

Climbing the last couple of steps of the eastern gate tower, he took a deep, calming breath. Things were happening faster than anticipated.

Keeper of the Jewel

The horns sounded again, startling the Duke of Grim. He turned a dour gaze on the captain of the Grim Guard and made a slashing motion across his neck.

The captain nodded and barked an incoherent order. The fanfare died away, echoing off the castle heights. Overhead, barely visible unless one knew where to look, two dragons patrolled the wide plains—one to the east and the other in the west.

Looking down from the outer wall, Orlythe recognized the captain of the Home Guard, Gerrant Wood. The captain had been a pompous fool for as long as Orlythe could remember. How he had managed to attain such a high rank in the queen's private guard spoke volumes as to the state of affairs in South March.

Riding behind Gerrant, Ouderling's unmistakable, thigh-length, white-blonde hair bobbed upon the flanks of a chestnut quarter horse—the princess appearing as disgusted as he was about her arrival at Grim Keep.

The head of the procession disappeared beneath the portcullis. Orlythe strode to the inside of the wide battlement in time to see Captain Gerrant lead the princess and the rest of the Home Guard into the bailey. He was surprised by how heavily the princess was guarded. As far as he knew, she would have travelled by ship to the lower end of the Ors Sea. Other than circumventing Grim Ward Island, Orlythe couldn't imagine her being in any danger at all. There was obviously more to Khae's insistence that Ouderling needed to spend time in Highcliff than just a coming-of-age education.

The presence of so many Home Guard had the potential of becoming problematic if Afara were to have any chance of completing his assignment.

Keeper of the Jewel

A cold wind blew across the ramparts. Orlythe shivered, deeper than what would normally be called for. If he were to heed the words of the wraith, the Duke of Grim would have to revisit his grand scheme of ascending the Willow Throne.

Keeper of the Jewel

Orly

Fanfare announced Princess Ouderling Wys' entrance into the crowded throne room of Grim Keep. Illuminated by hundreds of sconces mounted on dark stone walls and the arching pillars that held aloft a cobwebbed ceiling high overhead, the pall of deathly shadows draping the vast chamber exuded a surreal atmosphere of impending doom.

Keenly aware of everything that went on around her, Ouderling didn't miss the fact that Jyllana had placed her hand on the hilt of the dagger protruding from the front of her tunic as they entered the throne room. Nor did she miss the tension straightening the shoulders of the Home Guard following on her heels, or that of Captain Gerrant's unease on her left.

The captain looked across Ouderling and gave Jyllana a disapproving glare. Jyllana ignored him, keeping her hand at the ready.

Intense heat emanated from a bizarre structure comprised of lava stone just inside the throne room's main entrance. It hadn't been there the last time Ouderling had visited Castle Grim. She tried to get a better look at the fountain of flowing magma but the press of the bodies from behind kept her moving across the dank stone floor toward one of the largest elves she knew.

Orlythe Wys didn't appear any different than the last time he had attended court in Orlythia—a sour-faced boor with

77

scraggly, black hair held in place by a golden circlet denoting his station. Long, black sleeves full of folds, draped her uncle's arms, setting the stage for the hairiest of hands.

The elf regarded her with sinister, black eyes on either side of a prominent, angular nose. Starkly different in appearance than most elves, his thick mustache and unruly beard resting on his thick upper chest set him apart from the usual, refined demeanour of elven heritage. Taking a deep breath to steady her nerves, Ouderling thought the Duke of Grim aptly named.

Captain Gerrant brought the procession to a halt before a pair of elven guards larger than Orlythe. The Grim Guard stood stiffly at the base of two broad steps fronting the throne podium. The way they held their long-bladed halberds gave Ouderling the impression that the weapons were anything but ornamental.

Gerrant and Jyllana took a knee, their eyes lowered.

"Duke Orlythe. By order of Khae Wys, Queen of the Elves, I deliver into your care the future heir of South March, Princess Ouderling," Captain Gerrant said with the utmost respect.

Orlythe yawned and raised his eyebrows at Ouderling. "Welcome to Grim Keep. I trust your journey was uneventful. Had I known you were close, I would've sent an honour guard to provide an escort befitting a member of the royal house."

Ouderling forced a smile. She knew how court politics worked. Her uncle lied through that mangy beard of his. She dipped her head in thanks, mustering the mental fortitude required to hold his intense gaze. "I thank you, Duke of Grim. You had no way of knowing the time of our arrival." She motioned Captain Gerrant to his feet and said, "Though a small force awaiting our imminent arrival on the southern

Keeper of the Jewel

banks of the Rust Wash would have been appreciated, it was not required. Our good captain has seen us safely delivered into your capable hands."

"Of course, princess. And what do we owe the honour of your presence in the southland?"

Ouderling frowned. "Have the ravens not arrived?"

Orlythe raised bushy eyebrows and sat back in his lava glass throne. "They have indeed, but your mother's message was rather vague. Something about you visiting the resident wizard at Highcliff to begin your training."

The sarcastic lilt in her uncle's voice caused her to react stronger than usual given the formal decorum expected while addressing the Duke of Grim before the nobility of the region. "That would be Queen Khae, to you, duke."

"Of course. Of course," the duke sputtered. "I forget myself holed up in this…" He made a point of scanning the entire chamber. "This inhospitable keep that is unbefitting one of my station. I'm sure you agree."

As much as Ouderling despised diplomacy and everything that comprised court life, she had been around it for a long time. She knew how to carry herself. "Grim Keep is a valuable asset to the crown. Its strategic location wards Highcliff, and that provides the crown peace of mind knowing that our sacred grounds are well protected. Aside from Queen Khae herself, there isn't anything more vital to the security of our people than the existence of Highcliff."

Orlythe's voice belied his darkening eyes. "I assure you, princess, I take my duty seriously. I live only to serve our people and the queen."

"The queen will be pleased to hear that."

Had no one else been present in the throne room, Ouderling had no doubt that her uncle would have thrown her over his knee and spanked her for the impertinent way she spoke to him in front of his people, but with the chamber full of curious onlookers, the Duke of Grim knew his place. The fact that Captain Gerrant and a brigade of the Queen's finest fighters accompanied her, likely went a long way to temper the duke's reaction. Though, if Orlythe's eyes were capable, they would have slain her with daggers of contempt.

The duke clasped bejeweled fingers against his bearded chin, the priceless gemstones adorning each digit twinkling whenever their facets caught the rushlights burning around the podium. "If you'd be so kind, princess, explain exactly what the queen requires of her devoted vassal. And please," he directed his gaze to Jyllana, "your slave need not kneel all day."

Her uncle was purposely trying to provoke her. South March prided itself for its dim view on forced servitude. A tenet Ouderling doubted her uncle adhered to. "Jyllana is not my slave."

"Of course, *princess*. My apologies."

Ouderling bristled at the sarcasm in Orlythe's voice. She nudged Jyllana with a knee. "Get up."

Waiting for Jyllana to stand tall, Ouderling turned her attention on her uncle. "With regard to my *presence* in your humble fortress, I'm here against my will at the queen's request. Apparently, my parents believe I'm no longer safe at the palace."

"Is that so?" Orlythe sat forward and raised an eyebrow. "Do go on."

She couldn't tell whether he mocked her. Holding her chin high, she humoured him. "Mother claims to have encountered a spirit beneath Borreraig. One intent on causing me harm. She visited Grim Watch Tower and called forth the essence of her mother."

Keeper of the Jewel

"Nyxa?" Orlythe's brows came together momentarily, considering Ouderling's words. His face widened with comprehension. "Khae's been speaking to the faeries again?"

Ouderling swallowed and nodded, her earlier bravado all but dissipated as they fleshed out the truth of the matter.

"That sounds just like your mother. Always talking to things no one else can see." He nodded. "Aye. She's done that for as long as I can recall. Holding seances with creatures from a world quite different than our own, if you believe half the things she tells you when she gets in one of her moods."

Ouderling realized she was nodding along with her uncle's words. She didn't imagine many knew Khae better than her brother. Everything he said sounded remarkably similar to her own opinions regarding her mother's premonitions.

"Don't get me wrong." Orlythe's placating voice sounded odd coming from him. "Khae's an intelligent elf. The smartest one I've had the pleasure of knowing, but…," he raised his eyebrows and grimaced, commiserating with Ouderling, "she has a penchant for blabbering nonsensically, if you know what I mean?"

Did she ever. Her uncle painted her mother exactly the way she would describe her. Commonsensical to a fault, but subject to moments of absurdity.

Orlythe motioned with his chin at an unassuming elf standing in the shadows as he spoke. "Rest assured, princess. No harm will befall you under my roof. Of that, you can be certain."

Taller than average, the elf approached the dais and stopped beside Captain Gerrant, his beady eyes never leaving the ground before his feet. Devoid of the golden-hued armour of the elves bearing the polearms, the elf's clothes bore the same colours and markings of the uniformed troops of Grim Keep: studded, black leather tunic and black leather pants.

"Master Chamberlain Bayl will see to your comfort. You're welcome to stay as long as you like, but I'm guessing you're itching to continue on to Highcliff."

Orlythe's broad smile appeared out of place, but Ouderling didn't sense any malice behind it. "Thank you, Duke Grim."

Orlythe spread his hands in supplication. "Please, princess. In my court, you may call me Uncle Orly. Just like when you did when you were a wee lass, hmm?"

Ouderling smiled despite her mood. She had fond memories of her uncle as an elfling. He had always allowed her to sit on his lap at the head table during the high feasts even though elflings were not permitted. He even let her sip from his goblet when no one was looking. Had the king or queen found out, they would have been incensed. Feeding the future queen of South March alcohol at such a tender age would have been ample reason to expel him from court.

She bowed her head. Not prepared to revert to her elfling name for him, she met him halfway. "Thank you, uncle. Your gracious hospitality is welcomed by all. We don't wish to inconvenience your staff any more than necessary. My escort will re-provision tomorrow and be ready to leave for Highcliff the morning after if that suits my lord?"

Orlythe's face softened to a semblance of the cuddly elf she remembered from years gone by. "Of course, princess. We're humbled by your presence and are forever at your service. Now, let us speak on the arrangements that have been made."

Keeper of the Jewel

Strange Sensation

Jyllana paced back and forth in the cold tower chamber the Duke of Grim had set aside for Ouderling. The Home Guard were none too pleased with Orlythe's insistence that the entire contingent from Borreraig Palace was to remain within the confines of the southeast corner tower for the duration of their stay. Not even Captain Gerrant or the princess were allowed to wander Grim Keep without a Grim Guard escort. The duke had mentioned something about extensive renovations being undertaken in the drafty castle, but Ouderling hadn't noticed anything remotely resembling such an enterprise.

Sitting on a stone ledge fronting a narrow bay window, Ouderling stared through the iron-latticed glass at the white-capped waters of Lake Grim—the body of water so expansive it appeared as large as Ors Sea. Far across the waves to the south, black mountain peaks, taller than any in the land, rose stark against the late afternoon sky. Little snow stuck to the lofty crags; the Dark Mountains notorious for its perpetually erupting volcanoes.

She sensed Jyllana stop beside her, looking over her shoulder at the distant heights. Her personal guard had been given implicit instructions by Captain Gerrant that under no circumstances was she to lose sight of Ouderling while at Grim Keep. It had seemed like an odd request as they were

Keeper of the Jewel

under the protection of the queen's brother, but the captain of the Home Guard had been adamant.

"Quite a sight, that," Jyllana said. "Captain Gerrant claims that if the prevailing winds weren't funneled eastward by the contour of the land, the region surrounding Grim Keep would be buried under black ash all the way to Alywind. I can't imagine what it'll be like at Highcliff."

Ouderling kept her attention on the window. They would find out soon enough. She leaned forward and pressed her face against the dirty glass, trying to see the base of the ramparts as waves broke against the brooding stone of Grim Keep, but other than foam spewed from their impact, she couldn't make out anything notable.

She sighed. "How do you suppose we get there?"

"To Highcliff?" Jyllana blinked. "I'm not entirely sure. I've heard the journey involves a long trek through the heart of a mountain."

"Great. That's just what we need. Going to be fun dragging Buddy through there."

Jyllana regarded her like she'd lost her mind. "There won't be any horses where we're going."

"What do you mean, no horses? What about Buddy? I'm not leaving him behind."

Jyllana shrugged. "I don't know what to say, princess. I was led to understand that we'll be ferried across Lake Grim to a tunnel entrance and from there proceed on foot."

Ouderling gaped. She'd never taken the time to consider their route to the mountain aerie. As reality sunk in, she recalled someone mentioning years ago that there were only two ways to Highcliff—a long, subterranean tunnel through the Dark Mountains, or on the back of a dragon.

How her mother thought Highcliff safer than Orlythia vexed her to the point she wanted to spit. Now she faced a real dilemma. Leave Buddy in the hands of her uncle's grooms or…Or what? She had no other choice.

She grabbed Jyllana by the wrists. "Do you think Buddy will be okay if I leave him here?"

Jyllana swallowed. "I can't see why not. Its not like the Duke of Grim is a monster."

Ouderling held her gaze, wishing she could believe that. Her uncle hadn't done anything untoward to make her think otherwise but ever since they had arrived at the castle, she had experienced an odd sensation. One she couldn't explain. Nor did she know where it had come from. It was as if someone watched her. Not one of the nobility or the guards—someone else. Someone who exuded a malign aura. She dropped Jyllana's gaze and released her. How could she explain that to the Home Guard?

She admonished herself. She was being silly. Grim Keep was the second highest house in all of South March. If Buddy wasn't safe here, he wouldn't be safe anywhere. Sighing in consternation, Ouderling returned to the window alcove and fretted as the dying rays of the sun set the unsettled waters of Lake Grim on fire.

The throne room was empty in comparison to their arrival yesterday. A dozen officious-looking, older male and female elves milled about in knots around the spacious chamber between the Lava Throne and the magma fountain. Their voices lowered considerably as Captain Gerrant led Jyllana and Ouderling across the floor to stand at the base of the dais to await the Duke of Grim.

Gerrant had placed four Home Guard outside the throne room, an act that defied Ouderling's sensibilities but the choice of troop deployment was his call.

Keeper of the Jewel

She searched those gathered in the poorly lit room, their cold faces illuminated in the flickering glow of rushlights. She didn't recognize anyone who may have accompanied the duke on his last visit to Orlythia. How long ago that had been, she wasn't sure now that she thought on it. It had certainly been a while.

Keeping an eye on the nearest group of four men, she asked Gerrant, "Do you think Buddy will be safe here?"

The captain frowned, clearly caught off guard by the odd question. "As well as the rest of our horses until we return from Highcliff and make our way home. Why do you ask?"

"I don't know. No reason I guess." Ouderling hadn't thought about the fact that all of the Home Guard mounts would be left behind. She silently chastised her foolishness.

"Would you like us to take him home with us?"

Ouderling's eyes lit up. "Yes, please! That would make me very happy."

"Of course, Your Highness. Buddy will be safe with us."

The captain's simple assurance lifted the weight of the world from her shoulders. Buddy was her best friend. Her only friend if she cared to think on it now that Marris was a non-issue. Sure, she had many acquaintances, even a few girls her age she considered okay to hang around, but they were all back at the palace. She doubted the fact that she was a princess would do her any favours where she was going. Once the people of Highcliff realized who she was, they would treat her differently. They always did. Their usual carefree banter would become guarded and flat—as if afraid of saying something controversial and landing them in the dungeon.

She hated it. All of it. Court life and being a princess. She wasn't cut out for the endless hours of being on her best behaviour on the off chance she might offend one house or another. She absolutely dreaded anyone mentioning the fact that one day she would take her mother's place. South March would be a sad kingdom when that day came.

Surrounded by so many attentive people all the time, her life consisted of false comradery and the blatantly obvious attempts of shallow people wanting to gain the favour of the crown by being nice to her. Many were the days that she felt like little more than a conduit for lesser nobility to get closer to the queen. Being a princess had turned her into nothing more than a glorified conversation piece in most people's estimation—someone to be doted on like a prized artifact but never included in real life discussions or important decisions. She would give anything to live someplace where nobody knew her true identity. She wasn't looking forward to her stay in Highcliff.

Jyllana cleared her throat, alerting Ouderling to the change in atmosphere that had fallen over the ghastly chamber. Conversations had ceased and people stood straighter, their attention rivetted on the intimidating bulk of the black throne.

The spindly chamberlain, Bayl, appeared as if by magic behind the throne. He turned and waited—bowing low as the hulking figure of the Duke of Grim strode past him and stopped at the head of the steps.

Orlythe observed those assembled before nodding at four large Grim Guard standing near the glowing fountain. "Seal the doors."

The order made Ouderling jump. She looked around in surprise as the doors banged shut. For once, she was happy to have Jyllana by her side—the Home Guard's hand firmly clutching the hilt of her dagger.

Keeper of the Jewel

Ouderling didn't miss the fact that Captain Gerrant didn't take offense with Jyllana's action this time. The burly captain puffed out his chest and stared boldly at the duke.

The Duke of Grim gave Gerrant a false smile and waved a dismissive hand. "Save your bravado for someone who cares, Wood. This is my castle. You'd do well to remember that."

Captain Gerrant's cheeks visibly twitched at the dressing down, but he was experienced enough not to respond.

Ouderling's gaze went from the captain to Jyllana and back again before settling on her uncle. "I'm confused. What's going on?"

Duke Orlythe ignored her and stepped back to accept the embrace of the Lava Throne. Nodding to no one in particular, he said, "Fear not, princess. I am but heeding the gravity of your mother's message. If Khae fears there's treachery afoot, I'd be foolish not to take the appropriate steps to ensure the safety of South March's heir."

Ouderling bristled. The way her uncle spoke sounded as if he were mocking her mother's warning. Nor did she miss the slight to the queen when he referred to her as Khae in a public setting. No matter how close she had been to her uncle while growing up, it had dawned on Ouderling in recent years that perhaps he wasn't the fun-loving, jolly elf she fondly remembered.

She recalled travelling to Grim Town only once in her lifetime, and that was many years ago. Back then, she had been so enamoured with her uncle that her young mind hadn't appreciated how gloomy a place Grim Keep actually was. Thinking on it, the castle had always seemed cold no matter the temperature outside. Goosebumps riddling her skin gave testament to that memory.

Keeper of the Jewel

Swallowing an underlying fear, she vaulted the steps to stand at his feet.

The Grim Guard at the foot of the dais were taken by surprise. Concerned faces beseeched instruction from the duke. Nobody but his attendants were permitted to climb the dais without Orlythe's invitation.

Orlythe glared, his look promising reprisal for the Grim Guard's lack of vigilance, but he shook his head and they stood down. His broad face twisted into a tolerant smile, waiting for Ouderling to speak.

"I appreciate your concern for my welfare, Duke Orlythe, but..." She paused to collect her thoughts, "I find your security measures unduly harsh. Confining everyone to the tower seems a bit extreme if you ask me."

The duke folded his hands in his lap and tilted his head. "With all due respect, princess, no one asked you."

It was like her uncle had slapped her across the face. She stared in stunned silence at the impertinent duke who looked back at her as if daring a rebuke. She resisted the urge to look over her shoulder at Gerrant and Jyllana, humiliated by her uncle's remark. She opened her mouth to say something— anything, but words defied her.

The duke rolled his eyes. "Don't trouble yourself, Ouderling. Your presence in the south is but a temporary inconvenience. Tomorrow, the real elves of South March will be glad to see your backside."

A commotion arose behind her. She spun to see two Grim Guard physically restraining Gerrant and a third standing defiantly in front of Jyllana, thick arms crossed over his dark breastplate.

A smug grin split Orlythe's bearded face as he raised thick brows at Captain Gerrant. "Easy captain. You forget your place. In Grim Keep, I am the lord *and* master."

Keeper of the Jewel

"How dare you!" Ouderling managed to spit out. "The queen shall hear of this."

"No doubt she will." The duke's steely eyes turned on her. "In fact, I'm counting on it."

Flabbergasted, Ouderling didn't know how to respond. Seeing the captain of the Home Guard being restrained defied her sensibilities. She turned a dark glare on the duke, her eyes red. "Order your thugs to unhand the captain this instant."

"Or what, Your Highness?"

"Or...Or..." The challenge left her speechless. What recourse did she have besides threatening the wrath of the crown on an elf who obviously didn't care about the repercussions of his actions? Even if she were able to dispatch a raven, it would be many days before help arrived. Given the way her parents had been in such a hurry to be rid of her, they might not bother.

She swallowed. She couldn't believe they would sit back and do nothing if they knew the reality of how the Duke of Grim openly flaunted his position.

She wished she had paid more attention at court during her uncle's last visit to the palace. There had been an argument about something or other the duke had insisted on, but for the life of her, she couldn't recall what. She remembered being so bored by the pomp and circumstance of the official meeting between the nobility in the north and those from the south that she had found a way to excuse herself long before the proceedings were over.

Looking back, her parents hadn't been themselves for a few days afterward. Glaring at the duke who rose to his feet and looked down at her, almost knocking her from the dais, she could understand why.

Keeper of the Jewel

"That's what I thought," the duke muttered when Ouderling didn't say anymore. He stepped past her and nodded at the guards restraining Captain Gerrant. They released him and stepped back, their hands going to their sword hilts, prepared to engage the incensed elf if need be.

Gerrant stumbled forward, catching himself before he tripped over the first step, his purple face livid.

"This is the first and last time that attitude will be tolerated within my hall, captain. Is that understood?"

Captain Gerrant glared at the duke, the struggle on his face clearly apparent, but he didn't respond.

"Very well," Duke Orlythe continued as if the captain had answered him. "You may return to the south tower and gather your troops. Their service is no longer required."

Gerrant's eyes bulged. "What? Queen Khae has given us implicit instructions. The Home Guard are to see the princess to Highcliff. We're entrusted to deliver her into the hands of High Wizard Aelfwynne."

The duke's face darkened. "Are you refusing a direct order from your duke?"

Captain Gerrant lifted his chin high. "No, my lord. I'm refusing to shirk the responsibility bestowed upon me by the Queen of the Elves."

"You do so at the risk of punishment for refusing the counter-order of the ruler of the south. Is that what you're telling me, captain?"

Gerrant nodded. "As long as we're capable of drawing breath, I speak for the entire contingent from Orlythia. For you to counteract the queen's order is nothing short of treason."

Ouderling was certain the duke was about to order the captain's execution as he digested Gerrant's threat. The Grim Guard around the dais bared weapons and surrounded the captain and Jyllana, ready to strike—the scenario so outlandish it was as if Ouderling watched a nightmare unfold before her eyes.

Movement from behind the Lava Throne distracted her. The appearance of the corpse-like form of Afara Maral stepped from the shadows. She swallowed her discomfort, certain that the bony-framed man clothed in long black robes hadn't been there moments before.

The human wizard had accompanied the duke to Orlythia on his last visit, an occurrence that had raised many eyebrows and stirred up a lot of unfavourable commotion amongst the nobility and common folk alike. Humans weren't well-liked by the inhabitants of South March, but the idea of a human wizard attending a royal court was reprehensible. It had taken her many nights afterward to shake the image of the sallow-faced magic-user from her dreams.

Captain Gerrant and Jyllana both tried to pull their weapons free but sword tips directed at their chests stayed their hands.

Afara shuffled to the duke and whispered something into his ear.

The duke listened, nodding occasionally.

As soon as Afara had imparted whatever it was he had to say, he shuffled back to the shadows behind the Lava Throne.

Duke Orlythe waited until the scuffing of the wizard's feet ceased before addressing Ouderling directly. "Your entourage may escort you to Highcliff." He turned his gaze on Captain Gerrant and spoke as if nothing had happened. "You will return to the south tower to await the morn."

Keeper of the Jewel

The duke held Gerrant's defiant stare for a few moments longer before nodding to the head chamberlain standing off to the side.

Bayl raised his hands, long sleeves falling down his sticklike arms, and clapped wrinkled hands.

The Grim Guard barring the exit burst into action and the great door sealing the chamber swung open.

Duke Orlythe bowed his head to Ouderling. "That is all, princess."

Speechless, Ouderling could only gape after the arrogant duke as he spun and made his way into the shadows behind the Lava Throne.

Of the wizard, Afara Maral, there was no sign.

Keeper of the Jewel

Run with the Herd

"**Where** are you going?" Jyllana looked up from the edge of the large bed in the spacious room allotted Princess Ouderling near the top of the southeast corner tower of Grim Keep.

Ouderling stormed around the lavishly furnished chamber, stopping frequently to stare out over Lake Grim. She inhaled deeply twice, deciding whether she wanted to let the Home Guard in on her thoughts. Considering everything that had happened over the last few days, perhaps Jyllana might be just the one to provide the distraction she needed.

Ever since returning from their audience with the duke, Ouderling had worried about how the duke's elves were treating the horses—Buddy in particular. If her uncle's behaviour was any indication of how his staff carried on, she had good reason to be afraid. The fact that seeing her trusty steed once more would also help settle her rising anxiety made her mind up.

She spun on Jyllana, a mischievous smile creasing her cheeks, her finger on her chin.

Jyllana noted how she scanned her from head-to-toe. "What?"

"Stand up."

Jyllana frowned but did as she was asked.

"Turn sideways."

Keeper of the Jewel

"Okay?" Jyllana said, the word long and drawn out as she faced the back wall.

Ouderling nodded to herself and left Jyllana standing there as she rummaged through the first of three large armoires along the wall across from the window. Not finding what she sought, she opened the second mahogany cabinet and inspected several outfits. She put them all back, about to give up and try the third armoire, but a flash of black leather caught her eye.

Supple and smooth, the tunic and matching pants felt nice to the touch. Spinning around, she held them up for Jyllana to see. "You like?"

Jyllana shrugged. "They're nice, I guess."

"Try them on."

"Huh?"

"Just do it."

Jyllana gave her a skeptical look, but Ouderling knew the Home Guard would do anything she asked.

With no regard for Jyllana's privacy, Ouderling helped her remove her bulky Home Guard leather armour and set the stiff pieces on the bed one by one.

As Jyllana stripped down to her undergarments, her shapely figure confirmed what Ouderling suspected. The meek Home Guard was in incredible shape, complete with curves that would provide the distraction Ouderling hoped for.

Jyllana accepted the thin pair of leather breeks and set about working them up her legs.

Ouderling feared her protector's muscular thighs would be too large but as the waistband slipped over Jyllana's hips, she smiled. "Perfect."

Leaving Jyllana to shrug into what appeared as a two-piece tunic that clung to her upper contours like they had been painted on, Ouderling returned to the first armoire and located a small leather vest she had seen—the material closely resembling the suit Jyllana now wore.

Ouderling admired the amazing fit of the leather apparel and handed Jyllana the vest. The colouring was perfect to blend in with the Grim Guard. "Try this."

Without questioning her charge, Jyllana slipped the vest on and worried the red bauble necklace she liked to wear from beneath the tunic's neckline. Cheeks red, she spun a slow circle. "What do you think?"

Ouderling nodded her approval. "Just as I thought. Stunning."

Jyllana couldn't hold her gaze. Clearly embarrassed, she swallowed and looked at the floor between them.

"Do you think you're up to working that amazing body of yours?"

Startled, Jyllana looked up. "Do what, Your Highness?"

Ouderling grabbed Jyllana by the hand and pulled her toward the door. "Come on. I'll tell you on the way."

How they made it down to the third floor without having to explain themselves to any of the Home Guard who might happen to see them as they descended the southeast tower was anybody's guess, but Ouderling wasn't complaining. She was thankful they hadn't bumped into Captain Gerrant. She didn't relish the thought of lying to the elf who was ultimately responsible for her safety.

She pulled Jyllana close, her heart beating fast as they faced a thick, wooden door strapped with iron. This was where the plan got tricky. There would likely be patrols wandering the ramparts. As casual as the patrols might be, seeing that Grim Keep was located in the heart of South March, Ouderling was under no illusion. Her uncle would

Keeper of the Jewel

have given his troops orders to ensure that nobody from Orlythia had free reign of the castle. What the Duke of Grim was trying to hide was a mystery, but given his state of mind, it wouldn't be wise to dig too hard.

She put her hands on Jyllana's shoulders. Looking into her protector's eyes, she saw fear—something she wasn't used to seeing in the trustworthy guard. "You've got this."

Jyllana lowered her eyes. "I don't think I can. I'm gonna botch it all up, I just know it."

To hear strong and confident Jyllana speak in such a manner threw Ouderling. "If someone stops us, make sure they get a good view of…" Ouderling stepped back and held her palms out toward Jyllana, "…this."

Jyllana looked frightened. "And then what?"

"I don't know. Act sweet and innocent."

Jyllana gaped.

Ouderling laughed despite her rising skepticism. "Bat your eyelashes and look demure. Whatever you do, I need you to distract the guard long enough for me to slip away."

Jyllana's stare darkened. "I don't like the sound of that. If the captain finds out I let you go off on your own, he'll have me flogged." Her voice dropped to a whisper. "Or worse."

Afraid she was losing her, Ouderling grabbed Jyllana's hands and pouted for effect. "Please. I need you to do this for me. If the captain finds out, I'll take full responsibility."

Jyllana shook her head. "Captain Gerrant won't care. He'll smile and listen to you because you're the princess, but as soon as you're finished with him, he'll come looking for me and it won't go well."

"Jyllana!" Ouderling put her face close to her protector's. "Don't. Worry. About. The. Captain. I'll make sure nothing blows back on you. Okay?"

Keeper of the Jewel

For the briefest of moments, Ouderling thought Jyllana would balk at the promise. In the end, her protector nodded.

Ouderling smiled for Jyllana's benefit. "Besides, I'm not asking. Understand?"

"Yes, Your Highness."

That settled, Ouderling faced the door. From her memory of her previous visit to castle Grim, she was fairly certain the reinforced door opened onto a walkway that ran along the top of the castle walls—vaguely recalling the tour she was given years ago by one of the castle's chamberlains while her parents attended to business in the throne room. If she was right, the ramparts flanked the inner bailey around the keep proper and would lead them to an access stairwell along the inside of the thick wall to the stable yards below.

Ouderling took one last look around, listening for sounds of other Home Guard wandering close by. Satisfied they were alone, she took a deep breath and grabbed the door handle. "Ready?"

Jyllana nodded, her paler than usual countenance telling Ouderling she was anything but.

The door hinges squealed as Ouderling pulled the heavy, wooden barrier open. To her satisfaction, this end of the defensive wall lay in the shadows of the bulky keep, but the natural light still made them squint.

The section of wall they stood on led in a slow arcing curve toward the northeast tower in the distance—the long span interrupted by two minor towers breaching the rampart's length in equal distances from one another and the main towers—the lesser towers no higher than the top of the wall. The walkway widened atop the mid-towers, housing an array of defensive paraphernalia, from buckets of pitch to a minor catapult and a ballista.

Keeper of the Jewel

Ouderling didn't have to say anything. Jyllana saw it too. Their first test would happen at the junction of the first mid-tower. Two Grim Guard had stopped whatever they were doing, straightened their posture, and watched their approach.

Ouderling put on her friendliest smile. "Hello. Nice day for a walk."

The guards bowed, recognizing the princess. The older of the two stepped forward. "Good day, Your Highness."

The lead guard looked around as if for support but only saw his counterpart. He nervously gazed at Ouderling. "I beg your forgiveness, Your Highness, but we're under strict orders from the duke. No one's to leave the south tower today." He turned a chagrinned look on Jyllana. "And who would you be, m'lady?"

Ouderling feared Jyllana would freeze and throw away any chance they had of reaching the stables but the Home Guard surprised her.

"I've been appointed as the princess' escort while she resides at Grim Keep."

The guard frowned. "I've heard nothing about a personal escort. Nor do I recognize you. I'll have to check on it. If you'll be so kind as to wait here."

Jyllana's face darkened. She stepped boldly up to the man. "You dare question my master's order?"

The guard stammered, "W-who? The duke?"

"The duke?" Jyllana raised her voice. "Hardly. I take my orders from Afara."

The wizard's name struck a chord with the elf. He looked back at his partner, his confidence shaken. His partner shrugged and stepped back, wanting nothing to do with it.

"Ask Afara if you must," Jyllana insisted. "But make it quick."

Keeper of the Jewel

The lead guard swallowed his discomfort, obviously hesitating as he debated his next move.

"I warn you," Jyllana growled. "Master Afara isn't one to suffer kindly anyone questioning his orders."

She indicated for Ouderling to wait against the outer, crenellated wall. "My apologies, princess. Afara will be incensed when he finds out someone has interrogated the heir to the Willow Throne. I dare say this won't take long once old 'zap 'em' gets his dander up." Raising her eyebrows at the guard, she smirked and flicked her hand. "Go on, then."

Ouderling wasn't sure how successful she was at keeping a straight face. Nor was she certain she could refrain from bursting out laughing at the discomfort twisting the guards' faces. She imagined Jyllana's black leather outfit had gone a long way to sell the charade. The redhead certainly didn't look like one of the regular visitors to Grim Keep, nor did she resemble the Home Guard from Orlythia. The tight leather shrouded her with a dark, sinister appearance—one that fit exactly with the perceived persona of the Duke of Grim's human wizard.

The lead guard stared long and hard at nothing in particular, struggling with how to deal with the situation. He turned his gaze on Jyllana. "I'm sorry. I didn't get your name."

Without hesitation, Jyllana stared him in the eye. "Ryona."

The guard frowned and was about to say something else but Jyllana spoke over him, "Ryona Maral."

The guard's ashen face spoke volumes. "You're his...?" He was at a loss as to how to finish the question.

"Great-granddaughter."

The guard nodded as if it were obvious, but it wasn't lost on Ouderling how his gaze focused on Jyllana's ears.

Keeper of the Jewel

Jyllana raised her eyebrows in a smug-like manner, as if daring him to question her about not appearing human, but the guard stammered, "Yes…Yes, of course. I'm sorry. I hadn't realized you were in Grim Town."

"Great-grandpappy prefers it that way." Jyllana raised her eyebrows. "If you know what's good for you, you'll forget you ever saw me."

The guard bowed deeper than he had for the princess. "Of course, m'lady. It will be as you wish." He stepped aside and gave his partner an admonishing look, until he too, backed against the chest-high battlement; both elves lowering their eyes as Jyllana and Ouderling skipped past.

Wonder flushed Ouderling as they made their way toward a set of stone stairs that descended the inner wall halfway between the two mid-towers; just as she remembered from long ago. She put a hand on Jyllana's shoulder and turned her so that she could see her face.

Her protector smiled shyly, careful not to let the guards see. "How'd I do, Your Highness?"

"Not quite the way I'd envisioned you making use of that suit, but very well done. You were amazing."

"Thank you." A pretty smile lifted Jyllana's reddening cheeks. "I thought I was going to soil myself."

Ouderling gaped, barely able to restrain a boisterous laugh. "Ryona Maral! That was brilliant. Did you see their faces fall when they thought you were related to the wizard?"

Jyllana nodded, a pretty smile lighting up her face.

Ouderling slapped her on the shoulder and impelled her toward the top of the steps, a new respect for the elf she had until recently begrudged as her constant companion.

In another life, Jyllana and her might even have been friends.

Keeper of the Jewel

Several stables lined the base of the castle wall. It took a few inquiries before the Home Guard, Scale, came around a corner and greeted them with a surprised look. "Oh."

He dropped to a knee and bowed his head. "Your Highness. No one informed me that you would be visiting the stables."

"The princess," Jyllana spoke for Ouderling, "wishes to see her horse."

Scale hesitated, as if pondering his response. Swallowing hard he stood and nodded. "Of course. This way."

The flustered Home Guard led them into a long, low building, its interior lost in shadow. The only illumination came from late-afternoon sunbeams filtering through gaps in the wallboards.

A euphoria like none other filled Ouderling's heart as Buddy's white blaze caught her eye. Smiling from ear-to-pointed ear, she forgot her worries and ran down the hay-strewn aisle. Hugging Buddy's head, she laughed as he nuzzled her shoulder.

She had half a mind to mount him and ride away from Grim Keep. If only Marris hadn't seen fit to betray her confidence. They could have fled Orlythia and made a proper life for themselves far away from the life-sucking responsibilities that threatened to claim her existence.

Other than Jyllana and Scale, who respectfully waited near the stable's entrance, and a groom working in the relative darkness farther along the aisle, Ouderling was alone with the horses. She scanned Buddy's stall and frowned. Searching the immediate area, the strangest feeling tingled her senses. Similar to the one she had experienced just before her mother had come bursting into her bedchamber.

She hadn't thought much about it at the time, putting it down as the remnant of an odd dream she couldn't recall upon awakening, but standing in the dingy, Grim Keep stables, an eerie feeling troubled her profoundly.

At the head of the aisle, Jyllana and Scale still conversed as if nothing untoward was happening. The way Scale fawned over Jyllana implied her outfit was having the effect Ouderling had hoped for now that it wasn't required.

Ouderling tried to brush the strange sensation aside, but three stalls up the aisle toward the exit, Captain Gerrant's midnight black whinnied. The horse sensed it too.

The building erupted in a chorus of stamping and loud whinnies. The lone groom deeper in the stable backed into the aisle and closed the stall door he had been working in, wild eyes searching for the cause of the commotion.

Jyllana started toward Ouderling, dagger in hand. "Your Highness? Is everything alright?"

As soon as the odd phenomenon gripped her, Ouderling shuddered and it was gone. Whatever had caused the disturbance had left.

For some strange reason, Ouderling envisioned her mother hovering over her bed in Orlythia, tears streaming down her cheeks—very much like she had a few days ago. Ouderling could hear her as clearly as if the queen were in the stable with her. *"I just had a fright is all. I was worried something had happened to you. Not to worry. Everything will be alright. I promise."*

A chill tingled Ouderling's spine. She turned to Jyllana. "I need to get Buddy out of here."

Jyllana regarded her like she had lost her senses. "You need to do what?"

Ouderling grabbed the wrist of the frightened groom who was attempting to slip up the aisle and past them, his chores abandoned. "Quick. Where's my blanket and saddle?"

Keeper of the Jewel

The young elf, likely in his mid-teens, stared blankly, his mouth dropping as he realized who hung onto him. He dropped to a knee and bowed his head, forcing Ouderling to bend over, still clutching his arm.

She yanked him back to his feet. "No time for that. Where's my gear?"

The young elf swallowed, afraid to meet her gaze. "They've been taken to the keep, princess."

"To the keep? Why would someone go to the bother of lugging our saddles and tack away from the stables?"

"I don't know, princess," the groom whispered, sounding as if he expected to receive a whipping for not knowing the answer.

Scale walked up behind Jyllana and cleared his throat. "If I may, Your Highness?"

Jyllana's intense glare mirrored Ouderling's as they spun on him.

"The duke requested that we take everything to a storage area in the castle."

Ouderling stepped beside Jyllana to confront Scale directly. "Why would he do that?"

Scale shrugged. "That I can't say. If you'll allow me a little time, I can find out."

Ouderling's initial thought was to say yes, but she caught herself. An inquiry would raise questions. She would prefer to avoid another confrontation with her uncle. Whatever the reason made little difference at the moment, but as she thought more on the subject, her worry for Buddy's safety grew.

"Don't bother. There's no need. I'm sure the duke has his reasons."

"Yes, Your Highness." Scale bowed and walked back up the aisle.

Keeper of the Jewel

"Wait." Ouderling raised a hand to indicate Buddy's stall. "I want to exercise my horse."

Scale looked from Ouderling to Jyllana and back again.

"Is there an issue?" Ouderling pressed.

"Um. No, Your Highness. Of course not. It's just that I was under the impression that everyone from Orlythia had been confined to the tower."

"Why are you here then?"

Scale sputtered, "I-I...Captain Gerrant was adamant that at least one of the Home Guard were left behind to tend to the horses."

Ouderling frowned. "Doesn't the captain think my uncle's people are competent enough to feed and clean them?"

"I don't know, Your Highness. I'm simply following orders."

Ouderling mulled that over. "Is there anyone else watching over the stables with you?"

Scale swallowed and looked around. "Not that I know of. Other than him," he indicated the groom with a tilt of his head, "I haven't seen or heard anyone down here for some time now."

"So, you think I might be able to exercise my horse in peace?"

"Um, sure, I guess. Do you expect to ride him?"

"Don't know yet."

"Let me fetch you a saddle, in case you do." He bowed his head. "If it pleases Your Highness, I'll nip next door and see if I can find one of the Grim Guard saddles that might befit your station."

Ouderling wanted to take exception to how Scale framed his offer, but let it go. "Very well. Make it fast."

"Yes, Your Highness." Scale strode with purpose past the groom. Not stopping, he ordered the quaking teenager, "You stay here until I get back. Make sure they get whatever they want."

"Yes sir," the groom replied, terror on his face as he regarded the princess of South March.

A slow smile crept across Ouderling's face; the intent not lost on Jyllana.

"What are you up to, princess? I know that look."

Ouderling raised her eyebrows twice in quick succession. "Just see to it that Scale doesn't come back too quickly."

Jyllana hesitated, appearing like she wanted to ask more, but took a deep breath and started up the aisle, not sparing a glance for the terrified teenager who stood motionless, not knowing what to do.

"What's your name?" Ouderling asked as she unlatched Buddy's stall and urged her horse into the aisle.

The quaking groom wouldn't look at her. "Donel, my liege."

"That's it? Just Donel."

"Aye, my liege. My mother doesn't know who my father is."

The way Donel explained his situation in such a straightforward manor left Ouderling staring. She couldn't imagine not knowing who her father was. Swallowing her discomfort, she remembered what she had set out to do. If she didn't hurry, Scale would return and ruin everything.

"Is there another way out of Grim Keep? One that doesn't involve the main gates or tower gates?" She leaned in and whispered, "You know, one that's a little more…*discreet*?"

The wide-eyed shock on Donel's face as he considered how to answer the Princess of the Elves without upsetting her was endearing.

Keeper of the Jewel

"It's okay, Donel. As princess, I'm ordering you to show me a private way out of the castle. I desire to ride my horse one last time before I'm whisked away to Highcliff."

She cupped his quivering chin in her fingers and lifted his face to meet her gaze. "You wouldn't deny me such a little request as that, would you?"

The terror on Donel's face screamed that he wanted nothing else than to be absolved of any further dealings with her.

"Not to worry, handsome. This'll be our little secret. I'll be back before anyone knows I'm gone."

Saying nothing, Donel nodded into her hand and pulled away, leading her toward a storage closet near the stable's entrance and opened its door. "If it pleases Your Highness, you can use my saddle and reins."

The astonished look on his face as she kissed him on the cheek was priceless.

The afternoon sun lay low over the grassy plains fronting Grim Keep by the time Ouderling turned Buddy back to the south and headed for the castle walls. She had done a lot of soul searching as the leagues of flat terrain had disappeared beneath steady hoof falls. As much as she wanted nothing more than to ride him into the sunset and never look back, she knew she couldn't do that to Jyllana or the young groom, Donel. If she weren't to return, their lives would be forfeit for facilitating her escape. Likely Scale's as well.

She brought Buddy to a halt a longbow's shot from the steep banks supporting Grim Keep's bulk and looked around one last time—an inner voice urging her to flee while she still had the chance. She dismounted and held his head in her arms, her face close to his, whispering sweet nothings.

Keeper of the Jewel

Buddy nuzzled into her and dropped his head to the ground to crop at the swaying, knee-high grasses. Taking advantage of his distraction, she removed the ties binding his braids and did her best to straighten his mane.

She patted his flank, lovingly running a hand beneath his cinch strap, noting how sweaty the ride had made him. A heavy sigh escaped her. She didn't think she could go through with this no matter what her parents thought. Training with the Highcliff Guardians wasn't something she had ever aspired to do. Being the princess, she had well-trained troops at her disposal to do the fighting for her. Wasn't that one of the privileges of being high-born?

Her vision shimmered as if something moved in the distance to her left. She whipped her head around but was met with nothing but empty grassland.

She stared at the far away spot, her long hair blowing in the gusts that bent the grasses in waves of green. She had been at Grim Keep for little over a day and already her nerves were getting the better of her.

Inhaling deeply, she let her breath out slowly. It was time to return to whatever fate awaited her. It didn't matter how she felt about the path her life was taking, there would always be those who would dictate how it really went.

A cold sensation riddled her with goosebumps. The feeling struck her as odd since the wind had abated, leaving her to bask in the last rays of the day. The word, 'phantasm,' came to mind with alarming clarity.

If she hadn't been so afraid, and equally disgusted, she would have laughed. She was becoming more like her mother with each passing day.

Eyes red with growing frustration at how she was losing control of her life, a distant rumble, almost indiscernible at first, drew her attention to the east.

She stiffened.

Keeper of the Jewel

A dust cloud billowed on the horizon, growing in size as the tell-tale thunder of hundreds of hooves shook the ground beneath her feet.

The Herd of Bascule galloped toward her. Before she could think of remounting and getting out of their path, they surrounded her and Buddy; forming ranks six deep and more, and proceeded to run a wide circle around them.

To her surprise, Buddy stamped, but not in agitation or fear, but like he was urging her to let him join the procession.

A stunning thought occurred to her. It was as if fate had stepped in to offer a solution to her greatest concern.

Ignoring the pandemonium around her, she grabbed Buddy's bridle and undid the buckles, her hands shaking at the prospect of what she was about to do. Heart breaking, she knew without a doubt it was the right thing to do. In order to save her best friend, she must set him free.

Choked with emotion, she could barely see to undo the belly cinch and slide the saddle from his glistening back. Letting the cumbersome leather hit the ground, she pulled the protective blanket free and let it fall away. Wrapping her fingers in his mane, she hugged his wide neck, pressing her face into him, deeply breathing in his scent.

"I need to set you free." The building lump in her throat barely allowed her to say the words, "I love you, Buddy. It's time you ran with the herd."

Buddy stamped and leaned his face against the top of her head. Emitting a long whinny, he walked slowly away until her trailing hand fell from his posterior. He picked up speed and trotted to the inner edge of the circling horses, watching them run past until a white mare broke rank and came up beside him.

They played strange at first, tentatively sniffing each other. The white mare nickered twice, stomped her front hooves,

Keeper of the Jewel

and started toward the circling herd. She slowed long enough to look at Ouderling, as if to thank her, and then whinnied at Buddy.

Ouderling didn't think he would go—selfishly hoping he wouldn't.

But, with a last, longing look her way, Buddy held his head high and neighed. Joining the mare, they picked up speed and joined the procession.

Ouderling turned slowly, watching Buddy run circles around her with the Herd of Bascule, her heart swelling with joy as much as it was breaking.

They circled twice more before galloping off to the west, disappearing behind a cloud of dust that shrouded the setting sun.

Shoulders shaking, Ouderling dropped to her knees. She pulled her tiara free, not caring how much hair she took with it, and tossed the priceless talisman away. Stupid bit of metal. The last thing she wanted was to be reminded of who she was or where she had come from.

Grabbing hold of Buddy's discarded blanket, she clutched it to her face, inhaling deeply of her best friend's aroma.

A smell she would never forget for as long as she lived.

Keeper of the Jewel

Wraith's Wrath

Patience was a virtue never mentioned in the same breath with the Duke of Grim. Waiting on a meeting that had consumed his every waking thought since the last encounter had taken its toll on his nerves. Few were the times Orlythe felt out of sorts when faced with a confrontational conversation but, on this occasion, he was at a loss as to how to subvert the outcome to meet *his* needs. Even Afara standing before his magma fount portrayed as apprehensive—and this was the type of creature he envisioned his dark wizard liked to consort with.

As much as Orlythe had prepared himself for the inevitable, the icy tendrils creeping across the nape of his neck nearly had him leap from the Lava Throne in fright. Whipping his head back and forth, he couldn't identify how the evil being had entered the throne room undetected.

Dark banners hanging off the walls rustled in unison with pennants strung between the thick pillars as if someone had opened a window. Afara Maral turned and locked eyes with the duke in the windowless chamber.

A shiver shook Orlythe's jowls. Standing between the duke and Afara in the middle of the floor was the wraith— the apparition's true identity hidden beneath a ratty black cowl. Red, piercing eyes were the only indication anything lived within the voluminous folds of the creature's flowing

Keeper of the Jewel

cloak. With nary a sound, the wraith glided across the stone floor and ascended the dais.

Not much in life intimidated Orlythe, but if not for the throne's thick, lava glass backrest, he would have slid from the backside of his seat. Swallowing his discomfort, he admonished his cowardice. Although Afara shuffled up the steps to stand at his side, Orlythe couldn't shake the impression that they were nothing more than an annoyance should the wraith decide they weren't worthy of its energy. The power radiating from its essence left no room for any other consideration.

A voice, more of a grating of metal on metal, made Orlythe cringe as he tried to make sense of the strange way the ethereal being spoke.

"Why is she who bears the mark of the Dragon Witch still alive?"

It took everything Orlythe had to meet those fiery red pinpricks of light within the cowl. "She'll be taken care of, trust me, but if I'm to be of any use to you, it must be done with the greatest of discretion."

"You assured me she'd be dealt with."

"And she will be." Orlythe swallowed in an attempt to thwart his notorious temper from overcoming his rational thought process. It likely wouldn't end well if he succumbed to its ugly release. He sat up straighter, his angst at being manipulated hardening his resolve. "She travels with a large contingent of Home Guard. One cannot simply assassinate the heir to the Willow Throne without assuring the appropriate safeguards are in place. Should the Queen of the Elves think for a moment that I had anything to do with her daughter's demise, Grim Keep would know the entire might of South March. Where would that leave us then?"

Keeper of the Jewel

The wraith seemed to hover a little higher, its long robes unfolding around where its feet should be. Its fiery orbs shone brighter, illuminating a hint of white skin stretched over a veiny skull.

Orlythe shrunk back on the Lava Throne, expecting to meet a grim fate.

"I demand it done at once or the queen's wrath will be the least of your concerns."

"Yes…Yes, of course." Orlythe's white knuckles kept him from jumping from the throne and screaming in terror. Drawing on the last of his reserves, he forced himself to speak with a tone that bordered on insolence given the present danger. He glanced at Afara who nodded in return. "With your assistance, the death of Ouderling Wys will happen midday tomorrow at the earliest—"

The wraith grew in size, and leaned over the cowering duke. Long, dangling sleeves reached outward; tips of bony fingers emerging from the folds.

"Wait!" Orlythe held his hands up in a desperate attempt to fend off the creature's touch. He exchanged a quick glance with his wizard, but Afara's indifference showed neither fear nor anger in the wraith's presence. If Orlythe survived the encounter, his glare promised he would be having words with the useless finger-wagger.

The wraith halted its approach.

Orlythe grasped the slim opportunity to explain. "The princess is heavily guarded. Queen Khae sent along an elite squad to see to her safety. Short of a fire-breathing dragon, there isn't anything capable of getting close to her while she's under their protection." He swallowed again. "But, with your assistance, Afara has foreseen a way."

The wraith hissed its displeasure, but didn't respond.

Keeper of the Jewel

In that briefest of moments, a revelation made itself known. It rose in the back of Orlythe's mind and flitted amongst his darker thoughts. The slightest of grins tugged at the duke's lips. Something prevented the wraith's wrath from claiming what it so desperately sought. The newfound knowledge that the wraith needed him if it were to achieve its own goal, bolstered his confidence.

Orlythe sat up straighter. "That's it, isn't it? You need me to do your dirty work."

The wraith's orbs flared brighter but Orlythe leaned toward it. "You lack the means to dispose of what threatens you. Without me, you're helpless."

The wraith shrunk in size. It floated to the edge of the step, its bony fingers disappearing into its sleeves. But that was as far as it retreated. It raised an arm to point at Orlythe. "Do not become too arrogant with your delusionary knowledge, Duke of Grim. I may not be able to get at Ouderling…yet. But, let me assure you, there's nothing that can prevent me from bringing you to your knees and destroying this castle should you not follow through with your end of the bargain."

"Nothing but my ability to perpetrate that which you cannot," Orlythe said before he could think better of it. He rose to his feet and pointed a ringed finger at the wraith's cowl. "I said I'd deal with it and so I will, but it has to be on my terms, not yours. What good is what you offer if the queen brings a war to my gates?"

The wraith hissed long and deep until its words began to make sense. "I know what your wizard has in mind, and I'm warning you. Don't lose sight of what you're requesting. Once invoked, it cannot be undone."

Orlythe worried he had stepped over the line when he had agreed with Afara that they needed to enlist the resources of the wraith to rid him of the first obstacle. Fighting back words that might spark the wraith's wrath, he grunted, "I refuse to allow it loose within these walls. It'll have to wait until the morrow. Until then, begone from here."

The wraith's eyes flared twice. Without a word, it drifted past Orlythe, circled the throne, and melted into the shadows.

Though he couldn't be sure, Orlythe was fairly confident the wraith had left the chamber. How, he had no idea. He took the time to breathe deeply many times to calm his pounding heart. Considering his near brush with death, he turned a malevolent eye on his supposed trusty accomplice. It was time for a heart-to-heart talk with his human wizard.

Keeper of the Jewel

Passage of Dolor

Jyllana stared across the choppy surface of Lake Grim at the black sentinels rising straight up off the horizon to disappear into a thick layer of brooding clouds. Beside her, the princess sighed; Ouderling's mind more than likely on her horse. The whip of the sails from their ship and the escorting brigs keeping pace on either side, along with the wind in their face, made conversion difficult on the choppy surface of Lake Grim.

She couldn't blame the princess for what happened. She had been lucky enough to have shared a similar bond while growing up and training for the Home Guard. If not for an ill-timed decision to venture along a treacherous side path high in the northern reaches of the Steel Mountains, she might still be enjoying the company of her first horse to this day. The day Amber had stepped into an unseen crevice and shattered her leg had broken Jyllana's heart along with it. There weren't many days the horrifying event didn't haunt her.

The sky directly ahead was darker than the surrounding area—black clouds roiled above the heights. According to the lessons of the Chronicler, Highcliff was situated in the heart of the Dark Mountains, an area riddled with active volcanoes. Jyllana couldn't imagine anyone living in such a hostile environment. She didn't envy Ouderling's plight.

Keeper of the Jewel

Having to learn whatever the high wizard thought to teach her while living in constant fear of a volcano erupting.

Jyllana scanned the Home Guard assembled on the deck searching for Scale. She had rather enjoyed his company yesterday. At least until they both realized that Ouderling's absence had become apparent to those who had the authority to make their lives miserable. Though she didn't know all of the Home Guard personally, she was familiar with everyone who had journeyed with them from Orlythia. Of Scale, there was no sign.

Captain Gerrant's voice rose above the wind cutting across the bow. She stiffened, but his loud words weren't meant for her this time.

A shudder wracked her. Perhaps Scale had born the brunt of the captain's wrath last night. Shortly after Ouderling had returned to the castle late in the afternoon, the captain had taken Jyllana down a notch for *her* part in the princess' ill-advised foray. Even after the princess had vouched for her. She could only imagine the punishment that might have befallen Scale. Daring to snatch a glance at the dour faced captain, she didn't have the nerve to inquire about Scale's fate.

Everything had gone without incident yesterday until the arrival of the Herd of Bascule had caught the attention of the Grim Guard manning the walls. The resulting disturbance of hundreds of hooves thundering upon the plains had stirred up quite a commotion, bringing attention to the princess' antics. Curious onlookers gathered upon the battlements to take in the spectacle. Unfortunately, the Duke of Grim had joined them.

Duke Orlythe had stormed into the south tower and tore a strip off Captain Gerrant for allowing the princess to escape the protection of the tower—the duke's tirade and promise of reprisals had vexed the captain to no end.

Captain Gerrant had been quick to seek out those directly responsible. He had been adamant about Jyllana's punishment due to her implicit involvement. Her days as a member of the Home Guard were about to come to an unceremonious end. As soon as they finished escorting the princess to Highcliff, Jyllana was to return to Orlythia and resign her role as the princess' protector.

Just thinking about how humiliated she had been when the captain had dressed her down in front of her peers made her want to cry anew. Nor could she forget the day not long ago when the king had berated her for allowing Ouderling to escape into the mountains unprotected. Her time with the princess was drawing to a close.

Though her placement as Ouderling's personal protector for the last three years had been nothing but professional, casting a glance at the maturing young elf beside her, Jyllana was going to miss being part of her life. The princess had made no qualms about how much she detested being watched over. As such, she hadn't made any attempt to get to know Jyllana—as if the princess despised Jyllana personally for performing her duty.

She sighed. If not her, someone else would have been assigned to shadow Ouderling's every move. Likely, Ryona. Jyllana winced. The thought of Ryona keeping up with Ouderling lifted her sullen cheeks momentarily. She didn't think too many people were up to the task of keeping Ouderling in sight while trying to be inconspicuous at the same time. The princess possessed a knack for losing her guards.

Whoever the captain referred to the queen to take Jyllana's position when they returned to Orlythia was in for a big surprise. They would have their eyes opened and their hands full. The heir to the Willow Throne's mannerisms were nothing but rife with impetuous urges. A fine line was required if they wished not to induce Ouderling's ire. With any luck, the princess' stint at Highcliff would help tame her.

And yet, Jyllana was crushed at having lost her position. Up until recently, if the queen had asked the captain to assign someone else to take her place, she would have graciously bowed her head and thanked her, but something had happened in recent days to alter how she felt about her role as the princess' protector. Despite the eventual outcome, she recalled yesterday's events with fondness—at least until the princess had fled the castle unguarded.

It was like they had bonded while holed up in the south tower. Allowing Ouderling to persuade her into donning the tight leather outfit she ironically still wore, much to the obvious consternation of Captain Gerrant, had felt like they had shared an intimate moment. As if the princess had unconsciously accepted her as a friend instead of despising her as someone who watched over her every move. It shocked Jyllana to realize how much she was going to miss keeping tabs on the high-spirited, young elf.

The bow broke through a whitecap, dousing them with a generous spray of cold water.

The disgusted look Ouderling shot her—long, royal locks clinging to her sullen face, her sodden cloak snug against her slight form—almost made Jyllana spit out a laugh. Almost.

Jyllana knew better. Pretending nothing untoward had happened, she returned her attention to the approaching cliffs and the gloomy haze shrouding the heights.

"Jyllana! Stay close to the princess!" Captain Gerrant barked from the head of the gangplank as Jyllana and

Keeper of the Jewel

Ouderling walked toward him. "Do *not* allow *anyone* to get between you. Do you understand?"

The way the captain spoke to her made Jyllana feel like a five-year-old. She glared at the large man; something she would never have dared before. Knowing her place in the household Home Guard would be taken from her in a matter of days, she found it increasingly difficult to control her pent-up frustration at how things had turned out.

Captain Gerrant held her gaze as they walked past, chewing his lower lip and folding thick arms across his chest as if to keep from lashing out at her.

"What's up with him?" Ouderling muttered as she followed Jyllana down the bowing exit ramp to the rock shelf carved from the base of a towering cliff face. "Still mad at you?"

"Beats me," Jyllana lied. She knew full well what bothered the captain. Her dereliction of duty could have proven catastrophic. If something serious had befallen the princess, the entire contingent of Home Guard might have lost more than just their position in the queen's court.

Half of the Home Guard had already disembarked and formed a protective semi-circle around Princess Ouderling as the two accompanying ships divested themselves of heavily armoured elves from Grim Keep.

Ouderling scanned their surroundings, a puzzled look on her face. "Why all the swords? I thought the duke's ships were acting as an escort across the lake. Surely the Home Guard can handle anything we might encounter. It's not like we're travelling into the northlands."

Jyllana followed Ouderling's gaze. "Not sure, Your Highness. I can ask."

Keeper of the Jewel

Ouderling grabbed Jyllana's wrist and held her back. "You'd better not. I'm thinking mister grumpy pants wouldn't like that."

"Ya. You're probably right."

The troops parted to allow Captain Gerrant access to the shore. He proceeded to where a heavy iron door was set into the base of the cliff, its dark face coated with a layer of rust. Easily twice Jyllana's height, the curved-top barrier to the tunnel beyond squealed eerily on great hinges as the door swung outward with the help of two straining men-at-arms draped in the Duke of Grim's black surcoats.

Captain Gerrant shook hands with a duke's elf very much his equal in bearing and stature. They exchanged a few words before Captain Gerrant faced those assembled on the shelf rock. "The duke has graciously provided us with two squads of his best troops to ensure our safety while we march through the Passage of Dolor. No matter what you may hear in the tunnel, under no circumstances are you to break rank."

Jyllana exchanged glances with the princess, both of them shrugging at the same time. Jyllana smiled despite her apprehension. She wasn't sure what the princess knew of the Passage of Dolor, but she had been privy to the briefing before departing Orlythia. The tunnel system they were about to enter was reportedly infested with dangerous creatures—many that defied description. According to the old Home Guard who had given the talk, these creatures preferred to hunt on their own. As a consolation, any sizable force would, in all likelihood, be left alone. There were the ever-present trolls of course—communal beasts that were rampant in the catacombs of the vast cave systems honeycombing the interior of the Steel Mountains, but according to the wizened veteran, the shaggy creatures were the least of their worries.

122

Keeper of the Jewel

Even so, the old elf's assurances hadn't sat well with Jyllana. Crossing the threshold into the infamous tunnel, she locked arms with Ouderling. The princess frowned and shrugged free but Jyllana made certain her charge was never more than an arm's length away.

Keeper of the Jewel

Beneath the Surface

Princess Ouderling forced her way through the troops ahead of her and grasped Captain Gerrant's shoulder. "Captain, I demand a word with you."

The captain spun on her; face twisted in anger. He stammered as he realized who confronted him and bit back whatever was on his mind, but he couldn't keep the venom from his voice. "My apologies, Your Highness." He cast a dark look at Jyllana. "I hadn't realized you'd broken rank."

The animosity between the captain and Jyllana would have to be addressed another day. Right now, Ouderling wanted to know why a sizeable number of the duke's troops had disappeared up various side tunnels. They had been marching for a long time, following a wandering passageway, the imperfect stone floor ascending at varying degrees of steepness. After passing an intersection a while back, the scuffing of boots created by their passage over the stone tunnel floor had diminished noticeably—as if the duke's troops had abandoned them.

The captain called a halt to the procession to keep those in front from getting too far ahead. He held his temper in check, but his face retained a look of annoyance. "What can I do for you?"

"Where have the others gone?"

"I'm sorry?"

Keeper of the Jewel

Ouderling stepped past him and scanned the heads of those visible up the tunnel. "My uncle's troops. Where have they gone?"

Comprehension softened the captain's expression. "Ah. Yes. They've ventured down side passages that parallel this one. Scouting them to keep us safe."

Ouderling raised an eyebrow. That made sense. Chagrinned, she forced a smile. "Very good, captain. Carry on."

The captain didn't appear pleased to have to take orders on an expedition he led—his corresponding smile obviously forced. Ouderling didn't care. She was the princess.

"Of course, Your Highness." Gerrant bowed his head and barked the command to resume the march.

Muted boot falls thumped unseen in the distance. The captain turned his back on Ouderling, falling into step between the male and female elves who marched on either side of him.

Jyllana grasped Ouderling by the elbow. "We should fall back into line, Your Highness."

Ouderling looked at the young elf's hand, about to tell her what she thought about being grabbed, but something in Jyllana's eyes stopped her. Her personal Home Guard, still dressed in what she could only classify as a provocative, leather suit, had never been anything but respectful toward her. Unlike the captain. She nodded and allowed Jyllana to pull her back to where they had been placed in the procession for her protection.

Most of the troops travelled three wide as the tunnel allowed, but no one had taken it upon themselves to walk with her or Jyllana. Whether due to their discomfort at her being a princess or something to do with whatever had

Keeper of the Jewel

transpired between Jyllana and the captain last evening, she wasn't sure. Likely a bit of both.

She had smiled this morning when Jyllana opted to dress in the supple leathers but hadn't put much thought into why Jyllana would have done so. Considering her protector's role in the Home Guard, it seemed strange now that she thought about it. An open defiance of the procedural tenets of the members entrusted to oversee the security of the queen's house. Jyllana was proving to be a cheeky thing.

A mischievous grin lit up Ouderling's face. Perhaps her shadow's company wasn't that bad after all.

Keeping her own company as they trudged deeper into the mountain, Ouderling shuddered as she thought about who could have been assigned to watch over her for the last three years. Before Jyllana's appointment, the princess had been subjected to two overprotective Home Guard in a row. Ones who openly meddled in her affairs and bossed her around as if she were a wee elfling who deserved a good scolding.

She studied Jyllana's pretty profile and smiled. Locking arms with her personal protector, she held her chin high and strutted along the passageway, determined to appreciate the redhead's company during the little time they had left together. Beneath the surface of the earth, Jyllana was beginning to remind her of herself.

Ouderling pulled up short. "Did you hear that?"

Jyllana had stopped as well and was searching the ranks of Home Guard behind them. Everyone looked around, baring steel. Jyllana nodded, dagger in hand.

Feeling useless, Ouderling swallowed. Not wanting anything to remind her of the life she had left behind, she had decided not to bring her ceremonial dagger of office.

Keeper of the Jewel

The spooked eyes of those around her made her second guess that decision.

Whatever the guttural sound had been, it hadn't been natural. More shocking was the fact that the Home Guard ahead of them hadn't turned around. Blades held at the ready, they faced the opposite direction.

The growl came again, louder this time and from both directions.

"Ward the princess!" An echoing cadence repeated itself as the order filtered down the line. Packed in the tunnel three wide with weapons drawn, there was little room for anyone to move. The command that followed: "Hold your rank," seemed to Ouderling like a silly thing to say.

Jyllana grabbed Ouderling's upper arm and forced her against the wall, eyes darting everywhere at once. "Whatever happens, hang onto me."

A roar boomed up the tunnel from the rear of the procession. Startled cries of seasoned veterans reached them just before the tunnel lit up in a blinding flash and pandemonium broke out.

The Home Guard ahead of Ouderling's position turned in time to witness a ball of fire roll through the rear lines. As soon as the deadly flames hit, the ranks of Home Guard backed up the tunnel as fast as the close confines permitted; all semblance of order forgotten.

A muscular, red-bearded guard grabbed Ouderling's arm on the opposite side of Jyllana and propelled her into the backs of the troops ahead of them. "Make way for the princess! Save the princess!"

His pleas were drowned out by another roar from behind, closer than the first. Wrapped around Ouderling's elbow, the big elf's hand encompassed her thin arm as he practically lifted her from her feet and forced her up the tunnel.

Keeper of the Jewel

Wild-eyed, Ouderling ran as fast as the Home Guard ahead of her permitted, trying not to step on anyone's heels or get cut by an absently held blade. Wincing at the pain the male Home Guard inflicted, she was comforted by the pressure of Jyllana's palm on the back of her shoulder, her fingers entwined in the top of Ouderling's cloak. Her faithful protector wasn't about to allow anything to separate them.

Ouderling looked over her shoulder, only to wish she hadn't. The light from the many torches carried by the Home Guard scrambling along behind them paled with the insurgence of a fireball tumbling up the passageway, its path filling the tunnel. Flames lapped at the heels of the ranks not far behind. Elves fell writhing to the tunnel floor, their skin blackening instantly.

The flames fell short of Ouderling but she didn't miss the blast of heat that accompanied them. And then she felt the creature's presence. The passageway trembled under her feet. She cried out and looked down, expecting the ground to crumble beneath her, but the rock held firm.

Impelled by the red-bearded guard and Jyllana, Ouderling leaned into the elf in front of her, hopelessly urging him to move faster, but he could only run as swiftly as the ranks in front of him.

Another roar incited a cold dread deep within Ouderling's soul, so loud she cringed. She expected to be able to see the creature by now but a quick glance behind showed her nothing but blackness and the terrified faces of a male and female Home Guard bringing up the rear. Of the rest of the troops who had been following, there was no sign.

Horrified, Ouderling ran sideways, afraid to witness what came after them but unable to take her eyes from the tunnel; the darkness dispelled in the distance by the remnants of what could only be the burning bodies of fallen Home Guard.

Her breath caught. A shadow filled the tunnel, passing over the last of the burning corpses and dropping the tunnel behind them into total darkness.

The trailing guards called out a warning.

The red-bearded hulk who had her in his grasp, stopped long enough to yell at Jyllana, "Keep her moving. We'll stall it."

Jyllana never missed a step, dragging Ouderling after the retreating backsides of the forward troops.

The female Home Guard and her partner turned to face whatever stalked them, their torches held high in one hand, and brandishing thin, elven blades in the other. Red-beard stepped beyond them, his shining, thin-headed warhammer at the ready.

A roar shook the tunnel.

Ouderling stopped, too terrified to take another step for fear of what was about to happen.

Jyllana pulled on her, causing her to stumble backward but the princess refused to take her eyes off the three brave warriors—two courageous males and a female who had run toward the danger in a desperate attempt to give her a chance to escape.

She tried to break free of Jyllana's grasp. Scared as she was, Ouderling refused to let elves she'd never taken the time to get to know, throw away their lives on her account.

"Run!" She screamed after them.

Red-beard turned long enough to shout at Jyllana, "Get her out of here!"

A faint glow took shape in the darkness, manifesting into a searing brightness. Roiling flames formed as if out of thin air. It was then that she saw it.

Keeper of the Jewel

Deep within the mountain, a scaly leviathan that had no business tracking them through the underground passageway, opened its fanged maw and spewed forth a magnificent wave of fire. She was certain it would engulf them all.

Bracing for the impact of the wall of fire, Ouderling hunkered down, hands over her head in an attempt to prevent her skin from melting off her bones.

Beside her, Jyllana screamed, but if the Home Guard meant to say anything intelligent, Ouderling couldn't hear over the roar of doom.

Keeper of the Jewel

The Responsibility of Power

Molten rock oozed out of the wall and into intricately carved channels that directed its flow into two small basins near the top of the lava fountain. The pools of lava coalesced almost to the point of hardening before overflowing the small basins' front lips and funneling into two wider channels that dropped into a larger catch basin at the height of Afara's waist. With glacial speed, the orangey-reddish glowing magma swirled and seeped into a wide, shallow channel fronting the central bowl and dropped slowly into a catch basin that spanned the fount's wide base. The lava flow coalesced at the base of the fount, slowly turning in a small whirlpool of liquid rock. Its surface blackened as it hardened in the open air, but it never quite had time to solidify before it was sucked into a hole at the bottom of the lower basin and dropped out of sight.

When questioned about how the mesmerising fountain withstood such extreme heat, Afara had simply stated that the blood of the earth served to stoke the furnaces of his underground forge. Orlythe had raised his eyebrows at that but the dark wizard never expanded upon his explanation.

Captivated by the oozing flow, Orlythe jumped when Afara's voice sounded beside him. "It is done, m'lord."

"For the love of everything you hold dear, you blasted wizard! Stop sneaking up on me like that." Orlythe glared at the sallow-faced man.

Keeper of the Jewel

Afara acted like the duke hadn't said anything at all and pulled a blackened stick from the folds of his robe. Examining the lava flow, he inserted the end of the stick into one of the upper channel entrances, wiggling it several times before removing it. The tip of the stick glowed bright red, a wisp of smoke drifting into the air between them.

Orlythe studied the stick. He didn't know for sure, but he was fairly certain it was the same length of polished wood Afara used every time he played with his fountain to adjust the flow. If he wasn't mistaken, the stick had never gotten any shorter as a result.

He shook his head. There were so many things about the wizard he didn't understand. He put most if it down to the fact that Afara was from the kingdom of man. For that reason alone, his magic-user was shunned by most everyone in South March. And for good reason if there were any truth to the practices of mankind. That was one of the reasons Orlythe valued his resident wizard. As long as Afara was in attendance at Grim Keep, most of the busy bodies who comprised the South March nobility preferred to avoid having anything to do with the region and that suited him just fine.

Orlythe calmed himself. "Walk with me."

Afara bowed his head and replaced his lava poker.

The duke frowned, thinking the smoking tip would cause the wizard discomfort, but Afara merely stared at him, waiting to be led.

Orlythe cleared his throat and exited the throne room. Passing by the guard stationed outside the doorway, he held up a staying hand. Though overly cautious when moving about in public—there were many elves he had crossed over the years—he was confident no one would try anything while in the company of his mystical colleague.

Keeper of the Jewel

A long, black marble hallway led them from the middle of the ground floor of Grim Keep to the connecting corridors circumventing the far reaches of the keep's exterior walls. Mounting a long flight of granite steps, they emerged onto a high balcony overlooking the southern corner tower, and were treated to a commanding view of Lake Grim.

The duke followed Afara's shrewd gaze to the gloomy horizon, the skies above the Dark Mountains perpetually obscured by swirling clouds of volcanic activity. He shuddered to think what might happen should one of the mountains engage in a full-scale eruption. It was hard enough now to keep the outside walkways clear of ash whenever the witchy, east winds blew.

A smug expression twisted the corners of his pepper-grey mustache. If things played out according to plan, he needn't worry much longer about the angry peaks. Orlythia lay in the hospitable northern reaches of the Steel Mountains, its yearly temperature swings nowhere near as severe as those in the south. "I'll wait until my units return before I celebrate."

Beside him, Afara's gaze never wavered from the distant cliffs. "You needn't worry. We've invested a lot in its summoning. Nothing escapes a wyrm of the deep. I'd be surprised if your troops made it back."

Orlythe didn't have to be told who *we* were. His wizard and the wraith had been busy preparing for Ouderling's journey through the Passage of Dolor. The off-handed remark about the safety of his own troops came as a shock. "That wasn't part of the bargain."

"What the wyrm does while in the thrall of the wraith is not my concern. You're the one who condoned the conjuring of the hell-spawned creature. You can't be surprised if events don't play out exactly as planned."

Keeper of the Jewel

Orlythe sensed colour flushing his cheeks. "As my wizard, I expect you to be forthcoming about such matters."

Afara raised his eyebrows. "As the Duke of Grim, I was under the assumption that when you agreed to be a party to the wraith, you appreciated the danger involved. A summoning of this magnitude cannot be undertaken lightly."

"Ya, ya, ya. I've heard those words before. But why *my* troops? The plan was to have them split off and return to the lower exit."

"*After* the wyrm locates the delegation *and* does what is necessary. Timing in matters such as these is not precise. In order to keep the captain of the Home Guard oblivious, the Grim Guard must ensure they travel along the main tunnel. If Gerrant suspects something amiss and orders the Home Guard down one of the side passages, our beast won't be able to follow. And then where would we be? As much as you despise the captain, Gerrant is no fool. If he walks out of there alive, you can bet the queen will respond with the full weight of South March's army.

"Nor will it take Aelfwynne long to become aware of the wyrm's presence. Even if he doesn't detect it outright, I'm sure his bevy of dragons will inform him soon enough. The Grim Guard's role is to keep everyone confined to the main tunnel for as long as possible."

Afara paused, considering the duke with a shrewd gaze. "Fear not. Between the wyrm and the troll army we have assembled, the demise of the Orlythia Home Guard shouldn't be a problem."

Orlythe's laboured breathing made it hard to talk without an edge to his voice. "No matter the outcome, when word makes it back to the palace, I'll *need* every fighting unit I have!"

Keeper of the Jewel

"Such is the responsibility of power, m'lord. A consequence you'll have to deal with in due course, at any rate." Afara shrugged but held up a staying finger as Orlythe teetered on the verge of outrage. "Perhaps, in the end, it will prove a fortuitous circumstance."

Orlythe frowned, barely able to contain himself. He couldn't see the upside in having the full might of the Willow Throne come down on him. At least not yet. "How so?"

"Surely, you must suspect the wraith isn't here to simply rid the world of the measly girl. Granted, preventing the princess from spawning offspring is paramount in the grand scheme of things." Afara scanned the horizon, not offering anything further.

Orlythe was so irate he wanted to spit. No wonder nobody trusted wizards. If their extraordinary power wasn't bad enough, trying to carry on a normal conversation with one was worse. They spoke in riddles and half-truths, as if everything they did was nothing more than an elaborate game.

If not out of respect for what Afara Maral was capable of if crossed, Orlythe might have pitched the impertinent wizard over the battlement and delighted in his frail body breaking on the jagged rocks abutting the base of the lakeside walls.

Keeper of the Jewel

Pecklyn

Flames lapped at the writhing forms of three elves, their agonized cries cutting through Ouderling's brain like a battle-axe. If not for the death grip Jyllana maintained on her, she would have run to their sides and attempted to put the fire out. If not for Jyllana, she would have shared the same fate.

"Your Highness! We have to run!" Jyllana shouted, an edge of hysteria in her plea.

For an elf of Jyllana's petite stature, her strength was incredible. Ouderling couldn't prevent Jyllana from dragging her up the tunnel.

"Help me!" Jyllana yelled at the backsides of the nearest Home Guard.

Two burly elves grabbed Ouderling by the arms and pulled her off her feet. The retreating ranks of Home Guard slowed to allow them through their lines before filling in the gaps behind them.

Captain Gerrant met them halfway, all the while encouraging his troops to keep moving. "Princess Ouderling. Thank the gods you're okay." He took the place of one of the elves holding Ouderling and spirited her up the tunnel.

A series of higher pitched roars rumbled through the tunnel from somewhere ahead.

"Engage the trolls!" The captain ordered. "Push through!"

Keeper of the Jewel

"Trolls?" Jyllana asked as she struggled to keep pace. "How many?"

Ouderling caught the dire look the captain gave Jyllana. His refusal to answer didn't bode well.

Metal clanged off metal. An intense battle was being waged up ahead.

The tunnel gave way to a large cavern, its stalagmite infested floor teeming with creatures towering over seven feet tall. Bodies covered in mangy, black fur, sported long gangly limbs tipped with leather-rending claws. Feral, red eyes, and yellow fangs dripping with saliva, made the fearless beasts scarier than Ouderling had believed possible.

Two tunnels emptied into the cavern's far side; their mouths choked with trolls charging into the fray. They were trapped.

A quick look behind them made Ouderling flinch. The impenetrable darkness receded on the cusp of a new barrage of flames.

If not for Jyllana's warning shout and moving to pull Ouderling and the burly Home Guard against the cavern wall, the fire would have incinerated them.

Captain Gerrant dodged to the far side of the opening, wild eyes scanning their surroundings as the volley of flames crackled into the backsides of the Home Guard battling the trolls. When the fiery onslaught abated, his gaze settled on a spot along the cavern wall beyond Jyllana. He pointed. "There! Take the princess. Get her out of the cave!"

Not waiting for a response from Jyllana, the captain spun on the burly Home Guard. "And you! Prepare to engage that creature!"

Jyllana didn't hesitate.

Keeper of the Jewel

Ouderling feared Jyllana would dislocate her shoulder, the Home Guard pulling on her arm as they stumbled across the cave mouth.

The press of the countless trolls drove the remaining Home Guard back toward the advancing creature in the tunnel. Ouderling couldn't imagine what kind of beast lived beneath the ground and spewed fire like a dragon, but she knew if they didn't move fast, they would soon find out.

Jyllana led her to the narrow cleft in the rock the captain had indicated and pulled a torch from where it rested in a loop on her belt. It took a couple of strikes of her rapier against a flint stone, but a lick of flame caught and quickly spread to engulf the torch's head.

Screams and screeches, roars and battle cries thundered in the cave, but nothing compared to the guttural growl of the creature that slithered after them. Ouderling tried to get a better look at it, but Captain Gerrant ran up and pushed her and Jyllana into the recess.

"Does it go anywhere?" He asked, frantically flicking between the battle raging in the cavern and where the creature would emerge.

Dust sifted past the upper edge of the crevice opening as a ground shaking roar caused everyone fighting in the cave to stop and take notice.

Judging by the captain's eyes, whatever had entered the cavern was enough to shock the veteran warrior.

Jyllana's muted voice from down the narrow side tunnel was barely audible. "It looks like it does."

"Then go! Get the princess as far away from here as fast as you can!"

"How will I know where to go?"

Keeper of the Jewel

On the verge of joining the battle, the captain paused long enough to answer. "Wherever it goes, just keep turning right! If we make it, we'll follow. Now run!"

Ouderling didn't have to be coerced. She chased Jyllana toward a bend in the fissure, trying hard to pick out the nuances in the rock face so as not to bash her body off the unforgiving stone.

A crackling roar filled the crevice. Jyllana's body blocked the light of her torch but she had to cover her eyes as the passageway lit up—a colossal gout of flame filling the cavern beyond.

The firestorm lasted mere moments. When it was over, most of the noise from the raging battle had been reduced to the dying cries of whatever still lived within the cave.

Captain Gerrant ran into the crevice, stumbled, and fell; facial hair singed and skin blackened. He gazed at Ouderling who had run back to help him, holding up a burnt hand— intense pain twisting his face.

Ouderling carefully grasped his hand, afraid of inflicting more pain, but he pulled hard and righted himself. The touch of his damaged skin made her shudder.

He released her hand and pushed her toward the bend. "Go!"

It was a tight squeeze to round the corner but the fissure widened considerably on its far side, opening into what appeared like a tunnel that rose into the mountain's core.

Jyllana waited until Ouderling passed by her and went back to assist the captain.

"It's no use. I can't get through," he said, his leather chest armour wedged into the gap.

Jyllana examined the crevice. Dropping to her knees, she bent toward him. "Get on my shoulders. It's wider at the top."

Keeper of the Jewel

The captain didn't hesitate. Driving a heavy boot into Jyllana's shoulder, he scraped his body up the rough wall. "Higher!"

The strain on Jyllana's purple face twisted her features into an ugly sneer as she struggled to straighten up. Veins bulged on the sides of her forehead and sweat beaded upon her brow, but the slight elf didn't give up. Taking a deep breath, she steadied herself for a final push.

A high-pitched cry of exertion escaped Jyllana's lips, her muscular thighs driving upward.

The captain's chest armour scraped through the gap and he tumbled after it, hitting the ground hands first and rolling to a stop at Ouderling's feet.

He didn't waste time worrying about Jyllana. Faster than his condition would have suggested, he stood and shoved Ouderling away from the high-pitched roars filling the crevice from the direction of the cavern. "Run!"

Jyllana grabbed her torch from where it sputtered on the ground and hazarded a look back around the bend, her face terror stricken. "Trolls!"

The tunnel walls narrowed and expanded all along its twisting course for no apparent reason but remained wide enough to run single file without much interference. Despite the faint light of Jyllana's torch, Ouderling continually banged into the irregular walls, scraping her elbows and knees.

Though hidden in the darkness that followed the torch's light, the muted sound of claws clicking on stone intensified. As big and ungainly as the trolls were, they moved through the unlit passageways with ease. It was only a matter of time before they caught up.

Having just learned what an enraged troll sounded like, Ouderling's blood ran cold as one grunted from somewhere ahead of them. She stopped and gaped, pointing up the tunnel at something she couldn't see.

Jyllana assisted the captain to her side. The battered elf laboured more with each step, but he refused to release his hold on his rapier. Torchlight illuminated everyone's face in eerie light; Jyllana and Captain Gerrant's terrified expressions coinciding with how Ouderling felt.

"They must be coming from the other end of the cavern. Most of the ones inside were incinerated along with…" The captain couldn't finish his statement. Coughing profusely, he grabbed Jyllana's torch and cast it past Ouderling, the faint light not extending far up the twisting tunnel.

"There." Captain Gerrant pointed to the left and hobbled up the tunnel to stand before a dark recess. "Another tunnel."

He shone the torch up the side passage and leaned in to listen. Satisfied, he handed the torch to Jyllana and pulled the two he carried from over his shoulder—lighting them both from her flame.

"Take the princess down there," he said, and propped his torches against the wall across from the side tunnel's entrance. "I'll hold them off."

Jyllana mirrored Ouderling's incredulous stare, shaking her head. "You can't fight them on your own. You can barely stand."

The captain shrugged. "Ain't got much choice. No use you two dying as well."

"But, but—" Ouderling stammered.

"But nothing, Your Highness!" Captain Gerrant cut her off. Eyes crazed; his tone was harsher than expected considering who he was talking to. "If anything happens to you, I'd rather be dead anyway. I owe my life to your grandmother."

Keeper of the Jewel

Ouderling wanted to protest but the captain turned to Jyllana. "I'll give you as much time as I can, but I'm thinking I won't last long. Take the princess and run. Run hard. Don't stop."

Jyllana nodded. "Yes, captain." She indicated for Ouderling to enter the byway.

Ouderling couldn't keep the tears from falling. Shaking her head in disbelief, she swallowed and started up the side tunnel. Trolls sounded from both directions, so loud she feared they were already too late.

Jyllana slipped into the passage and pushed Ouderling ahead. The princess stumbled until her feet caught up to her momentum.

A loud roar chased them into the unknown. Afraid to look back, Ouderling wasn't sure if the cry had originated from the trolls or the captain. Whoever had issued it, the noise of an intense scuffle followed them down the dark passageway—quickly muted by the closeness of the tunnel walls and the pounding of their footfalls on the descending tunnel floor.

Ouderling wasn't a dwarf, but her sense of direction niggled at her that they were going the wrong way if they intended on reaching Highcliff. Besides descending deeper into the heart of the mountain, they had taken the left tunnel. She yelled over her shoulder between heavy breaths. "Didn't he say we're supposed to keep turning right?"

Jyllana's grim look spoke volumes.

Jyllana pulled her final torch over her shoulder, waiting to light it until the last possible moment. It had been a while since they had abandoned the captain to his fate. They had encountered several places where the passageway came to a vee. Each time they stopped to listen and proceeded up the right fork. After the third intersection, the floor levelled out and began to climb. Though relieved they appeared to be travelling in the proper direction, the increasing grade of the tunnel wasn't doing their tired legs any favours.

Ouderling stared at the newly lit torch. "What happens when that one burns out?"

Jyllana shrugged. She had no answer. It was obvious they would be in deep trouble if that came to pass, but she had neither the heart nor the energy to give the princess a sarcastic response. She forced a smile and started to jog up the tunnel. "Let's not let that happen."

Never having been to Highcliff, Jyllana had no idea how far the dragon enclave was from the docks at the base of the cliff. Rerouted through side tunnels, she wondered if they had travelled farther than was necessary to reach the settlement that was rumoured to be nestled above the shores of a large, mountain lake. For all she knew, they might be under the lake and running in the wrong direction, but she didn't know what else to do.

Going back was out of the question. Not afraid to fight, she didn't fool herself. Her dagger wasn't going to fend off their pursuit if the trolls ever caught up to them. She silently hoped the captain had prevailed, but if she cared to be realistic, the brash elf lay dead many leagues behind them.

Fingers of torchlight crept ahead of Ouderling, revealing another intersection. The princess froze, her eyes widening. The meagre torchlight illuminated a set of claws, and what appeared to be an odd stick protruding from the ground, tucked into a recess in the wall.

Jyllana saw it to. She grabbed Ouderling by the shoulder and hauled her back. Putting a finger to her lips she handed the princess the torch.

Keeper of the Jewel

Dagger in hand, she soundlessly padded up to the creature's hiding place and lunged, thrusting her blade into the space.

A shockwave jarred Jyllana to the elbow; the point of her weapon impacting rock. A pair of red eyes looked up at her above a large mouth brimming with pointed teeth. She shivered as its malicious jaw curled up in satisfaction.

Jyllana screeched and jumped back. Slamming her back against the opposite wall, she repositioned her blade and dove in for the kill.

The creature didn't flinch as her dagger arced through the space between them, its point aimed at the dark green skin covering the creature's large head.

A hand appeared out of the darkness, gripping her wrist and stopping her assault in mid-swing. The force of the impact sent Jyllana's arm across her body, pivoting her off balance and knocking her against the wall beside the green-skinned creature. She hit the stone hard. Before she could recover, another hand reached out and held her in place.

"Easy, my lady. You're in good hands." The green-skinned creature said with a throaty voice. No taller than Jyllana's waist, it hobbled from its hiding place with the aid of a short cane and stared at Ouderling. "What have we here, Pecklyn? Two damsels in distress, if I have the right of it."

The face of the second creature in the tunnel came into view in the torchlight—the significance of his pointed ears and long, flowing, white hair shocked Jyllana's senses. What was an elf doing with this...she regarded the creature with revulsion...this thing?

"And a princess, no less," the elf replied, releasing his hold on Jyllana's shoulder; allowing her to step away from the wall, but he maintained control of her dagger bearing wrist.

Jyllana pulled hard, but couldn't break his grip.

Keeper of the Jewel

The green-skinned creature cackled. "You may release her."

Pecklyn gave her a disarming smile and let go, not appearing to fear any reprisal she might offer. He crossed his arms and tilted his head, taking her outfit in from head to toe and back again. "Nice leather. We hadn't expected an assassin to escort Princess Ouderling."

Ouderling stepped between the two. "Who are you? How do you know who I am?"

Pecklyn dropped to a knee and grasped Ouderling's right hand. She tried to pull it away, but he held firm and drew it to his lips. "You're lovelier than the last time we met, Your Highness. How could I forget such an exquisite sight?"

Pecklyn released her, his gaze extending beyond Jyllana and Ouderling to the dark tunnel they had travelled along. "If you'll kindly follow Master Aelfwynne, I'm thinking we need to be free of these tunnels before your hairy friends catch up."

Jyllana and Ouderling stared after the receding goblin, both mouthing at the same time, *'he's the wizard?'*

Pecklyn nodded, a great smile cleaving his clean-shaven face. He indicated they should go ahead of him, and muttered under his breath as they passed, "Shh. He doesn't know he's different."

Jyllana glared at Pecklyn, making sure she kept herself between the smug elf and the princess as they followed the strange little creature up the passageway.

Emanating from hard to distinguish carvings etched along the length of the goblin's cane, a mysterious, green glow illuminated the tunnel ahead.

Keeper of the Jewel

Earth Blood

Highcliff, at first glance, wasn't anything like Ouderling had expected. The tunnel that the odd-looking creature claiming to be South March's all-powerful wizard, and the muscular elf, Pecklyn, had led them out of, emptied onto the western edge of a large, rock platform extending out from a sheer cliff face high above the blue waters of an immense mountain lake. Eddies of volcanic ash swirled in random places across the wide expanse. After a weary climb through numerous side tunnels to avoid the wider Passage of Dolor and a possible encounter with the fire breathing wyrm, they had finally stumbled out of the warrens.

Pecklyn folded his arms over his chest and nodded at the lake. "Impressive to behold, hmm? A body of water this high in the mountains equal to that of Lake Grim. Except that Crystal Lake is much deeper. Bottomless if you believe the creatures lurking within its depths, waiting to take you down."

A bitter wind whistled across the expansive rock shelf, buffeting everyone's hair, including the wispy locks barely visible atop Aelfwynne's large head.

Ouderling pulled her cloak tight and hugged herself to ward off the chill. "Is it always this cold up here?"

"Nah," Pecklyn smiled and started across the platform. "Colder, usually."

Keeper of the Jewel

Ouderling watched the spry elf bounce away, his gait more of a skip than a walk. She cast Jyllana a puzzled glance.

Her exhausted protector shrugged.

Pecklyn turned a lazy circle in the middle of the platform, scanning the sky. Raising two fingers to his mouth, he emitted a shrill whistle.

Aelfwynne hobbled along between Ouderling and Jyllana, a malicious smile parting his barely discernable lips. "You think it's drafty out here now. Just you wait."

Grey clouds limned with the dying rays of the day clung to the mountain peaks surrounding the vast lake, but curiously not a wisp hung over the water's centre.

Pecklyn skipped to the edge of the platform, oblivious to the deadly drop at his feet, his passage stirring up a thin layer of volcanic ash. His attention focused on something below the platform. Judging by the movement of his head, it moved quickly.

"Here she comes," Aelfwynne pointed, his rough-skinned, claw-tipped hand appearing too large to belong to a creature his size.

Ouderling frowned at the wizard but before she could ask, her attention was drawn to Pecklyn.

The smiling elf jumped into a run, spread his arms wide, and leaped over the edge of the platform—falling out of sight.

Ouderling matched Jyllana stride for stride as they raced toward the edge of the promontory. Before she could breathe again, a swooshing sound rose above the wind—again and again. From out of nowhere a dragon appeared, lifting itself and the prone form of Pecklyn above the ledge, his legs scrambling to right himself as the pale purple dragon flew him out over the lake.

Keeper of the Jewel

Easily five times Pecklyn's size, the dragon flapped its great wings with an odd sort of grace. On a command from Pecklyn, it turned back toward them, its ridged head regarding them with disconcerting red eyes.

If Ouderling's breath had not deserted her, she would have screamed as the platform burst into life. Several dragons of differing shapes, sizes, and colours appeared, shrieking as they rose above the platform's lip. In that moment, she knew fear beyond any she had ever experienced in her life.

Of all the dragons, Pecklyn's was one of the smallest, but certainly not the least scary. Thick legs and neck, covered by leathery scales, supported a massive head bristling with horns and spiked teeth.

A wicked grin exposed rows of Aelfwynne's pointed teeth. "Welcome to Highcliff. The magical aerie where everyday choices determine whether you live to see the morrow." He pointed a crooked finger at several of the dragons circling overhead. "Behold. Your first decision awaits. Choose wisely or be eaten."

Ouderling gaped at the bizarre wizard, but Aelfwynne didn't take notice. If he did, he wasn't overly concerned that his peculiar behaviour was directed toward a princess of South March. Instead, his lips curled upward, revealing a set of teeth similar to the dragon Pecklyn flew.

Stunned, Ouderling watched the goblin wizard shuffle across the back of the platform toward a goblin-sized opening in the middle of the cliff face.

Jyllana raised an arm to protect her face from the ash churned up by dragon wings, and grabbed Ouderling's elbow. "Follow Master Aelfwynne before we get blown over the edge!"

Ouderling allowed herself to be led along the wide, rock shelf, her mind whirling with Aelfwynne's words. Though not a common sight in northern South March, she had seen dragons before. Emissaries from Highcliff and Grim Keep had flown them to Orlythia on occasion.

She tried to place Aelfwynne, but couldn't recall ever seeing the wizard before, though she was sure she had been introduced to the high wizard back home. Puzzled, she would have remembered seeing the goblin at Borreraig Palace.

Being the high wizard of South March, her parents would have entertained his counsel during the larger, annual functions back in Orlythia, but for the life of her, she couldn't place him. There couldn't be more than one high wizard called Aelfwynne.

She sighed and considered the flying leviathans. Her parents had taken her to see the dragons whenever they visited the palace. The brief contact she had had with them hadn't prepared her for the cacophony and chaos circling the platform. Ear-piecing shrieks forced her to cover her ears and cringe. Despite the fact she wanted nothing more than to get off the ledge to make it stop, she dug in her heels and shrugged off her protector.

"Princess!" Jyllana shouted and made to grab hold of her again. "You need to get off the ledge!"

Ignoring her protector's advice, the crackling of flames drew Ouderling's attention to Pecklyn's dragon—beast and elf hanging in the air as if on a rope. The dragon reared back and emitted another long burst of fire—the heat discernable above their heads.

Pecklyn adjusted his grip on his dragon's neck and laughed. He said something, but his words were lost to the din of dragonsong.

Keeper of the Jewel

The purple-hued dragon turned a narrow-eyed gaze on Ouderling. Two wing-flaps and a sudden flutter of its leathery span allowed it to settle on the platform before her.

Jyllana stepped in front of the princess and spread her arms wide, a dagger in each hand.

Pecklyn leaped from the dragon's neck and landed with the deftest of movements. Seemingly unconcerned by Jyllana's aggressive stance, the dragon craned its thick neck to observe them overtop of Pecklyn's shoulder.

"Princess and brave assassin. You needn't fear the Highcliff Guardians. I have assured them you're welcome here, so no harm will befall you." Pecklyn smiled wide, blonde locks blowing around his face. "As long as you don't threaten the Crystal Cavern, of course."

Ouderling was unable to look away from the dragon's intense stare. "Are they always this noisy?"

"Ha! Not always. Most are quiet by nature, but when they sing together, they tend to shake the rocks loose from the heights. It's a natural response when they are agitated…" He trailed off.

Ouderling stepped back and pressed her body against the rock wall behind her, the sudden movement causing Jyllana to stumble against her.

"*Or*, when they're happy." Pecklyn held out a hand to extricate Jyllana from Ouderling's arms. "It's not often they get to meet a princess." He turned and whispered something to the purple dragon and the noise of the accompanying dragons fell away.

Captivated, Ouderling watched a few of the dragons settle onto the promontory, folding their wings—colourful eyes watching her.

"See?" Pecklyn swept an arm out wide to include the dragons before leaning in close. "They anxiously await your approval, Your Highness. It would mean the world to them if you spoke a few words."

Ouderling swallowed. She gave Jyllana an apprehensive look and stepped around her, cautiously inspecting Pecklyn's dragon. Giving it a wide berth, she moved into the middle of the crowded platform, captivated by the nearness of the incredible creatures.

Green, yellow, red, blue, and orange dragon eyes followed her every step. Awestruck, she struggled to keep her limbs from quaking.

The wind gusting across the promontory swirled ash in eddies—its passage the only sound disturbing the surreal atmosphere. Rumours of her uncle's ideals regarding the magnificent beasts slammed into her. She couldn't deny the potential for death and destruction exuding from the indescribable beauty of the dragons watching her.

Being this close to them, her uncle's reasoning made sense. If he were to command a squad of dragons, the Duke of Grim would be godlike in battle. Who would dare stand in the face of such a strike force? And yet, for some reason, her parents were against training the dragons to that end.

She swallowed, the other side of the argument sinking in. In the wrong hands, such a powerful army would be able to take-over South March and the other lands as well. In the wrong hands, a dragon army would be catastrophic.

Her concentration so completely on the fire-breathing beasts, Jyllana's voice directly behind her almost made Ouderling scream in fright.

"Beautiful animals, Your Highness, but do you think it wise to be as exposed as you are?"

Unable to break free of the dragon stares, Ouderling nodded. Mustering every bit of nerve she had, her voice came out as a croak. "Greetings…" She cleared her throat, not sure how to address a group of dragons. She gave them a timid wave. "Greetings. I'm happy to meet you. I, um, extend the gratitude of my parents, the Queen and King of the Elves. They, uh, send you their best wishes…"

Ouderling faltered but Pecklyn stepped up on her other side. He bowed and spoke with the confidence of someone used to being around creatures capable of snapping an elf in half, "Dragon friends. It's my privilege to introduce Princess Ouderling Wys, heir to the Willow Throne. I trust that while she…" he paused and winked at Jyllana, "and her associate are in Highcliff, that you will afford them the same protection and respect you bestow on the Crystal Cavern."

Pecklyn side-stepped and took a knee in front of Ouderling. "Know that the princess is every bit the precious jewel as those that gave rise to Grimclaw."

A strong gust of wind buffeted the promontory, whipping hair and clothing about; ruffling a few wings.

The platform shook with the motion of dragons lowering their chests to the ground, bowing their heads. If not for Jyllana's steadying hand, Ouderling was sure her legs would have given out beneath her.

Aelfwynne spied them from the shadows of the small entrance tunnel farther along the back of the ledge. With a grim look, he disappeared from view.

"No matter what they say or do, I wouldn't trust them completely," Pecklyn said as he walked beside Ouderling down a wide passageway hewn into the mountain face, following the distant figure of Aelfwynne who had emerged from a small side tunnel that appeared to have been built for someone his size.

"Who? The dragons? Why not?"

Pecklyn raised dark eyebrows. "Because they're dragons."

Keeper of the Jewel

Ouderling didn't know what to say to that. She couldn't imagine living amongst so many deadly creatures if she couldn't trust them.

"Don't get me wrong. They're faithful to a fault. As an emissary of Queen Khae, you needn't worry. Unless, of course, you violate their law. Rest assured, each and every one of us at Highcliff have been personally appointed by the crown to oversee the carrying out of that law."

"And what law is that?" Jyllana spoke up.

"Grimclaw's Law."

Ouderling exchanged a questioning glance with Jyllana; forcing a smile when Pecklyn said no more. "Do you care to enlighten us? What's Grimclaw's Law?"

Pecklyn chuckled. "Oh, that's simple. Protect the Crystal Cavern with your life."

"You mentioned the cavern before. What's so special about it." Ouderling had heard the Chronicler speak of such a place, but her mind had been elsewhere while the teacher had droned on and on about something she hadn't cared less about at the time.

Pecklyn stopped, his usual smile absent. "The Crystal Cavern contains the biggest source of earth blood in the world as far as we know. Rumour has it there's another one far to the north, but Aelfwynne doesn't know of its location. Earth blood helped give birth to Grimclaw. Simply put, in the wrong hands, the power contained in the Crystal Cavern is sufficient enough to destroy life as we know it."

He nodded at the almost indiscernible form of Aelfwynne hobbling into the shadows far ahead. "That's why he's here. And the dragons. And a handful of the most trusted elves in the realm. To ensure that power doesn't fall into the wrong hands."

Keeper of the Jewel

"I imagine life up here must get pretty boring," Ouderling said, and then worried she had offended their escort. "I mean, who in their right mind would attack a place guarded by dragons?"

"That's exactly the problem," Pecklyn said with a serious tone and began walking again. "It's those not in their right mind that we worry about the most."

Ouderling fell into step beside him. Considering his statement, the Duke of Grim came to mind.

Jyllana kept pace on Pecklyn's far side, her soft leather swishing in the relative quiet of the broad tunnel. She waited until a knot of elven males passed them going the other way; curious stares taking in Pecklyn's charges. "Has there been many attempts on the caverns?"

"Cavern." Pecklyn corrected. "There's only one. And not for centuries, but signs point toward another assault."

"Signs?" Jyllana and Ouderling asked at once.

Pecklyn ignored their question, his attention on Aelfwynne standing outside a small doorway obviously built for someone his size.

Pecklyn bowed his head. "Master."

"Show the Home Guard to the princess' quarters. I hadn't expected on housing two of them." He turned his attention on Ouderling. "I'm sure you're good with your guard sleeping in your quarters until I make other arrangements."

The high wizard's request wasn't a question.

"Of course...Master Aelfwynne." The title of respect felt strange to say, but Ouderling decided it best to respect the high wizard's stature. "Jyllana has been underfoot for years. I'd feel naked if I wasn't tripping over her."

Her attempt at humour was lost on the wizard.

Keeper of the Jewel

Pecklyn smiled and winked at Ouderling as he held out a hand for Jyllana to proceed with him deeper into the mountain.

Jyllana hesitated, not sure what to do.

"It's okay. I'll be with Master Aelfwynne. I'm sure he'll prove almost as capable as you are at keeping me safe." Ouderling chuckled and spared a glance at the wizard.

He wasn't smiling.

"So, what do you do here?" Jyllana asked, walking a step behind Pecklyn and looking around as he led her along several different tunnels; some sloping up while others sloped down. She ran a hand along the relatively smooth, shiny black walls that arched overhead; their bottoms curving underneath stone floors that had obviously been added after the formation of the circular passageways.

"You and I are much alike..." He paused, prompting Jyllana.

She pulled her hand from the wall and answered his unspoken question, "Jyllana."

"Ah. That's it? Just, Jyllana?"

Her dimpled cheeks flushed. "Jyllana Ordalf."

Pecklyn nodded. "Makes perfect sense. Ordalf is the ancient elven name for spear. It fits you well, as you're the princess' spear."

Jyllana laughed shyly. "Aye. Kind of a fluke that. Not many remember its meaning anymore."

"What's important," Pecklyn stopped outside a curved-top door, "is that you do. Don't ever forget the importance of your role. As Ouderling's protector, your safety is more important than anyone else in all of South March. Save the queen and king, and the princess, of course."

155

Keeper of the Jewel

Jyllana shook her head. "Oh no. I'm a minor member of the Home Guard, I'm no—"

"Minor member?" Pecklyn laughed and crossed his arms over his chest, appraising her. "You're the personal protector of the heir to the Willow Throne. There isn't anyone as vital to the succession as you."

Jyllana wasn't sure how to respond. Gooseflesh washed over her skin. She had never thought of it that way before. This perpetually smiling elf with the habit of crossing his arms over his chest seemed wiser than his years suggested. Before she could stop herself, she blurted, "How old *are* you?"

Whatever Pecklyn was poised to say caught in his throat. He tilted his head. "Forty-eight name days. Why?"

"That's awfully young for someone charged with the protection of the high wizard, isn't it? What happened to his previous protector?"

"Aelfwynne killed him."

Jyllana choked on what she was about to say and sputtered, "He what?"

"It's complicated."

Jyllana stared into his amber eyes, not sure what to make of that. "Still, forty-eight's pretty young to be in charge of the high wizard's safety."

Pecklyn snorted. "And you're, what? Twenty? Charged with the safety of South March's future queen! You're one to talk."

"Twenty-five," she muttered sheepishly, the very thought stunning her. She had never thought of her role that way before. Back in Orlythia, she was just another member of the Home Guard. She had been appointed as the princess' protector when the previous Home Guard had…She frowned. Had what? Come to think of it, she had no idea why the previous protector had been removed from her position.

She looked at the floor, embarrassed. "I guess you're right."

"That's nothing to be ashamed of." Pecklyn lifted her chin in his hand and smiled warmly. "You should be proud. Obviously, the queen has seen something in you that has elevated you above your peers."

Dumbstruck, Jyllana gaped. That presumption had never crossed her mind. She wanted to look away from his amber eyes but the warmth reflected there held her rapt. She muttered, "Whatever the queen sees, I hope I prove worthy of her trust."

"From what little I know, you already have. You got her here safe and sound, didn't you?"

"Ya, but—"

"But nothing. You survived some ungodly creature and eluded a horde of trolls. No one else in your group managed to do that."

Jyllana felt tears welling up as the significance of what had happened in the Passage of Dolor slammed home. The panic. The chaos. The death of so many elves, some she had considered friends. She cast sad eyes to the ground. "I didn't do anything. I followed orders and ran while everyone died around us. I'm no hero. I abandoned my mates."

Unable to keep from crying, her weakness disgusted her. She tried to pull away from the pressure of Pecklyn's consoling hand on her shoulder, but didn't have the strength to resist.

He pulled her into a tight embrace and rocked her, whispering into her ear. "What you witnessed was something so horrific I'm surprised you were able to move at all. You did what was expected of you. You honoured their commitment to saving the princess' life. You got her away from a monster born in the depths of the fiery abyss. Had you remained behind, you would be dead, along with the princess. From wherever you believe their spirits have gone, take solace in the knowledge your mates' sacrifice wasn't in vain."

As much as Pecklyn's words were meant to ease her grief, her shoulders shook violently. Everyone was dead. Captain Gerrant and the rest of the elite Home Guard. How could she ever face the queen again?

Aelfwynne watched the princess of South March over the brim of a stone goblet, savouring the steaming effervescence of the spicy concoction he had brewed with the aid of the magical fire burning within a ring of ornate stones.

Resting on a low, stone bench within a small chamber carved into the mountain rock, its roof not high enough for Ouderling to walk upright, she tried to still her fear of the odd creature. Even seated, she had to bend so as not to scrape her head on the rough-hewn ceiling—the chamber eerily illuminated by glowing crystals embedded into the rock around her.

Ouderling sniffed at the goblet she had been given. Its contents exuded a heady, earthy aroma that turned up her nose. She waited for her host to sip at his before working up the nerve to do likewise. Following his lead, she slurped enough to taste it, the liquid tart and hot in her mouth. Daring to swallow, her face twisted in what she could only surmise was an ugly expression. Though she had prepared herself for anything the strange brew might offer, the pungent afterbite was nothing like she had experienced before.

Keeper of the Jewel

Pointed, yellow teeth glinted across the magical firepit as Aelfwynne smiled, the grin making him look more nefarious than usual.

Ouderling didn't think she would ever look at the high wizard without revulsion. Her gaze on her hands wrapped around the goblet, she appreciated the warmth infused in its stone composition, but she could feel the wizard's beady, red eyes burrowing into her. Swallowing her discomfort, she cast her attention to the glittering gemstones radiating soft light. "Is this the Crystal Cavern?"

Aelfwynne stared long and hard. Taking a deep pull of his drink, he placed it on the ground beside him. "What if I were to say yes?"

Ouderling met his soul-searching gaze and shrugged. "I guess I'd say it's not what I expected."

"Were you not taught about Highcliff as an elfling?" His cynical gaze examined her from head to toe. "Or perhaps you aren't old enough yet."

"Of course I am. But…" She sighed, barely able to think straight. Sitting alone in a cramped burrow inside a mountain wore on her frayed nerves. The events of the day seeped into her thoughts, haunting her. Accompanied by the horrific noise of elves suffering and dying a tortuous death she couldn't escape the ghastly visions of their burning bodies. She doubted she'd ever get the stench of burnt flesh from her nostrils.

If Aelfwynne suspected her turmoil, he never let on. His intense glare implored her to elaborate.

"I wasn't a good student. My mind was always elsewhere."

Aelfwynne held her stare a while longer. When he finally nodded, Ouderling was sure his demeanour had hardened even further.

"You know who you are, do you not?"

159

Keeper of the Jewel

The question threw her. A nervous chuckle preceded her reply. "Of course. I'm Ouderling Wys. The first princess of South March."

"You have a sister, then?"

His query dripped with sarcasm. She could tell he already knew the answer.

"Well, no, but…" The wizard's overpowering presence cowed any chance she had of carrying on a normal conversation with the creature. It was like he judged every word she spoke.

"Then you're the *only* heir to the Willow Throne."

"I guess."

"No! Never guess. That is twice you have done that since you sat down. As a future leader, you must know. Always. Even when you don't, you must profess that you do. The masses expect this. Never display weakness. Lead by example or lose your way."

Try as she might, Ouderling couldn't disengage from that penetrating gaze. She swallowed, not knowing whether to speak or not.

Aelfwynne picked up his goblet and drank deeply, closing his eyes in appreciation of the soothing effect it appeared to have on him.

Without knowing why she did so, Ouderling did likewise. The liquid burned going down, as if searing her throat and boiling within her stomach, but even as she was about to cry out in shock, a wave of calm overcame her. She searched the dark liquid, wondering what the wizard had put in it.

Aelfwynne's unsettling grin grew wider. "Your first real taste of earth blood. If you prove unworthy, it will kill you."

Keeper of the Jewel

Learn to Fly

Stunned, the stone goblet slipped from Ouderling's fingers and broke on the ground in front of her—the viscous liquid sizzling and smoking as it seeped into the stone floor of Aelfwynne's little chamber.

Ouderling jumped to her feet in alarm but a hard knock on the back of her head dropped her back to the low bench—the rough stone ceiling unforgiving.

"You *are* the one Khae claims you are," Aelfwynne's raspy voice hissed, nodding his over-sized head in satisfaction. "Else you would be lying on the ground struggling to take your last breath. Only dragonborn may consume earth blood and live to speak of its nasty taste."

Rubbing the back of her head, a stickiness met Ouderling's probing fingers as they inspected the length of a painful lesion to her scalp. She glared at the wizard. "You mean you might have knowingly killed me? Wait until mother finds out. Why she'll…she'll…" So incensed, she couldn't come up with a fitting punishment.

"She'll thank me for carrying out her order," Aelfwynne said as a matter of fact.

Ouderling's jaw dropped. Flummoxed, she sputtered incoherently, unable to articulate her angered thoughts.

"Aye. Your mother has what it takes to be a true leader."

"But…But…I could've died." Her anger waned as his previous words sunk in. *'Only dragonborn may consume*

161

Keeper of the Jewel

earth blood and live to speak of the nasty taste it leaves in their mouth.'

Aelfwynne shrugged his indifference. "If you had died, it would've saved me a lot of trouble."

In the uncomfortable silence that ensued, the immutable silence of the wizard's den pressed in around her. Vulnerable and alone, Ouderling's knees shook of their own accord; bent at a sharp angle to allow her to sit on the hard bench without toppling over or getting too close to the magical fire burning silently between them. What did this strange creature mean by only the dragon born would survive? Surely, he couldn't be referring to her. Despite the heat radiating from the circle of rune etched stones of the small firepit, she shivered.

Aelfwynne's raspy voice made her nerves jump. "To answer your question, no, this isn't the Crystal Cavern. I'm not worthy to claim that as my own. Only the dragons and their handlers are permitted access to the ancient lair for any appreciable length of time."

Ouderling fought hard to maintain his gaze. "So, there are still dragon riders then?"

The goblin's face twisted into a sneer. "What if I said yes? Would that surprise you?"

Ouderling held his intense stare but couldn't keep it long. She lowered her gaze to the mystical flames. "Um. No. I guess not. It's just that—"

"There you go guessing again," Aelfwynne growled, his eyes narrowing. "That's three times. There is no allowance for maybe where you're concerned. You're either surprised or you're not." He sat back, a deep scowl on his wide mouth. "It is as I feared. You're weak. You don't possess the mentality of a Highcliff Guardian. Guessing is a fault that will never bode well. It leads to hesitation. A condition that

Keeper of the Jewel

gives rise to unforeseen difficulties for one who is destined to rule the realm. It's unfortunate this quality thrives in you. The earth blood test isn't always conclusive. I fear my faith in Khae's judgement has led me astray."

She could feel his beady eyes bore into the top of her head. Thankful her long locks prevented Aelfwynne from seeing the hurt twitching her facial muscles, she dared not wipe at her eyes and give away the fact that she was on the verge of crying, she was so scared.

"I'll make the arrangements to have you escorted back to your uncle on the morrow," the high wizard's low growl set her nerves on end. "Leave me."

Pecklyn stepped aside to allow the princess access to her quarters, his smile greeting his partner, Balewynd, who had escorted Ouderling from the high wizard's chamber. Though quiet in demeanour, Balewynd was known amongst her peers as one of the fiercest defenders of Highcliff. Pecklyn had sparred with her many times. He could count on the fingers of one hand how many times he had gotten the better of her with either melee or ranged weapons.

Between Pecklyn and Balewynd, it wasn't often High Wizard Aelfwynne was left unguarded, even while in their cliffside home. Whenever they were elsewhere, however, the old wizard was usually in the most capable hands of the eldest elven member of the Highcliff Guardians, Xantha.

Aelfwynne's bitter tolerance of their constant presence was a source of amusement for Pecklyn and Balewynd, but the former Queen of the Elves had insisted from the outset of the crown's arrangement with the grumpy, old goblin that he should be, and would be, guarded at all times.

For years, that duty had seemed an unnecessary endeavour, but recently, signs were pointing to the need for heightened

Keeper of the Jewel

vigilance surrounding the security of the Crystal Cavern. Subsequently, Aelfwynne had grudgingly taken on Pecklyn and Balewynd to augment his security—albeit he insisted it be done from a distance.

"Your Highness," Pecklyn said as he and Balewynd bowed deeply. "If it pleases you, Balewynd and I shall leave you and the lady Jyllana to acclimatize yourself with your quarters. If you require anything, someone will be posted down the hallway to attend to your needs."

The princess observed him with downcast eyes. It appeared like she had been crying, but there was something strange about the colour of her eyes. Pecklyn was positive they had been brown when they had first met. He didn't want to bother her further with his curiosity, so he resisted the urge to stare. But, if he didn't know better, he would say the colour of her eyes had turned a peculiar shade of orange. He blinked several times and shook his head. No one had orange eyes. At least not an elf.

It was Jyllana who answered him. "Thank you, Pecklyn." She nodded at the blue-eyed, brunette Guardian and added, "Balewynd."

Dressed in black leather, similar to the outfit Jyllana wore, except not as tight fitting, Balewynd returned the nod and exited the small chamber.

Pecklyn closed the door softly behind him and fell into step with Balewynd. "Is everything okay with the princess? She looks troubled."

"Aelf is sending her home." In typical Balewynd fashion, she spoke directly, without emotion; keeping her attention on where she was headed.

Pecklyn had fancied a relationship with the aloof Guardian a few years back, but Balewynd had been colder than the edge of a finely honed rapier. However pleasant, the taciturn

Keeper of the Jewel

Guardian was rarely known to participate in anything aside from furthering her skills as an elite fighter.

Pecklyn raised his eyebrows, almost stumbling on the smooth tunnel floor. "Home? She just got here."

"Ya? Well, she's about to leave again."

Pecklyn stared at Balewynd's profile and frowned, but she didn't meet his gaze. "I thought Queen Khae had sent her to be trained in the ways of the dragons and Fae?"

Balewynd shrugged bare shoulders. "Not my concern."

It was a wonder the thin Guardian never froze to death wearing what she did. Though conservatively clothed, her bare shoulders and arms weren't conducive to the cool temperature of the tunnels, nor the cold winds perpetually buffeting the heights around Highcliff. The slender elf showed no sign of body fat on her lean frame. If not for her well-developed musculature, she would be nothing but skin and bone.

"Did he say why?"

"Nope."

If an outsider observed their conversation, they would believe Balewynd was mad at Pecklyn, but he knew better. Her flat personality had always been this way. She never spoke a word to most of the Highcliff Guardians unless it was duty related. He considered himself fortunate that she spoke to him at all. As such, he made it his mission that whenever he was in Balewynd's company to try to make her smile. She had such a pretty smile.

"He just said, send her home? What about the queen? And the wyrm?" His voice squeaked as he mentioned the atrocity that had besieged the Home Guard and the contingent from Grim Keep. He had to walk fast to keep up. "How does Aelfy-boy think she's getting home? On the back of a dragon?"

Keeper of the Jewel

Moonlight filtering through the opening at the end of the tunnel highlighted Balewynd's high cheeks as they approached the exit. She stopped to look Pecklyn in the eyes. "He didn't say. He asked me to prepare a Wing, so I assume he's planning on flying her out."

"Has he lost his mind?" Pecklyn gaped. "The dragons won't agree to that. They'll eat her."

"She's the princess."

"So? Since when did our stature hold sway with dragonkind? Our politics' shortcomings lie at the root of the dragon dilemma. Princess or not, the dragons won't contravene Grimclaw's Edict."

Balewynd stared him in the eye but didn't respond.

"Ya, ya. I know. He never told you how he was going to remove her, did he?"

She shook her head and pulled aside the strands of shoulder blade length hair that had blown across her face as a gust of wind swept down the tunnel.

"Great. If we force her on the dragons, they eat her. If we take her through the Passage of Dolor, we'll get eaten along with her. Either way won't be a positive experience for the princess. We have to find a different way."

Balewynd's serious demeanour softened. "What do you suggest?"

"I have no idea. Seems I'll have to strap her to my back, flap my arms hard, and hope I learn to fly before we hit the lake." Frustrated, he threw his arms up in disgust and tromped into the night.

Balewynd watched him stomp out of the tunnel, the semblance of a smile on her lips.

Keeper of the Jewel

Old Guard

Inadequate. That was the kindest thing Ouderling could think of to describe the cramped quarters she and Jyllana had been given to sleep in. Imagine. The heir to the Willow Throne sharing a thin layer of scratchy straw with a member of the Home Guard, the bed barely as wide as her shoulders, all cramped into a grotto no bigger than her closet back in Borreraig Palace. If she wasn't so intimidated by the green wizard, she would have marched straight back to his cave and demanded accommodations more befitting her office.

She sighed hard, venting her annoyance at the whole ordeal. At least they were only staying for one night. As strange as it seemed, that was what bothered her most.

She wanted to storm around and stamp her feet, but there was little room to move. Disgusted, she sat on Jyllana's rucksack and glared at the door. There wasn't even a window in the cursed place.

A loud knock startled them both. Jyllana pulled one of her daggers free of its sheath and exchanged glances with Ouderling. Ouderling nodded.

Her back against the door, Jyllana asked, "Who is it?"

"My name is Xantha, Your Highness. I'm a Highcliff Elder. May I have a word with you?"

Jyllana looked to Ouderling for guidance.

Ouderling didn't feel like company. Not that she had wanted to come to Highcliff in the first place, but she certainly didn't want to be here anymore. Not after the goblin had called her out.

Thinking on how things had evolved since being rescued from the mountain depths, she should have been ecstatic about going home. That's what she had wanted all along. To be left alone to do as she pleased. But the thought of facing her parents and explaining she hadn't met the high wizard's standards was something she wasn't looking forward to.

Her eyes widened. Buddy! She had let him run free with the Herd of Bascule. A fresh wave of tears threatened to streak her cheeks. She shook her head at Jyllana, imagining what a disaster she must look.

Jyllana nodded and spoke to the door. "Princess Ouderling doesn't wish to be distur—" Her voice rose an octave as the door opened, knocking her aside.

"Hey!" Jyllana grabbed the edge of the door and threw it the rest of the way open, her dagger held at the ready. "I said…" She trailed off.

The most muscular, female elf Ouderling had ever witnessed stood in the doorway.

Long, grey hair tumbled in no apparent order past the elf's broad shoulders. Muscles a female normally didn't have rose above her collar bone to support her thick neck. Pointed ears protruded beyond a wild mane of thinning, coarse hair that framed her wrinkled face. Though her beauty had been tattered by time, Xantha radiated an air of someone not to be trifled with.

A thick sword hilt extended above her left shoulder, the grip resembling one of the crude blades the humans north of South March liked to employ when hacking their foes into submission. Wearing nothing but a thick, leather armour bra and long, black suede pants that disappeared into knee-high, fur-cuffed, leather boots, Xantha appeared barbaric. Skin withered and blemished by years of exposure to the elements, the muscles ridging her slim waist belied the age her face exuded.

"Please. Put that away. The last thing I want to do is hurt an emissary of my dearest friend, Queen Khae," the old elf purred.

Ouderling frowned. "Dearest friend of my mother? I've never heard of you before."

Xantha winced. "Ouch. That pains me worse than if your lady-in-waiting were to stick me with her cute eating utensil." She grasped the sides of Jyllana's blade with a wrinkled pointer finger and thumb, and forced the blade out wide. "Please. I'm getting too old to be killing one as pretty as you."

Jyllana yanked her dagger free of Xantha's grasp, her quick motion matched by the speed of Xantha pulling her hand away.

"I'll have you know I'm the princess' personal protector," Jyllana growled and repositioned her dagger for a strike.

Ouderling feared Jyllana had cut the old elf, but Xantha didn't react.

The princess put a hand on Jyllana's weapon arm and squeezed. "It's okay. I'll listen to what she has to say." She stood to meet the Highcliff elder and mumbled, "I got nothing better to do."

Jyllana held firm a moment longer, sneering. Heaving a disgusted sigh, she lowered her weapon but didn't put it away.

Hopeful that Jyllana wouldn't react without provocation, Ouderling turned her attention squarely on Xantha and was immediately captivated by the old elf's pale, purple eyes.

Xantha tilted her head. "I see I'm not the only one with odd-coloured eyes."

Keeper of the Jewel

Ouderling didn't know what to say. In Orlythia, everyone knew of the unique ability her moods had on changing the pigment hue in her eyes. Because of whom she was, most never bothered to bring it up lest they offend her. As she grew into adolescence, she had often wished she could consciously alter their shade to match her attire, but hadn't yet figured out how to do so on command. Other than her parents, Marris, and a couple of elfling girlfriends, she had never really spoken about the odd phenomenon. It was just part of who she was.

Intimidated by the old elf's confident bearing and forthrightness, Ouderling struggled to hold Xantha's inquisitive stare. Being the heir to the Willow Throne, she shouldn't have been daunted by anyone, but she freely admitted to herself that the old elf frightened her. "Say what you have to say, Lady Xantha. My Home Guard and I are tired and require sleep."

"I'm hardly a lady," Xantha muttered, scanning the small chamber. "Would you care to walk with me? Alone."

Jyllana bristled.

Ouderling placed a calming hand on Jyllana's shoulder. "I go nowhere without Jyllana. Either speak to us both or not at all."

"What I have to say should only be heard by someone of…" Xantha ran her tongue behind her upper lip, clearly looking for the right word, "Import."

Ouderling stepped between Jyllana and the elder; having to look up to hold her gaze. "There isn't anyone more important to me than my spear."

Xantha considered her words. She nodded and backed through the open door, stopping on the far side of the tunnel with a hand held out for Ouderling and Jyllana to start down the wide passageway. "Very well, Your Highness. Don't say I didn't warn you."

Falling into step with the Highcliff elder, Ouderling allowed herself to be led deeper into the complex. Jyllana walked a pace behind, keeping off centre of Xantha's tracks in case she needed to react. At least, Ouderling mused, her faithful Home Guard had sheathed her dagger.

Highcliff was a confusing honeycomb of warrens and tunnels—some large enough for a dragon to traverse; others clearly carved into the stone to accommodate the elves. A few smaller tunnels piqued Ouderling's interest; too small for anyone but a large dog. Or a certain goblin wizard.

"Master Aelfwynne has his own tunnels?" Ouderling said to break the silence as the passageway they travelled opened on the main corridor and descended toward a peculiar glow.

"Indeed. There are places in Highcliff only privy to his kind."

"His kind?"

"You don't think he's the only goblin in the world, do you?"

"Well, no. Of course not." Ouderling was caught off guard by the snide comment. Her irritation mounted at the elf's attitude, but one look at the Highcliff elder set her mind at ease.

Xantha smirked, a warmth radiating from her eyes. "Our little green friend isn't alone here in Highcliff. Much to the chagrin of the South March nobility, your uncle included, many of Aelfwynne's people live and work here. In fact, without their keen attention to detail, I dare say Highcliff wouldn't be the marvel it is today. Their stone craft equals that of the dwarfs from Sarsen Rest."

Ouderling found herself nodding at the mention of the dwarven stronghold northeast of South March. Her grandparents had formed a loose alliance with their onetime, bitter enemy—banding together to prevent the human horde from overrunning South March and the eastern lands centuries earlier, in an era known as The Rebirth.

The soft glow ahead intensified the farther they walked. If Ouderling hadn't known that South March now lay beneath a blanket of stars, she would have thought they approached an exit tunnel.

The bright light seemed to pulse. Not all at once, but certain hues within the colour spectrum blinked in different cadences. She wanted to ask about the cause but as she looked at Xantha, the elder gave her a broad smile and indicated that she should look forward.

Xantha stopped and nodded for Ouderling and Jyllana to proceed her into the light. "Behold. South March's greatest treasure. And indeed, the world's, if I have the right of it. I present to you, Princess Ouderling Wys, the Crystal Cavern."

Shielding her eyes from the painful brightness, Ouderling stepped across the threshold of an enormous cavern; its walls, ceiling, and floor a jagged conglomeration of multi-coloured crystals, jutting at various angles into an open space toward its centre.

"Wow!" Jyllana exclaimed, spinning in circles, taking in the dazzling cavern.

Ouderling absently realized that she was reacting the same way. All around them, the enormous chamber buzzed with the sound of wings flapping and the chatter of a language the princess had never heard before. More a series of grunts, clicks, and squeaks than spoken words.

It took a moment for her vision to adapt to the kaleidoscope of colours emanating from countless shards, but as everything came into view, Ouderling marvelled at several

Keeper of the Jewel

flying beasts, similar to dragons but noticeably distinct. "Those are...?" She said in awe, not quite able to put a name to them.

"Wyverns," Xantha answered for her.

"Yes. Wyverns. Wow. They're beautiful. The way they hover in midair..." Ouderling trailed off, squinting to see better. She pointed to the nearest wyvern, the brown creature holding its altitude about halfway up the cavern wall next to a large outcropping of crystals. Something small was on its back. Something green. "Is that Aelfwynne?"

"Hardly!" Xantha laughed. "Though I wouldn't put it past the old spellcaster to worry himself over the cavern. No, that is..." She squinted and leaned forward as if that might help her see better. "Eolande, I believe."

Ouderling's gaze flitted from one wyvern to another, all around the cavern. "This is incredible. What are they doing?"

"Maintaining the crystals. Polishing them mostly. Keeping their luster from fading. They check for flaws or cracks that might require the attention of the high wizard."

Xantha's words meant little to Ouderling. Other than appreciating the exquisite beauty of the place, she had no idea what she was looking at.

Something the Chronicler had taught her many years ago came to mind. Wide-eyed, she met Xantha's smiling face. "This is where Grimclaw was born."

"That it is." Xantha stepped past Ouderling and wandered through a maze of subtle walkways that ran at angles between jags of thick crystals sticking up through the floor of the cavern. Her skin and hair changed colour as she strolled through fields of pulsing light.

Ouderling hurried to keep up. "How come the light flickers?"

Keeper of the Jewel

Xantha spoke as she walked, lovingly examining the surfaces closest her. Though multi-hued, the more they made their way toward the centre of the cavern, the more the crystals took on a bluish tint. "We fondly refer to the pulse as a heartbeat. The Crystal Cavern is a direct by-product of the largest source of earth blood known."

Ouderling's legs felt weak—her recent experience with the high wizard sapping her newfound exhilaration. "There's earth blood in h…?" She trailed off as her jaw dropped.

Xantha stepped aside, giving her an unobstructed view of a large basin carved into the centre of the cavern floor; its edges protruding with smaller crystals, as if they were climbing out of the bluest of water.

A wispy, white, vaporous cloud hung over the basin. The pool of earth blood was large enough for four elves to bathe in at once, though judging by the sharp fringes of the crystals surrounding it, Ouderling doubted it would be a relaxing experience.

She recalled the substance Aelfwynne had given her. "I was under the impression earth blood was darker in colour."

Xantha frowned.

"While I was with Master Aelfwynne, he made me drink something he called wizard's tea."

Xantha spit out a laugh. Rolling her eyes, she shook her head. "Sounds like something he'd do. Wizard's tea is earth blood alright. Taken from its natural environment, its properties die quickly, thus the dark hue. If you were to drink earth blood directly from the source, you'd die a horrible death."

Ouderling wondered who had been the first one to test that theory. Better yet, who had decided that since earth blood was lethal at its source, that it would be a good idea to see if they could survive its affects in its darkened state?

Keeper of the Jewel

She shook her head, curious as to why Xantha was taking the time to show her all of this. "You know I'm being sent home tomorrow, don't you?"

Xantha held her gaze, her chiselled features formidable beneath her wrinkles. "Don't you worry about the high wizard. I'll deal with him."

The elder's concern for her was puzzling. Whatever relationship Xantha had shared with her mother must be the reason why she was taking the time to show her the wonders of the Crystal Cavern. But was it out of a sense of debt or humility, or perhaps something deeper? Diabolical even, Ouderling mused, her hackles rising.

"You claim you know my mother."

"It's true. I know her very well." Xantha nodded. "In fact, I saved her life once, long ago, when the Reaper came to steal her from the cradle."

Ouderling gaped.

"Aye. And again when she was much like you are now." She nodded, a warm smile lifting her wrinkled jowls. She extended her hand and traced a finger along Ouderling's jawline. "If I were an artist, I don't believe I could create a more accurate likeness of Khae than the one standing before me now."

"Who are you?" Ouderling asked full of wonder.

"The last of the Old Guard."

Forgotten by the princess and the force to be reckoned with who called herself, Xantha, Jyllana was mesmerized by the activity inside the Crystal Cavern. A place she had only read about or heard mentioned around campfires while training to become a Home Guard. No one she considered a friend had ever been to Highcliff, let alone witnessed the extraordinary spectacle of the magical cave.

Keeper of the Jewel

Winged leviathans hung in midair as only a hummingbird could; great wings undulating faster than the eye could follow. The resulting thrum instilled in her a sense of what it might be like if she stood inside an agitated beehive. Perhaps more remarkable were the sure movements of the goblin folk walking around the wyverns' backs to access the protruding, glowing shards of glasslike rock.

Wresting her mind from the spellbinding stupor the grotto held over her, she swallowed hard. Ouderling and Xantha were nowhere to be seen.

Dagger in hand, she scanned the nearest clusters of crystals, wondering if they had climbed above the meandering path, but couldn't detect any movement beside that of the wyverns and their riders. Running as fast as she dared between glowing rock formations, she breathed a sigh of relief when she stumbled upon Xantha's broad backside blocking the path—the elder's skin cast in blue.

Beyond Xantha, Ouderling stood with her back to a wide basin brimming with iridescent, blue water. "There you are. I thought I'd lost you."

Ouderling smiled and squeezed past Xantha. "Not to worry. Xantha and I were just discussing how she knows my mother."

Jyllana waited for the princess to elaborate but Ouderling offered no more.

Xantha's purple eyes flicked toward the exit, indicating that Jyllana should retrace the path that had brought them here.

The princess impelled Jyllana with a gentle push as she spoke to the elder. "Do you honestly think you can convince the high wizard to teach me? He was pretty adamant he wanted nothing more to do with me."

Keeper of the Jewel

Xantha nodded. "Just by being in the Crystal Cavern you have proven yourself worthy. If what you say about your experience with the wizard's tea is true, I can't think of anyone better suited to become the next Highcliff Guardian." She looked at Jyllana. "Apparently, your Home Guard is proving promising as well."

"I don't understand."

"Drinking the earth blood is a special test. One that's generally used to mete out prospective dragon riders, but it can be performed anywhere."

Xantha's voice sounded more like a purr from where Jyllana stood. Perhaps a result of the thrum of wyvern wings.

"Most elves don't have what it takes to undergo such a test and survive," Xantha went on. "The rare outsiders who visit Highcliff generally aren't allowed this deep into the complex, and for good reason. Only a special few can withstand venturing more than a few steps into the Crystal Cavern without suffering serious harm." She gazed at the high ceiling. "Had you not proven worthy, your presence would have brought the wrath of the wyverns down upon you. Not to mention that of their handlers." She raised her eyebrows and nodded. "Our goblin friends may not appear threatening at first glance but let me assure you, you'll never forget it if you ever tangle with one. Should you survive the encounter, that is."

"They sound...nasty." Ouderling's voice barely reached Jyllana as she led the princess and Xantha around the last corner in the path before the exit.

"When provoked. For the most part, they're gentle, peaceful creatures who seek nothing but to make others happy. You needn't fear them, but if for some inexplicable reason you earn their wrath, I advise you to run the other way."

Keeper of the Jewel

Jyllana stopped at the mouth of the cavern to let Xantha and Ouderling precede her up the tunnel. She cast a longing glance backward, wondering if she would ever bear witness to such an incredible sight again.

Thankful to have been given such a unique opportunity, she skipped up the tunnel after the princess and the mountain of an elf known as Xantha.

Keeper of the Jewel

Grim Fate

Pecklyn's knuckles rapped off the door of Princess Ouderling's temporary living quarters. It was time to take the young elf to the landing platform and discover what the high wizard had in mind with regard to her return to Grim Keep.

Last evening and all through the night, the warrens, tunnels, caverns, bottomless fissures, and heights surrounding Highcliff had been abuzz concerning the brutal events that had heralded the arrival of the princess and the subsequent rumours of her impending dismissal. It had been a long time since the last member of the royal family had trained at Highcliff. Two decades almost, if what the whispers claimed were true, but the topic of Ordyl Wys was a subject best left alone when in the company of the Highcliff elders, especially where Aelfwynne was concerned.

"Who is it?" Jyllana's muted voice came through the thick wood.

"Pecklyn Ors and Balewynd Tayn. We're here to escort you and Her Highness back to Grim Keep."

A long silence followed.

Pecklyn glanced patiently at Balewynd, his partner looking none too pleased by the lack of response.

Poised to knock again, Pecklyn pulled his hand back as the latch snicked and the door opened. He smiled for the princess' benefit. "I trust you'd like to eat first?"

Keeper of the Jewel

The unpleasantness emanating from Ouderling's orange-tinged eyes made him step back.

"I'm not hungry," she muttered.

Pecklyn glanced at Jyllana, but the Home Guard looked away, clearly unhappy with how things had worked out.

"Alright. Well, if you'd care to grab your stuff and accompany us outside, we can await Master Aelfwynne on the platform." Pecklyn raised his eyebrows at Balewynd, prompting her into motion. "You'll be happy to know it's a rather pleasant day outside."

Receiving no response, Pecklyn waited until the princess and the Home Guard had gathered their meagre belongings and followed Balewynd down the winding passageway toward the main tunnel. He searched the corridor in the opposite direction to ensure no one untoward was close by— a habit that had been instilled into him by the grizzled elder, Xantha. Though he had never known the elf in her prime, tales of her prowess on the battlefield, however exaggerated they might sound, left him in awe of the aged elf.

Dawn crept over the eastern summits abutting the blue waters of Crystal Lake far below. Balewynd led them to where several, long, stone benches were carved into the cliff face three layers high along the eastern edge of the platform.

Instructing the princess and her protector to take a seat, Pecklyn walked to the edge of the platform lost in thought of what the day might bring. Who knew what the high wizard would deem appropriate to transport the princess back to Grim Keep? He wouldn't put it past the old goblin to send Ouderling and Jyllana into the Passage of Dolor on their own and be done with it. He grimaced. Not even Aelfwynne would be that heartless. Or would he?

"How's your arm flapping coming along?"

Keeper of the Jewel

Pecklyn jumped, his perpetual smile absent. He didn't appreciate anyone sneaking up on him—taking pride in his ability to remain constantly alert. Seeing Balewynd standing behind him with her arms folded made him realize how helpless he felt at the moment. He didn't know Ouderling or Jyllana personally, but he couldn't help feeling bad for them. Finding oneself on Aelfwynne's wrong side was never a pleasant experience. He wished he knew what had happened in the wizard's cave that had made the old goblin react the way he had.

He spun away, disgusted with himself, and scanned the still waters far below. "It's not. I hope Her Highness can swim."

Balewynd stepped up beside him, following his gaze. "That's a long way down."

Pecklyn sighed and shook his head in frustration. "The old fool can't be serious. With the wyrm patrolling the upper tunnels, there's no way we can get them off the mountain."

"There's always the Path of the Errant Knight."

Pecklyn cast her a dark look. "I'd rather take my chances flapping."

A dark shape detached itself from the side of a steep slope far to the east, followed by another, and then a third.

"Looks like there's to be quite the send off, whatever he has planned," Pecklyn mumbled, watching the distant dragons grow in size. Several more fell into formation behind the original three, emerging from cliffside grottos along the steep mountain slopes.

Pecklyn turned to stare at the forlorn figures on the front bench. "I hope the queen doesn't take exception to our treatment of her heir."

Keeper of the Jewel

Dragons, wyverns, elves, and goblins filled the great, stone promontory jutting high above Crystal Lake, their cacophony reverberating off the surrounding heights, making it difficult to hear one another speak.

Ouderling's stomach rumbled in protest at her hasty decision to skip breakfast. She ignored the pangs, impatiently anticipating the arrival of High Wizard Aelfwynne. The arrogant spellcaster had a lot of nerve making the Princess of South March wait on him. Had this happened in Orlythia, she would have cancelled his visit and had him escorted from the palace for his cheek.

The din died off as if the platform had dropped out from underneath them.

Ouderling looked up from her brooding, searching for the reason. Following the attentive gaze of every creature on the promontory, she laid eyes on the tunnel they had exited earlier. The purple-eyed elder, Xantha, stepped into the sunshine, her large frame dwarfing a persnickety-looking goblin who hobbled in her wake with the assistance of his gnarled cane—little heads of misshapen creatures with faces that appeared to have a life of their own carved into its surface.

The Highcliff Guardians on duty snapped to attention, scanning the surrounding cliffside. Wyverns and dragons ruffled their wings as they settled into the nooks and crannies of the rock face, while several of the larger dragons lined the edge of the platform, vigilantly examining the lake and distant mountains.

Overhead, the flap of leathery wings reached them from on high. Pairs of dragons soared into view from beyond the heights behind Highcliff, turning lazy circles and disappearing from view.

Keeper of the Jewel

Squinting in the sunlight, Ouderling thought she saw riders straddling the dragons' shoulders.

If Ouderling had to guess, she would say there were at least a dozen visible dragons and wyverns, counting those in the sky. Where they had all come from, she couldn't imagine. She had never really thought much about what went on outside of her small world at Borreraig Palace. During her lifetime she had travelled as far south as Grim Keep as an elfling and had been as far east as Erline, on the shores of the Niad Ocean. As part of her parent's retinue, she visited the capital city of Urdanya twice a year to visit her mother's sister, but never once in all that time had she considered the fact that the world didn't revolve around the palace.

The noise of soft-souled boots lifting their wearers to their feet grabbed her attention. She and Jyllana followed suit as one of the smallest creatures present shuffled toward them, leaving a faint trail in the ever-blowing volcanic ash. If she had the right of it, the high wizard was the oldest of them all.

Xantha walked a step behind the wizened goblin and stopped when he did. Resplendent in grey leather armour, cinched at the waist, Xantha's black belt held her sword on her left hip. A small quiver of precisely arranged arrows and a stringed, polished bow, etched with runic characters, protruded over opposite shoulders. The elder Guardian dipped her head at Ouderling in greeting, but her purple-eyed gaze continually roved the elves and goblins around them, as if expecting treachery.

"Greetings, Princess Ouderling Wys, daughter of Khae Wys, and heir to the Willow Throne. I trust Highcliff's hospitality has been fitting one of your royal pedigree." Aelfwynne's rasping voice echoed off the cliff face.

Ouderling maintained the high wizard's beady stare. She couldn't be positive, but it was as if he regarded her with a malevolent sneer. It was plainly obvious that her cramped quarters and poor reception were anything but fitting a member of royalty—not to mention the fact that he was about to throw her out.

Jyllana squeezed her hand, reminding her to watch her tongue.

"Yes, High Wizard Aelfwynne. Thank you for your gracious hospitality," Ouderling snarled. "I only wish my stay could have been longer."

A row of spiked teeth protruded above the wizard's upper lip, his underbite making his face appear nastier than usual. "Though I have determined the state of your presence at Highcliff..." Aelfwynne turned sideways to glance up at Xantha. "My trusted advisor had the gall last night to inform me that I may have erred in my assessment."

As the words sunk in, Ouderling gaped. Xantha took a moment away from scrutinizing the crowd to wink at her.

"I'll have you know, I'm rarely mistaken. Especially when it comes to dragon magic. *But...*" His voice peaked, emphasizing his last word as he held up a bent and twisted bony finger tipped by a dark green nail. "When I am, it tends to be catastrophic."

Ouderling frowned, having no idea what the strange little creature was on about.

"It has only happened two times before, that I can recall. Once, long ago, and once, two decades past. The first nearly cost the elven nation its collective life."

The wizard trailed off. His hard gaze seemingly delving into Ouderling's soul as if searching for something.

In an effort to prevent herself from openly squirming, Ouderling blurted, "And what of the second?"

As the words left her mouth, she wished she could have them back.

Keeper of the Jewel

Xantha's disapproving glare fell on her, but it was the goblin's twisted features that invoked genuine fear. The pain behind those beady eyes was nothing short of frightening.

Aelfwynne jutted his chin farther than usual.

Just when she thought she would bear the brunt of the wizard's wrath, it occurred to her that Aelfwynne wasn't mad at all. Never having met a goblin before, it was difficult to comprehend what he was thinking.

Aelfwynne broke eye contact, staring at the ground between them. "Ordyl was murdered."

Ouderling wasn't sure she heard him correctly. "What? You mean, my brother?"

Aelfwynne didn't look up, his nod almost imperceptible.

"I thought Ordyl drowned."

Ouderling couldn't be sure, but it looked as if he shook his head.

"That's what mother told me."

Aelfwynne glanced at Xantha's hand as she placed it on his shoulder; the large elf squatting at his side. He shook his head again.

Xantha's stern gaze implored her not to dig deeper, but she couldn't help herself. "Why would she lie about something like that?"

A cool breeze swept across the platform, playing with Ouderling's locks and ruffling the wisps of sparse hair on top of Aelfwynne's head. Silence gripped the promontory, the eerie atmosphere unsettling.

Aelfwynne patted Xantha's hand. "It's okay, my pet. She has the right to know."

Xantha stood up straight. Face dour, she recommenced scanning those assembled.

"You may look like your mother, but Ordyl *was* your mother. At least in the way of the Fae. Ordyl had a unique aptitude for communicating with the sprites as a wee elfling. Your mother claimed that he had shown signs of it earlier in life than she had, and that was significant as your mother is the most capable practitioner of nature's essence I have ever encountered.

"To spare you a history lesson, I'll just say that because of my obsession with Ordyl's ethereal omniscience, I put into motion events that ultimately led to his death. I took him to Grim Watch…Rather, I summoned him to Grim Watch, unbeknownst to your parents.

"Ordyl had so much potential. I honestly believed he was the one to breach the plane between our world and the Fae. The one to open a direct link to the all-knowing faery folk. In my lust to achieve what no other wizard ever dreamt of, I called on magics, that in hindsight, were better left alone. In the end, my manipulation of the dark forces instilled within the foundation of Grim Watch Tower alerted the one creature I had striven so hard to elude. The one I have devoted my life to destroying.

"Suffice it to say, our subsequent battle upon the shores of Grim Ward Island nearly brought the ancient warlock tower down upon us. I sent Ordyl to fetch your parents, hoping they would provide me with much-needed assistance and magical backup to defeat my nemesis. Alas, my foe knew I wasn't its biggest concern. Ordyl's ability had the potential to align forces beyond our comprehension. If Ordyl had been permitted to fully appreciate his gift, my enemy would have been powerless to prevent its own demise.

"I refer to my enemy as *it*, for surely, he has no soul. Anyway, my struggle with *it* left me exhausted and spent in the bowels of Grim Watch Tower. *It* found your brother's boat floundering in rough seas and slew him, eliminating its biggest threat. I can only hope that Ordyl had no idea what had hit him. That he died never knowing he'd been the victim of a much greater struggle."

Ouderling ignored her protector's hand and sat heavily on the bench, the breath taken from her. She had been told her brother's death had been the result of an accident at sea. Nothing more. She forced herself to look into the goblin's eyes. "Do my parents know?"

Aelfwynne held her stare. "Mmm, in a roundabout way. That's why the queen never returned to Grim Watch Tower after that night." He dropped her gaze and mumbled, "Because of the forces I brazenly conjured, the Fae refused to answer your mother's pleas to answer for Ordyl's death. She vowed to never speak with them again. I effectively killed two people that night. Khae loved the Fae. My actions stole that joy from her heart. Though I never intended such a travesty, I effectively eradicated Khae's desire to ever seek their counsel again."

"But she did go back. That's why I'm here. She went to seek the advice of nature's essence and was visited by the shade of my grandmother. Nyxa brought her tidings from the Dragon Witch."

Aelfwynne nodded. "She said as much in her missive."

Ouderling frowned. "Then you know why she sent me. Mother believes its imperative I train with the Highcliff Guardians. She believes it'll help me deal with whatever portent the Dragon Witch alluded to. In her mind, Highcliff is the only place I'll be safe. I'm supposed to learn how to divine my own nature's essence, though I can't imagine what good that'll be. Speaking to bits of light." She rolled her eyes, her rising anger putting an edge to her words. "How can you justify sending me home? Mother will be livid. She'll...she'll..."

Keeper of the Jewel

Ouderling couldn't come up with a just punishment for the wizard's insubordination. To deal with Ouderling the way he had so far was perhaps forgivable. He was the high wizard of South March and she nothing more than an elfling when it came to the ways of the world, but to go against the wishes of the queen was reason for dismissal from his role as high wizard. Was reason for imprisonment or exile.

Letting her anger simmer, she realized she didn't care about anything her mother believed. Her parents had betrayed her by sending her away from the only life she knew. The hurt cut sharper than any message imparted by an otherworldly spectre. As much as she wanted to be home again, she wasn't sure she could face her parents.

Aelfwynne's soft words brought her up short. "You're soft. You don't possess the right attitude, nor the mettle required to remain in Highcliff. The queen will thank me for not making a third error. The last thing I want on my head is the knowledge that I sentenced the world to a grim fate."

Keeper of the Jewel

The Difference

Xantha's look of utter contempt shrivelled Ouderling where she sat.

Without having to look around, Ouderling sensed everyone on the platform had squeezed in a little tighter to make sure they were privy to everything that transpired between her and the high wizard.

Jyllana put a comforting arm around her as if to protect her from a fate no one knew. No one except Aelfwynne.

Suppressing her apprehension, Ouderling accepted Jyllana's assistance and stood. She took two steadying breaths with the hope of keeping her voice free of the raging emotions threatening to make her scream and cry at the same time. "You have little faith, high wizard. I should be the one who decides my own fate. It should be up to me as to whether I do as you fear and destroy the world."

Xantha stiffened, her glare intimidating.

Ouderling licked dry lips. "I don't know what you think I'm capable of, but as the future leader of South March, don't you think I should be given the opportunity to prove myself?"

Aelfwynne maintained her hard look, his soft reply belying his malevolent appearance. "My apologies, Your Highness. My reasons may be selfish, but they are not without merit."

Keeper of the Jewel

The wizard's eyes misted up. He looked away. "I couldn't bear to be the source of the death of Khae's only surviving elfling. I've caused her enough pain."

A single tear ran down Aelfwynne's cheek.

Ouderling swallowed the lump building in her throat. Before she realized what she was doing, she cupped the wizard's chin, his skin rough in her hand, and lifted his head to look at her. "Mother holds nothing but the greatest of admiration for you, High Wizard Aelfwynne. Please don't disappoint her by sending me home."

Aelfwynne tried to step back but Ouderling refused to release him.

"If what you said about Ordyl is true, you owe Mother that much. Instead of allowing me to ruin the world, why don't you help me do whatever it is you think needs to be done to prevent that from happening."

A tear dripped down Aelfwynne's opposite cheek. "My queen doesn't know what killed Ordyl. I couldn't bring myself to tell her. As the years went by, I never found a good time. She's the daughter of my best friend. I lost Nyxa long ago. I can't bear to lose Khae as well."

Even if it means the end of the world? Ouderling wanted to ask, but couldn't bring herself to do so. Barely able to speak past the emotion Aelfwynne's words had evoked in her, Ouderling forced herself to say, "Will you help me prevent whatever it is you have foreseen from happening? I can't do it alone. Without your help, Master Aelfwynne, I'm thinking that what you mean to prevent will happen even sooner."

The flap of dragon wings patrolling the skies overhead filled in the uncomfortable silence that ensued. Finally, Ouderling felt, rather than saw, the old wizard nod. Relieved, she used her free hand to wipe the second tear from his cheek before it reached the wart near the edge of his mouth.

The wizard's claws clasped her wrist and removed her hand from his chin. He straightened his shoulders in what appeared to be an effort to compose his dignity. When he spoke, his question surprised her. "Tell me princess. Do you honestly think you're worthy enough to be here?"

"Honestly?" Ouderling wanted to reply with the haughty arrogance of the spoiled, seventeen-year-old princess she was, but she caught herself. She had so much to learn about the real world. A fact that had been slowly sinking into her psyche since their recent visit to Grim Keep. If asked, she would claim she had matured greatly since being forced from her easy life at the palace. A grim determination had made itself known deep inside her soul. Like a part of who she was had died to allow for the birth of a new outlook on life.

"Worthy of Highcliff? No, Master Aelfwynne, I am not. But we'll never know what I'm capable of if you don't give me the chance." She spoke with as much sincerity as she could muster, the words sounding strange passing her lips.

Taking in those around her, a slow, genuine smile transformed her face. "With the invaluable assistance of yourself, Xantha, Pecklyn, Balewynd," she nodded at each person in turn, "and everyone else here at Highcliff, I'm confident that someday I might earn your praise. *If*," she raised a finger in the air, "I let go of who I am, and learn to become who I feel I'm supposed to be."

Aelfwynne tilted his head, the semblance of puzzlement on his odd features. "And who might that be?"

"The difference, Master Aelfwynne. The difference."

Keeper of the Jewel

King of the Elves

Wizard's tea didn't taste quite as revolting the second time around. Ouderling didn't think she would ever enjoy the distilled remnants of earth's blood, but she couldn't begrudge its soothing effect. After a couple hesitant sips, she mused that her clarity of thought had improved as a result.

She examined the contents of her stone goblet in the poor light of Aelfwynne's chamber; shoulders slumped so as not to scrape her head as she sat with her legs folded on the low, stone bench. "What's in this? I know what you say it is, but what's it made from?"

Aelfwynne regarded her over the brim of his goblet, much the same way he had the first time they had sat on opposite sides of the magical fire. "The earth's essence."

A chuckle escaped Ouderling as she sipped a little deeper, her face twisting with the afterbite. "That doesn't tell me much."

Aelfwynne nodded. "Sometimes simplicity is all we need to know. Appreciate it for what it is, not what you think it may or may not be. Leave judgement to the elders and leaders…" He paused as she raised her eyebrows. "Neither of which you are. Yet."

Ouderling laughed. For the first time in a long while, she felt happy. As repulsive as the high wizard had first appeared, she considered him in a different light now. He was actually cute, in a bizarre sort of way. He still looked

192

every bit the demon she had first thought he was, but getting to know him a little better, his persona was perhaps due to equal parts of his natural appearance and his reputation as a no-nonsense magic-user.

Being the high wizard, she suspected there were many who coveted his position within the elven hierarchy. Because he wasn't an elf, attaining such stature in the first place had most likely been quite an undertaking. Elves enjoyed their privacy; were untrustful of other races. She knew from gossip overheard at the palace for as long as she remembered, the fact that a goblin had been appointed high wizard over prominent elven wizards had not sat well in many houses around South March. And yet, her mother, and indeed Queen Nyxa before her, had seen beyond his outward appearance.

She imagined that during the era of The Rebirth, the final battle that had brought about the kingdom had solidified Aelfwynne's position. She recalled bits of the Chronicler's lessons that claimed that along with the Dragon Witch, and the warlock known as Grimlock, Aelfwynne had been instrumental in deciding that battle.

A common contempt for their northern neighbours fostered a lingering resentment between the elves' and their shorter-lived aggressors. That sentiment had spilled over to include all races. But, for as long as Queen Khae lived, Ouderling was sure the crown would never beseech Aelfwynne's deserved place in South March.

Ouderling blinked several times, wondering where that introspection had come from. She studied her half-drank goblet. Wizard's tea was potent stuff.

The soothing effect of her drink had allowed her mind to relax. For the first time since her harrowing journey, she allowed herself to reflect on the many lives lost the previous day. "What was that thing that attacked us? It breathed fire like a dragon."

Aelfwynne lowered his goblet. "I don't know for certain. I didn't see it myself. I believe it was a grotdraak."

Ouderling tried to pronounce the word, "Grot drack?"

"Aye. An ancient wyrm. A cave dragon if you will. A wingless serpent that dwells deep within the bowels of the world. At least, that's what I concluded from Balewynd's description."

"Wait. What?" Ouderling was about to sip her wizard's tea but did a double take. "Balewynd was there?"

"You don't expect me to venture into the world without my protectors, do you? I would never hear the end of it from your mother."

"Balewynd saw it and lived?"

Aelfwynne's eyes seemed to blaze brightly with the help of the flames. "Ain't many creatures going to detect Balewynd's presence if she doesn't wish them to."

Ouderling mulled that over. Pecklyn's companion was definitely someone she would have to find out more about. "Xantha was there too?"

"No. She remained behind. I don't trust anyone else when it comes to protecting the Crystal Cavern."

Something wasn't making sense. "How did you know where to find us? Did my uncle tell you we were coming?"

Aelfwynne didn't respond straight away. He sipped at his tea and grunted a couple of times as if talking to himself. He put his goblet on the ground between him and the smokeless fire.

"Your uncle and I don't speak."

Ouderling nodded. Though she had no idea why, it made sense. Her uncle was a different sort of elf. Gruff and brooding. Now that she was older, she would even go as far as to say he was an arrogant blowhard.

She smiled. "I can see why you don't get along. You're very much alike."

The high wizard had never appeared more malign than he did at that moment in the flickering half-light of the chamber.

Ouderling corrected herself, "I didn't mean that as an insult."

"I take it as one," Aelfwynne growled.

She sipped at her drink, afraid she had undone the fragile rapport they had recently built. Changing the subject, she asked, "Do you have to evade that thing every time you travel, or is there another way off the mountain?"

"There is another route, but it's too risky, and takes too long to traverse."

"More dangerous than confronting a...a grodack?"

"Grotdraak."

"Ya. That."

"The Passage of Dolor is fraught with danger, but generally, a well-provisioned escort is more than enough to deter anything that may think of waylaying it. The advent of a grotdraak is troubling indeed. I have given it much thought and can't for the life of me figure out why it has come so near the surface."

"Did..." Ouderling found it hard to broach the subject. "Did anyone make it out alive?"

Aelfwynne steepled his clawed fingers in front of him appearing reluctant to answer. "Of the Home Guard? Not that we know of."

He hadn't answered her question in full. She went over the events in the tunnel. Her uncle's troops hadn't been with them when the attacks had come. "What about the Grim Guard?"

Aelfwynne raised hairless eyebrows. "Reports tell of three ships sailing back to Grim Town bearing troops in the duke's colours. How *many* made it out, we don't know."

The news that anyone had survived besides herself and Jyllana should have made Ouderling happy, but it didn't. She considered the wizard's serious stare. "Are you thinking what I'm thinking?"

Aelfwynne picked up his goblet and downed its contents. He heaved a great sigh. "I'm loath to go down that road, but your account of the Grim Guard venturing down separate passageways is troubling. In all my years at Highcliff I've never heard tell of such a course of action."

The wizard confirmed what she feared. "You think they knew about the grodark?"

"Grotdraak," Aelfwynne corrected. He nodded. "It doesn't benefit us to jump to conclusions, but the actions of the duke's troops are indeed odd. Something I must lend my mind to. I can't fathom for the life of me why your uncle would ordain such a move. To send the heir to the Willow Throne knowingly into a trap is an act of high treason. As much as I dislike the elf, I struggle with the notion that Orlythe condoned something this heinous. What would he hope to gain?"

Ouderling mulled that over. She wasn't convinced her uncle would stoop that low either. Though they hadn't been as familial lately as they had been in the past, Ouderling had nothing but fond memories of him.

She sipped her tea, attempting to down the rest, but was unable to do so. An odd thought came to mind. "What would Uncle Orlythe need to do to assume the throne?"

Keeper of the Jewel

Aelfwynne considered her with a critical eye. "What you're suggesting is blasphemous."

"Perhaps, but…humour me."

The wizard's brow came together. "In order for the Duke of Grim to become King of the Elves, he would require the removal of three key players."

"Three?"

"Well four, actually, because I wouldn't stand by and allow it to happen. You, your mother, and—"

It came to Ouderling as Aelfwynne spoke. "Aunt Odyne!"

Aelfwynne nodded. "Aye. If something were to happen to you and your mother, your aunt would be next in line."

"What about Father?"

Aelfwynne shook his head. "No. Hammas could only rule if Khae had died before you reached the age of sixteen. He would have become your Queen Regent. Elven law requires a female to occupy the Willow Throne."

Ouderling thought long and hard. Other than a few female cousins on her father's side and Aunt Odyne's late husband's family, the Wys family name had no other direct female descendants. "What if all three of us were removed? Me, Mother, and Aunt Odyne. Who would rule then? Wouldn't it then fall on my father?"

"Your father? No. He married into the family. He's not a direct descendant of Nyxa, but you raise a valid question. Since your mother is only the second queen of South March, we haven't had to deal with such a possibility before." He met her gaze, a hint of shock belying his calm demeanour. "If what you propose comes to pass, it stands to reason that the Duke of Grim would be the only remaining direct descendent of Nyxa Wys. If that were true, he would become King of the Elves. You're right."

Keeper of the Jewel

The old goblin's eyes bulged as the inference of what may be happening settled in. "It's a good thing your mother saw fit to send you to Highcliff." His voice dipped to a harsh whisper. "Fear not, princess. Nothing will harm you as long as I still live."

Keeper of the Jewel

Wraith's Soul

Grim Keep was abuzz with the news coming out of the Passage of Dolor. Princess Ouderling's entourage had been set upon by a creature from the depths of the mountain. Only a handful of the accompanying Grim Guard had made it out alive.

Servants and nobility alike tied a black ribbon to their attire to mark the passing of South March's heir—the colour of the ribbon matching Duke Orlythe's mood. Though the wraith had assured Orlythe that this course of action was the best route forward to achieve his ultimate goal, he wondered what price his beloved niece's death would cost him in the end.

But what was done, was done. He had to plan for the future. Aelfwynne and the queen would be formidable enemies should the truth behind the debacle in the Passage of Dolor ever come to light. Reflecting on the outcome, he couldn't help worrying that those who survived might prove to be a liability going forward. It would only take one slip of the tongue and everything he had worked for would come to naught.

Chin in hand, he sighed. He hadn't known a time in his life that he had felt as poorly as he did at this very moment. To attain the Willow Throne, the princess had to be removed from the picture.

Now that the deed was done, he wasn't sure he could live with the guilt wrenching the pit of his stomach. He and

Keeper of the Jewel

Ouderling had shared some magical times when she was younger. Whether he wanted to admit it or not, he couldn't keep her angelic face from plaguing his thoughts. She had been the daughter he always wished he had. It wasn't her fault she had grown up to be like her mother.

The Grim Guard manning the exterior door to the throne room snapped to attention.

Orlythe's anxiety rose.

The Grim Guard parted and in walked Afara Maral, the wizard's robes remarkably similar to the wraith who hovered along beside him. The Grim Guard standing in the shadows on either side of the dais straightened, grasping their weapons a little tighter.

Afara mounted the dais and turned to regard the wraith, its face hidden within a voluminous cowl. Two red embers in an otherwise field of shadow gave the ghastly visitor a sense of something more daunting than just an animated corpse.

"It is done, Duke of Grim," the wraith rasped. "It's time to invite the high wizard to Grim Keep."

Orlythe grimaced. Being a hard elf with little conscience, the fact that he was having second thoughts gave him pause. Visions of young Ouderling bouncing on his knee assailed him.

Worse, however, was the knowledge of the next step in the wraith's plan. Entertaining a meeting with the wretched high wizard of South March made his skin crawl. There was nothing more un-elven than hosting a foreign magic-user within the walls of one's own home. A goblin, no less.

His gaze focused on Afara and he sighed at the hypocrisy of his previous thought. Searching for a reason to delay the proceedings, he asked, "How can you be certain the princess is dead? Have you seen her body?"

Keeper of the Jewel

The wraith hissed, "I can't go near the Crystal Cavern. If I could, your services wouldn't be required."

Not appreciating the wraith's flippant attitude, Orlythe stewed. "Nevertheless, I insist on a visual verification before I allow the goblin vermin into my hall. I'd rather peel my eyeballs than parlay with one such as he."

The wraith's red eyes flared. "That can be arranged."

Orlythe clenched the arms of the Lava Throne, desperately trying not to be goaded into a confrontation. His eyes flicked to Afara who remained stoic beside him. If things escalated between him and the wraith, he wondered where the wizard's loyalties lie.

Not one to suffer a threat, he rose to his feet. "Don't threaten me. Not in my house."

The Grim Guard on the inside of the door, alert as always, came up behind the wraith.

If the wraith was cowed by their presence, it never let on.

Bolstered by the implacable loyalty of the Grim Guard, Orlythe growled, "Before we proceed, I demand to hear your name. If what you seek is so important, you can at least allow me the privilege of knowing whom I'm casting my lot in with."

"Names are of little consequence. I'm a kindred spirit in all things that matter. You and I covet something neither of us can attain without the other. Something of such import that both of us are willing to kill for it. In fact, our end game is a mutual one."

"Bah! I seek what should rightfully be mine. If not for the ludicrous laws enacted by my overzealous mother and my spineless father, I would have no need for the likes of you."

A throaty chuckle resounded throughout the throne room, emanating from deep with the wraith's cowl. "And yet, you do. Which brings us to the crux of the matter. As for proof of the princess' death, I implore you speak with your wizard. If you fully realized the nature of the beast Afara and I conjured from the fiery depths, you'd appreciate that the likelihood of ever finding her remains, or anyone else's for that matter, are slim. Be grateful we summoned the grotdraak to the far side of Lake Grim; else displeasing me would be the least of your worries."

If it were anyone else speaking to him thus, Duke Grim would have murdered them on the spot with his own hands. The fact that he was reluctant to act against the one he had struck an uneasy accord with frightened him. What had he done?

The wraith's cowl bobbed as if nodding. "Yes. Only now do you appreciate the gravity of what we have set into motion. In order for the Duke of Grim to ascend the Willow Throne and thus conquer the realms of man, you must first provide a means for me to acquire that which is out of my reach. It is time you did your part and deliver unto me our mutual bane. The death of High Wizard Aelfwynne will open up the path to your deepest desire. Only through the elimination of dragonkind can you hope to rule the world."

The bluster of Orlythe's angst left him as quickly as it had come. He slumped into the unforgiving embrace of the Lava Throne, defeated. Princess Ouderling's death had sealed his fate. He had embarked upon a treacherous path that he could no longer deviate from. Like it or not, he was at the mercy of the soulless thing hovering before him. As much as he yearned to rip the wraith's soul from its corporeal essence, that would have to wait.

An almost imperceptible smile twitched the edges of his hair covered lips. If he remained vigilant and stayed the course, there would come a time in the not-too-distant future that he would tear the wraith's soul from the depths of its

Keeper of the Jewel

ratty robes and crush it underfoot. And he would do it *with* the dragons' assistance.

Orlythe straightened, hard eyes locking on Afara. "Fetch the Chronicler. I have a raven to dispatch."

Keeper of the Jewel

Dawn of a New Era

𝕺𝖚𝖉𝖊𝖗𝖑𝖎𝖓𝖌'𝖘 tension eased from her weary muscles. She hadn't realized until sitting in Aelfwynne's chamber what a toll the last few days had taken on her. The wizard's tea had been a welcome tonic, but Aelfwynne's professed fear of the supposition regarding the Duke of Grim's ascension to the Willow Throne had her relishing more of the magical elixir.

She held up an empty goblet.

A rare smile crossed the old wizard's lips. "Acquired a taste for wizard's tea, have you?"

"A taste for forgetting, more like."

Aelfwynne stood and decanted half a goblet from a crystal urn. Carefully setting the urn on a raised rock ledge beside his bench, he cautioned, "You mustn't drink too much at one time. Possessed of dragon magic or not, earth's blood can be hazardous if abused."

Ouderling's goblet paused at her lips, but Aelfwynne nodded. She sipped sparingly, thinking she would never get used to the afterbite despite the tonic's therapeutic properties. Digesting their earlier fear, she asked, "Do you really think my uncle would harm my mother? Or my aunt? What kind of animal would do such a thing?"

"You have much to learn about the deliberations and machinations of those in power. Most are never content with their lot no matter how well life has provided for them."

Ouderling frowned at the cryptic response.

Keeper of the Jewel

"Take the Duke of Grim for example. He's the master of southern South March. He has his own castle and sits upon his own throne. He has more riches than he knows what to do with. To most anyone else in the realm, your uncle possesses happiness beyond their wildest imagination, and yet, he's forever preoccupied with what he doesn't have. He wants for nothing but lusts for more."

"But to kill his own sister?" Ouderling's eyes flared red. "I'm still struggling to believe he tried to have *me* killed."

Aelfwynne held up a hand. "Aye. We can't allow ourselves to jump to conclusions. What happened in the tunnels is a matter to be investigated, for sure, but the quickest way to incite the wrath of those in power, or anyone for that matter, is to assume the worst before the facts are known."

"But that…That, grotdraak. I may not be the wisest when it comes to the way of the world, but you said yourself it isn't a creature that lives near the surface. Why else would it have been in the Passage of Dolor if not summoned?"

Aelfwynne raised his eyebrows but didn't speculate.

"The timing is too much of a coincidence." Ouderling looked around the wizard's tiny grotto as if expecting the grotdraak to be lurking within the shadows. "I can't believe it! It makes sense. My uncle tried to have me killed. Why, if that's true, he…he…he's responsible for the death of everyone in the Home Guard. Captain Gerrant had been my mother's personal protector while she was growing up in Urdanya. When she finds out what happened, she'll raze Grim Keep to the ground."

She rose into a crouch and looked down the passageway leading into the heart of Highcliff where her humble quarters lie. To where Jyllana awaited her return. "We need to warn my mother."

205

Keeper of the Jewel

Her goblet forgotten on the floor, she took a crouched step toward the exit.

"Ouderling Wys!" The booming voice sounded bizarre coming from Aelfwynne. "Sit down!"

Looking over her shoulder, the wizard's vicious glare held her frozen in place. She swallowed and returned to the bench, careful not to overturn her goblet.

"I'll dispatch ravens to Orlythia and Urdanya as soon as we're done here."

"Yes, Master Aelfwynne." Her meek voice sounded strange to her.

Aelfwynne stared at her long and hard. When he spoke, it was like nothing had happened. "If it comes to pass that the Duke of Grim has had anything to do with the tragedy in the tunnels, I'll deal with him. With the blessing of the queen, of course. Until we discover the truth, Highcliff must act as if we don't know anything untoward has happened."

"Let me speak to him. He wouldn't dare lie to me." As soon as the words left her mouth, she realized how silly she sounded. If her uncle had conspired to kill her, lying to her wouldn't come as much of a stretch. She was about to admit the short-sightedness of her request, but Aelfwynne's stern voice brought her up short.

"No! If the duke *is* behind the attack, we must allow him to think you perished. The best way to keep you safe is to convince whoever summoned the grotdraak that you're dead."

"What if they saw me escape? Someone must've seen me run down the side tunnel. They'll report…" She trailed off, seeing Aelfwynne shaking his head.

"Anyone who was with you when the grotdraak attacked is dead. Nothing can escape the beast once it has their scent."

Keeper of the Jewel

Ouderling muttered, feeling no more than a petulant elfling as she did, "Jyllana and I did."

If Aelfwynne heard her he never let on. Instead, he took a deep swallow from his goblet, his face twisting with the burn. "I'll dispatch an emissary to root out the source of the recent trouble. Until then, I suggest you prepare yourself for the likelihood of the dawn of a new era."

Keeper of the Jewel

Revelations

𝕻ecklyn's eyes followed Ouderling around the inside of the small chamber she shared with Jyllana. He had been summoned by High Wizard Aelfwynne to keep an eye on the princess. She hadn't stopped pacing since they returned.

Though he didn't say it in so many words, Aelfwynne made it understood that from this point forward, the danger the Highcliff Guardians had been preparing for was at their doorstep. The wizard was adamant that the princess' life was their paramount concern, and that, surprisingly, included the Crystal Cavern.

The last statement had visibly shaken Pecklyn. Born and raised in Highcliff, never once had anyone's life taken precedence over the protection of the world's most precious resource—the dragon crystals. Tied directly to the dragon community and responsible for the survival of the elves in centuries past, Pecklyn couldn't recall the Chronicler ever mentioning that one person's life was worth more than what the Crystal Cavern represented. That had all changed with Ouderling's arrival.

A rap sounded on the door. Jyllana jumped up from where she sat on the end of the bed, but Pecklyn put his hand up. "It'll be Balewynd."

Sure enough, Balewynd strode into the chamber bearing a wooden platter laden with food. She waited for Pecklyn to clear the top of the lone cabinet at the foot of the bed and deposited the tray. "I'll be back."

Pecklyn closed the door behind Balewynd's departure and spun to appreciate the amount of food she had managed to scrounge together. "Ya gotta love that girl," he said, motioning for Ouderling and Jyllana to help themselves.

Jyllana waited for Ouderling. The princess didn't seem interested, but after a moment, she grabbed a bowl and filled it to overflowing.

By the time Pecklyn helped himself and sat on the floor against the wall across from where princess Ouderling devoured her meal, another rap sounded.

Balewynd pushed into the chamber without waiting for a response, carrying four stone goblets and a pitcher; slopping water as she struggled to place her burden next to the platter.

Pecklyn laughed at Balewynd's plight but Jyllana rescued her.

Balewynd shot Pecklyn a dirty look before filling a bowl and sitting next to him on the floor, her hard shoulder knocking him sideways.

Pecklyn laughed and rolled his eyes for Ouderling's benefit. He could tell the princess fought to supress a smile, but in the end, his efforts won out. He snatched Balewynd's goblet off the floor and raised it to Ouderling. "Here's to the princess of South March," he turned to Jyllana, "and his most capable protector. May your stay in Highcliff be without hardship or woe."

He hadn't missed the fact that the princess had seemed distracted since her second visit with the high wizard. Whatever they had discussed had affected her deeply. He had hoped that with Aelfwynne's acceptance of Ouderling, the princess would have been happy, but undoubtedly, that wasn't the case.

Keeper of the Jewel

He leaned in to whisper his concern to Balewynd, not wishing Ouderling to hear, and immediately regretted it.

Balewynd digested his words and blurted, "Is something bothering you, princess?"

Pecklyn scowled, his cheeks reddening. He should have known better than to say anything to the mischievous elf. When it came to couth, Balewynd had none.

Ouderling held Balewynd's stare, a strange colour in her eyes. Pecklyn was sure her eyes were a pale brown moments before. The princess appeared upset, but he didn't think she was going to say anything.

And then she did.

"I've only been here a short while but I feel like everyone is afraid of who I am."

"And who is that, Your Highness?" Balewynd asked.

"That's just it. I'm a nobody."

Jyllana, Pecklyn, and Balewynd all began to protest but she cut them off.

"Yes, I'm a princess, but beyond that, I'm no more special than any one of you." Ouderling looked at each of them in turn, her gaze lingering on Balewynd. "Less special more like. But, because of my title, I've been uprooted from my home, whisked clear across South March under the protection of an entire, elite battalion, stashed within a tower in Grim Keep for my own safety, and finally escorted to Highcliff through a mountain brimming with trolls and a creature whose name I can't pronounce that was waiting for me. If I'm to believe a two-foot, magic-toting goblin, the only reason Jyllana and I are alive today is due to the heroic efforts of you two." Her gaze encompassed Balewynd and Pecklyn.

Pecklyn expected Balewynd to respond so he waited, but surprisingly, Ouderling's words had left his partner speechless. He forced a smile for the princess and bowed his head. "We're only doing our duty, Your Highness."

"Ouderling! I have a name. I'd appreciate it if you used it. We're not in Orlythia." Ouderling's emphatic outburst dropped off. "Even if we were, I'd be happier if everyone would just treat me as a normal elf."

"Understood." Pecklyn spoke for all of them, his gaze including Jyllana. "All *three* of us will call you Ouderling. From this point forward, you'll be treated like every Highcliff Guardian trainee, but," he raised an eyebrow, "I warn you. We're rather harsh on new recruits. We don't get many these days, so we tend to lean heavily on them. You and Jyllana are in for some of the worst days of your lives. At least from a physical standpoint."

"Me?" Jyllana sounded dumbstruck.

Pecklyn frowned. "Of course. Why not you?"

"I'm just…just…a Home Guard who is about to lose her position when I return to Orlythia."

Ouderling's frown matched Pecklyn's. "Return to Orlythia? How? The Home Guard were slain beneath the mountain. There's no way you're leaving Highcliff on your own."

"But that was Captain Gerrant's order."

Ouderling stood and glared at her protector. "You take your orders from me. I insist you remain in Highcliff for however long I'm stuck here." She glanced at Pecklyn and Balewynd. "No offence intended."

Pecklyn dipped his chin. "None taken, Your Highness."

His remark earned him a dirty look.

He laughed. "None taken, Ouderling."

"That's better." Ouderling refilled her bowl and returned to her place on the bed. Speaking around a mouthful of food, in a not so ladylike manner, she muttered to Jyllana who settled in beside her, "Besides. No one would expect you to face that beast in the tunnel again."

"The grotdraak." Balewynd nodded. "No, I don't suppose the Passage of Dolor will be deemed safe for some time. I imagine Master Aelfwynne will send me out to assess the situation in the days to come."

Ouderling's gaze fell on Balewynd. "Alone?"

Balewynd shrugged as if it were no big deal. "I move faster on my own." She dug an elbow into Pecklyn's ribs, making him readjust his hold on his bowl to prevent it from spilling onto his lap. "Don't need anyone giving me away."

Pecklyn hurriedly chewed what was in his mouth and swallowed, a sly grin on his face. "Don't wish to give the grotdraak indigestion, more like."

He leaned sideways to avoid the worst of Balewynd's punch to his shoulder.

Ouderling smiled at them. "Master Aelfwynne told me that nobody can escape a grotdraak once it has their scent. Is that true?"

Pecklyn looked in question at Balewynd.

Balewynd shrugged. "Not that we're aware of."

"Then how did Jyllana and I escape? And you too, for that matter. Master Aelfwynne told me you actually saw the creature."

Balewynd nodded. "I did. I watched it enter the cavern where your Home Guard were squaring off with the trolls. Not a pretty sight."

Jyllana spoke up, "You were there? Where? How did you even know we were in trouble?"

"A few of the wyverns working the Crystal Cavern picked up on the grotdraak's presence. Don't ask me how." Balewynd's sad smile matched her tone. "I observed the battle from a side tunnel high in the opposite wall from where your group entered. The tunnels below were full of trolls, so I took another route. I knew something big was happening but I couldn't get to you in time to warn you. I was about to find my way to the cavern floor to help with the trolls when the grotdraak showed up. I saw you two, and an elf who had picked himself up from the cavern floor after suffering a blast of fire, slip into a fissure. Whoever he was, I imagine he must have died shortly afterward."

Jyllana locked stares with Ouderling. "Captain Gerrant!" She turned back to Balewynd. "No, he didn't…Well, at least not then. He kept us moving away from the cavern until he couldn't walk anymore. He sacrificed himself so we could escape."

"The elf was a hero," Pecklyn said. "That explains how you evaded the trolls for as long as you did. The hairy beasts know the tunnels like no one else."

"But," Ouderling's intense gaze held Pecklyn's, "that still doesn't explain our escape from the grotdraak." She emphasized the last word with the satisfaction of having pronounced it correctly.

"That's because the high wizard of South March covered your tracks. There are only three people I know of who can elude a grotdraak once it has their scent. This one," Pecklyn nudged Balewynd, "Master Aelfwynne, and old Xantha."

"Master Aelfwynne thinks somebody summoned the beast," Ouderling muttered, picking at her food.

That caught Pecklyn's attention. "Summoned? A grotdraak? Really? I don't think even Aelfwynne is capable of performing such a feat." He looked at Balewynd. "Who do you suppose can summon an earth dragon?"

Balewynd's eyes searched the chamber as if looking for the answer. She shrugged.

"We think the Duke of Grim had something to do with it."

Keeper of the Jewel

Everyone in the chamber gaped at Ouderling. "Aye. Though, unless he's more gifted than I give him credit for, I'm thinking he had help."

Everything was beginning to make sense. Ouderling's mood since returning from Aelfwynne's grotto, the appearance of the grotdraak, and the fact that the high wizard had changed his mind about sending the princess home. Pecklyn couldn't recall a time in his forty-eight years at Highcliff that Aelfwynne had ever changed his mind.

Jyllana relieved Ouderling of her empty bowl and placed it on the platter. "You know what troubles me?"

Everyone looked at her.

"If the Crystal Cavern is so special, why are there so few elves protecting it? From what I can tell of Highcliff, there may be what…twenty, thirty elves max?"

Pecklyn put Balewynd's discarded bowl in his and got up, setting them with Jyllana's. He thought about how to answer her question in a way that made sense.

"The Crystal Cavern is an anomaly. It's a place where earth blood and dragon magic comingle in perfect harmony. A sacred ground, that when visited by the highest magic-users in the land, can be employed to do wondrous things."

He searched his memories for something that Ouderling and Jyllana ought to know. "You've heard of the great dragon, Grimclaw, haven't you?"

Both elves nodded.

"Good. For lack of a better way to explain the cavern's importance, it was the combination of the earth blood and its effect on the crystals lining the cavern that gave rise to Grimclaw. His birth heralded the return of dragonkind to South March; his rise subsequently led to the formation of South March. Does that make sense?"

Keeper of the Jewel

Judging by their confused faces, he surmised his message had been lost somewhere in the translation.

"Anyway, when dealing with the confluence of earth blood and dragon magic, there are only a few that can get anywhere near Highcliff without being harmed by its purity. Believe me when I say that were either one of you not attuned to both the elements the crystals and earth blood offer, you'd rue the day you set foot in the cavern. You would've fallen ill. If not removed from the area, a grim death would have followed."

"Grim," Ouderling chuckled nervously. "There's that word again. It seems everything is grim when it comes to the dealings of southern South March."

"Depends on how you look at things." Pecklyn sat down beside Balewynd and placed an arm over her shoulder, pulling her into an embrace she didn't appear happy about receiving.

Balewynd ducked out from beneath his arm and gave him a two-handed shove, knocking him onto his side.

"What?" He laughed and sat back up. "You make me happy." He broke away from her scowl and smiled at Ouderling and Jyllana. "Everything about Highcliff makes me happy. Trust me when I say, there's nothing quite like forming a bond with a dragon."

Ouderling and Jyllana gaped at each other, unable to contain the wonder gripping their faces.

"Aye. In due time, you might even fly one."

Jyllana's eyes grew wide. "Me too?"

"I don't see why not. According to Xantha, you both entered the Crystal Cavern without trouble. That's the first step. If you're still here next year, you'll witness hatching season."

An uncharacteristic squeak escaped Jyllana as she wrapped her arms around Ouderling and squeezed.

Keeper of the Jewel

Ouderling put up with the embrace, rolling her eyes, but she couldn't help the semblance of a smile from banishing the melancholy from her face.

Pecklyn crossed his arms and sat back, enjoying their happiness. Revelations of riding a dragon always had that effect on new recruits.

At least on those who weren't terrified by the prospect.

Keeper of the Jewel

The End of All Things

An odd buzz sounded amongst the elves of Highcliff the following afternoon. Ouderling had looked forward to seeing Pecklyn again but neither he nor his serious companion came by the quarters she shared with Jyllana.

Instead, they had been led around the intricate tunnel complex of Highcliff by two male elves who didn't appear much older than Ouderling. Though pleasant, and seemingly having received the message that they weren't to treat Ouderling as a princess, their escort appeared pre-occupied, matching the mood of the entire enclave.

Ouderling had been under the impression that whatever training regimen she and Jyllana were about to undergo should have commenced this morning. So far, other than their escort, nobody bothered so much as to look their way. Trying hard to remember the names of their guides, she grabbed the arm of the elf with long, black hair and a wisp of a mustache. "I'm sorry, I can't remember your name."

"Cynder."

"Cynder." Ouderling nodded, inwardly rolling her eyes. What else would you call someone from this volcanic hole in the wall? "I'm a bit lost. Can you take us to see the Crystal Cavern?"

Cynder looked uncomfortable. "That's off limits."

"We've already been there. Xantha took us." Ouderling was fairly sure she knew how to get to the cavern, but they were in a tunnel she wasn't familiar with. She started back the way they had come. "It's okay. I think I know the way. Come, Jyllana."

"Your Highness!" Cynder said louder than he meant to, judging by how his face flushed.

Nor did Ouderling miss the fact that he had reverted to calling her by her official title. She sighed. It would be next to impossible to separate herself from who she really was. She stopped, raising her brow to urge Cynder to say what was on his mind.

"The cavern is off-limits to everyone today."

"Oh." Ouderling's frown took in Cynder and his male counterpart, whose peculiar grey locks hung straight to the middle of his back. "Why's that?"

Cynder looked at his companion and shrugged. "Might as well tell them, Ashe. They're going to be training here anyway."

Ouderling almost choked. Ashe. How ironic. Cynder and Ashe. Names given to elves living in the volcanic region of South March. How original.

Ashe nodded. "Don't see why not." He flashed a big smile. "Master Aelfwynne received a summons from Grim Keep last night. He's preparing Highcliff for his departure."

Ashe spoke as if what he imparted was common knowledge. He turned and continued up the tunnel.

Warning bells clamoured in Ouderling's head. If the duke had been complicit in the ambush in the Passage of Dolor, it would be dangerous for the high wizard to attend Castle Grim.

She fell into step behind Jyllana and followed Cynder and Ashe through the complex. They had been on their way to the promontory overlooking Crystal Lake at the bequest of a senior elf who had caught up to them during their midday meal.

The more Ouderling considered the implications of the summoning, the wilder her thoughts became. What if Aelfwynne was in league with her uncle? She shook her head at the absurdity, but couldn't get it out of her mind. Orlythe's choices had always been a sore point with her parents. The duke's human wizard, Afara Maral, was proof of that. It wasn't much of a leap to assume Orlythe might also be in league with a goblin wizard.

Her breath caught. Visions of Aelfwynne haunted her. His evil face, grotesquely half-hidden in the flickering shadows of his grotto, assailed her.

She swallowed, hoping she wasn't attracting attention to herself. If Jyllana were to look over and take note of her struggle, there would be endless questions.

Inhaling deeply, Ouderling fancied a goblet of wizard's tea would hit the spot right about now. It was all she could do to put one foot in front of the other without tripping.

Xantha forced a sad smile for the benefit of the handsome face staring back at her, holding her wrinkled cheeks between strong hands. Gazing into the eyes of the only one she had ever loved in all of her seven centuries, she couldn't escape the fact that the last few decades hadn't been kind to her. If the love of her life hadn't been holding onto her as hard as he did, she would've turned her head so that he wouldn't have to look on her aged complexion.

She fought hard to keep her shoulders from slumping, a posture that had become a part of who she was lately. The winds of change were blowing hard and would soon be whisking her away. If not for the fact that she never wanted to leave her best friend's side, she'd welcome the journey into the next world so that she might catch up with old friends.

"Do be careful, my sweet," she whispered, unable to stop her eyes from welling up. "I don't like what the crystals are telling me."

The male elf smiled; his perfect skin illuminated in the pulsing blue glow of the earth blood pool bubbling beside them; translucent mist wafting around his lower legs. He wiped at the tears rolling down her cheeks with his thumbs. "I will never leave you for long, my beautiful angel. I'll be back before you know I'm gone."

"What if the portents speak true? What will you do?"

"I'll do what I've always done. My duty."

"Will you inquire of the queen?"

"I guess that all depends on if things go sideways."

"You? Guess?"

He laughed and released her face, but never dropped her loving gaze. "Don't tell anyone. Especially not Khae's daughter. I'll never hear the end of it."

As much as Xantha wanted to laugh with him, her breaking heart wouldn't allow it. Standing before her, the pillar of strength she so relied upon to see her through the days and long, dark nights that so often brought with them the haunting memories of centuries past, she couldn't imagine living if he ceased to exist.

Oblivious to the wyverns flitting about the chamber with their goblin riders, she sighed and stared at the earth blood bubbling in the pool at their feet. All the power in the world at their fingertips and yet, she doubted it was enough to avert what they both feared was coming.

The duke's summons had spiralled her mind into depths of despair she hadn't known since the last days of the Dragon Witch.

Keeper of the Jewel

Gentle arms wrapped around her waist and pulled her into a tight embrace. She leaned her head back, enjoying the touch of his soft cheeks against her own. His long, white hair itched her skin. She didn't care. "If only the world would stop and leave us in this moment forever."

"I wish that too, my pet." He released her and turned her to face him, his love for her beaming from his angelic face. "But you know that cannot happen. At least not yet. Today I travel to Grim Keep. With any luck, the sun will rise tomorrow and shine on us both."

Xantha swallowed. Not trusting herself to speak, she hugged him, squeezing hard. Unable to keep her body from trembling, she cried.

Light at the end of the tunnel snapped Ouderling out of the palsy her mind had mired itself in. She had no idea how long they had been walking, but they were in the familiar wide tunnel that emptied onto the promontory.

"Is everything okay, Your Highness?" Jyllana had stopped and was waiting for her.

"Um, yes," Ouderling muttered. She willed herself out of the last of her stupor and said more emphatically, "Yes. Everything is fine. Why?"

"No reason. You just don't seem yourself."

"I said, I'm fine!"

"Yes, Your Highness." Jyllana dropped her gaze as Ouderling passed by; dutifully falling into step behind her.

Ouderling sighed. Her protector hadn't deserved that, but she was in no mood to apologize.

Cynder and Ashe shaded their eyes with forearms as they strode into bright sunshine and stepped aside to allow Ouderling to pass between them.

Keeper of the Jewel

Dragons of all sizes and colours lined the arcing edge of the expansive ledge high above the rolling surface of Crystal Lake. The benches carved into the cliff face rising from the rear of the promontory were lined with elves conversing in groups of two or three, their hushed words indiscernible in the gusting wind.

Ouderling stopped between Cynder and Ashe. "What's happening?"

Cynder nodded toward the ghastly-looking, purple hued dragon Pecklyn had flown when they had first arrived at Highcliff.

Ouderling couldn't help thinking that of all of the majestic creatures, that particular dragon was the ugliest by far. Smaller in stature than its brethren, the dragon's front legs were thicker than its hind legs. Bright red eyes devoid of pupils were sunk within overly large eye sockets beneath a high-ridged brow. Two thick horns curved back from its temples, extending beyond smaller horns protruding backward from its scaly cheeks.

Ouderling swallowed her revulsion for the beast, not wishing to have anything to do with the pointed, yellow teeth lining its slavering jaws.

As much as her attention was drawn to the squat dragon, she couldn't help but notice the white-haired elf who stood before it, his golden armour glistening in the sun.

Pecklyn Ors had no way of knowing that she stared at him from across the expanse, but he turned his head, his amber eyes locking with hers. He nodded slightly, his demeanour serious. She had only known him for a couple of days but she couldn't recall a time his handsome face had worn anything but a smile. The hard line of his features startled her senses. Something significant was happening.

Keeper of the Jewel

Conversations ceased and all eyes turned to the tiny alcove on the far side of the carved benches. Ouderling's hackles rose as the high wizard of South March emerged from his private egress.

A dragon shrieked overhead, the piercing cry sending shivers across Ouderling's skin in the wake of a blue dragon soaring by the edge of the promontory.

Brown hair fluttering in the wind, Balewynd's bright eyes glinted in the sunshine atop the blue dragon's shoulders, her muscular legs holding tight. Offering Pecklyn a thumb's up, her dragon's flight took them out over Crystal Lake.

Pecklyn awaited the goblin hobbling out to meet him with the assistance of his gnarled stick. He said something to Aelfwynne, his words indecipherable from where Ouderling stood, and assisted the high wizard onto the scaly shoulders of the purple dragon.

Satisfied Aelfwynne was properly seated, Pecklyn wasted little time scaling the dragon's shoulder and placing himself behind the high wizard. With a nod to those who had come out to see them off, Pecklyn urged the dragon into flight.

The behemoth crouched momentarily before leaping into the sky, its massive wings slowly flapping, pushing great volumes of air as the dragon and its riders dropped out of view beyond the lip of the rock shelf.

Ouderling walked closer to the edge and squinted, staring toward the western mountains. Through a gap between a yellow dragon and a knot of elves, she caught a silhouetted glimpse of two dragons flying side by side into the setting sun; the winged beasts covering distance so fast their riders were nothing more than mere specks on their backs.

A glimmer from Pecklyn's golden armour was the only way the princess could tell which dragon was which as they banked sharply and disappeared behind a distant crag.

Keeper of the Jewel

A deeper shiver crawled up her back.

She wondered if she was witnessing the beginning of the end of all things.

Keeper of the Jewel

The Essence of Nyxa

"**Dragons,** m'lord."

Orlythe looked up from a scroll stretched out upon the surface of a polished, volcanic rock table in a well-lit chamber known as the war room. The head chamberlain awaited his response.

"Very good, Bayl. Fetch Afara and meet me on the steps."

"Aye, m'lord." Bayl bowed slightly, turning to leave.

"And Bayl."

"M'lord?"

"Alert Captain Drake."

"Already done, m'lord."

Orlythe nodded. What would he ever do without Bayl? "Excellent," he muttered and turned his attention back to the chart depicting the west coast of South March.

Tracing a route up from where the Rust Wash joined the Scale River, he followed the main road to the outlying reaches of Urdanya. The capital city was massive. Nowhere in all the lands that he had visited did a city even remotely match the utter scope of South March's industrial centre.

Home to the finest ship builders and metal smiths in South March—in all the world if he had the right of it—the sprawling city was also a breeding den for the seediest of characters. Characters that might prove useful going forward.

Keeper of the Jewel

Not as elegant as the royal residence in Orlythia, Urdanya Castle dwarfed Borreraig Palace. Rumored to have been carved from a lone mountain that had once stood on the shores of the Niad Ocean, any semblance of its former likeness had all but been eradicated.

The noise of growing activity in the halls of Grim Keep precluded him from concentrating anymore on the next steps that were required for him to secure the Willow Throne. He sighed, perturbed by the rising tension the imminent meeting with the high wizard instilled in him.

A clatter of metal boots came to a halt outside the war room door. Without looking up, Orlythe said, "Come in, captain."

Captain Drake entered the windowless chamber and stood at attention in front of the table. "The Elite Grim Guard is in position, m'lord. Afara has set up wards and awaits your arrival."

"What of the wraith?"

"No sign, m'lord."

Orlythe sighed. He wasn't sure whether that was good or not. Dealing with that creature was going to prove the death of him.

He removed a set of lava stone dragons from the corners of the scroll and let it roll back on itself. Putting the parchment in its place in a mahogany shelving unit pock-marked with dozens of pigeonholes, he nodded for the captain to lead the way. "Very well. Let's get this over with."

It was a fair walk from the war room to the main entranceway fronting Grim Keep. The captain remained quiet, the elf's mind forever on his duties. Orlythe only had himself to blame for his anxiety, but he didn't think the wretched wizard would actually come. They hadn't been on speaking terms for hundreds of years. The advent of the

Keeper of the Jewel

Dragon Witch had driven an irrevocable chasm between them.

Not that their differences bothered Orlythe. Their resentment of each other meant he didn't have to see the spineless creature who had subverted the royal family and led them astray. If everything went according to plan, he would finally put things right.

The fact the high wizard came at all spoke volumes as to Aelfwynne's knowledge of the fight within the Passage of Dolor, or lack thereof. If Aelfwynne had known of Princess Ouderling's death, he doubted the high wizard would make himself susceptible to the one who was likely responsible...

He stopped to stare at the back of Captain Drake's head. Or *did* Aelfwynne know?

Grim Guard in the hallway ahead snapped to attention, opening a broad set of double doors; the black wood awash in bright sunlight. The duke's crack troops lined either side of the entranceway, their ranks spanning several steps that led down to the bare scrub bailey between the keep and the outer walls.

Black pennants heralding the Duke of Grim snapped in the brisk breeze that lifted the hems of the Grim Guard surcoats.

Curiously, the outer gates remained closed.

Aelfwynne studied the imposing dark stone of Grim Keep's outer walls. His eyesight wasn't what it used to be, but he didn't miss the well-armed troops manning the battlements as far as the eye could see.

He grunted. "What's the fool worried about?"

Standing a pace behind the high wizard, next to his dragon, Pecklyn shook his head. "Maybe he knows you're aware of what happened."

Keeper of the Jewel

"Afraid I might know, perhaps." Aelfwynne cupped his chin in thought. "Unless we have a traitor amongst the Highcliff Guardians, there's no way he can know she's safe. Something else is in play here. I can feel it."

Standing beside Pecklyn, Balewynd's keen eyes searched everywhere at once. "We should go back." Her blue dragon's growl imitated her own but on a much deeper level.

"Balewynd's right, Master Aelfwynne." Pecklyn patted his dragon in an attempt to calm it. "The dragons sense something amiss."

"No. This is something I must do. The queen's life may depend on what I discover within those walls."

Balewynd lifted her chin and squared her shoulders, her fists clenching. "Then we're coming with you."

Aelfwynne spun on her. "No. You are not. I forbid it. If there's treachery afoot, Highcliff will need you two more than ever."

Pecklyn's gape matched Balewynd's. "If there's treachery afoot, Highcliff needs *you* more than the rest of us combined."

Balewynd crossed her arms, nodding her agreement.

The high wizard of South March wasn't accustomed to anyone standing up to him. There was only one elf with whom he was willing to tolerate such outbursts and her days were long behind her. He smiled ruefully. Oh, to have her by his side again. He would march through those gates and put the Duke of Grim in his place before the greasy-haired fool knew what was happening.

Aelfwynne's anger normally surfaced in the face of such insolence, but a heartfelt smile softened his features. Balewynd and Pecklyn. Other than Xantha, there weren't two more competent elves in all of South March. All the world even. He'd bet his life on it.

228

Keeper of the Jewel

With as much compassion as he could instil in his gravelly voice, he said, "No. There's one amongst you with the potential to do great things. I need you to promise that if anything happens to me, you'll train Ouderling Wys in the old ways."

"The princess?" Balewynd asked.

"Aye. I sense in her a greatness I've never felt before. I was hesitant at first. Afraid, even, for she possesses the ability to cause great harm if left to her own devices." Aelfwynne tilted his head, searching the depths of his experience. "She *is* the embodiment of the essence of Nyxa. Perhaps even the Dragon Witch herself, but her strength lies along a different path than either one of them travelled. I only hope she is given the opportunity to complete her journey."

Both Guardians swallowed, uncomfortable with the import of what he said. That's what he admired most about Balewynd and Pecklyn. Though carefree in their attitude toward life, they took their responsibility to heart. Either of them would willingly sacrifice themselves rather than see something bad happen to anyone in Highcliff.

"Of course, Master Aelfwynne, but—" Balewynd's voice dropped away.

Aelfwynne shot her his notorious, *'that's all there is to say on the matter,'* look.

She nodded in respect. "It will be done."

"Excellent. Now, if you'll excuse me, I have a meeting with someone I haven't seen eye-to-eye with for many, many years. May the Dragon Witch's spirit grant me the wisdom to afford the Duke of Grim the decorum he deserves."

A cold wind swept across the grassy plains fronting the dark walls of the sinister castle. Fine wisps of Aelfwynne's dishevelled hair danced around his over-sized head.

Keeper of the Jewel

Without another word, the high wizard leaned on his exquisitely carved walking stick and hobbled toward Grim Keep. A two-and-a-half-foot creature bearing the weight of the world upon hunched shoulders.

Keeper of the Jewel

You Should Not Have Come

"I don't care," Ouderling opened their living quarters' door to look up and down the passageway beyond. "I want to see the Crystal Cavern."

Jyllana shook her head and hurriedly pulled her boots on. "Then at least wait for—"

The door closed behind Ouderling, cutting off her protector's words. Something monumental was happening in Highcliff. Something they weren't telling her about. It was no coincidence the secrecy revolved around Aelfwynne's summons to Grim Keep.

Pecklyn's demeanour out on the platform as he had awaited Aelfwynne had spoken volumes. In the short time she'd known the Guardian, the smiley elf had never been anything but happy. It occurred to her that perhaps the high wizard had berated him for something, but even were that the case, she doubted Pecklyn would let it bother him. No. Something else was happening. Whatever it entailed, it had rattled the jovial elf.

"Your Highness!" The exasperated voice of her personal protector reached her, followed by the bang of the door to their quarters. Jyllana's usual light footsteps hammered up the tunnel as she ran to catch up.

Reaching Ouderling, she scanned the corridor in both directions. "Cynder said the Crystal Cavern is off limits to everyone."

Keeper of the Jewel

Most people would have wilted under Ouderling's scathing glare, but not Jyllana. She was used to such treatment at the hands of the princess.

"I'm not just anyone. I'm Ouderling—" She trailed off as Jyllana spoke the words she knew so well.

"—Wys. Princess of South March." Jyllana's eyes widened as she vocally imitated Ouderling. She cast her gaze to the floor. "Sorry, Your Highness."

Ouderling would normally have torn a strip off her cheeky servant, but she took a deep breath, the reality of her situation inherently apparent. In her own words, while at Highcliff, she was just Ouderling. Nothing more. There was a new hierarchy to be followed. One that didn't include sovereigns. In the eyes of the Highcliff Guardians, Jyllana was Ouderling's equal. Perhaps her superior considering Jyllana's training with the Home Guard.

She offered Jyllana a genuine smile. "While you and I spend time at Highcliff, I'm no longer a princess. I'm nothing more than a green recruit who, like you, will observe the rules and show respect to those who have come before us. We're equals, you and me. In fact," her gaze took in Jyllana's twin daggers, "your ability with your weapons puts you above me."

Jyllana's jaw dropped. She shook her head. "Oh no, Your Highness—"

Ouderling interrupted, reinforcing she was to be called by her given name only. "Ouderling."

"Ouderling," Jyllana capitulated. "I don't feel right considering you anything but my princess. Why…why I'm sworn to protect you. That's my job."

Ouderling considered that. "Weren't you supposed to have returned to Orlythia as soon as the Home Guard dropped me off?"

Keeper of the Jewel

"Yes, but—"

"But nothing. As soon as we stepped foot in Highcliff, your duty to me was done. Had things played out differently in the Passage of Dolor, you'd already be on your way back to Orlythia with the rest of Captain Gerrant's troops."

"Ya." Jyllana lowered her gaze. "To be discharged of my service to you."

"Exactly!" Ouderling said more enthusiastically than the situation called for. As much as she wanted to get her point across, she hadn't taken the time to consider how Captain Gerrant's punishment had affected her protector. She stopped and grabbed Jyllana's hands. "Look at me."

It took her a moment but Jyllana raised her head, a hurt expression on her pretty face.

"I, Ouderling Wys, princess of South March—I know, I know, I said to forget about my title, but humour me. As the heir to the Willow Throne, I hereby countermand the edict of Captain Gerrant Wood and reinstate you to your position in the Royal Home Guard of Orlythia as my personal protector for as long as you wish to serve me. In fact, let it be known, that I *insist* you be forever more my permanent personal protector from this day forward. My order can only be revoked by death."

Jyllana gaped.

Ouderling laughed. "*Or,* whenever you decide to move on."

If Jyllana had been trying to hold back tears, she was unsuccessful. Her bottom lip quivered as she held her chin high. "Thank you, Your Highness. That means more than you'll ever know. I'd be honoured to stay on as your personal protector. I vow to remain out from underfoot and not be intrusive in any way during the course of my duties."

Keeper of the Jewel

Ouderling squeezed Jyllana's hands. "You're never underfoot. As a matter of fact, I've recently realized I quite enjoy your company. You may shadow me day and night…" A vision of Marris came to mind. Her smile faded but she raised her eyebrows and chuckled, "Unless I'm in the presence of someone I might wish to know a little more intimately, if you get my meaning?"

Jyllana's glossy eyes searched Ouderling's face. A look of understanding widened her eyes. She spat out a wet laugh. "Of course, Your Highness. I would never."

"I know. Now that that is settled, you must remember, I am Ouderling. Nothing more. At least until we return to Orlythia." She thought of her parents. "Hopefully, that'll be a long time coming."

She released Jyllana's hands and started down the tunnel. "Now, back to what we were about. And don't think of talking me out of it. There's someone I need to see."

The telltale glow in the tunnel up ahead informed Ouderling and Jyllana that they had chosen the proper corridor to arrive at the Crystal Cavern. Once in it, the passageway was hard to miss. It was by far the grandest of the tunnels in the Highcliff complex—big enough to accommodate the largest of dragonkind.

The heightened activity around the exit tunnels was non-existent this far into the shadowy warrens. Ouderling and Jyllana's stroll to the Crystal Cavern had been uneventful, but as they neared the magical cave, Ouderling's confidence in why she sought it out had waned.

Standing across the entrance to the infamous cavern were several goblins. The fact that they wore full battle armour and presented drawn weapons was overshadowed by the presence of three wyverns growling at their backs.

Keeper of the Jewel

Jyllana grabbed Ouderling's elbow. "Um, I'm thinking we might want to reconsider."

Ouderling stopped and stared, taking a deep breath. She and Jyllana were part of Highcliff now. Recently accepted, but she didn't think that should change how they were treated by their peers. She pulled free of Jyllana's grasp and approached the blockade of cavern guardians.

Hands held out before her, Ouderling tried to keep the worry from her voice. "Greetings. Not sure if you know who we are?" She held out a hand to Jyllana and pulled her forward. "Jyllana and I have been accepted by Master Aelfwynne to begin training as Highcliff Guardians."

The unwelcoming reaction they received did little to bolster her belief that she belonged. If the goblin folk and the brown, winged beasts behind them understood her, they made no effort to respond.

She sighed and glanced sideways. She had just finished telling Jyllana that her position in real life had no bearing on her standing at Highcliff but she couldn't help herself from blurting out, "I'm Ouderling Wys."

The sentinels glared their indifference.

"The princess of South March."

Nothing changed.

"Maybe they don't speak our language?" Jyllana offered, her hands clenching and unclenching near the hilts of her daggers.

"I don't think they care," Ouderling muttered under her breath. She moved a couple paces closer.

With each step, the goblins became increasingly agitated.

The wyverns stood straighter, ruffling their wings as if positioning them for what was about to happen.

"I'm thinking we came at a bad time," Jyllana said, her eyes flitting from one goblin to the next. "Let's go back."

Keeper of the Jewel

Even as she spoke, Jyllana placed herself between Ouderling and the serious creatures glaring at them.

The middle wyvern shrieked.

Jyllana's daggers jumped into her hands, daring the creature to come at them before Ouderling knew her protector had drawn them.

Helpless to offer Jyllana support, it wasn't the first time Ouderling wished she hadn't been so rash when she had departed Orlythia. Though she doubted her ceremonial dagger, especially in her hands, would deter the creatures facing them, it would have given her something to use so that Jyllana didn't have to fight them on her own.

The wyverns shrieked and lowered their heads, but surprisingly, they turned and entered the Crystal Cavern. Six of the seven goblins followed, not bothering to look back, but the oldest looking one of the bunch, if Ouderling had to guess their ages—she was learning that with goblins, like dwarfs, it was hard to tell—started toward them.

When the goblin spoke, her female hiss surprised Ouderling. "Follow me and do not stray." Was all she said as she spun and hobbled toward the cavern's threshold.

The wonder of the Crystal Cavern was no less captivating than it had been on their first visit to the awe-inspiring grotto.

Ouderling expected to be confronted by the wyverns and the rest of the goblins, but as her eyes adjusted to the pulsating radiance of the multi-hued crystals, the only one she saw was the backside of the older female goblin as she rounded the first bend in the zig-zagging trail across the cavern floor.

Ouderling increased her pace. Rounding the first outcropping of crystals, she lost sight of the goblin. She spun to look past Jyllana. Other than the darkness of the outside tunnel, there was nothing to see.

Keeper of the Jewel

Overhead, the flutter of leather wings snapped rapidly. A wyvern hovered alongside an outcropping of crystals near the cavern's ceiling. The flight of several others caught her attention at varying heights around the vast interior of the cave, but none of them showed any interest in her or Jyllana. Just as doubt began to gnaw at the fringes of her mind, a voice made her jump.

"Ouderling Wys. Just the one I was regretting to have met." Xantha rounded the next bend in the erratic path cutting through the crystals, her narrowed, purple eyes red around the edges. "Because of you, I'm about to lose the one most precious to me."

Ouderling's brow scrunched up. "Because of me?"

"Aye," Xantha growled and pulled a wickedly curved blade from the folds of her fur-lined, brown robes. "You should not have come."

Keeper of the Jewel

The Prisoner

Bayl met Aelfwynne within the cold shadows of the gatehouse tunnel fronting Castle Grim. Waiting for the outer, iron-latticed portcullis to descend and entwine its great spikes into the channels set into the cobblestoned entranceway, the tall chamberlain bowed low. "High Wizard Aelfwynne. Welcome to Grim Keep. May your visit deliver you from what you fear."

As welcoming a sight as Balewynd's father was, Aelfwynne had no illusion that his presence within the Duke of Grim's castle was anything but welcome. The head chamberlain's greeting gave him pause, but his attention remained on the eight, fully armoured and armed Grim Guard who had surrounded him the moment he stepped into the gatehouse. The disciplined reception party's no-nonsense attitude attested that not everything was as it should be.

Orlythe's assertion of building an army of dragon riders to expand the elven borders had been a bone of contention between his supporters and those loyal to Queen Khae for as long as she had been on the throne. Aelfwynne conceded that harnessing a dragon's superior combat presence had been a necessary evil when they had defended South March from the human rabble north of the border, but to subjugate the majestic creatures to brutal campaigns rife with needless deaths to assert elven superiority was not the best way forward.

The winches of the inner barbican protested under its weight, the metal gate disappearing into the heights of the gatehouse ceiling. Ranks of well-drilled Grim Guard escorted Aelfwynne across the inner baily to a set of broad, obsidian steps fronting Grim Keep—their devotion to the duke an ugly reminder that there were many like-minded military leaders within the queen's ranks who would support Duke Orlythe's ambitions if the elf ever made a move to usurp the ruling house of South March.

The high wizard sighed and checked his composure as he stopped at the base of the steps and beheld the pompous fool staring down at him. If not for his devotion to Nyxa's daughter, Aelfwynne would have smote the arrogant duke then and there. Alas, he owed it to the queen to confirm his suspicions before executing her brother.

"Ah, the infamous green wizard has lowered his high and mighty standards and answered my summons." Duke Orlythe's black eyes regarded Aelfwynne from on high. "Castle Grim is humbled by your presence. It must be quite a sacrifice for Khae's high wizard to demean himself so."

Aelfwynne refused to be goaded into meaningless posturing. Not only would such an endeavour prolong his stay at Grim Keep, but he was certain he would find no sympathisers within the black walls. Holding his chin high, he choked back a scathing retort. With measured breaths, he glanced at the head chamberlain for instruction.

Bayl, forever cordial as his station demanded, remained stock straight, shoulders back, and eyes trained ahead. He noted Aelfwynne's hesitation and nodded for the wizard to proceed up the steps.

Keeper of the Jewel

Something in the chamberlain's manner made Aelfwynne hesitate. Never one to be accused of being overly friendly, Aelfwynne and Balewynd's father had shared the odd goblet of spirits over the years. Upon greeting Bayl in the gatehouse, the chamberlain had demonstrated none of that past familiarity—acting as if Aelfwynne were nothing more than a foreign dignitary paying homage to the duke.

Aelfwynne snorted. As if. He placed his cane on the bottom step and was about to start up the broad flight of flagstone stairs but a subtle shake of Bayl's head warned him to proceed with caution.

"Do you require assistance, high wizard?"

Orlythe's mocking voice jarred Aelfwynne's senses. He had to concentrate to keep the faces carved into his walking stick from coming to life. Mustering all the dignity he could, Aelfwynne clumped up the lava steps, his short legs forcing him to step sideways and lean heavily on his cane as he made his way to the top.

A breeze kicked up as Aelfwynne ascended the last few steps. To his right, atop a low tower, Afara Maral oversaw the proceedings in the courtyard—a hooded black cowl fluttering around his bony frame. Aelfwynne harboured no illusions that the human wizard's presence was out of respect for his magical ability. No doubt the master of dark arts observed the proceedings with a spell at the ready.

Aelfwynne's decision to leave Pecklyn and Balewynd outside appeared to have proven a good one. If what he suspected was to come to pass, their added presence would have done little to alter the outcome. The Grim Guard and Afara Maral were more than enough to deal with two Highcliff Guardians and himself.

Aelfwynne bided his time mounting the last step as he considered his options. Out in the open, surrounded by the duke's troops, he didn't stand a chance of leaving the castle with his life were he to lash out. Inside an enclosed room, however, an opportunity might present itself to use the environment to his advantage.

He crested the top step and bowed low. "My duke."

Captain Drake stepped forward. "High wizard, your staff."

Aelfwynne looked into the captain's humourless eyes. Disarming visitors before entering the castle in the duke's presence was a matter of protocol, but to ask the same of the high wizard of the land, one who was also the Master of Highcliff, was an egregious assault on Aelfwynne's station. The captain's demeanour let Aelfwynne know there would be no clemency on his account.

Aelfwynne bowed his head but didn't offer his cane willingly, gripping it firmly and forcing the captain to wrest the gnarled stick from his hand.

"After you, wizard," Captain Drake snarled, clearly angered by the resistance.

"I'm going in."

Pecklyn stared at the black ramparts of Grim Keep. He wanted nothing more than to climb aboard his dragon and drop inside the walls, but Master Aelfwynne had forbidden it. He sighed, his worried gaze falling on Balewynd's matching expression. "We can't. We gave our oath. You know how testy Aelfy gets when someone goes against his orders."

Balewynd's hard glare was enough to shrivel a hardened warrior. "He should've been back long ago. What's taking him so long?"

Shadows crept across the grassland as the sun sank below the western horizon, bringing a chill to the air.

Keeper of the Jewel

Out upon the plain, there was little fuel with which to make a fire. Burning the long grasses would prove a never-ending endeavour to keep the flames alive. Nor did Pecklyn like the thought of the wind igniting everything around them should they get a sustainable fire burning. "You know how longwinded the old wizard can be."

"With someone he likes. Aelfy detests Duke Orlythe."

"True." Pecklyn raised his eyebrows and considered Grim Keep. "What're you thinking?"

Balewynd's shoulders slumped. She shook her head and followed his gaze, her eyes moist with emotion. "If I weren't afraid of the Grim Guard taking down the dragons, I'd land Mirage in Duke Orlythe's lap and see how he likes it when a dragon holds *him* captive."

Pecklyn observed Mirage, Balewynd's sky-blue dragon. He knew for a certainty that the male dragon wouldn't hesitate to do what his rider asked of him. Pecklyn looked into his own dragon's fiery orbs. Dawnbreaker glared back, clearly agitated as she listened to the conversation.

"Balewynd has the right of it. We should strike fast and hard. Me and Mirage aren't afraid of the duke's defenses." Dawnbreaker's voice sounded in Pecklyn's mind.

"I know you aren't, m'lady." Pecklyn forced a smile, patted Dawnbreaker between the nostrils, and considered Balewynd's taller dragon. Mirage would be an easy target for the duke's ballista crews. With his long body and enormous wingspan, the big blue was more of an elegant flyer than a smash and grab raider like Dawnbreaker. "None of us are, but we can't risk you. Aelfwynne holds your life above his own."

"My life is mine to do with as I please. Should I choose to risk it to save the goblin's sorry, green hide, then that's for me to decide."

Keeper of the Jewel

Mirage stomped on the ground, a puff of smoke escaping his nostrils. *"We would gladly die for Master Aelfwynne."*

Balewynd spun and hugged Mirage's face. "I know you would." She let out an exasperated sigh. "But Pecklyn's right. Master Aelfwynne gave us implicit instructions to remain here. You need to keep out of ballista range until he returns."

"How long must we wait?" Dawnbreaker asked, readjusting her wings. *"A day? A week? If something's gone wrong, how will we know?"*

"That's a good question, my scaly friend." Pecklyn sensed his eyes welling up with the frustration of his inability to do anything. "We'll wait for as long as it takes."

Cold steel chafed Aelfwynne's thin wrists; a creeping numbness mercifully dulling the shooting pain in his arms. Hanging by a set of rusted manacles embedded in a rough dungeon wall far below Grim Keep, he wasn't sure how long he had been imprisoned. He had passed out on more than one occasion—his delirium addling his ability to think straight.

The duke had never admitted to his role in the attempt on the princess' life, but Orlythe's actions when Aelfwynne had entered Grim Keep's throne room were nothing short of a glaring testament that he had stepped beyond the bounds of his duties as the Duke of Grim. No sooner had Aelfwynne passed Afara's lava fountain, than he was set upon by a hulking Grim Guard. Roughly thrown to the ground, his wrists were bound, and he was imprisoned in the musty catacombs of the dungeon levels beneath the castle.

Groans had accompanied fetid odours emanating from behind rusted cells doors as the Grim Guard dragged him down to the deepest part of the dungeon levels. Every now and then, a Grim Guard would pound on a random cell door and threaten an unpleasant fate to whoever was inside if they didn't stop whimpering.

Struggling to focus his thoughts, Aelfwynne envisioned the young princess sitting across the fire in his cramped quarters, her face twisted in the afterbite of wizard's tea. The recollection hardened his resolve. Nyxa's granddaughter's life hung in the balance. He cared little about himself, but he owed it to the memory of his dear friend to ensure that Ouderling Wys didn't come to harm. If his gut feeling served him well, the heir to the Willow Throne was paramount to the future of dragonkind and the world in general.

A stool scraped outside his cell, followed by a gruff voice, "Who's there?"

If someone answered, Aelfwynne couldn't hear, but shortly the metallic scrape of a key being inserted into the cell door and the subsequent clicking of the lock mechanism drew his attention.

Torchlight flooded the dark cell, blinding Aelfwynne. Squinting against the dazzling light, three figures passed a grizzled guard who had been stationed outside, and entered his cell. Duke Orlythe himself, and two figures clad in hooded black cloaks.

The smaller of the cloaked figures shuffled up to him and lifted his chin, the torch in his hand dangerously close to Aelfwynne's face.

"Afara Maral," Aelfwynne growled despite his dry throat. "I'd recognize your stench anywhere."

The human wizard's hold on Aelfwynne's chin intensified, wrenching the goblin's head one way and then another, studying Aelfwynne's beady eyes.

"Still wasting your life hanging out with this lot, I see," Aelfwynne said through clenched teeth. Waiting for the right moment, he lunged with his head and snapped his pointed teeth at Afara's hand.

Faster than Aelfwynne would have given him credit for, Afara jerked his hand from harm's way.

The human wizard chuckled, eyeing Aelfwynne's restraints. "A strange choice of words, high wizard, given your current situation."

"Wait until the queen hears of this." Aelfwynne spat and lunged again; the action twisting his face in pain as his fetters prevented his movement.

The Duke of Grim stepped in beside Afara, turning up his nose in repulsion. "Oh, not to worry. Khae will know of your demise soon enough." His fist struck Aelfwynne's cheek, splitting his lip. "I intend on telling her myself."

"Enough!" The raspy voice of the third member of the duke's party hissed.

The cool air in the cell became noticeably colder. "He's no good to me if you kill him too soon."

Duke Orlythe's chest rose and fell with great heaves—his clenched fists trembling.

"Cut him down," the third one to enter the cell ordered.

Afara and Orlythe spun on the cloaked figure, their faces agog as if such an action was ludicrous.

Aelfwynne didn't experience fear very often. He had lived many centuries battling all sorts of terrors, but as the cloaked figure drifted toward him, fiery eye sockets blazed within a ratty cowl, sending a cold dread up his spine. The soulless creature he had striven to eradicate from the world had survived its encounter with the Dragon Witch. He had feared as much. Everything that had happened recently, including the appearance of the grotdraak, began to make sense.

"You heard me!" The wraith hissed.

Keeper of the Jewel

"He's dangerous," Orlythe protested. "He's the high wizard."

"I know who he is. My little goblin friend and I have much to discuss, don't we Aelfwynne?"

Orlythe shook his head in disgust and motioned for the burly guard standing outside the cell along with the unobtrusive form of the head chamberlain, Bayl, to release Aelfwynne.

Free of the manacles, Aelfwynne dropped to the cell floor in a heap.

"Leave us," the wraith hissed. It turned its head to stare at the high wizard's cane. "And take that vile stick with you. Cast it into Crag's Forge and destroy it before it does any more damage."

Duke Orlythe nodded and Afara grabbed the gnarled cane carved with misshapen faces. Together, they followed the dungeon keeper to where Bayl awaited in the dim passageway. The human wizard handed the cane to Bayl, disgust on his face at having handled the high wizard's talisman, and started down the passageway, leaving Aelfwynne to his fate.

Keeper of the Jewel

Xantha's Lament

Xantha's purple eyes stared into Ouderling's orange gaze, a curved dagger brandished between them.

Jyllana's twin daggers jumped into her hands, the startled Home Guard acting on instinct. She stepped between the princess and the keeper of the cavern.

Xantha laughed, but there was no joy on her haggard complexion. She dropped her blade to the ground, the gleaming steel rattling on the floor of the Crystal Cavern. Stepping toward Jyllana, she lifted her chin to expose her chicken-skinned neck. "Use your knives. It makes no matter. The princess' presence has already sealed my fate."

Jyllana swallowed, rocking back and forth on the balls of her feet, unsure what to do. She glanced at Ouderling for guidance.

Ouderling examined Xantha's discarded blade at her feet and then the old guard's face. "I'm not sure what you mean."

Xantha responded by exposing her neck further.

Ouderling motioned for Jyllana to lower her daggers. "What would make you think we came to kill you?"

Xantha let her chin drop and slumped dejectedly against an outcropping of pink crystals. "Oh, I would never think that of Your Highness. I'm asking you to end my suffering."

Ouderling crouched to retrieve Xantha's blade, only taking her eyes off the old guard for the time it took to snatch the weapon from the floor. Standing tall, she contemplated what to do, the ancient blade heavy in her grasp.

She lowered the dagger to her thigh. Xantha wasn't making sense. Unless her first impression of the old guard had been dead wrong, Xantha possessed more fortitude than anyone else at Highcliff. Her bizarre attitude was puzzling to say the least. "I don't understand. Suffering from what?"

"The death of the only one I've ever loved."

Ouderling searched her memory, knowing full well she hadn't killed anyone. At least not knowingly. "I'm not sure what you mean…" Her eyes widened. "Oh. You mean someone who was killed in the Passage of Dolor?"

Jyllana tensed as Xantha scowled and pushed off the wall, wagging a finger in Ouderling's face.

"No! Your arrival at Highcliff has upset the harmony. You brought the shadow of death with you. It's only a matter of time before our staunchest defender is killed." Xantha threw her arms in the air and glanced at the wyverns hovering along the cavern walls. "Do you have any idea what Aelfwynne's death will mean to dragonkind?"

Ouderling's legs felt weak. The Highcliff Guardian's ramblings made no sense but the urgency and pain in Xantha's words left her reeling.

Xantha spun on Ouderling. "Think, Your Highness! What will happen when Aelfwynne attends Grim Keep?"

Ouderling's brow creased deeper.

"Duke Orlythe tried to kill you. Surely you realize there's no way my soul mate will be allowed to leave the black keep with his life. Aelfwynne answered the duke's summons on your behalf because it's the only way to prove the truth of the duke's treason. A truth we already know."

Ouderling stepped back, stunned. She swallowed as Xantha's lament became brutally clear.

Keeper of the Jewel

Aelfwynne was not only the high wizard of Highcliff, but he was also Xantha's mate.

Cast in the blue iridescence of the earth blood pool bubbling in the centre of the Crystal Cavern, Ouderling sat upon a jut of pulsing, purple crystal, her arm around Xantha's shoulder in a vain effort to comfort the aging elf.

Jyllana leaned against an orangey-blue crystal a few steps away, her daggers back in their sheath. Her hands jerked momentarily as Ouderling presented Xantha with her curved blade.

"Take your dagger. I don't think we'll be using it today," Ouderling whispered and patted Xantha's back. It felt strange to comfort someone several centuries older than herself. If the queen could see her now, she doubted her mother would believe her eyes.

Xantha stared at the blade Ouderling placed on her lap for a long time before she took it and placed it on the crystal shard beside her. "I'm sorry, Your Highness."

Ouderling squeezed the old guard's muscular shoulder. "There's nothing to be sorry about. Aelfwynne will be back soon and we'll forget this ever happened." She glanced at Jyllana for help.

"Yes. Exactly." Jyllana blurted.

"You see?"

Xantha nodded.

Listening to the thrum of wyvern wings about the chamber, Ouderling couldn't help wondering how a union between an elf and a goblin was even possible. As she gave Xantha the quiet she needed, her thoughts jumped in many directions.

She wasn't any less confused about the whole ordeal she had been subjugated to since that fateful morning her mother had sensed the phantasm. Her talk with Aelfwynne in his chamber came back to her. They had suspected her uncle must have had help if he had anything to do with the grotdraak's appearance.

She took a great intake of breath, not quite believing what her instincts were telling her were true. The phantasm her mother had sensed was in league with her uncle. She peered through the misty vapor emanating from the pool to scan the glowing crystals, hoping to find confirmation in the palpable magical essence of the cavern, and yet, something deep inside her stirred, telling her she was right.

"What is it?" Xantha's voice startled Ouderling back to the present.

Not wanting to stress the old Guardian any further, Ouderling wracked her brain for something to say. Staring into Xantha's troubled eyes, it struck her that she vaguely remembered seeing the Highcliff Guardian at Orlythia many years ago. "You've visited the palace at Orlythia."

The worry on Xantha's face lessened. "Yes. It's a beautiful place. Why?"

Ouderling shrugged, trying to keep the distracting conversation going. "I thought so. How about Master Aelfwynne? I don't recall seeing him at court."

A bittersweet smile played on Xantha's lips. "Oh, he was there alright. Every time I was and many times on his own."

Ouderling pondered that. "Odd that I can't remember him. No offense, but I'd remember seeing a goblin in my home."

"That's because you didn't know what to look for."

"How's that?"

"Aelfwynne is conscious of how different he is from the elves. He was a great friend of your grandparents, and indeed your mother, but he never wanted them to feel uncomfortable while performing their duties as sovereigns of South March. So, whenever he attended court, he came in disguise."

Ouderling spit out a short laugh. She covered her mouth, embarrassed. "Sorry. I don't mean to laugh, but even in disguise, I think I'd be able to pick him out. Why, he'd look like an elfling."

"Ah," Xantha's face lit up, a faint smile driving away the last semblances of what had been bothering her earlier. "Aelfwynne is a powerful wizard. He's mastered spells well beyond the norm of most magic-users. Chief of them is an ability to transform his physical self into something quite different from his usual form. Given the proper amount of time to cast the spell, he can transform into an elf. At least in all outward appearances."

Ouderling blinked several times as she digested Xantha's words. "So, that's how you two first met?"

Any happiness Xantha was experiencing at telling the tale of Aelfwynne fell away. She glared at Ouderling. "Absolutely not. I fell in love with Aelfwynne long before he learned that spell. I love him for who he is not who the rest of South March wishes he were. Aelfwynne spent many years devising that spell. Decades. Not wishing to give the king and queen any trouble, nor me, though I could care less, he learned how to transform his appearance."

Jyllana moved in closer. She gazed at Xantha in wonder. "How is that even possible? I mean, for an elf and a goblin to…" Her cheeks reddened. "Oh, I'm sorry. I didn't mean to be so bold, I-I just—"

Xantha spit out a harsh laugh. "It's okay. I can only imagine how strange this all seems, but trust me, if there's a will and a love that's deep enough, there's always a way." She smiled sheepishly. "But yes. Whenever he assumes his elf form, it makes things much less complicated."

Keeper of the Jewel

The wonder on Jyllana's face matched her voice. "Wow. If Master Aelfwynne was afraid of what the elves thought of him being a goblin, why doesn't he remain an elf?"

"Two reasons. The first being that it takes a lot of effort to change his appearance. To maintain it for long periods of time is exhausting. The second, and more important reason, however, is, why should he? To those who genuinely care about him, they love him for who he is, not who others deem he should be. He's Aelfwynne. That's it. Why should he pretend to be anyone else? I'm Xantha. You're Jyllana. He's Aelfwynne. End of discussion."

Jyllana nodded and looked at the ground between them. "My apologies, Xantha. I meant no disrespect."

Xantha stood and lifted Jyllana's chin with wrinkled fingers. "I know you didn't. You're pure of heart." She directed Jyllana's gaze to the glittering cavern surrounding them. "You wouldn't be permitted in here if you weren't. Beautiful, isn't it?"

Jyllana nodded into her hand.

"Only the purest of souls may enjoy the Crystal Cavern for what it represents. The coming together of earth blood, dragon magic, and one other thing that most elves will never admit to."

Jyllana and Ouderling hung on her words, not daring to interrupt.

"Do either one of you know what that might be?"

Ouderling shook her head. Jyllana did likewise.

"Mankind."

The very word shocked Ouderling to the core.

Xantha nodded. "Aye. Don't be so surprised. When I say mankind, I mean elves too. Dwarfs. Giants. Goblins. Gnomes. Like it or not, we're all related. Bipedal creatures that, though different in outward appearances, are fundamentally identical. We're all capable of independent thought."

"Trolls too?" Jyllana wondered aloud.

Xantha shrugged. "Who knows? Perhaps on a basic level. But none of that's important. What matters is this." She spread her arms to include the Crystal Cavern. "Nowhere else in the world, that I'm aware of at least, can all three magics coexist in perfect harmony. Much as the outside world should coexist were it not for the disparaging forces that seek to eliminate all that's beautiful in life."

If Ouderling's mind wasn't buzzing before, it now teemed with questions on a wide variety of subjects. Not wanting to bother the troubled Guardian, she thought better about broaching many of them in case they caused her grief, but given the speed at which her life had spiraled out of control, she decided she dare not let the opportunity pass her by. According to Xantha, Aelfwynne's life was in question. If the high wizard were to perish at the hands of her uncle, only the spirits knew what that would mean to Highcliff. Not to mention her and her family.

Ouderling poised herself to ask Xantha about the details involving Aelfwynne's summons to Grim Keep. She stopped herself as the saddest look crossed Xantha's face.

Tears rolled down the old elf's cheeks.

Ouderling hated seeing anyone cry, but witnessing the pain on the face of someone who had lived for over seven hundred years was too much to bear. She put a comforting hand on Xantha's wrist and squeezed gently. "Master Aelfwynne will be fine. I know he will."

Xantha's shoulders shook, her muffled response indecipherable.

Ouderling exchanged a questioning glance with Jyllana.

Jyllana shrugged.

Keeper of the Jewel

Leaning close, Ouderling said, "I'm sorry. I couldn't hear you."

Xantha's sobs sputtered. She wiped her aged face on the shoulders of her robes. Facing Ouderling, she inhaled deeply. "There's something I wanted to tell Aelfwynne. I was waiting for the right time and now I fear it's too late."

Ouderling put on her bravest face, trying not to cry herself. She patted Xantha's wrist. "Nonsense. Tell him when he gets back. Pecklyn and Balewynd will make sure he doesn't come to harm."

The look on Xantha's wizened features bespoke she knew different. "I know Aelfwynne better than anyone. If he suspects treachery at the hands of the duke, he won't put their lives in jeopardy. He'll face the duke alone."

"You can't know that."

The look on Xantha's face spoke otherwise.

"Whatever it is. I'm sure he already knows," Ouderling said in an effort to pacify the Guardian. "He *is* the high wizard."

Xantha shook her head, fresh tears threatening to fall. She sniffed loudly. "I'm pregnant."

Ouderling wasn't sure what she expected to hear, but Xantha being pregnant was amongst the last things she would have thought. Her cheeks flamed hot as she realized how badly she gaped.

Xantha nodded. "Aye. Now you know."

Unable to speak past the lump in her throat, Ouderling couldn't fathom Xantha having Aelfwynne's baby, but she had no reason to suspect the old elf would lie about something like that.

"I realized it the day Aelfwynne went into the Passage of Dolor to rescue you. He's had so much on his mind since your arrival that I dared not distract him from the task at

Keeper of the Jewel

hand." Xantha lowered her chin to her chest. Her voice dropped to a whisper. "Aelfwynne always wanted a family but due to our mixed races, he never believed it possible."

The old Guardian looked away, her voice cracking. "And now he'll never know."

Keeper of the Jewel

Old Stomping Ground

"**See** that his body follows his staff into the fiery abyss," the wraith hissed and drifted from the cell. It stopped on the far side of the cell door, its red orbs staring straight at Orlythe. "When I return, I expect your strike force will be ready."

Orlythe shuddered under the wraith's scrutiny—the cold left in its wake gave him the chills. He swallowed, his voice weak. "It'll be ready."

"Excellent," the wraith's rasp filled the corridor as it disappeared from view, a maniacal laugh marking its departure.

Orlythe forced himself to stop staring at the spot the wraith had vacated and turned his attention on Afara Maral. Grim Keep's wizard was bent over the motionless body of the high wizard of South March. "Is…is he dead?"

Afara straightened up. "He clings to life, but his essence fades quickly. If we don't hurry, he'll be dead before I can perform my spell."

"Very well." Orlythe nodded, fed up with the whole ordeal. "See that it's done quickly. Once you have what we need, feed him to your furnace."

Afara bowed his head. "Aye, m'lord. It will be done."

The wizard gestured to two acolytes waiting patiently in the tunnel. They rushed in, each grabbing Aelfwynne by a wrist, and dragged him out of the putrid cell.

Keeper of the Jewel

Orlythe turned up his nose as the assistant's passage stirred the obnoxious aroma of the cell—not all of it due to Aelfwynne's loss of bodily functions. A look of disgust twisted his face as he followed Afara Maral down the tunnel in the opposite direction the wraith had taken.

Deep beneath castle Grim, far below the dungeon levels, Afara Maral stoked the fires of his lava forge. In order for his transference spell to take effect and capture the magic contained in Aelfwynne's being, he needed to raise the temperature far above that of mere magma.

Lying unconscious on a carved granite bench, close to the open face of the wizard's roaring forge, Aelfwynne's body clung to life. Chest falls so shallow, Orlythe was left wondering whether his nemesis had the strength to see him through the procedure Afara had in store. "Are you certain this will work?"

Afara never looked up from tending the forge, sprinkling some unknown dust into the flames, and chanting magical phrases at prescribed intervals. If he heard Orlythe, he never let on.

The wizard had informed him that the spell required to transfer the magic ingrained in Aelfwynne and his cane into a broach Orlythe could wear to gain control of a magic beyond his capability would take the better part of the night.

He sighed. He should never had allowed the wraith first crack at the goblin. Whatever it had wanted from the high wizard, it had exacted a grievous toll.

No matter. Provided Afara and his gaunt, young apprentice, who worked silently at a side table, could keep Aelfwynne alive long enough to complete the augury, or whatever the finger-wagger was up to, it would be worth it in the end. With Aelfwynne's magic at his command, centered and channeled through the focal point of the ruby broach, the wraith's days were numbered.

He would wait, of course, until the wraith completed the next step of their plan, but once free of the familial restraints that prevented him from attaining his rightful place on the Willow Throne, ordering the wraith's death would be his first, royal decree.

"Well, I don't like it. Not one little bit." Pecklyn bit at his lower lip and ran his fingers through his long, white hair as he observed the dark hulk of Castle Grim in the partial moonlight of the overcast sky. "We go together or not at all."

Balewynd's bright blue eyes caught the moonlight, her chin set in defiance. "Too risky. Two of us will be easier to detect than one. Besides, once I'm on the ground, not even Aelfwynne will know I'm there unless I wish him to."

Pecklyn clenched his fists, wanting to shout his frustration at the full moon. The fact that Balewynd was right didn't make it easier to digest. It was bad enough not knowing what had happened to the high wizard. The last thing he cared to entertain was risking his best friend's life as well, but Balewynd was right. As usual.

"Fine!" Pecklyn blurted, his outburst out of character. "Fine. But Dawnbreaker and I are taking you."

The look he received from Balewynd made him throw his hands up between them. "Just to drop you off. We won't stay."

"I'm Balewynd's dragon," Mirage growled. *"My rider. My responsibility."*

Pecklyn forced a smile. "Not this time. Bale must be dropped off quickly and quietly. If someone even suspects she's in the castle, her life will be in danger. Dawnbreaker is better suited to get her in unobserved."

Keeper of the Jewel

The blue dragon growled. The noise he made was bad enough but Pecklyn feared Mirage was about to spout a burst of fire. If he did, the Grim Watch would know they had returned.

Just before nightfall, a rider on horseback had left Grim Keep to inform them that the high wizard would be staying the night and that the duke would send a raven to Highcliff when Aelfwynne was ready to return home. He had made it clear that Duke Orlythe wished for them to return to Highcliff.

Neither Pecklyn, Balewynd, or their dragons believed the elf was sincere when questioned about Aelfwynne's wellbeing, but they knew better than to take the elf to task. Especially with the ramparts lined with ranks of Grim Guard keeping a close eye on the dragons at their gate.

A quick stop at Highcliff to inform Xantha of the situation and a change of clothing to better suit night flying, Pecklyn and Balewynd had flown their dragons back onto the plains fronting Castle Grim. They had set down north of the main gatehouse, hoping to remain out of sight, but whenever the cloud cover thinned, they worried the dragons' bulk would be visible in the moonlight.

Balewynd shrugged free of her bow and quiver, and slipped out of her fur-lined tunic. She secured them on a harness draped around Mirage's midsection and nodded to Dawnbreaker. "Let's do this."

Pecklyn made to mount his dragon but Dawnbreaker stepped sideways. *"It'll be easier if I take her on my own."*

Pecklyn frowned at Dawnbreaker and gaped as Balewynd gave him her smug smile.

She stepped up beside Dawnbreaker and paused. "At least your dragon has sense."

Keeper of the Jewel

Before he could say anything, Balewynd jumped up, settled on Dawnbreaker's shoulders, and patted her between her temple horns. "Come in low over the lake from the western end of the castle. There shouldn't be many guards patrolling that section. The southwest tower shadow will aid in hiding our approach."

Dumbfounded, Pecklyn considered what Balewynd jokingly referred to as her assassin's gear. Black boots, black leather pants, a snug fitting black leather, sleeveless top, and a peculiar pair of black leather gloves secured around her wrists by matching, thick leather bracelets. A utility belt equipped for scaling cliffs—or in this case—castle walls, completed her wardrobe. He had to admit, when it came to subterfuge, there were none better suited to it than the aloof elf.

He stepped back and covered his face to avoid having grit flung into his eyes as Dawnbreaker's wings churned the dust around them when she leaped into the air and flew north across the grassy plain, away from Castle Grim.

Stepping close to Mirage, Pecklyn placed a hand on the base of the blue dragon's neck as the they watched with more than a little trepidation.

Balewynd and Dawnbreaker meant the world to them. Should anything happen to either one of them, they would be crushed.

"Drop me there. On that rooftop." Balewynd readjusted her hold on Dawnbreaker. Not accustomed to flying Pecklyn's dragon, the flight across the plains north, and the subsequent trip to the west and back south again, had tested her skills as a dragon rider. Dawnbreaker didn't fly anywhere near as smoothly as her bigger blue.

"Do you think it'll hold me?"

Keeper of the Jewel

"I don't know." Balewynd's eyes watered in the cold wind, her hair whipping around behind her. "Don't stop, just in case. Swoop in close enough for me to jump."

Dawnbreaker flapped twice more, gaining altitude, and spread her wings wide, gliding noiselessly on the thermals toward the rapidly approaching castle. *"That roof is steep. Do you think it's wise?"*

Balewynd rose into a crouch. "Just keep it steady."

The castle had appeared as little more than a dark blot against the shimmering lake moments before. In the blink of an eye, the rooftops rushed up to meet their flight.

Dawnbreaker adeptly swooped out of the sky, her wings catching wind and slowing her descent as she drifted across the last league of shoreline.

Balewynd admired Dawnbreaker's mastery of flight. Her years of experience flying dragons allowed her to appreciate that gliding upon wind currents for a creature this large wasn't as easy as a hawk or falcon made it appear. Keeping their great bodies aloft without the assistance of wing flaps was a skill all in itself. She was thankful the prevailing winds of southern South March had cooperated tonight. If the wind had been still, she doubted Dawnbreaker could remain aloft for as long as she had without taking a wingbeat.

Despite the powerful dragon's skill, bringing Balewynd close enough to the castle's rooftop so that she could safely jump free without alerting the Grim Guard was not an easy feat. Balewynd was glad Pecklyn insisted she ride Dawnbreaker.

She loved Mirage with all her heart, but she knew of his limitations. There was no way her big blue could have flown as deftly as Dawnbreaker. Mirage was an elegant flyer. His wider wingspan and large body better suited for a long, comfortable flight. He didn't possess the strength to match

261

the speed the more compact, beefier Dawnbreaker was capable of achieving.

Hidden within the southwestern tower's shadow, Dawnbreaker skimmed low across the lake. At the last moment, she tilted her wings and swooped over the ramparts, barely missing the high wall's crenelations.

Balewynd leaned out. Picking her spot, she sprung into the air. For the briefest of moments, she feared she had misjudged her leap. She hit the steep roof hard, rolling twice before she arrested her tumble and concentrated on keeping herself from sliding down the slick slate roof tiles glistening with dew.

She clung to the steep pitch with every ounce of strength she possessed—pressing the soft soles of her boots and palms of her supple gloves against the moist stone surface. Abating her downward slide, she clung to the tiles and listened. She didn't fool herself. Dawnbreaker's approach had been flawless, but there was a good chance someone had witnessed the dragon's flight.

A commotion arose farther along the ramparts toward the southeastern tower—the one the princess claimed the duke had held her and the Home Guard prisoner in during their recent stay at Grim Keep. She stared at where she estimated the uproar originated. Hoping the duke's troops would be caught off guard and not be able to get a volley of ballista bolts into the air fast enough, she didn't breathe again until Dawnbreaker's silhouette crossed in front of the partially, cloud covered moon.

The dragon's wings beat fast, distancing her from Grim Keep with every stroke.

Balewynd dared to breathe. Scanning the barren rooftop, she hadn't anticipated tumbling as much as she had. Ever so carefully, she crawled headfirst to peer over the edge. Sure enough, the window enclosure she sought was off to the west.

Attentive to the sounds around her, she made her way to a spot above the window.

A quick scan confirmed no one was visible below. Her legs slid over the edge, followed quickly by her hips. She flexed her torso to build momentum and swung the rest of her body over the eave, landing deftly in the arched window enclosure.

Crouched on the wide sill, she inspected the darkened room, its interior partially illuminated by the full moon rising above the eastern ramparts.

Being the daughter of the head chamberlain, Balewynd knew Castle Grim better than most. She had spent her youth getting into mischief in the numerous rooms of the sprawling fortress.

The room she selected was a little used library. One the castle's healers used when searching for an answer to a malady they couldn't explain. The dust and cobwebs clinging to the shelf-lined walls stuffed with musty tomes testified to the fact that the library entertained few visitors.

She recalled her time at Grim Keep as an elfling while her eyes adjusted to the darkness within. She hadn't seen her father in years. As much as she wanted to hug him and know that he was well, she didn't dare look for him. She knew where his living quarters were—had lived with him there for many years—but doubted she would find him there. Bayl was a lifelong servant, strictly devoted to his duty. She wasn't convinced of her father's personal feelings regarding the duke, but she knew how he prided himself for his professionalism and the execution of his high position at Castle Grim. It would be better if they didn't meet tonight.

Keeper of the Jewel

Adjusting her utility belt in such a way that the metal carabiners wouldn't clink as she moved about the shadows, Balewynd padded through the musty library and stopped in

Keeper of the Jewel

front of a non-descript selection of tomes. It took her a couple of tries to locate the ones she sought. Remembering how she used to stand on a stool to do this, she smiled as she pulled back on one book and simultaneously pushed on another several books away. Grim Keep was her old stomping ground. She knew the layout of the castle like few others.

Although she had done this many times as an elfling, she sighed with relief as the bookshelf lurched into the thick, stone wall, its left edge parting enough to expose a dark passageway beyond. The seldom used servant byways.

She paused to listen, ensuring no one had noticed her entrance into Grim Keep. Satisfied, she plucked the unlit torch she knew would be sitting in a metal ring near the ground just inside the passageway.

The head of the cloth-covered brand felt dry to the touch, but still exuded an oily aroma. Three strikes of her dagger on a piece of flint brought the torch sizzling to life—the flame languishing momentarily before it engulfed the torch's head and illuminated the musty tunnel that ran inside the castle walls.

Pushing the bookshelf closed behind her, she slunk along the secret byway, trying to remember the paths she would have to take to reach the various rooms she thought the duke might hold Aelfwynne in. She swallowed and pushed aside the dire thought that rose to the forefront of her mind. She had to hold on to the belief that he was still alive.

Her pace picked up as her instincts told her she may already be too late.

Keeper of the Jewel

The Harrowing

Aelfwynne's head lolled to the side. He blinked his eyes, his bleary mind trying to focus on where he was and how he had gotten there. Vaguely recalling being roughly cleansed by two Grim Guard before he had succumbed to unconsciousness at the spindly hands of the Soul, it dawned on him that he lay upon a stone slab, wrists and ankles bound tightly in iron fetters behind his back. As the flickering light of the room came into focus his nose filled with the acrid smell of sulfur and burning rock.

The black robes of who could only be the human wizard, Afara Maral, hunched over an open-faced furnace built into a magnificently carved chimney of polished lava stone that spanned the entirety of the chamber's rear wall.

They had taken him to the infamous, Crag's Forge—named after the Sarsen Rest dwarf who had built it long before South March had become a kingdom. Back in the early days of the Dragon Witch. He didn't recognize many of the newer effigies carved into the shimmering, glassy surface, but there was no mistaking they held him captive far below Grim Keep, offering him little hope of escape.

Not far from the wizard, a wiry elf clad in immaculate, red robes, worked at a side table, mixing potions, and crushing powders—Afara's apprentice, Ryedyn, hard at work.

A deep voice on his far side said, "Ah, Bayl. There you are. Hurry. Afara is nearly ready."

266

Keeper of the Jewel

Aelfwynne rolled his head to look at the large form of the Duke of Grim. Beyond the malicious elf prince, the slender form of Bayl shuffled around the foot of Aelfwynne's stone slab and approached Crag's Forge with a short length of wood in his hands. The Staff of Reckoning!

Shimmering light blazed and died, illuminating the chamber in varying colours. An incessant litany of ancient phrases reached Aelfwynne as Afara enacted a transference spell.

The spell was one Aelfwynne had never learned, but he knew of it. Afara had become more powerful than Aelfwynne cared to admit. Only an elite practitioner had access to the powers the duke's wizard attempted to command.

He doubted Orlythe appreciated the peril of being anywhere near the forge during such an enactment. If Afara's conjuring deviated in any way during his delicate attempt to blend earth magic with the magic of mankind, the resulting conflagration would be felt throughout Grim Keep and beyond. Considering his predicament, Aelfwynne hoped Afara *would* lose control of the spell.

Never looking up from his casting, the wizard must have sensed Bayl come up beside him. "Place it in the forge and be gone."

Bayl nodded. From the folds of his robes, he produced the cane and carefully positioned it over Afara's head to access the opening.

"Now, you fool!" Afara hissed.

The cane disappeared into the fire and Afara chanted in earnest. Spreading his arms wide, a pendant dangled at the end of a delicate chain from his right hand—the ruby gemstone sparkling in the light of the roaring fire.

Keeper of the Jewel

Aelfwynne winced, not sure what to expect as his staff disappeared into the roiling mass of fire. The destruction of the irreplaceable artifact sealed any hope of foiling the duke's dastardly scheme. Many souls had gone into the construction of the Staff of Reckoning—their faces immortalized along the wooden shaft. He expected to hear the cries of the great people whose death had instilled the magic in the talisman but the hellfire of Afara's furnace devoured it without a trace.

Shuddering at the loss, Aelfwynne followed the slow arc of the ruby pendant. A deep foreboding twisted his insides, shaking him to the core. Even from where he lay, he recognized the ruby as a piece of the Crystal Cavern. Unless he was gravely mistaken, there was a traitor within the ranks of the Highcliff Guardians.

Orlythe leaned over Aelfwynne, a smug grin parting his hairy face. "Ah, high wizard. You're just in time to witness the end of everything you've fought so hard for over the last millennium. A misguided era that will soon be expunged from the annals of time."

If Aelfwynne's dry throat would have permitted him to spit he would have hocked a wad into the insolent elf's face. As it was, he held the duke's stare, defiance firmly entrenched on his goblin features.

Bayl stopped behind the duke. "If you no longer require my services, m'lord, I shall put in for the night."

The duke's face twisted in annoyance at the interruption. Without looking at the chamberlain, he waived a dismissive hand. "Begone."

"Very well, m'lord." Bayl bowed, unseen by the duke. He lingered momentarily to look directly at Aelfwynne before leaving the chamber.

An anguished cry sounded from the direction of the forge.

Keeper of the Jewel

Orlythe looked up. "What?"

"I don't understand," Afara bemoaned, his back to them. "I did everything I was supposed to do. I added a little more, just to be sure, but nothing happened. The Staff of Reckoning should have been the catalyst to unlock the magic."

Ryedyn had stopped what he was doing, his pale face concerned.

"What're you talking about?" Duke Orlythe left Aelfwynne's side and confronted his wizard. His eyes darted from the pendant dangling from the end of Afara's outstretched arm to the wizard's perplexed expression. The significance darkened Orlythe's surly mood further. "You mean you failed?"

Afara didn't meet his gaze.

"After everything we've done, you're telling me you can't deliver what you promised? That pendant cost me a lot of good men." The duke's incredulous voice rose to a shout. "If I ever wish to crawl out from under its thumb, I must possess the power! Do you understand what I'm saying?" He leaned in closer. "Get me that magic!"

Afara turned on the duke.

Ryedyn stepped back from where he worked.

Aelfwynne tensed in anticipation of the wizard's wrath, but it never came. An odd sense of disappointment filled him. His life was over but he would have died content knowing the human wizard had incinerated the traitorous brother of the Queen of the Elves.

The wizard's chest falls were laboured. He turned his shrewd gaze on Aelfwynne, an evil smile twitching his hairless lips. "There may be another way, m'lord."

Keeper of the Jewel

"Another way?" the duke asked. "What? With him? I thought you needed him alive to divine the magic of his staff?"

Afara nodded. He cupped his chin in his free hand and tilted his head. "I think I can do both."

"Both what?"

Afara ignored the question. "With a bit of luck, I think I can pull off one of the greatest spells known to wizardkind."

The duke swallowed; his bluster gone. "Is it dangerous?"

The wizard nodded. "Of a certainty."

"What's this spell called?"

Aelfwynne's beady eyes widened as he realized what Afara suggested. He mouthed the words Afara spoke to the duke.

"The harrowing."

Keeper of the Jewel

Caught

Balewynd slunk through the hidden byways of Castle Grim, avoiding contact with all but the odd servant she came across. When confronted, the servants cast their eyes downward, thinking Balewynd to be a member of the Grim Guard as she certainly wasn't a servant. On a couple of occasions, she noticed a familiar face, but thankfully, they never let on that they recognized her.

Now that she was safely inside the castle, she put her mind to where they might be holding Aelfwynne. If her suspicions weren't unfounded, she would find him either in the throne room or housed in the nobility wing overlooking the southern ramparts abutting Lake Grim.

She paused, allowing a meek female servant to pass her by, the dirty-faced elfling barely a teenager. The servant dared to look her in the eye before lowering her head and pressing against the rough stone wall to squeeze past.

It had been a while since Balewynd had travelled the labyrinth of tunnels within the walls. She waited for the glow of the elfling's torch to disappear before setting out toward where she hoped to find a narrow stairwell that would take her up to the third level.

It was so quiet within the walls. Every so often she could hear muffled conversation on the other side of the wall beyond a movable panel into the room in question, but it was impossible to tell what they were saying.

Keeper of the Jewel

The stairwell she sought came up on her right. Narrow steps carved out of the wall disappeared into the gloom above and below a small landing. Listening for anyone in the tunnels with her, she hurried up the steps and found herself in a similar passageway at their summit. She looked left and right, unable to see anything beyond the torches' glow.

She was about to step out and go left but a faint light bobbed down the passageway toward her. She pulled back into the recess of the stairwell and peered around the corner.

The glow grew into two distinct torches. A male voice reached her, accompanied by the hushed laughter of a female. Two elflings, no older than the last servant she had seen on the level below, stopped and stared at her in surprise as they reached the stairwell landing.

The male elf scanned Balewynd from head to foot. "I'm sorry, m'lady. We had no idea anyone was still awake."

The embarrassed look on the shy female elfling spoke volumes as to what the two were up to skulking about the hidden walkways.

Balewynd faked a smile. "Working late, are you?"

"Um, yes. Just, uh, seeing to the tapers, m'lady."

Balewynd winked at him. "I see. Well, don't let me slow you down."

"Thank you, m'lady." The male bobbed his head and pulled his companion after him.

Their receding forms soon became nothing more than a faint light—the laughter of mischievous youth followed them as they rounded a corner and disappeared.

Balewynd sighed. She missed those days.

The corridor running behind the nobility wing was exceptionally quiet. She paused at each access panel to listen but didn't hear anything for the entire length of the passageway. Stopping at the far end, the corridor terminated

Keeper of the Jewel

within the structure of the double, sea gate tower. A wooden door barred the end of this section of servant tunnels, presenting her with a decision to make.

To pass through and enter the public corridor beyond would put her at greater risk. Most everyone in Grim Keep had known her as an elfling. If anyone came across her, questions would be raised as to her presence in the castle— especially skulking about in the wee hours of the morning dressed as she was. But the fact that it *was* late, also meant that other than night servants, no one else should be awake.

Ear to the exit door, the handle gave way in her hand. She cracked it open enough to peer into the long room spanning between the gatehouse towers. Two-open-aired windows looked out onto the lake and the distant blot of the Dark Mountains surrounding Highcliff. Satisfied no one was in the gatehouse parapet, she eased into the bare room and closed the door behind her.

A main corridor ran beyond the room and out into the open air along the higher, western battlements toward the southwest corner tower, but that wasn't the route she wished to travel. Though hard to discern in the moonlight, she knew where to look for the hidden mechanism that would open the next section of servant passageways.

It was as if she had never left the castle. Everything about its grandeur and design came back to her with heightening clarity the more she explored. Her fingers located the secret switch and the door panel sunk into the otherwise nondescript wall.

She slipped inside and padded along the corridor, debating whether it would be better to return to the gatehouse and visually inspect each of the nobility chambers. For all she knew, Aelfwynne might be sleeping comfortably and all of this was for nothing.

Keeper of the Jewel

She grinned, thoroughly enjoying herself. Even if she and Pecklyn had blown everything out of proportion, she relished the chance to flaunt her ability. Being Highcliff's primary spy came with a heady responsibility. She needed to keep her skills up. She couldn't think of a better way to do that than sneak around Grim Keep—a castle full of wary Grim Guard and boasting the presence of a powerful wizard—even if he was human.

A soft 'snick' behind her froze her in mid-stride. She spun around just as another 'snick' sounded farther along the passageway.

Light flooded the hidden byway on either side of her. She dropped her torch to the stone floor and tried to extinguish it by rolling it beneath her foot but it wouldn't go out. The heat radiated through the sole of her boot. Horrified, she pulled her foot away. She had inadvertently set her boot on fire.

Stamping the ground between the open doorways, her commotion attracted the quizzical stares of the Grim Guard watching her from either direction.

"Balewynd Tayn?" A Grim Guard with a blonde goatee asked, stepping into the passageway.

Balewynd pulled her curved, black-bladed dagger free of its sheath, the blade an exact replica of Xantha's except on a smaller scale. The elder Highcliff Guardian had been Balewynd's mentor while training to become one of the elite protectors of the Crystal Cavern.

A black-haired Grim Guard ducked into the passage from the opposite door, pushing a tower shield ahead of him. "Don't make this harder than it needs to be."

There was no way past the large Grim Guard's shield in the tight confines. She spun back to where the blonde elf waited, only his head and shoulders visible above his shield. Her feet drove into the ground as she sprinted up the passageway toward the gatehouse tower. Her boots slipped on the smooth stone as she tried to avoid running into the tower shield the blonde Grim Guard came at her with.

As soon as she stopped the chasing Grim Guard slammed into her, squishing her between his shield and that of the blonde elf who had braced himself for the impact.

She was thrown against the opposite shield so hard that her head rang off its unforgiving surface. Held tight between the shields, the press of the Grim Guard was unrelenting. With all the strength she could muster, she wrenched her dagger arm down to her hips, but there was no way to use her weapon. It was all she could do to prevent the shields from crushing her. She screeched in frustration at her stupidity. How had she allowed herself to be caught? Aelfwynne depended on her.

"Release her," a deep voice sounded from beyond the blonde elf.

The Grim Guard eased their pressure but immediately applied it again as Balewynd drove her hands and feet against the shields, causing their bearers to stumble backward.

"Baley dearest. Desist," the deep voice commanded.

Balewynd's eyes grew wide. "Daddy?"

"Yes, Baley. You're amongst friends."

The blonde elf's shield tipped aside, allowing her to see the open doorway. Framed in torchlight flickering from the room beyond, the tall form of head chamberlain Bayl smiled grimly back at her.

She swallowed. The pent-up anxiety of the past day and the excitement of stealing around Castle Grim released their grip on her emotions. Her eyes welled up. She hadn't seen her father in years. She sheathed her dagger, not sure how to respond. Her father was the duke's head chamberlain. He might not be as receptive once he discovered what she was up to.

Bayl extended his hands, motioning with long fingers for her to come out of the passageway.

That simple action prompted her to run to him, wrapping her arms around his neck and hugging him like she would never see him again. Her momentum made him stagger backward into the room, but he caught his balance and returned her embrace—holding her bodily off the floor.

Leaning her head back, she stared into the warmth emanating from his beady eyes. The only true love she had ever known lay behind those eyes. Cold as a dagger to anyone else, Bayl's gaze contained nothing but devotion and adoration for his only elfling. In that moment, Balewynd's swelling heart knew true happiness.

She kissed his weathered face several times—the lines of his responsibility etched deeper than she remembered. Grey hair streaked his temples. The strain of his position at Castle Grim had exacted a toll on his sagging features. Once so handsome and chiselled, her father had aged faster than their years of separation warranted. She could only imagine the rigours he had been subjected to while attending to the duke's high demands.

Ever so gently, Bayl lowered her to the ground and held her at arm's length. "I trust Highcliff's been good to you."

"Yes daddy. I've learned so much. Master…" She trailed off, not sure whether she should mention the high wizard.

Her father knew her. Another rare smile crossed his clean-shaven face. He nodded, his smile fading. "He's in trouble."

Balewynd stepped free of her father, her eyes going to the chamber's main door. "We must free him."

As soon as she spoke, she cast a worried glance at the Grim Guard stepping from the servant's byway. Her hand went for her dagger but Bayl reached out and prevented her from pulling it free.

"They're with me."

She frowned, unsure what to think. "How did you know I was here?"

Bayl raised thick eyebrows. "It's my job to know everything that goes on in Grim Keep."

"But...But..."

"But nothing, Baley. Nothing goes on within these walls without my knowledge. The duke expects nothing less. I have eyes and ears everywhere. No one is ever truly alone while under this roof."

Balewynd glanced nervously at the Grim Guard, their uniforms off-putting. "Who else knows I'm here?"

"Only those who need to," Bayl said and nodded to the two elves. They nodded back and stepped into the public hallway, scanning the quiet corridor in both directions.

"Where's Master Aelfwynne? What're they doing to him?"

Bayl held his hands out, pleading with her to lower her voice. "He's beyond help."

Balewynd started for the door but her father's hand clasped her forearm and wrenched her back—his strength belying his frail appearance.

"Daddy! Let go. I have to save him." She tried to wrest her arm free.

Bayl's grip was relentless. He shook his head. "Only death lies where he has gone. It's too dangerous here at the moment." His free hand reached into his black robes and withdrew a small packet bound by a wax seal. He shoved it into her free hand. "If you wish to help him, you must get free of the castle and return at a later date."

Keeper of the Jewel

He steered her toward the servant's passageway. "Now go, before it's too late."

Balewynd pulled free of his grasp and bumped against the edge of the secret opening. She studied the folded paper in her hand. Looking up, her eyes pled with her father to explain himself, absently wondering at his peculiar robes. Her father had never worn anything like that before.

A challenge sounded in the public corridor.

Balewynd and her father both stared at the door.

The noise of a scuffle reached them, followed by metal rattling off stone.

"Come no closer!" A male voice shouted.

Bayl nodded at the servant's passageway and said under his breath, "You must go. Now!"

Balewynd hesitated.

"You mustn't be seen!"

Balewynd took a deep breath. Her instincts told her to rush into the hallway and help, but she couldn't deny the urgency in her father's voice. He had never led her astray before. Even counting Master Aelfwynne and Pecklyn, who she had gotten to know quite well over the last few decades, there wasn't anyone she trusted more than her father.

She jumped up and kissed his surprised face before ducking into the passageway. He winked at her like he used to do when she was an elfling, and nodded for her to close the panel.

She did as she was asked but stopped short of securing the secret door into its latches. Concerned for her father, she put an eye to the crack.

Bayl lifted the single torch burning in an iron ring on the wall and approached the main door.

Keeper of the Jewel

The blonde-haired guard passed in front of the doorway, his sword held in front of him, his face splattered with blood. He staggered backward, pain twisting his youthful features.

"Hold!" Bayl commanded.

Someone in a ratty, black cowl and black robes came into view. They paused at the doorway to regard Bayl.

Balewynd couldn't be certain, but the newcomer's eyes appeared to burn with the intensity of small fires, as long, dangling sleeves stretched toward Bayl.

Bony, white fingers extended from the newcomer's sleeves. With a rapid stabbing motion, the fingers drove into her father's midsection.

Balewynd gaped, the shock so complete she couldn't utter the scream that lodged in her throat. She jammed her fingers into the crack, trying to pull the door open but her father's urgent plea stopped her. "Run, Baley! Run!"

Frozen with indecision, she watched incredulously as a second rapid jab drove skeletal fingers clear through her father's body, ripping through the back of his robes, dripping red.

Bayl exuded a loud gasp, crumpled over the figure's outstretched hand, and hung limp in its grasp.

The skeletal fingers withdrew and Bayl fell dead to the floor.

Balewynd dropped to her knees, hands clutching her face in horror. Her father lay unmoving on the floor, a growing pool of blood expanding around his midsection.

The creature, for that was all she could think of referring to it as, scanned the dark room. Its fiery orbs fell on the panel she hid behind, its hand dripping with the blood of her father, gripping something Balewynd couldn't recognize.

Keeper of the Jewel

A coldness swept into the passageway as if on a breeze as the creature floated across the threshold, moving on her position, but a commotion in the hall drew its attention.

The bloody-faced Grim Guard let out a crazed bellow and ran at the creature with his sword raised.

The creature lifted his arms and uttered words unknown to Balewynd.

The guard's advance stopped as if he had run into a stone wall and froze in place. He tried to break free of whatever held him, his face twisted in agony. A horrendous scream escaped his lips for the briefest of moments before he dropped to the floor—his sword clanging uselessly beside his lifeless body.

Balewynd rose shakily to her feet. Her father's last words screamed at her from beyond the grave, *"Run, Baley! Run!"*

Her legs pumped harder than they had ever carried her. She was through the end door and across the gatehouse before she had time to think about what she was going to do now that the only person who really mattered in her life had been taken from her.

Keeper of the Jewel

A Thousand Excruciating Deaths

Khae looked up from the Willow Throne, taking her attention off the blackened cornstalk leaf in her hands. She gazed curiously at the farmer standing before the twin chairs of state. Weary from dealing with the long line of weekly petitioners from all over South March, she asked, "And you say this is abnormal?"

The meek farmer kept his eyes directed to the ground between them. "Yes, Your Highness. If we can't find a way to prevent its spread, we'll lose the entire harvest."

"We? You mean you and your family?"

The weathered elf dared to meet her inquisitive stare. "Oh no, Your Highness. I speak for every farmer south of Ors Spill."

Khae's brow furrowed. "You're talking about half the kingdom."

The farmer broke eye contact and lowered his gaze to his folded hands. "That's correct, Your Highness."

Khae exchanged glances with her husband. Hammas raised his brow and rolled his eyes.

As rulers of South March, they had heard it all before. Merchants and farmers looking to increase profit margins by playing on the sympathy of the crown. "So, corn will be at a premium this year. Is that what you're telling me?"

"Why no, Your Highness."

Keeper of the Jewel

Khae had been ready to lecture him about the dangers of misleading the queen of South March, but his reply shocked her.

"The disease is spreading like wildfire across *every* crop in the south. Corn. Wheat. You name it. Nothing's immune. If something isn't done soon, I'm afraid no amount of gold will buy anything worth eating."

The king sat up straight, his undivided attention on the farmer.

Khae gaped. If the farmer's prediction came to pass, South March would soon be in the midst of a famine.

Whispers filtered down the line of those still in attendance; all eyes rivetted on the queen, awaiting her response.

A commune with nature's essence might help get to the root of the problem. It seemed like the natural course of action, but Khae shuddered at the thought of returning to Grim Watch Tower.

A commotion arose on the steps outside the main entrance. The head falconer nodded at the guards who had momentarily detained him, and marched with purpose up the marble aisle, along the edge of the petitioners; a finger-sized scroll in his hands.

"Waryn, what an unexpected pleasure," Khae's words dripped with sarcasm, but she couldn't bring herself to reprimand the elf for interrupting the petition. The tall, angular faced elf rarely left his aerie atop the northern mid-tower where he tended the royal aviary. For Waryn to make the long trip down to the throne room didn't bode well. "I expect the tidings you bear warrant the disruption of the weekly petition?"

Not afraid to speak his mind, Waryn remained unusually quiet, his dun-coloured tunic showing signs that it had begun

Keeper of the Jewel

to rain. He chewed his lower lip and offered Khae the parchment.

As soon as Waryn extended a hand toward the queen, a halberd with wide, curving blades atop a dark polished shaft, chopped down. If Waryn hadn't been quick to react, the blades would have severed his hand. He glared at the large Home Guard stationed beside the queen.

Khae wasn't sure who jumped more, her or Waryn. She swallowed her fright and spoke with as much decorum as she could muster—the Home Guard was only doing his duty. "It's okay, captain. He may approach."

The vigilant Home Guard kept his concentration on Waryn but he raised his halberd and returned to attention.

The falconer scowled, wary eyes on the polearm. "Grave news out of Highcliff, Your Highness."

A wave of cold flushed Khae. She accepted the tightly bound scroll with a shaking hand. Leaning to the side, she broke the wax seal of High Wizard Aelfwynne and held it open so that Hammas could read it as well.

My dearest Khae. I'm writing to inform you of the most interesting development out of Grim Keep.

Though I have no way to prove my suspicion, I'm of the belief that your brother recently conspired to ambush Princess Ouderling on her way through the Passage of Dolor. She's fine but I regret to inform you that the entire Home Guard contingent from Orlythia was killed. Including Captain Wood.

I fear a malign magic is being employed here in the

Keeper of the Jewel

southlands. I travel to an audience with Orlythe
but am mindful of what such a meeting might
hold in store. If my intuition proves correct, may
the gods watch over the princess and keep her safe.

Your faithful servant,

Aelfwynne

A cold sweat soaked Khae's attire. She had no way to see her own face, but she imagined it reflected Hammas' pale skin. Dumbfounded she stared at him.

Hammas held her frightened gaze for a moment. His handsome features hardened. Rising to his feet, he ordered, "Clear the room and seal the doors." He turned to the guard beside Khae. "Fetch the commander!"

The large elf nodded and forced his way through the confused crowd that was being ushered from the throne room, herded by the many Home Guard stationed around the lofty chamber. Bewildered petitioners and noble spectators alike squeezed through the large double doors and disappeared down the steps beyond.

Hammas paced circles around the veined marble podium the Willow Thrones sat upon, both chairs identical in every aspect except one. The queen's intertwined, willow branch throne was padded with a burnt orange, velvet cushion, whereas the king's was red—the seat and back contrasting sharply with the shiny shellac coating the surrounding willow wood.

Khae stared at the entranceway. The rain had picked up but her thoughts weren't on the elves shuffling into the afternoon deluge. Her concern lay hundreds of leagues to the south.

Keeper of the Jewel

Images of Aelfwynne confronting her ornery brother with his accusations within the black walls of Grim Keep left her breathless. It would turn into an argument. Given her brother's temperament, that wouldn't end well for the high wizard.

Shuddering, she considered all of the wonderful members of the Home Guard who had escorted Ouderling. She tried to envision Captain Gerrant's rugged face—one she knew almost as well as her dear husband's, but for some reason, it eluded her. The only thing preventing her from fainting due to a wave of overwhelming grief was the mention that Ouderling had survived.

For now.

She swallowed her fear. The cold gripped her tighter. She had experienced the most horrific of pains twenty years ago with the death of Ordyl. She didn't think she would survive the pain if she had to bury Ouderling.

Hammas passed in front of her, intelligent eyes narrowed in dark contemplation. She knew that look well. Her soft-spoken husband rarely uttered a cross word, but on the occasion he did, it was as if all of his pent-up frustrations boiled over. When that happened, it was dangerous to look at him the wrong way.

The unsubstantiated rumour of an attempt on his Little Sprite's life had him on the verge of just such an outburst. As calm and sensical as the king had proven himself to be, Khae dreaded to witness the darkness that had understandably taken hold of him. If anything happened to Ouderling, Hammas would burn South March to the ground.

He rounded the podium again and stopped to stare at the entrance as the great doors banged shut. Everyone had cleared out, leaving them alone with the elven Home

Keeper of the Jewel

Guard—hand picked by Captain Gerrant to oversee Khae's safety.

"I can't see his face anymore," Khae whispered, not caring about the tears running down her cheeks.

If Hammas heard her, he didn't let on.

"Oh, Hammas, what have I done?"

The king turned dark eyes on her. His Adam's apple convulsed. He shook his head slowly. "I knew this would happen."

Khae held her breath, waiting for what was to come next. They had had this discussion many times. Hammas was convinced that Orlythe would someday do something so egregious that they would have no choice but to act. If not for overstepping her authority as the queen of South March, she was certain Hammas would have put an end to the duke a long time ago.

The two elves had fallen out long before Queen Nyxa's death. Though not privy to what had been said behind closed doors, as Hammas never discussed it, their differences had driven a wedge between them. Orlythe hadn't been the same since. Once their mother followed their father to the grave, Orlythe only attended the ceremonies of court that were considered mandatory from that point forward.

Khae suspected it had something to do with their differing views on the dragon question, but recently she suspected her brother's discontent went much deeper than that.

Still, she clung to her memories of Orlythe while they were growing up. He had been charming and elegant. A true prince of the realm. Suitors adored his dark locks while military admirers appreciated his proficiency with all types of weaponry. Not to mention that his command of basic magic had elevated him amongst the most talented in the land. His namesake, King Orlythe, had proudly boasted about his son's prowess and The Prince of the Elves had quickly become the realm's favoured son.

King Hammas knelt before Khae and gripped her hands. "We'll deal with this like we do everything. As husband and wife." He squeezed. "As queen and king."

Khae wiped her eyes with the back of her hand. "I must go to her."

The king's eyes narrowed to slits. "Not without an army at your back."

As much as Khae knew she should accede to his wishes, she needed to hold on to the belief that it hadn't come to that. She shook her head. "No. That'll only aggravate matters."

"I insist!"

Hammas' tone got her hackles up. She was the queen. She tilted her head. "Really? Perhaps my husband forgets his place."

She pulled her hands free of his grasp, expecting a tirade, but he surprised her.

"No, I do not. You're the queen. You've the final word with regard to all matters of state." He pulled a folded handkerchief from inside his royal tunic and dabbed at her tears. When he was done, he cupped her cheeks. "But you're also my wife. When it comes to your safety, or that of our daughter, we're equal partners. As your husband, I'll not allow you to step one foot out of Orlythia without the full might of the army at your back."

Captivated by the penetrating stare of his deep green eyes, Khae swallowed at the lump in her throat. Staring back at her was the greatest love she had ever known. She nodded ever so slightly.

Maintaining his hold upon her face, he leaned in and kissed her lips. "The gods be warned. If anyone disturbs so much

Keeper of the Jewel

as a hair on Ouderling's sweet head, they'll die a thousand excruciating deaths."

Keeper of the Jewel

Staff of Reckoning

"What do you think's going on?" Ouderling asked, staring at Xantha across the cold firepit in Aelfwynne's living quarters.

A sad grin crossed Xantha's face. "Knowing Aelfwynne, he's worked the duke up into a lather."

Ouderling smiled briefly for the old Guardian's benefit, but there was nothing about their present situation that warranted happiness. Had things not have been so dire, seeing Xantha's large frame hunkered low on Aelfwynne's stone bench, her head bowed so as not to scrape the roof, Ouderling imagined she and Jyllana, who was stuffed against the side wall, would have laughed at the comment.

Jyllana sipped tentatively at the contents of a stone goblet, her face twisting in disgust as she swallowed. Recovering from the afterbite, she said softly, "Its gotta be close to dawn. I would've thought we would've heard something from Pecklyn and Balewynd by now."

Ouderling watched her protector with concern, ready to catch her if need be. "Do you think it wise for Jyllana to drink wizard's tea?"

Xantha shrugged, attentive eyes on the Home Guard. "I spoke with Eolande. He thinks she's got what it takes."

"Eolande?" Ouderling frowned for a moment and then her eyes lit up. "Oh. Right. One of the caretakers of the Crystal Cavern. How can this Eolande tell? He's never met Jyllana."

Keeper of the Jewel

"One doesn't live over a thousand years without acquiring certain knowledge."

Jyllana gaped. "A thousand years? Wow. That's old."

"He's the oldest living creature known." Xantha nodded. "Older than any of the dragons even."

"How can someone live that long?" Ouderling said in awe.

Xantha shrugged again. "He attributes his longevity to his closeness with the earth blood. He's worked the cavern since he was old enough to fly a wyvern."

Ouderling couldn't keep her jaw from dropping. "You mean he's done nothing other than polish rocks for a thousand years? I find that hard to believe."

"That's what he says." Xantha sipped at the goblet wrapped in her age-spotted hands. "I've been here for…" she pursed her lips and looked at the ceiling for the answer, "at least six of those centuries. He's always been here as far as I remember."

"That's insane." Ouderling sipped at her wizard's tea, trying hard not to scrunch her face.

"Lady Xantha?" Pecklyn's unmistakable voice sounded from up the small tunnel that led from Aelfwynne's quarters to the passageway connecting the promontory to the Crystal Cavern.

"In here," Xantha answered.

The distant sound of scraping metal on rock drew near. As the tunnel darkened, the elves in Aelfwynne's chamber were surprised when Balewynd's head appeared in the light of the wall sconces. The pretty elf's hair was dishevelled; her face smeared with traces of dirt as if she had been crying.

Xantha picked up on her distress and held out a hand. "What is it, dear Bale?"

An ominous feeling rippled through Ouderling, fearful of what Balewynd was about to impart. She glanced at Xantha with concern, but the elder remained rock solid. After their episode in the Crystal Cavern, Xantha's mood had resumed its former, confident self.

The usually emotionless Balewynd allowed herself to be pulled into the cramped quarters and accepted Xantha's tender embrace. The young Guardian's shoulders began to shake visibly as she buried her face into Xantha's neck.

Where the old Guardian got her strength from, Ouderling couldn't imagine, but she was thoroughly impressed by Xantha's ability to hold her own emotions in check. "What is it? Aelfwynne?"

Balewynd didn't respond verbally. She shook her head.

Bewilderment crossed Xantha's face. Pecklyn had obviously made it back. "One of the dragons?"

Balewynd shook her head again.

Xantha forced a little separation between them so as to look into Balewynd's watery, blue eyes. "Then what, Bale? What has affected you so?"

Balewynd struggled to find her voice. Her bottom lip trembled.

In one of the most pathetic voices Ouderling had ever heard spoken by an adult, Balewynd whispered, "Daddy."

Xantha's eyes grew wide. "Head chamberlain Bayl?"

Balewynd's chin dipped with the saddest of nods.

"Oh, Bale." Xantha embraced her, allowing the worst of Balewynd's grief to play out.

The sconces had burned low by the time Pecklyn scraped down the entrance tunnel on hands and knees and poked his head into the high wizard's quarters. He whispered to Jyllana who was closest to the exit. "How is she?"

Keeper of the Jewel

Jyllana shrugged. "Okay, I guess." She lowered her voice and leaned close to Pecklyn. "Who's head chamberlain Bayl?"

Pecklyn studied his partner being held in Xantha's embrace, gently rocking Balewynd back and forth. His eyes welled up and his voice broke. "Her father."

Shocked, Jyllana hadn't been able to hear what Balewynd had said to Xantha with regard to who had died.

Pecklyn nodded and dragged himself into Aelfwynne's chamber, squeezing between Jyllana and where Xantha held Balewynd.

Ouderling couldn't help thinking it was good the high wizard wasn't with them. There was no room for anyone else in his quarters.

Pecklyn placed a consoling hand on Balewynd's shoulder and gave Xantha an appreciative nod.

Xantha whispered, "Pecklyn's here."

Balewynd lifted her head from Xantha's shoulder and found the male Guardian's face. She released Xantha and fell into Pecklyn's arms.

Pecklyn embraced her as well as he could given the tight confines and rubbed her back. "You're amongst family, Bale. We've got you. All of us. You'll never be alone at Highcliff."

Balewynd nodded against the side of his head. She sniffed loudly and broke the embrace, allowing Pecklyn to dab at her cheeks with the edge of his long sleeve. "I must look a mess."

Pecklyn laughed. "You've looked better." His face grew serious. "Have you shown her?"

Balewynd shook her head.

Keeper of the Jewel

"She might know what it means," Pecklyn's smile was obviously meant to help cheer Balewynd. "Besides, she deserves to know."

Balewynd nodded and sighed. She withdrew a small wad of paper, interestingly folded into a packet. The remnants of a dark crimson wax seal stuck to the fold in its centre. She stared at it in her hands, a shudder visibly shaking her. She held it out for Xantha. "Daddy gave me this before he…" Her face darkened. "Before he was murdered."

The thick parchment unfolded in Xantha's fingers. She read its message aloud; her eyes welling up and her hands shaking.

The many-faced staff lies shrouded.

Aelfwynne lies beyond help in Crag's Forge.

Orlythe is controlled by the Dragon Witch Wraith.

Not sure of Afara's affiliation.

My time draws nigh.

Convince the princess of her danger.

Only the queen can save us now.

The elder Guardian stared at the parchment a long while afterward, tears dropping onto its surface as she murmured several times, "Dragon Witch Wraith? Dragon Witch Wraith?"

When she looked up, she locked eyes with Balewynd. "Do you know what this means?"

Balewynd shook her head.

"My dearest heart is alive, and his most powerful weapon has eluded capture by Duke Orlythe and his wizard." She glanced at the message again, her lips moving as she reread it. Her voice lowered to an ominous growl. "Your father has hidden the talisman sought by an ancient wraith."

Xantha's wet gaze fell on each person in the room as if sizing up their merit. Crushing the parchment in her wrinkled hand, her trembling voice was so quiet everyone had to lean in to hear, "Aelfwynne is being held prisoner deep beneath Grim Keep. The soulless creature the Dragon Witch gave her life to defeat has returned...From the dead, apparently."

She looked up, her lower jaw firm. "We must go to the castle."

Everyone in the wizard's chamber hung on her every word.

"There's only one thing the wraith fears more than the power of the Crystal Cavern." Fierce determination shone from her narrowing, purple eyes. "The combined magic of the souls trapped in the Staff of Reckoning and the Dragon Mage himself."

The elder's eerie stare fell on Jyllana, her voice dropping to a husky rasp. "And you're going to help us get them back."

Keeper of the Jewel

Unforeseen Magical Presence

Scale shook out his long, dirty-blonde hair, thankful to be out from underneath the sackcloth cowl. The supple, studded, Grim Guard leather armour he had confiscated from a locker in the stables felt surprisingly comfortable.

He scanned the darkness beyond the meagre light of his handheld sconce and listened, all the while wondering how the resident holy elves could stand wearing such uncomfortable clothing. The coarse fibres of the sackcloth had itched his skin to distraction.

Assuming he was alone in the dank passageway far beneath Grim Keep, the Home Guard put the sconce on the dirt floor and shrugged free of the rest of his disguise. He hoped the holy elf wouldn't have too much of a headache when he came to upon the altar of Grim Cathedral.

A sudden dread shot up his spine. If someone happened upon the unfortunate victim of his sword hilt, it wouldn't be long until the Grim Guard were alerted to his presence.

He lifted the sconce and patted the hidden pocket sewn inside his studded, black leather armour tunic as he listened some more. The reassuring bulk of what he hid there gave him all the reason he needed to sneak around the castle of the Duke of Grim. If the rumours were true about the princess' demise, he had to find a way to speak to the high wizard. The queen would expect nothing less.

Keeper of the Jewel

At the end of Scale's sword, the holy elf he had stolen the cloak from had mentioned that the high wizard had been taken to Crag's Forge, accompanied by the duke's human wizard. When asked how to get to the forge, the holy elf had indicated a trap door around the side of the altar, but when asked if he knew where the key was to unlock the marble hatchway, the holy elf had shrugged and turned his back, clearly uncomfortable with the conversation. Without considering the ramifications, Scale had knocked the elf unconscious, smashed the lock with the aid of a marble bust, and stolen down the steep stairwell into the depths of Grim Keep's foundation.

It had taken many wrong turns, and a couple of nervy conversations with random elves he had passed, to get him this far. Sneaking through the foul odours of the dungeon level had nearly stolen his nerve.

He stared down the foreboding tunnel he stood in, the earthen floor dipping into darkness beyond his sconce light, and swallowed. If he were caught now, he wouldn't be able to explain his presence beyond the dungeons. He pulled his dagger free of its plain scabbard and started down the passage.

The tunnel wound around juts of dark granite, inevitably running beneath Lake Grim, if he had the right of it, though by now, any sense of direction was long lost to him. The utter silence in the tunnel and the fact that hundreds of thousands of tons of rock loomed overhead threatened to smother him.

A tight space caused him to bang the sconce against a jag of rock. His knee-jerk reaction to keep from losing his grip on the metal and glass light smashed the failing sconce against the opposite wall. The stub of a candle bounced free of its resting place and rolled underneath a section of projecting stone.

Keeper of the Jewel

He cursed his rotten luck. Turning sideways, he tried to bend down within the tight confines, but his fingers couldn't reach the ground. In the relative darkness, he straightened up and toed at where he imagined the candle had landed but, try as he might, he couldn't retrieve it.

The candlelight sputtered and went out.

Oh great. Now what? Scale's eyes widened at the relevance, though that didn't help him see the nose on his face. He could likely fumble his way back to the stone steps leading up to the dungeon level, but he feared that sooner rather than later, someone would discover the holy elf. When that happened, his time beneath Grim Keep would become complicated.

Left with little choice, he decided it was time to find out if he was as competent as he desperately wanted to believe. Years ago, the wizard's guild at Gullveig had brushed him off as someone below their station. As a low-ranking member of the Home Guard, the wizard he had spoken to had had no time for him, telling him to stick to playing with swords and other crude weapons fancied by those without the gift.

He sighed. Unseen in front of him, he held his palm upward, willing his questionable magic to life. Nothing happened. He grunted in frustration, but the bulk of the hidden object pressing against the inside of his arm renewed his determination. He couldn't live with himself if he didn't return it to its rightful home. But first, he had to get to the high wizard.

Staring hard at where he knew his hand trembled in the air before him, he concentrated. Not sure he was up to conjuring the simple spell, he gulped.

Had he imagined it?

Keeper of the Jewel

He focused his effort, pushing beyond his self perceived limits. From along the periphery of his mind he sensed a tingle of something he had always known had lain in wait deep within his subconsciousness.

His eyes grew wide in wonder. A faint glow illuminated the dirty skin of his palm—the lick of a flame wavering on the cusp of going out. Digging deeper, he willed his mind to ease—to put aside his self-doubt. As a surreal sense of calm flushed through him, washing away his anxiety, the flame coalesced into a thumb-sized ball of fire.

Sweat dripped down his face with the exertion, but no matter how hard he tried, the flames refused to grow any further. Grunting his disappointment, he fought to maintain the spell.

The light flickering above his outstretched hand was barely enough to expose the uneven stone walls, but he didn't care. It would suffice. It was time to find the high wizard.

Dimmer than the handheld sconce, his conjuring allowed him to see enough to not to trip over the uneven floor. If only he could stop from banging off the walls—his complete concentration on the semblance of a fire roiling in his palm.

He had no idea how far beneath the surface he had descended but the cold permeating the tunnel lessened. An odd smell of brimstone turned up his nostrils. Several steps ahead, a wave of warm air raised the fine hairs on his exposed skin. He stopped and looked both ways, afraid he might have inadvertently walked into a lava vent. Crag's Forge was rumoured to have been built into the wall of such a channel.

Standing motionless and holding his breath, he listened to the soft hiss of his conjuring as he scanned the walls. He couldn't be sure, but on the edge of his senses, he thought he heard something else. Something akin to a muted rumble.

Keeper of the Jewel

Sweat soaked his clothing, more from fear than the increased temperature. Princess Ouderling and the entire Home Guard had been killed by a beast that one of the grooms in the stable yards claimed to have been a wingless dragon. A beast that now prowled the warrens and fissures deep within the Dark Mountains.

Scale doubted he had travelled far enough to put him on the far side of Lake Grim, but the irrational fear began to play on his mind, nonetheless. Ever so slowly, he made his way farther along the tunnel.

The passage levelled out beneath his feet. In the distance, a soft glow lightened the way ahead as the tunnel veered left, its roughly hewn walls flickering in more than just torchlight. Scale fought to curb his mounting tension. Unless he was mistaken, he had found Crag's Forge.

He allowed his pitiful magic to disperse and regripped the hilt of his dagger—its heft instilling him with a sense of valor, quelling the unknown fear festering along the edge of his mind. If the duke and the dark wizard were present, he would need every bit of courage he could muster.

Ducking low, he peered around the rocky edge of the opening. A large chamber, bathed in warm, yellowy-orange, greeted him; the intense light causing him to squint. As his vision adjusted, his breath caught. Strapped to a carved stone plinth in the centre of the roughly hewn chamber was the strangest of creatures.

Scale had never seen a goblin before, but from the tales his father had related to him while growing up around Orlythia, and the recent rumours in Castle Grim, the green creature could be none other than High Wizard Aelfwynne.

Beyond the prone high wizard, an opening in the far wall silhouetted a black cowled figure. The remainder of the irregular shaped chamber consisted of shelves carved into a mixture of granite and rougher-appearing, solidified magma. Wooden cabinets were scattered along the walls—their surfaces heaped with a wide assortment of tools, scrolls, and multi-coloured vials. A low table lined the far wall close to the forge, its top littered with what appeared to be vials of multi-hued sand and other materials he didn't recognize.

Being around horses and fighters most of his life, Scale had witnessed all sorts of forges in local smithies, but aside from the fiery furnace, there wasn't much within Crag's Forge that resembled anything he was used to. Excitement tingled his senses. This was a wizard's forge.

His first impression told him no one else was in Crag's Forge. With practised grace, he slipped into the chamber and ducked into the shadows between two, tall cabinets, conscious of the extreme difference in temperature inside the forge.

Heart hammering, he listened to the hiss and crackle emanating from the forge—the only sound that disturbed the otherwise absolute quiet.

Sweat beaded on his forehead. He couldn't imagine how the figure tending the forge tolerated the heat of the roaring fire.

He almost yelped as a soft moan directed his attention back to the plinth. Beady, red eyes stared at him, similar to those of an albino rat. He wanted to look away. Wanted to run from the forge to get out from under the goblin's scrutiny. Its lips parted, revealing dozens of pointed teeth, but as afraid as the creature made him, he couldn't keep from staring.

Frowning as the goblin shook its head, he stared harder. Was the goblin trying to warn him of something?

Beyond Aelfwynne, the figure attending the forge appeared oblivious to the world, engrossed in whatever the spellcaster was doing to the flames. Odd colours lit up the forge, the attendant's ministrations manipulating the fire's hue.

Gooseflesh riddled Scale's skin as the relevance of what the goblin was trying to tell him sank in. The three of them weren't the only ones in Crag's Forge.

Forcing himself against the wall in a futile attempt to disappear, a wave of cold wafted by his hiding spot.

Another black cowled being moved across the chamber, its passage suggesting it glided along rather than walked.

Locking eyes with the high wizard, Scale knew at once that whoever the newcomer was, its unforeseen magical presence meant death.

Keeper of the Jewel

In Her Master's Absence

Balewynd shrugged free of Pecklyn's comforting arm and strode into the morning light, making her way to the edge of the expansive, stone shelf fronting Highcliff. Heavy with moisture, grey clouds scudded across Crystal Lake lower than the level of the promontory. She gazed forlornly at the advancing front. Blowing in from the southeast, the imminent storm matched her brooding emotions.

Her stomach ached as if she hadn't eaten in weeks, but food was the last thing she wanted at the moment. The heartbreak of her father's murder bunched up her insides and squeezed, stealing her breath away.

She swallowed, uncaring of the tears that wouldn't stop. She had never felt this way before. Not even when her mother had left her as an elfling; her sudden death never fully explained. Though she had an inkling her father suspected something unnatural had been at the root of her mother's passing, at the time, she hadn't known any better.

Blame, denial, and bitterness intertwined, twisting her dark thoughts and leading them down paths she had previously been afraid to entertain. If not for the ever-watchful presence of Pecklyn, she believed she would have climbed aboard Mirage and stormed the castle in search of the one responsible for her pain.

She was certain whoever had murdered her father wasn't from South March. The sensations she had experienced during the horrific few moments in which she had laid eyes on it made it obvious it wasn't elven.

She took a deep breath. As a Highcliff Guardian, she had a duty to perform. Speaking past the lump in her throat she said to the wind, "I must oversee the training of the princess."

Pecklyn frowned.

"Aelfwynne bade us to train Ouderling in the old ways. Who else is capable of doing that properly? Xantha's too old to teach her many of the physical things she must learn. No one else besides you and myself know how Master Aelfwynne would prefer someone like the princess to be handled. Given the knowledge handed down by my father, that leaves me." She turned to regard her companion, trying hard to keep her voice from breaking. "You're good with swords and dragons, probably the best with both, so I'll need your help."

"Of course, I'll help, but—"

Balewynd shook her head. "There's no time for but. Despite what my father wrote, Xantha fears Aelfwynne may already be dead. There's little time left to us before whatever that thing that killed my father comes for us."

"She *assumes* he's dead, but we don't know that for certain."

Balewynd's no nonsense stare intensified. "If she honestly thought Master Aelfwynne was still alive, we'd already be down at the castle."

"Ya, you're probably right." Pecklyn sighed and looked away to watch the roiling clouds. "You know I'll help. But…" He faced her again, holding up a warning finger. "But we must hang on to the faint hope that Aelfy has survived." His features hardened. "I won't believe he's gone until I see his body."

Keeper of the Jewel

Balewynd held his gaze. "You didn't see what I did. That thing floated above the ground like a…a…ghost."

"I ain't afraid of no ghost."

Balewynd's eyes welled up. She lowered her gaze and muttered. "Daddy wasn't either."

"Ah, Bale." Pecklyn stepped toward her but she backed away.

"Daddy was the toughest elf I knew. If you had seen the look on his face as the creature stole his life, you'd agree that even the great High Wizard Aelfwynne wouldn't be strong enough to go against it."

"You keep calling it a creature. Help me understand what you mean. What exactly do you think we're up against?"

"That's just it. I don't know. It wasn't elven. At least not like any elf I know. It…it was as if it was already dead. Like it had no soul. My father referred to it as the Dragon Witch Wraith."

Pecklyn mulled that over and shook his head as he cupped her chin in a dirty hand and lifted it so that she would look at him. "Whatever it is, we'll face it together. All of us. That's what we've been trained to do. We're Highcliff Guardians. Heck, Bale, we've got dragons."

She held his concerned look for a moment, his handsome face blurred by tears. Pulling away, she wondered where to start. If Aelfwynne's suspicions were true, the duke had dragons too. The same ones that lived around Highcliff.

She sighed her frustration at not knowing what to do. She wanted desperately to believe Master Aelfwynne had survived, but deep down, like Xantha, she was convinced of his death.

Hardening her resolve, she recalled the high wizard's last words to her and Pecklyn before the gates of Castle Grim. *'I sense in her a greatness I've never felt before.'*

Keeper of the Jewel

She could clearly see the determination on Aelfwynne's face as if he stood before her now. *'The essence of Nyxa. Perhaps even of the Dragon Witch herself, but Ouderling's strength lies along a different path than either one of them travelled.'*

It was up to her to see to it that Master Aelfwynne's last wish was carried out. He was convinced their future lay in the princess' hands. In her master's absence, she vowed to hold fast to his belief and defend Ouderling with her dying breath.

It wouldn't be easy. The old ways were different from those the newer Guardians practiced. Nor did she fool herself. She wasn't even five decades old yet. She needed Xantha's help. She only hoped the old Guardian still had it in her.

Feeling lost, the weight of responsibility threatened to crush her. It was incumbent upon her to move beyond her father's death and do so quickly, but her knees wouldn't stop trembling. Daddy was dead. Her spirit had been cut adrift. She felt so alone.

Tears etched new paths through the grime clinging to her face. She cast a scared glance at her constant companion and swallowed.

Good old Pecklyn. Always by her side. The one elf she could truly be herself with. Her best friend.

She snorted. Her only friend.

Her breathing became ragged as she stared at Pecklyn's blonde locks blowing around his angelic face. She knew he smiled for her benefit. Knew he wanted nothing more than to hold and comfort her; protect her from the evil that had descended on their world.

Keeper of the Jewel

For some inexplicable reason, his concern infuriated her as the crushing grief gripped hard and wouldn't let go. She scowled. How dare he care?

Ripping her gaze from the one elf who would lay his life down for her without a second thought, she glowered at the approaching weather.

Lightning flickered at intervals throughout the brooding cloud cover.

A storm was coming.

It was going to be a bad one.

Keeper of the Jewel

Elusive

Penetrating cold wafted into Scale's hiding place as the floating creature swept by. Cowering in the shadows, the jarring sensation of something unworldly almost reduced him to a quivering lump on the ground. It was like death itself had entered Crag's Forge.

Upon the granite slab, the goblin's beady eyes narrowed at the newcomer's approach. "You'll never gain access to the crystals. Without the magic of my staff, you're powerless to go anywhere near Highcliff."

The floating figure paused on its way past Aelfwynne, its hooded cowl turning to regard the bound high wizard. A hoarse laugh scraped across the room, "Your traitorous mole has been dealt with. It's only a matter of time before I discover where it's hidden."

Scale struggled to quell the rising fear taking hold of his body as he took stock of the creature. Fiery orbs resided where its eyes should have been. Though he couldn't tell for sure, they appeared to look right at him—the hint of a white face visible around the light those fiery eyes emitted. More of a bare skull than skin around its sockets. He held his breath, fearing the worst, but the creature moved on.

It approached the forge. As the fire's attendant turned to greet the newcomer, Scale laid eyes on the dark wizard, Afara Maral.

Keeper of the Jewel

Withdrawing something from within its robes, the creature presented it to Afara. "Use this to discover where the chamberlain has concealed the Staff of Reckoning."

Scale cringed. Just the sound of the creature's voice grated on his nerves. He leaned out to get a better view of whatever the creature had placed in Afara's hand—the object dark and fist-sized; not quite solid, yet bearing weight.

Afara's response to the creature contained little patience as he sneered at Aelfwynne. "Do you realize what you've done? You've interrupted the Harrowing of *him*. The duke will be displeased when he discovers that the resources he paid dearly for have been wasted."

"I care little for your petty conjurings, wizard. Locate the staff and I'll see to it you have access to whatever powders and potions you require." The creature followed Afara's gaze. "The sooner we put an end to the goblin's reign, the better it'll be for all concerned."

Lingering on the edge of the shadows, Scale felt exposed, but he dared not move back lest his movement give him away. His chest swelled deeply, concentrating on a simple spell he had enjoyed invoking as an elfling. Hands raised in front of him, he spread his fingers and silently invoked the simple phrase, "Osteno revalara," while concentrating on the object in Afara's hand. As soon as he realized what Afara held, Scale wished he didn't know.

Both cowled figures' heads snapped to attention, as if sensing a disturbance in the chamber.

On the verge of wetting himself, Scale barely managed to keep from squeaking in fright. How could he have been so naïve? These weren't ordinary magic-users. They could sense another magic in the room. Fortunately, their attention fell on the goblin.

Keeper of the Jewel

Afraid to so much as blink, Scale gripped his dagger hard as the human wizard stepped away from the forge to confront Aelfwynne.

Keeper of the Jewel

"So, you still maintain the ability to perform minor tricks, do you? How quaint. I thought I'd beaten it out of you," Afara hissed and examined Aelfwynne's bindings. Satisfied, he turned to the cowled creature. "Harmless drivel. He's delirious. His old mind's likely reliving his training days as a pup."

The creature floated to Aelfwynne's side, fiery eyes brightening. It regarded Afara. "Don't underestimate him. He wasn't appointed Queen Nyxa's high wizard for nothing." Its burning orbs considered the object in Afara's hand. "I assure you, he'll pose a threat well after his heart pumps its last. Do *not* lose sight of that. The game you and Duke Orlythe are playing at is a dangerous one. If the Harrowing goes sideways, you'll bring the castle down."

"I know what I'm doing, wraith," Afara hissed. "Perhaps you should concentrate on whatever it is you're supposed to be doing to expedite the duke's plan."

Scale gaped at Afara's open hostility in the presence of the dangerous creature it referred to as a wraith. Although the name made sense, the revelation shocked him. He recalled what he knew of a wraith from centuries past. The head Chronicler of Orlythia had taught him about the wraith that had done battle with the Dragon Witch and the one known as Grimlock.

Scale's eyes widened. Surely this couldn't be the same one. A hiss of displeasure drew his attention to the dark wizard.

"It's only a matter of time before the queen comes against us, or have you overlooked that important fact. You should have dealt with her in the tunnel below the palace when you had the chance."

The wraith growled, its eyes banishing the shadows within its cowl, revealing a pasty white skull. "And the duke's elves should have seen to Ouderling's demise while she was in the castle. Summoning that beast was an unnecessary risk. Absolute power is not simply meted out. Setbacks are the norm when dealing with magic of this magnitude. It's how we overcome these unforeseen obstacles that provide testament to our magical prowess. Patience is required when things go awry."

"The duke's patience wears thin."

"Then so too will his grasp upon the throne become," the wraith's voice thundered in the chamber. "Unless you get me that cane!"

Afara walked away from what Scale had feared was about to erupt into a confrontation of epic proportion—two master magicians dueling it out far beneath the dungeons of Grim Keep.

The wraith watched Afara walk past where Scale stood frozen in place, afraid to blink. The wizard disappeared through the exit, his grizzly offering clenched in bloody fingers.

The wraith's stare lingered on the doorway a while before it leaned over Aelfwynne's head. "Your death has been a long time coming. Once I see to the siphoning of power from your pitiful staff, I'll find my way into the Crystal Cavern. With the aid of your magic, I'll rid myself of this corporeal form and reign over the world as the god I'm meant to be."

Aelfwynne's beady eyes stared at the wraith, but if the high wizard was lucid enough to understand, he never responded. His gaze tracked the wraith across the chamber as it followed Afara Maral from Crag's Forge.

Scale held his breath. A wave of cold preceded the wraith's passage, wafting into his hiding spot. He waited until it disappeared from view before he stepped from the shadows

Keeper of the Jewel

and moved silently after the wraith. If he was quick, he might surprise and disembowel it before it knew he was there.

Two steps brought him to the edge of the entrance. He leaned out but couldn't see beyond the light spilling over the threshold. Nor could he sense the cold sensation the wraith's presence had brought with it.

Not sure what to do, he considered his options. He didn't dare light a torch. Staring at the dagger shaking in his hand, he caught the high wizard's gaze.

Aelfwynne shook his head, a pathetic voice escaping his lipless mouth, "Let it go."

It took a lot to scare Scale to the point of not being able to move, but the wraith had intimidated him more than he cared to admit. A wave of guilt washed over him as he savoured the relief instilled by the high wizard's plea to not chase after it.

Aelfwynne nodded and closed his eyes.

Physically and emotionally spent, Scale slid down the rough stone door frame, landing on his rump; hands and knees trembling uncontrollably. His dagger slipped from his fingers and clanged on the ground.

He swallowed. The events he had just witnessed played out in his mind—the vision of what the wraith had handed to Afara forefront in his thoughts.

He shuddered, wondering who the freshly claimed heart had belonged to.

Keeper of the Jewel

No Going Back

Queen Khae appraised the regal troops assembled in the great courtyard fronting the northern gates of Borreraig Palace. Beside her, King Hammas sat resplendent in his official battle gear—golden plate draped in a flowing, light burnt-orange surcoat piped with golden thread. Her heart fluttered. He looked so regal; his wire tiara keeping his long, black hair at bay.

Though the southern skies were hidden behind the bulk of the royal residence, Khae couldn't escape the cold wind that snapped at the colourful pennants overhead depicting the many cities and towns of South March.

The affluent city of Orlythia sprawled on either side of the expansive green space nestled between the palace gates and the grand gatehouse bisecting the city walls. Hundreds of well-wishers had gathered to see them off.

Khae waved to the citizens calling out to her from beyond rank upon rank of mounted warriors and disciplined squads of pike elves. Outside the open city gates, files of South March's infamous archers sat astride well-trained mounts, ready to protect the army's flanks when it left the safety of the north wall.

A flutter of uneasiness tickled the queen's throat. Many years had passed since the last time the full might of South March's army had been brought to bear. Not since the great skirmish that had marked the death of the Dragon Witch had the elven kingdom prepared for war. Queen Nyxa had led that charge. Khae had been little more than a teen-aged elfling trying to find her place in the grand scheme of the world.

Goosebumps riddled her skin. She would have been around Ouderling's age. Everything her daughter was going through brought Khae up short, instilling her with a crushing wave of guilt. Perhaps she had overreacted by sending Ouderling away. Recalling her youth, she hadn't been any different than Ouderling when Queen Nyxa and King Orlythe had mobilized the troops to combat the invading human army from the north. She remembered how abandoned and unworthy she had felt at the time. Neither of her parents had deemed her mature enough to accompany the army, although they had entrusted an entire battalion of their best warriors to her brother.

"Hey!"

Hammas' voice snapped Khae out of her recollection.

She blinked several times, her hand absently waving at no one in particular. She forced a smile. "Give the order."

Hammas held her gaze a moment before nodding to a large elf dressed in his rank's traditional, purple-plumed helm.

Commander Keel in turn signaled to the standard bearer on his far side.

The lanky herald placed a curved, bone horn to his mouth and emitted a long, mournful note that reverberated between the palace and city walls—his white plumed helm shaking vigourously with the effort.

Booted feet and shod hooves resounded in a spectacular demonstration of what a well-drilled army sounded like when it marched in unison—troops breaking into narrower files as their passing thundered through the shadow of Orlythia's northern gatehouse and turned west.

Keeper of the Jewel

The warm sun on her face despite the cold air, Khae sat tall in her saddle, her shoulders back and her chest puffed out. No matter how badly her emotions spun in turmoil, twisting her stomach with doubt, she was the queen of South March. Like Nyxa before her, she must put on a brave face to maintain the people's faith in the crown. If the Duke of Grim meant to disrupt the peace and prosperity of the realm, it was her duty as queen to quash it before it got out of hand.

Proudly riding his black charger, Shadow, Hammas' eyes remained rivetted on the elven units preparing to advance before them.

It seemed to take a long while before the sheer number of troops ahead of them filed through the gatehouse before Khae spurred her mount into action. Hundreds of horses and foot soldiers were spread out to either side and behind where she and Hammas marshalled, patiently waiting to form the rear guard.

As soon as Faelnyr lurched beneath Khae, her horse's dirty white flanks rippled the burnt-orange surcoat draped across her mid-section. Drums boomed and horns blared from Borreraig Palace's ramparts, announcing her movement to the troops who were already long out of sight.

Catching the breeze, the tattered, burnt orange banner Queen Nyxa had carried herself on that fateful day her troops had routed the human horde and sent them back to their northern kingdoms, fluttered magnanimously ahead of her. She tried hard to suppress the smile that threatening to lift her cheeks, but as she entered the gatehouse tunnel, she allowed herself a brief respite in decorum. Being the sovereign of her people instilled within her the greatest sense of pride. She was the embodiment of the wishes, aspirations, and hopes of the elven nation. She was the daughter of Queen Nyxa, the War Dragon.

Keeper of the Jewel

Taking advantage of the few moments out of public, she drew a deep breath to calm her jittering hands as they gripped Faelnyr's reins. She hoped she could be half the war leader her mother had been.

"Do you think it wise? We'll lose a couple of days," Hammas asked Khae that night as she sat on a stool, clad in a simple shift. She worked vigourously at combing out her thick hair in front of a mirror that sat upon the top of a makeshift table within the royal pavilion.

She tugged at a stubborn knot and grunted, "Aelf thinks there's significant magic at play inside Grim Keep."

Hammas stopped behind her and peered at her reflection. "He suspects a malign magic, I believe were his words. Wizard Maral fits that description."

Khae nodded, her face contorted as she pulled hard on her mother's old, bone comb. "True, but we already know of his dark magic. I sense Aelf is warning us of someone else."

Hammas frowned. "Your brother? He's fairly adept."

"I don't think so," Khae said through gritted teeth as a chunk of hair tore free. She pulled the clump from the comb's teeth and started again. "I'd rather take the time now to enlist the aid of the wizards of Gullveig. If they aren't needed, then no harm done. Besides, it'll do them good to get away from that drafty keep of theirs for a while."

"What of Ouderling?"

"Aelfwynne said she was fine. As much as my decision to send her away has left me tossing and turning at night, I hold on to the belief there's no safer place than Highcliff."

Hammas drew a deep breath, his face giving away the fact he was trying to keep the frustration from his voice. "And what if Aelfwynne has the right of it? It's obvious he was worried about his meeting with Orlythe."

Keeper of the Jewel

The comb stopped its slow progress through Khae's hair. She regarded his reflection, locking eyes. "I can't think about what-ifs. Surely, by the Fae's gossamer wings, Orlythe wouldn't harm her." Her face darkened as she ripped the tangle she'd been worrying at free of her head and spun to face Hammas. "Why…Why…I'll tear his heart out!"

Hammas' face softened. "You're right, of course. Not even Orlythe would be that stupid."

Khae took a deep breath, her hands dropping to her lap. Though she dearly clung to that belief, her brother had given her ample reason to believe otherwise. "If he is, he'll rue the day the forces of South March arrive at his gate."

Hammas raised his brow. "Whether he's guilty or not, there may be no going back once he sees the army amassed against him. He'll not take kindly to the slight."

"I care little for what he may or may not like. I'm done catering to his dark moods. If I'd listened to him when mother died, who knows where we'd be now?"

Hammas nodded. "Without the support of the dragons, that's for sure. His plan to take on the northern kingdoms is nothing short of insane. Our immediate neighbours outnumber us ten to one. I shudder to think what dealing with the brutes living north of the Innerworld would entail. There's nothing but barren land up there. Ice and snow if the rumours are true."

Khae placed the hair-filled comb on the makeshift dresser and stood, the candlelight revealing a silhouette of her figure beneath her shift. She wrapped her arms around Hammas' neck and hugged him tight; her soft whisper causing his eyes to widen as long fingernails dug into his back, "If that bastard has proven unfaithful, I'll skin him alive with my own hands."

Keeper of the Jewel

Moment in Time

"For the love of all that's sacred, who the heck could that be?"

Jyllana sat up beside Ouderling, squinting blearily at the door. She swung bare legs over the edge of the bed they shared and spoke through a long yawn, "I don't know, Your Highness. I'll go see."

"Ouderling," Ouderling corrected her, but Jyllana paid her no mind.

Clad in nothing but a thigh-length, filthy, white shift, Jyllana snatched one of her twin daggers from her belt lying on top of the lone dresser and inquired at the door. "Yes? Who is it?"

"Guardian Balewynd. It's time to begin the princess' training."

"Ouderling," Ouderling muttered. She was never going to break them of the habit. "Ask her what time it is."

"Princess Ouderling demands to know the time of day?"

Ouderling rolled her eyes.

"Time is of no consequence. She trains when I say she trains. Evil sets no schedule. We must be prepared to deal with it whenever it arises."

Jyllana gave Ouderling a questioning look.

"Tell her we'll be out shortly."

Jyllana turned to the door, her mouth opening to relay the message but Balewynd's muted voice cut her short. "You're free to do as you like. I only require the princess' presence. Tell her to get ready at once."

Ouderling flew out of bed and ripped the door open. "*Ouderling* will be ready shortly!" Not waiting for a response, she slammed it shut again, shaking her head as she gathered up her leggings and turned them right side out.

Wiping at the sweat streaming down her face, Ouderling shivered in the cold morning air. Judging by the lightening skies in the east, dawn was close to breaking across the Steel Mountain Range. Though still shrouded in twilight, she imagined the dark blot toward the west of where she sat on the edge of a fallen tree that hung precariously over the glistening waters of Crystal Lake far below had to be the shelf of rock fronting Highcliff.

Not believing she would ever breathe properly again, she glowered at Balewynd pacing along the narrow animal track they had been following for some time. The elf looked as if she had just gotten up from a relaxing meal.

The very thought of a meal made her stomach growl. Breakfast would have been nice before the crazed Guardian had made her sprint all over the dragon gods' creation. She took a pull of the waterskin they shared and threw it back to Balewynd. "Why couldn't Jyllana accompany us this morning?"

Balewynd took her time sipping at the waterskin and reapplied its stopper. She threw its thong over her head and tucked it into her thin tunic. "Jyllana is a Home Guard. She went through this rudimentary training long ago."

"Rudimentary?" Ouderling rolled her eyes. "I doubt her trainers had her up before the birds."

Keeper of the Jewel

Balewynd acted as if Ouderling hadn't spoken. "On your feet. The easy part's behind us. With the dawn's early light, we can continue in earnest."

"In earnest?" Ouderling squeaked. "By killing me, you mean?"

Balewynd didn't so much as look her way as she started along the animal track and scrabbled higher up the steep ridge they had been ascending. She paused before disappearing beyond an outcropping of rock. "I suggest you keep up. I don't envy you finding your way back in the dark tonight by yourself."

Ouderling's jaw dropped. Swallowing her dread of what the Guardian had in store, she put her hands on her thighs and forced herself into a standing position. The tightness of her calves twisted her face with a grimace as she started after Balewynd Tayn, the daughter of the late head chamberlain of Grim Keep.

"Eolande, come down here a moment. I want you to meet someone."

Jyllana followed Xantha's gaze to where a ratty wyvern hovered next to an outcropping of dark purple near the centre of the vaulted ceiling of the Crystal Cavern. Hard to see in the multi-coloured hues shimmering around the great chamber, she thought something small skittered across the topside of the jut of rock and take up a place at the base of the wyvern's neck.

Separating itself from the wall, the wyvern turned in mid-air and flapped its leathery wings in such a way that it descended and landed gracefully in front of Xantha.

Jyllana didn't care that she gaped at the wondrous site. She held a hand toward the wyvern. "May I?"

Keeper of the Jewel

A severely wrinkled goblin, his skin more grey than green, scrambled down the wyvern's shoulder and alit on the cavern floor. Wearing nothing but a dun-coloured loin cloth and matching sandals that laced up his scrawny legs to just below his knees, Eolande's toothy smile was every bit as scary as Aelfwynne's. He adjusted the hem of his loin cloth, a well-used hammer and chisel swinging from a leather thong on either hip.

Eolande stepped to the side and bowed. "By all means, Miss Jyllana. Perch would much rather fly a beautiful elf than my old bones."

The goblin stared at Perch and laughed. "Aye. I suspect she would be."

Jyllana frowned as Xantha laughed with him. She had no idea what was so funny, nor how the goblin knew her name.

"Perch says you'd be a pleasant change," Xantha answered her unspoken question. "Says you appear much softer than Eolande's bony carcass."

Jyllana blinked in confusion. She knew a little about dragons, had even witnessed the odd one visiting Orlythia, but until she had come to Highcliff, she had never seen a wyvern. "The wyvern speaks to you?"

"Of course." Xantha rubbed at a scale behind Perch's ear. "There you go, old boy. Does that feel good?"

Perch leaned his head against her hand, eyes closed in satisfaction.

Eolande gestured with an open palm for Jyllana to approach; his rough skin callused and ingrained with dirt.

Jyllana hesitated. She had been close to dragons before but had never actually touched one.

Xantha smiled and stepped clear, a large smile brightening the sadness that had become a permanent look for the elder recently.

Keeper of the Jewel

Perch's eyes followed Jyllana, blinking at her approach, but he never moved.

Cold emanated from his scaley skin, clammy and rough on her fingers. She flattened her palm against the firmness of the wyvern's thick skin, exchanging wondrous looks with Xantha and Eolande. They smiled and nodded back.

Concentrating on Perch, Jyllana pushed past her inhibition and ran both hands down Perch's neck, aware that he was watching. She met his gaze and it was as if a hidden lock had clicked open. She was utterly smitten by the closeness of the magnificent creature. If it had been in Jyllana's power at that moment, she would have urged the world to pass her by and strand her in that moment in time.

As if he sensed her emotion, Perch startled her by wrapping the tip of his leathery wing around her shoulder, careful not to hurt her with the protruding length of ivory horn.

Jyllana froze, unsure whether she had offended him.

"Come, Eolande. Walk with me. I have something I need to discuss with you," Xantha put a large hand on Eolande's shoulder and urged him farther into the cavern, leaving Jyllana and Perch behind.

Jyllana stared wide-eyed at their departure. She tried to step away from Perch, but the wyvern's wingtip forced her back. Panic gripped her.

Perch opened his mouth to grin at her; rows of pointed, meat rending teeth flickering in the ever-changing light of the Crystal Cavern.

Jyllana swallowed, trembling in the grasp of the dragon-like creature. She wanted to cry out, but Xantha and Eolande had disappeared around a bend in the path.

"Do not be afraid, young one."

Keeper of the Jewel

Jyllana's wide eyes searched for the one who had spoken. She expected to see one of Eolande's ilk, but there was no one else. Just her and Perch.

Perch withdrew his wing and swung his head close to Jyllana's face, a toothy smile parting his great mouth. *"You are amongst friends in the Crystal Cavern. On behalf of every caretaker, I welcome you to our fold."*

On the verge of screaming, Jyllana's face twisted in confusion. She backed away a step, pointing at her chest. "Y-you're t-talking to me?"

Perch craned his neck one way and then another before stretching out to Jyllana again. *"I don't see anyone else. Do you?"*

"But...But how?" Jyllana trembled uncontrollably. "I'm not a magic-user."

Perch's mouth opened wider, a deep rumbling laugh escaping his throat. *"You don't need to be a wizard to speak with dragons. You're dragonborn."*

"I'm what?"

"Dragonborn. You have dragon blood in your ancestry."

"Me?" Jyllana continued to point at herself. "Dragonborn? I highly doubt it. I'm the daughter of peasant farmers from northern South March, nothing more."

"And yet, you have been charged with safeguarding the princess' life. Do you not think it strange that Queen Khae would entrust the future heir of the elven nation to a simple farmer's daughter?"

"I...I..." Jyllana frowned. "I never thought about it that way, I guess. I just figured Captain Gerrant saw my potential and appreciated my ability."

"You think those in the know don't invest more thought into who they entrust to oversee the important matters of state? They would be poor leaders indeed if they didn't make

it their business to know everything and anything about the elves they allow within their inner circle. I guarantee you were earmarked the day you were born to take up a place in the Home Guard."

Digesting the wyvern's words, Jyllana resented his implication. "I made a choice to try out for the Home Guard. I was accepted because I was good at what I did."

Again, the throaty laugh.

"You're as pretty as you're naïve, Jyllana Ordalf."

Jaw hanging open, Jyllana stared hard at the old wyvern. At first thought, she didn't think anyone in Highcliff outside of Princess Ouderling knew of her surname, but she recalled her conversation with Pecklyn about the meaning of her last name. Thinking on it, perhaps she had mentioned it to Xantha as well. She shrugged. "So you know my last name as well. That doesn't change anything. How would you know anything about my life? Xantha says you've been flying Eolande around this cavern for centuries."

"Nigh on a millennium."

"A thousand years?" Just thinking about that much time almost left her speechless. "I haven't reached my twenty-sixth name day. How could you possibly know anything about me?"

"One doesn't simply reach my age without garnering a great deal of knowledge."

"But you're stuck in here."

"One is never stuck when in the service of the Crystal Cavern. I'd rather not be anywhere else."

"Nevertheless, you're cut off from the real world."

"The real world now, is it? You speak as if you've experienced all there is to in life. At the tender age of twenty-five, I envy you your exploits."

Keeper of the Jewel

Jyllana couldn't comprehend the fact that she was actually talking to Perch. She paused to digest his words, not missing the sarcasm of his last statement. Her cheeks reddened. "I'm sorry. I forget my place. You're my elder and I shouldn't argue with you."

"On the contrary. You're curious, and rightfully so. I take no offense if that's what you're worried about. I value your conversation. Let me just say that when you've reached ten centuries, you may see life in a different perspective. To ease your mind, dragons talk. We know things most others do not. We share our knowledge to enrich others of our kind. One of us knew of your parent's heritage—likely better than your parents do. If they haven't been selected as dragonborn, then you can rest assured there's good reason. A reason that I, ironically, have not been made aware of."

Jyllana tried to digest everything Perch said but most of it was too hard to comprehend. She lowered her eyes to the ground. "Forgive me. I forget my place, Elder Perch. I will leave you now."

Ashamed that she had been bold enough to argue with the old wyvern, she prepared herself to be excused.

A gentle nudge on her shoulder startled her. Perch wrapped his wingtip around her and drew her in close.

"Nonsense. I look forward to telling you all about my life." A big smile exposed curved teeth longer than her forearm. *"I'm thinking it might take a while."*

Keeper of the Jewel

Unintentional Magic

Crag's Forge sputtered and crackled on the edge of Scale's numb mind. Vaguely aware of his body's uncontrollable trembling, he was powerless to still the wracking fear that had paralyzed him. He had come heartbeats away from dying—had unwittingly looked at what he perceived as death in the eye. If not for the high wizard bidding him not to chase after the wraith, his corpse would likely be shedding its last vestiges of warmth, descending into an everlasting cold; ironically matching that of the aura that heralded the wraith's presence.

He stared vacantly at the rough surface of the granite wall across the threshold from where he sat, a debilitating fright holding him tight. From somewhere close by, a raspy voice beckoned, but he couldn't draw his attention away from the dark tunnel. It was only a matter of time before the wraith or the human wizard returned. As much as a deep niggle urged him to pull himself together and escape before it was too late, he couldn't bring himself to move.

"Grim Guard!"

Scale blinked several times. Someone had spoken. Were they talking to him?

His eyes grew big. Grim Guard? They were coming back!

He pushed his body sideways, leaning out to stare into the impenetrable darkness of the tunnel.

"This way!"

Keeper of the Jewel

The raspy voice snarled behind him. How had the wraith gotten back into the forge?

He rolled his head ever so slowly against the stone wall and gasped.

Intense, red eyes glared back at him.

"Pull yourself together, elf."

The goblin's mouth opened and closed, exposing a split lip, and bloodied yellow teeth.

"What's a member of the Grim Guard doing skulking about the catacombs beneath the castle?" The high wizard demanded. "You obviously shouldn't be down here."

Scale stared hard at the green creature strapped to the top of the stone pedestal, the goblin's words slowly sinking in. He blinked again, wrapping his mind around what had happened. He shook his head as the recent events clarified in his mind. He was in Crag's Forge with High Wizard Aelfwynne!

His hands continued to shake, but he regained a measure of composure. Noticing his abandoned dagger, he picked it up and swallowed hard. He had come in search of the high wizard.

Heart hammering in his chest, it took everything he had to gain his feet. He took a deep breath and stepped into the tunnel, listening. Satisfied they were alone, he approached the high wizard and stammered as he patted his leather studded armour. "It's not what it looks like. I'm a member of the Home Guard. Sent to escort the princess to Highcliff, but my father decided it best to leave me behind."

The goblin stared long and hard, a subtle look of recognition crossing his strange features. "You're Gerrant Wood's son."

Scale wasn't sure what he had expected to hear but it surely wasn't that. He swallowed and nodded.

Keeper of the Jewel

"You must get free of this place," Aelfwynne whispered. "Find your way back to Orlythia and warn the queen that the Dragon Witch Wraith has returned."

Scale examined Aelfwynne's metal bindings. He slid his useless dagger back into its sheath and foraged through the contents on several shelves in search of the key that would free the high wizard.

"There's no time for that. Save your strength. My days are over. You're young, but you can't make a difference if you're dead."

"I can't just leave you here," Scale spoke to the shelf he ransacked, panic elevating his tone. "You're the high wizard. The queen will have my head if I let you die." He spun on Aelfwynne, his face ashen. "If I don't get you out of here, my days will be over too."

"The wizard has the key to my shackles. You're no match for him." Aelfwynne considered the molten rock and magma fires hissing beyond the hole in the back wall. "Afara Maral won't hesitate to feed you to his infernal forge."

Glass vials shattered on the ground as Scale swept his hand across a stone shelf in frustration. "There has to be a way."

He darted across the chamber to examine the tools assembled near the forge's mouth on a low table, exclaiming in desperation. "I know. I'll use this!"

The metal hammer was heavier than it appeared—a solid piece of cast iron. He carried it in two hands and plunked it down on the plinth beside Aelfwynne, careful not to catch the goblin.

Aelfwynne was tightly bound, both wrists and ankles secured to an iron ring embedded in the stone beneath him.

"Can you roll over a bit? I can't get at the chains."

Keeper of the Jewel

Aelfwynne made no effort to try. "These chains are forged with lava fire and magic. That hammer won't scratch its surface."

Scale glared at the hammer. Straining hard, he picked it up with two hands and flung it with disgust across the chamber. It bounced off the ground and careened against the wall with a resounding clang.

Aelfwynne rolled his eyes. "Brilliant. Now the whole castle knows you're here."

Scale stared after the hammer. It wasn't the smartest thing he had ever done. He cast a worried glance at the entrance, half expecting to see two cowled figures coming for him. One human, the other a beast from some nefarious nether realm.

"Go. Warn the queen before it's too late to save the princess."

It was as if Aelfwynne had risen off the slab and slapped him for all he was worth. "The princess is alive?"

"For the moment."

Scale teetered on the verge of panic at the startling revelation. The unexpected news made his decision all the harder. Aelfwynne would die if he left him, and yet he was being told that the princess' life hung in the balance if he didn't get word to Queen Khae. He leaned toward the doorway but his feet refused to move. There had to be a way to save the high wizard *and* inform the queen.

He pounded his forehead with the heel of his palm. *Think, Scale, think.*

Had his father not died in the recent ambush, he would've feared the hard elf's reaction were he to learn of his son's indecisiveness—the captain's voice sounding in his head as if he stood before him in Crag's Forge, *'You're lucky I'm a captain in the queen's guard else you'd be mucking barns*

Keeper of the Jewel

with the rest of the commoners. To think you aspired to the life of a wizard. Hah! You can't even figure out how to undo a set of manacles.'

A crazy idea jumped to the forefront of his mind. He produced a slim piece of metal from his waistband and confronted the high wizard with a tiny replica wand a girl had gifted him years ago. He had kept it in a pouch on his belt to remind him of the beautiful elf and the marvelous time they had shared—visions of her never far from his mind. "I need you to roll onto your side."

Aelfwynne sneered. "I told you, boy, it's magically bound. A master lockpick wouldn't be able to free me. Only the magic key can open it."

"What's it going to hurt if I try? I can't just leave you here." Scale forced Aelfwynne onto his side until the short chain prevented him from rolling farther.

Aelfwynne struggled, trying to resist. "Wait. You don't know what you're doing."

One hand firmly holding the high wizard, Scale ignored his pleas. The lock felt heavier than it looked. Twisting it so that the light of the forge lit up the keyhole, his tongue parted his lips as he concentrated on what he had to do. As soon as the wand's tip breached the opening, an audible zap accompanied intense pain. It shot through his hand and up into his shoulder. He yelped and threw his arm backward, losing his grip on the wand.

The metal stick tumbled slowly through the air toward the open face of Crag's Forge. It bounced off the wall, shy of the opening—a high-pitched 'ting' following its path to the ground in front of the lava chute.

Shaking the numbness from his hand, Scale rushed to retrieve his precious gift, his ears reddening as the high wizard's throaty laugh mocked him.

330

Keeper of the Jewel

A quick inspection revealed the lock's wards had scorched the wand's tip. He grimaced and attempted to polish its charred end to no avail.

"I tried to tell you." Aelfwynne rolled onto his back. "The bindings are a powerful construct of an experienced wizard. There's nothing a simple elf like you can do to the mechanism except harm yourself. And me."

Scale ran his fingers through his long hair, exasperated. He pointed the wand at Aelfwynne. "Instead of telling me what I *can't* do, why don't you help me figure out what I *can* do?"

"There's nothing to be done, you fool. Unless you're familiar with the type of spell Afara used to seal the lock, anything you do will only cause you, and *me*, harm. Now, do as I ask. Go, before it's too late."

Frustration, grief, and anger had consumed Scale from the moment his father had publicly disciplined him about his role in the princess' foray onto the plains abutting Castle Grim without an escort. He wanted to shout his anguish at the stubborn lock securing the high wizard, but held back.

Captain Gerrant had been well within his rights to issue the demeaning order for Scale to remain behind at the castle and watch over the Home Guard horses while the competent warriors oversaw the princess' well-being as she made her way to Highcliff.

Since then, shame and humiliation had been constant companions. When he heard of the ambush and loss of life in the Passage of Dolor, he couldn't escape the crushing guilt that accompanied not being there to help out.

A faint glimmer of hope broke through his dark mood. If what the high wizard said was true, perhaps his father had survived as well. He leaned in close to Aelfwynne, locking eyes. "Who else survived?"

The goblin's somber expression scuttled his hope.

Keeper of the Jewel

"Only the princess and her protector made it out." Compassion twisted the goblin's features—an odd expression on such an alien face.

Scale dropped to his knees, hanging off the granite slab by his elbows.

"If not for your father's heroic efforts, the princess would have died as well."

Scale swallowed the wave of grief threatening to consume him. His father had been a hard-nosed elf—unable to openly show love, but he knew by the way his father had watched over their family that deep down, they meant as much to him as his service to the crown. Although Scale had resigned himself to the fact that his father was gone, hearing it confirmed did little to soften the blow.

Aelfwynne's soft voice reached through his despair. "Now go, boy. Avenge his sacrifice. Make him proud."

Those simple words awakened a newfound determination in him. He stared at the tiny wand he gripped near the high wizard's shoulder. Rising to his feet, he glared at his hands as if seeing them for the first time. His father had doubted his magical ability—a major bone of contention between them. Scale had vowed years ago that someday he would prove the arrogant elf wrong.

Deep within his troubled mind, a spark of enlightenment flared to life. His breathing came in short spurts as he stared at the wand's blackened tip.

Without taking the time to consider the possible consequences of his actions, he forcefully rolled Aelfwynne onto his side; the chain and bindings visibly digging into the goblin's raw skin.

Aelfwynne fought against him. "No, you big galoop! You'll kill us both!"

Keeper of the Jewel

Ignoring the high wizard's plea, he concentrated on what he had to do. Similar to the sensation of conjuring his pathetic fireball, he embraced the essence of the magic he always knew he had. One that had eluded him for so long. It manifested into a sensation he had never experienced before.

Abandoning everything he knew about his gift, which wasn't much, he welcomed the power infusing his insides, and begging for release, as he positioned the wand's tip close to the keyhole.

Unaware of the potency of the magic flowing through him, energy crackled along the short length of wand and coalesced at its blackened tip. The finger-length metal shone brightly, forming a pinprick of white light for but a moment before discharging into the lock.

A resounding crack thundered through Crag's Forge and reverberated up the tunnel beyond.

Flying backward across the chamber, Scale held his arms over his head and tried the catch a glimpse of the ceiling, afraid to witness it crashing down on top of him. He hit the ground hard, halfway between the slab and the open forge.

A few moments passed before he allowed himself to breathe. Crag's Forge had withstood the blast. He stared dumbly at his empty hand, wondering where the detonation had originated from. Aelfwynne had been right to warn him about the spell the wizard had placed on the lock. If only he had had enough sense to listen.

A low moan came from the direction of the stone slab, but the goblin was nowhere to be seen.

"High wizard?" Scale croaked. Out of the corner of his eye he caught sight of his wand. Crawling to retrieve it, he heard another moan come from the far side of the plinth.

"Master Aelfwynne!" Scale scrambled around the platform on hands and knees to where the high wizard rolled on the ground in apparent agony, still fettered to a length of thick chain that dangled from the manacles binding his wrists. "Are you okay? What happened?"

Aelfwynne opened pain-laced eyes, the skin around his wrists and ankles blackened and raw. "You happened."

"Me?" Scale examined the blackened chain where the lock had been attached and then at the manacles still firmly restraining the high wizard. "I did it! You're free! Let me see if I can get those off."

Aelfwynne rolled out of Scale's grasp. "I've been the victim of enough of your unintentional magic, thank you."

Keeper of the Jewel

Once in a Lifetime

Jyllana flicked at the hair blowing across her face. Far below her dangling feet, white-capped waves frothed against crags of black rock where the mountainside plunged into the depths of Crystal Lake. To the southwest, a strange island broke the water's surface.

Goosebumps riddled her exposed skin in the dying rays of the day, but she didn't care. All she could think of was Perch. What a glorious creature.

She had wanted to ask if she could fly the old wyvern but lacked the courage to broach the subject. Instead, she had spent a magical afternoon speaking with him. She couldn't recall ever being this happy. Being told that she possessed what few elves had left her senses reeling, wondering what dragonborn really meant. If only Captain Gerrant had known who he had ordered out of the queen's house guard, she doubted the punishment he had meted out would have been so harsh.

Movement at the eastern edge of the vast rock shelf drew her attention. The aloof Balewynd bounded down the last stretch of a trail that led onto the heights. Of Ouderling there was no sign.

Jyllana scooched back from the edge of the platform and stood, watching Balewynd stroll toward the main entrance tunnel.

Keeper of the Jewel

Before the Guardian slipped inside, Jyllana called out, "Hey! Where's Ouderling? I thought she was with you."

Balewynd didn't appear to hear her above the ever-present wind, but paused on the threshold long enough to point to the heights above the promontory. Without a word, she disappeared into the complex.

Jyllana frowned. As far as she knew, nobody else had left with the princess and Balewynd during the early morning hours. She fast-walked to the edge of the stone shelf where it ended against the cliff and looked up the faint trail. Scrub brush and pines clung to barren rock, their scraggly branches blowing in the breeze.

She was about to start up the trail when a fist-sized rock careened over a ridge and tumbled down the steep trail. It skipped into the air and dropped past the edge of the platform, out of sight. Following the rock's path, the filthy countenance of the princess came into view, her feet slipping on loose scree.

Jyllana held her breath, fearing Ouderling might follow the stone to her death. She prepared to reach out and grab her but the bedraggled heir to the Willow Throne fell onto her backside to slow her slide.

Digging in her soft-soled boots, Ouderling bounced back to her feet and corrected her course, jumping the last few feet to the platform. If not for Jyllana's assistance, she appeared like she might collapse.

"Your Highness! Are you okay?" Jyllana pulled Ouderling away from the edge and steered her toward the entrance tunnel.

Ouderling's head bobbed on her neck, her orange-hued eyes bleary. "I'm close to death."

Startled, Jyllana gripped her by the shoulders, forcing the princess to look at her. "You're what? Are you hurt?"

Keeper of the Jewel

Ouderling's head lolled to one side, her body slumping. "That psychotic elf tried to kill me."

Jyllana supported Ouderling's dead weight with difficulty. "She did what?"

"If that's basic training, there's no way I'm going to survive advanced." Ouderling slumped against the cliff wall.

A wave of relief washed over Jyllana. A knowing smirk curled her lips. "Ah, I see." She positioned herself to support Ouderling's slight form and led her into the tunnel. "Come. Let's get food into you and then off to bed." Offering the princess a smug smile, she added, "Trust me. You'll feel worse in the morning."

Jyllana doubted the princess was even aware she was being undressed. The exhausted young elf had fallen asleep before her head dented the pillow.

Resuming her place on the edge of the platform, Jyllana enjoyed the peaceful tranquility of the incredible vista; the choppy surface of Crystal Lake set afire by the setting sun. As much as Ouderling's reaction to her first training day had made her laugh, she couldn't help but commiserate with the princess. If the initial training regimen at Highcliff was anything like the Home Guard employed, Ouderling was in for a long few weeks.

Jyllana's elation from earlier in the day waned as the sun dropped into the western heights, casting Crystal Lake and Highcliff in long evening shadows—the snow-capped peaks on the horizon illuminated in crystalline relief.

She pulled her cloak tight to ward off the tendrils of cold seeping into her bones and contemplated returning to the tunnels.

Echoes of Xantha's proclamation of her helping them recover Aelfwynne and his staff whispered in her head. What had happened to that plan? Nothing had been said to her since.

Shaking her head to rid it of the elder's voice, she rose to her feet and started for the tunnel but was brought up short by another voice sounding oddly in her mind. One that wasn't her own.

"Jyllana Ordalf. Wait."

The presence of a dragon, for she now knew instinctively where the voice originated, almost made her cry out in fright as it didn't belong to Perch.

She stared at the main entrance, squinting to see down the long corridor, its length illuminated by wall sconces. Other than three elves walking deeper into the complex, no one was around.

"Look to the west."

Alarmed, she did as instructed. At first, she didn't see anything, but as she stared, Pecklyn's dragon, Dawnbreaker, materialized from out of the shadow of the mountain overhead.

On closer examination, the Guardian's snow-white hair fluttered above Dawnbreaker's neck. Rising high over the lake, they caught the rays of the setting sun for the briefest of moments before Dawnbreaker altered her flight and dropped into a long, graceful arc, turning toward the platform.

Jyllana remained where she was, unsure of where Dawnbreaker meant to put down. She retreated a couple of steps as the squat dragon back-flapped and reared up close to where she waited.

Pecklyn vaulted from Dawnbreaker's shoulders before she had settled onto her front legs. "Ah, Jyllana. Just the elf I wanted to see."

Keeper of the Jewel

Jyllana frowned, unsure whether that was a good thing or not. She gave the handsome elf a shy smile. "Oh? And why's that?"

"Because..." Pecklyn walked right up to her, grabbed one of her hands, and led her toward the dragon. "Dawnbreaker and I have become aware that there's more to you than we originally thought."

Jyllana stopped her forward momentum. "Really? Do you care to tell *me*?"

Maintaining his hold on her hand, Pecklyn's broad smile lit up his face. "You're dragon worthy."

"Dragon worthy? What's that supposed to mean?"

"It means..." Pecklyn gestured at Dawnbreaker. "That you're dragonborn."

"How do you know that?"

"Perch told us. Well, he told someone, and someone told someone else, and...Well, you get the point. If you learn nothing else today, know that you'll never keep a secret from a dragon."

Trying hard to digest his explanation, she stared at Dawnbreaker. "Was that you who spoke to me?"

Dawnbreaker dipped her massive head.

"But how?" As soon as she asked, she knew the answer. Perch had explained it to her earlier in the Crystal Cavern. "You mean I can hear every dragon now?"

Pecklyn's shrug drew her attention back to him. "More or less. It depends."

"On what?"

"On whether *they* wish you to hear them." He patted the hand he still held and pulled her after him. "Just know that you are blessed."

"I don't understand. I don't have a magical bone in my body."

Keeper of the Jewel

Pecklyn stopped next to Dawnbreaker and stepped aside to allow Jyllana to get within touching distance of the dragon. "You don't need to be a wizard to possess dragon magic. For most of us, myself included, the latent magic will never manifest itself into anything more than a perpetual presence. But, as I'm sure you discovered while speaking with Perch, that is magical enough, don't you think?"

She realized she nodded as he spoke the truth. "Yes. Yes! It's incredible." She reached out and gently stroked the top of Dawnbreaker's front foot, mesmerized by the fact that she was patting a dragon.

Pecklyn puffed out his chest. "Amazing, isn't she?"

"Is she ever. She's an incredible creature."

"I told you I would like her."

Jyllana locked eyes with Pecklyn—her cheeks hurt she was so happy.

"You know what's even more amazing?" Pecklyn's grin matched hers.

Speechless, Jyllana could only shake her head.

His smile grew wider still as he lifted her hand toward Dawnbreaker's shoulder. "Flying one."

Jyllana was certain her legs were about to give out but Pecklyn's other hand reached around her waist to steady her as he urged her onto Dawnbreaker's foreleg. "This can't be happening."

"Trust me. You haven't seen anything yet." Pecklyn grabbed her hips and boosted her onto Dawnbreaker's shoulder. "Snuggle into her neck."

Jyllana's mind spun with elfling giddiness. So engrossed with the sensation of a dragon between her legs, she barely registered Pecklyn settling in behind.

His muscular body pressed against her as he wrapped his arms around her and took hold of her hands, guiding them to two of Dawnbreaker's neck scales. "Hang on tight. The take-off can be a little disorientating."

Dawnbreaker rose to her full height and turned to face the drop-off. Without warning, she crouched low and sprung into the air, her bulk dropping below the level of the rock shelf even though her great wings thrust great volumes of air beneath them.

Pecklyn hung onto Jyllana's hands, making sure she didn't lose her grip. He shouted into her ear to be heard over the rushing wind as Dawnbreaker's thrust propelled them far over the lake, "Don't worry! It'll take her a few wingbeats to compensate for the extra weight!"

Breathless, Jyllana couldn't respond. The feeling of weightlessness when they had first dropped off the promontory had stolen the breath from her lungs. The subsequent sensation of being compressed against Dawnbreaker's shoulders as the dragon's momentum increased with every wingbeat exacerbated her inability to breathe.

The distant, snow-capped peaks were no longer far away. The western edge of Crystal Lake soared by far below, quickly replaced by sprawling evergreen forests clinging to the side of a steep mountain.

Just when Jyllana feared they were getting too close to the towering cliffs, Dawnbreaker dipped to the right, and flapped harder than before. If not for Pecklyn's hold on her, she was certain she would have fallen to her death.

"Woohoo!" Pecklyn's cry of triumph pierced her ears as Dawnbreaker levelled out and he sat back, relinquishing his hold on her hands.

Jyllana tried to emulate Pecklyn's exuberance but her voice wouldn't come. Instead, she clutched Dawnbreaker's scales so tight her fingers hurt.

Keeper of the Jewel

The bone-chilling cold of dragon flight was but a fleeting sensation as the summit of one of the highest mountains in all of South March passed close by on their right and they burst into the blinding last rays of the orangey-red sun as it sank into the waves upon the distant horizon—the Niad Ocean awash in a spectacular reflection of the breath-taking sight.

The front of Dawnbreaker's wings angled downward. Weightlessness returned as they plummeted thousands of feet toward a great, aquamarine river that wound its way through the brown heights of the Mardeireach Mountains along the southwest coast of South March.

Jyllana's breath had barely returned, only to be snatched away again by a panorama of endless waterfalls along the watercourse, the fast-running waterway meandering between snow-capped mountain tors to empty into the ocean along a crag-filled shoreline.

Pecklyn held onto her waist to help keep her seated. Leaning in, he directed her attention to the winding river and a wide swath of what appeared to be a roadway high in the mountains. "That's the Path of the Errant Knight! The only other way to reach Highcliff besides the Passage of Dolor or on the back of a dragon!"

Jyllana considered the endless peaks stretching away in all directions. She turned her face to rub against Pecklyn's. "Is it travelled much?"

"Hah!" Pecklyn lifted his head and laughed at the sky. "Not unless you wish to die!"

His answer puzzled her. She'd have to ask him what he meant by that when they landed. Swallowing the question, her unbridled smile returned. Leaning forward and wrapping her arms around the bulk of Dawnbreaker's neck, she basked in the fading warmth of the sunlight on her face, her ponytail whipping around behind her. She laughed in the face of the wind, savouring the thrill of flying the sky on the back of a dragon.

Even if it proved to be a once in a lifetime experience, she would die content knowing there wasn't anything that could remotely compare to it.

Dawnbreaker's downward trajectory levelled off, the change in momentum squishing Pecklyn on top of her. She didn't care. She cherished the moment.

As they glided over the last of the dwindling crags and soared across the wavetops of the roiling ocean—so low their passage left a plume of froth in their wake—Jyllana let go of her inhibitions and relinquished her stranglehold on Dawnbreaker's neck. Leaning into Pecklyn, her cheek nestled against the side of his face.

She threw her arms in the air and exclaimed, "Woohoo!"

Keeper of the Jewel

Magic Drunk

Huffing more than he cared to admit, Scale couldn't believe the weight of the high wizard. Young and strong, he considered himself in excellent shape, but as he slunk through the upper tiers of Grim Keep's dungeons with the goblin bouncing unceremoniously over his shoulder, he felt the burden of the extra weight.

Voices up ahead gave him pause. If he and Aelfwynne were spotted by anyone, especially below the keep, he would have a difficult time convincing them he was a Grim Guard. They would have no choice but to fight their way free. Though he took pride in his ability to wield an effective sword, he was no match against a group of Grim Guard.

Nor could he afford to let anything happen to his burden. He had witnessed firsthand what Queen Khae and her forces would be up against. She needed the high wizard alive if she had any hope of defeating the treacherous duke's arcane accomplices.

The voices grew louder—feelers of torchlight banishing the darkness ahead.

Scale extinguished his pitiful wizard's fire and ducked into an open cell. A loud clang followed them in.

"Pay attention to what you're doing, you big galoop!" Aelfwynne complained, the goblin's voice coming from where his head bounced on Scale's back. "You trying to knock me out?"

Keeper of the Jewel

Scale realized the clang had been the high wizard's head ringing off the metal doorframe. "Sorry," he said as he crouched into a back corner of the cell and plunked the goblin on the damp, earthen floor amongst a scattering of small bones and other detritus he decided he'd rather not know any more about.

The cold cell rank of musty loam and urine mixed in with the rot of death. It was all he could do not to gag as the advancing torchlight encroached on their hiding place.

"What do you suppose that was?" a startled, high-pitched, male voice questioned.

"Beats me. I didn't think we housed anyone down this way. The human wizard…" a gruff voice answered, hocking and spitting as he referenced Afara Maral. "…doesn't want anyone housed along the route to his blasted forge."

"That's what I thought," the first voice agreed.

The torchlight slowed its advance. The sound of rusty hinges squealed, the grating noise echoing throughout the cellblock.

"Ain't seen anyone down this way in some time," the first voice said above the sound of a squealing hinge, this one closer.

"I doubt you'll find anything. Likely a rat," the deeper voice answered.

"Or something worse," the higher-pitched voice answered back. "Do you think something might have made its way up through the lower tunnels?"

Another squealing hinge grated on Scale's nerves—the voices almost on top of them.

"Like what?" The second voice asked with a cynical chuckle. "A grotdraak?"

The advancing torchlight stopped. "That's not even funny. You ever hear talk of those beasts?"

Keeper of the Jewel

"Bah! Old elf tales." A cell door banged against stone, the vibration against Scale's shoulder telling him the guards were checking the cell beside them.

A hinge squealed across the corridor as the torchlight intensified, the hissing of its flames devouring an oily rag wrapped around the head of the torch clearly audible.

As the door to the cell Scale and Aelfwynne cowered within squealed, the deeper voice spoke as if the guard stood right beside Scale. "Or are they?" Heavy footfalls rushed into the corridor, "Roar!"

Across the corridor, the high-pitched screech of the surprised guard sent shivers up Scale's backside. Daring to peek out from where he hid beneath the folds of his black tunic, a muscle-bound, big-bellied brute hovered in the passageway, his hands held over his head as if he were about to pounce on his skinnier companion—the flames of his torch blackening the stone ceiling.

The startled guard stumbled against the opposite cell door, face white with fear. He swallowed and gathered himself, scowling. "You're an ass, you know that?" With that said, he stomped away.

The huskier guard's deep laugh echoed inside the cell, fading as he followed his partner down the corridor. "I'm your grotdraak! Remember that."

"Oh, I'll remember it alright." A cell door squealed farther along. "As I slide the tip of me sword up your arse."

A deep-throated laughed rumbled down the passageway.

Aelfwynne groaned, "Get off me, you fool!"

The high wizard's muffled grunt snapped Scale's attention back to their cell. He jumped to his feet and cringed. The goblin lay crammed into the uneven rock of the cell wall and the back corner.

Keeper of the Jewel

He scooped Aelfwynne off the floor and positioned him over his shoulder. "Sorry, Master Aelfwynne."

"I'm beginning to think I would've been safer if you left me in the forge."

Scale stepped through the partially open, metal door and turned to look both ways, smacking the high wizard's head off either side of the door jamb. "What's that?"

Clearing the dungeon levels, Scale snuck along the lower levels of Grim Keep, his little fireball providing him a faint light in which to see by. If he remembered the way he had stumbled along on his way to Crag's Forge, the tight corridor he followed led beneath the inner baily and would come up below the cathedral. It certainly felt familiar. Provided there were no rites going on, he doubted he would meet anyone until he surfaced inside the vaulted-ceilinged building erected along the outer wall of Castle Grim,

A steep flight of flagstone steps spiralled into the darkness at the end of the passageway, confirming he had found his way back to where he had started.

"Do you know where you're going?"

The goblin's sudden voice behind him made Scale jump with fright. He swallowed an angry retort. "I think so."

"You think so? You realize there are enough passageways beneath the castle to keep someone walking for days?"

Scale ignored the question, his concentration on the trap door above. With any luck, the holy elf still lay unconscious beside the altar.

He paused to listen but couldn't hear anything on the other side of the stone hatch. A sinking feeling gripped him. If the holy elf had been found, perhaps those responsible would discover that the lock on the hatchway had been busted.

Keeper of the Jewel

Holding his breath, he pushed his shoulder against the heavy slab. It wouldn't budge.

He grunted in frustration and shoved again.

"What's the matter?" Aelfwynne asked, wiggling on Scale's back. "Put me down so I can see."

Scale sat the goblin on a step and stretched out his shoulder as best he could in the cramped quarters, hoping the numbness caused by Aelfwynne's weight would dissipate quickly. He used his little ball of fire to light a wall sconce set into an alcove in the stairwell wall and let his magic burn out. Worried who had secured the hatchway, he said, "It's locked."

"So? Open it."

Scale frowned. "The lock's on the other side."

"You know what end the latch is attached to?"

"More or less," Scale muttered. "It's not like I break it every day."

"That's good. You don't need to reach it. Use your magic."

Scale frowned. "I thought you didn't trust my magic?"

"Don't reckon we have much choice."

Scale rolled his eyes, but the goblin made sense. He considered the hatch, making sure he wasn't mistaken as to which edge held the lock. Judging by how the steps rose to meet it, the lock should be near the middle of the top step.

Taking a deep breath, he concentrated on what he remembered about the lock he had broken. The distinctive aura of his gift tingled deep within his core. Now all he had to do was channel it into something more tangible. That had always been his problem. Staring at the dark stone barrier, he had no idea how to turn the magical inkling into reality.

Dejected, he lowered his gaze to the steps dropping away into darkness. His father and the wizard's guild had been right all along. He was nothing more than a sword in the

Keeper of the Jewel

queen's personal guard. A position most elves aspired to obtain, but for Scale, his failure to become who he aspired to be had sapped the life from him.

Aelfwynne wriggled in obvious discomfort, his hands and legs bound by wizard's chains. "What's the matter? Why'd you stop?"

"It's no use. I can't do it."

The goblin's beady eyes narrowed. The scant light afforded by the sconce made his face nastier than its usual appearance. "What do mean, you can't? You almost blew my soul into the nether realm back in the forge. Now you just want to quit? Some magic-user you turned out to be."

"That's just it. I'm not a magic-user. Father was right. I should stick to what I do best." He pulled his sword free and jammed its tip into a small gap between the hatch and the top of the stone wall—the metal thumping and scraping as he twisted the blade to create a gap.

"Oh, that's swell. You might as well blow a horn and announce our location."

Scale paused to glance at the goblin but didn't respond.

"Stop. The only thing you're going to do is remove the edge from your sword. You think you're useless now?"

Scale glared. Had it been most anyone else, he would have punched their insolent face, but he shrivelled under Aelfwynne's scrutiny. He lowered his sword tip to the step by his feet and whispered, "What do you suggest?"

"Use your wand."

Scale frowned. "It's just a toy a girl gave me years ago."

"A powerful toy, if you ask me."

Scale sheathed his sword and pulled the wand free of the pouch, his puzzlement deepening as he examined its short length. No matter how he rubbed the tip, he couldn't erase the scorch mark. "It's a trinket. It's not real."

Keeper of the Jewel

"It's more real than you think." Aelfwynne raised thin eyebrows. "Or do you honestly think you were the one responsible for destroying the wizard's lock?"

"I…I guess I never thought about it."

"Never guess!" Aelfwynne hissed. "That's your first and biggest mistake. Know, or learn. Guessing will be your undoing."

Scale had no idea what the high wizard was on about. He imagined Aelfwynne was implying there was more to the replica wand than he knew. "You think it's a real wand?"

"Of a certainty. I sensed it as soon as you held it in your hand." Aelfwynne closed his eyes for a moment. "Mmm, I feel it now."

"That makes no sense. The elf who gave it to me was a farm hand. She wasn't a magic-user. I would've known."

"Appearances are best left at that. The second rule you need to take to heart is this: misconstrue someone, or *something*, based on your limited perception of them at your peril. It's the surest way to end up dead." Aelfwynne shook his head. "Do you know where she got it?"

Scale thought about that. "No, actually. She never said."

Aelfwynne's smug look silenced any further questions.

"Try again. This time concentrate on the lock, but channel your magic through the focal point of the wand. Allow it to control what you cannot."

Scale held Aelfwynne's intense gaze, digesting his words. Taking a deep breath, he placed the wand's tip against the edge of the hatch, the talisman's thin length allowing him to touch the spot in the dark shadow beneath where he believed the lock rested. His magical essence tingled deep within him, flowing easier than before. He couldn't be sure, but he believed he could feel a warmth infusing the metal.

Keeper of the Jewel

Just when he thought nothing was going to happen, a soft glow illuminated the wand's tip. Afraid he wasn't strong enough to maintain it, he focused on the odd sensation magic brought with it. The glow intensified, illuminating the step beneath the wand and the underside of the rough stone hatch.

A soft, blue-white tendril arced from the tip of the wand to the hatch, more a diffused light than a static charge—the stone darkening at the point of contact. Tiny wisps of smoke billowed into the space between his face and where the stairwell ended, but he couldn't tell whether the magic had penetrated the hatch or had merely fizzled on the surface. The more he worried about the effectiveness of his conjuring, the dimmer the light became until the arcing tendril winked out.

He tried pushing the hatch open to no avail. Slumping onto the steps, he hung his head in his hands. "It's no use."

A long silence filled the stairwell. He didn't have to look at the goblin to sense the high wizard's disappointment. He had failed. Again.

Biting his lower lip, he shook his head and stared into the darkness beyond his boots. They were going to have to fight their way out. He corrected himself. *He* was going to have to fight their way out. The high wizard was useless with his hands fettered.

Unable to resist, he glanced at his companion. The goblin's intense stare startled him so much he looked away in shame.

"Do you believe in yourself?"

Scale swallowed, considering how to answer the question. Up until recently, if someone had asked him, he would have responded with a resounding yes. But now, he wasn't so sure. Not in the mood for a lecture, he muttered, "I guess."

"Never guess! I already told you that. That's the root of your problem. You go through life unsure of yourself."

Keeper of the Jewel

"Ya." Scale rolled his eyes and looked away. "For good reason."

Aelfwynne adjusted his position, taking care not to roll off the step and tumble into the depths. The timbre of his voice dropped to a hair-raising snarl. "Do you believe in yourself?"

Shocked, Scale stuttered, "I...I...Um, yes. Yes, I do."

A quick glance at the goblin froze him. He couldn't break eye contact if he wanted to.

"It's as I thought. I sense untapped potential in you, Scale Wood. You just don't know how to release it. Yet."

Scale's eyes widened. "How do you know my first name?"

"I knew your father. He must've mentioned you once." Aelfwynne's dour mien softened. "He was gruff, no argument there, but don't you ever doubt his love for you. The Queen's Guard has suffered a great loss with his passing."

Eyes welling up, Scale chastised himself. Tears were the last thing he needed now. The high wizard already considered him a buffoon.

"According to Princess Ouderling," Aelfwynne continued, "Captain Wood gave his life to save hers. There'll be songs sung of him in taverns across the realm when news reaches Orlythia."

A couple of tears rolled down Scale's cheeks. "He was a hard man."

A silence settled between them within the stairwell; their faces flickering in the dim sconce light. Finally, Scale whispered, "I'm not my father."

"No, that you are not." Aelfwynne wriggled until he sat up as well as the chains permitted, the semblance of a sad smile cleaving his wrinkled face. "But it's because of who Gerrant was that I believe in you."

Scale blinked several times as the goblin's words sank in.

Keeper of the Jewel

"Yes." Aelfwynne grinned with a knowing look. "The third and final lesson if you're ever to become a shade of who your father was, is this. Magic is something few individuals are born with. Some call it a gift but I say nonsense. It's what you make it. A gift. A curse. A non-entity. It's up to you how you wish to behold it. Just like a bird can fly, or a fish draws breath underwater, it's who you are. A bird cannot fly unless it flaps its wings. Magic can't respond if you don't embrace its presence and truly believe. Do you think the fish doubts its ability to draw air? Until you come to terms with the simple truths, your magic will be lost to you."

Scale blinked in wonder at the cragged face staring back at him. It was as if the old goblin's odd words had opened a hidden compartment in his mind. A pinprick of understanding banished the darker shadows of his all-consuming doubt. As much as the captain in his father never believed in him, he felt he owed it to the elf's memory to rise up and embrace who he was meant to be. To prove Captain Gerrant wrong.

He looked up, his gaze intense. He owed it to himself.

The neglected wand rolled absently in his fingers as he considered it in a different light. Without a word, he faced the hatchway. Tingles of energy crept along his skin, surfacing from a place he had always known had existed inside him. A place he never had the courage to get acquainted with.

The little wand warmed noticeably. He squinted in light spilling from its tip. Three tendrils of wispy energy extended from the talisman and penetrated the stone.

His jaw dropped as he sensed the veins within the granite—thousands of years of history that spoke to the stone's unique story. Passing through the upper layer of the thin rock, he became one with the veined white marble attached to it as his magic penetrated the top of the hatch.

A foreign sensation drew his concentration to where an iron bolt scarred the marble—the anchoring hardware that held the lock in place. Up through the hardened steel the tendrils crawled, intertwining the hasp of the new lock— creeping into the shiny keyhole.

His magic located the mechanism holding the lock shut. With barely a thought, it sprung open. One with his gift, he directed the tendrils to manipulate the open lock and slide it free of the iron ring.

It took every bit of mental strength he possessed to disengage from the magic's allure. His mind returned to the stairwell where he teetered on the steps, almost losing his balance.

"Well done, boy," Aelfwynne hissed. "Now get a hold on yourself. You're magic drunk."

Keeper of the Jewel

Fan the Flames

Duke Orlythe brooded in his own company within the empty throne room, the lava fount doing little to warm the drafty chamber. Considering the attentive Grim Guard stationed around the chamber as nothing more than part of the room, visions of Borreraig Palace darkened his mood.

Strapped to the sacrificial slab in Crag's Forge, the high wizard had somehow managed to extricate the Staff of Reckoning from harm's way. According to the wraith, the cane Afara had burned in Crag's Forge had been a fake. Either the demented goblin had purposely not travelled with the real talisman or there was something dreadfully amiss within the ranks of the castle's inhabitants.

To make matters worse, Aelfwynne had found a way to escape the arcane shackles Afara had insisted were unbreakable. He nodded, his mood darkening further. The high wizard must have had someone in the upper echelons of Grim Keep's staff. Whoever the culprit, they would rue the day they crossed Orlythe Wys, the rightful ruler of South March and beyond.

He licked his lips, craving something to remove the acidic taste of betrayal from his mouth. Where was his ever-reliable head chamberlain? It wasn't like Bayl to neglect his duties.

A furtive movement behind the Lava Throne alerted Duke Orlythe to Afara Maral's presence—the human wizard appearing from the shadows. How Afara managed to position himself there without Orlythe's knowledge irked him to distraction, but he was in no mood to berate the wizard for his petty mischief. Afara had bigger things to answer for.

Not dispensing pleasantries, Orlythe got straight to the crux of his frustration. "Tell me again how the high wizard slipped your unbreakable bond."

The cantankerous wizard casually strolled to Orlythe's side and hissed, "As I said, Aelfwynne is in possession of a great wealth of arcane knowledge. It's doubtful he could break the spell on his own, but one can never be too sure when dealing with the goblin."

Duke Orlythe pointed at the broken lock lying on a small table on the opposite side of the throne. "And yet there it is. Judging by the shredded metal, a strong magical presence was involved."

Afara's shrewd gaze flicked to the offending lock. "Again, without the aid of his staff, I'd bet my life that Aelfwynne wasn't the caster. He had help."

Purple-faced, Orlythe snarled, "What you suggest is inconceivable. The only magic-users remotely as adept as yourself or the high wizard are cloistered in Orphic Den. Are you suggesting the headmaster of the magic guild had something to do with this? Or are you suggesting your apprentice might have freed him?"

"I'm not suggesting anything. Ryedyn was with me when the high wizard escaped. The identity of this rogue magic-user is as much a mystery to me as it is to you. Perhaps your bedfellow, the wraith, has ulterior motives."

Orlythe glared but there wasn't time to punish the impudent wizard. The insinuation of the wraith's involvement in Aelfwynne's escape unsettled him; something he was sure the wizard meant to do. Ignoring the remark, he asked, "Are you certain he escaped through the cathedral?"

"As certain as I can be. The lock sealing the underground passageway was definitely opened with magic. I sensed its presence on the opened device."

"But you can't sense who the magic came from?"

"That would be a neat trick. I can only speak to the strength of the magic employed, not to who performed it. There hasn't been a magic diviner in centuries."

"So that lock was magically bound as well?"

"No. It was an everyday lock."

"Then what makes you sure the goblin went that way? He could still be in the castle."

"Unless Grim Keep is infested with unknown magic-users, my conclusion is the obvious course," Afara hissed. "Nor can I sense Aelfwynne's stain anywhere in the castle."

Orlythe's festering rage came to a head. "If you can sense the high wizard's presence, how was he able to slip through layers of underground passageways, past the patrolled dungeon levels, and beneath the bailey to the cathedral without alerting you?"

"Detecting magic doesn't just happen. It takes deep concentration and the enactment of a high-level spell. I was in my tower gathering the necessary ingredients for another casting of the harrowing spell because your ghostly ally ruined my first attempt." Afara held the irate duke's glare. "Nor can I claim to know where the wraith was during the escape. Perhaps you should ask it."

As if on command, the tattered robes of the creature in question slipped between the large Grim Guard stationed outside the throne room's exit, not bothering to abide their challenge. It was as if the creature simply flowed through their crossed halberds.

Keeper of the Jewel

Recovering from their shock, the Grim Guard gave chase but Orlythe held up a hand and shook his head.

The wraith glided to his usual place halfway up the dais steps. "Ask me what, Duke Orlythe?"

The duke flicked an irritated look at Afara before addressing the wraith. "Where have you been since leaving us in the forge?"

The wraith's fiery gaze brightened slightly. It nodded toward Afara. "Attending to matters both of you should've dealt with a long time ago. You had a traitor in your midst."

Orlythe gripped the arms of the throne and leaned forward. "You found the rogue magic-user?"

The wraith tilted its head, a throaty chuckle escaping the shadows of it cowl. "Your chamberlain was hardly a magic-user."

"My chamberlain?"

The wraith nodded. "The one you call Bayl."

"You think Bayl facilitated the high wizard's escape?" Duke Orlythe was so irate spittle flew from his lips. Nor did he miss the odd smirk on Afara's face.

The wraith stiffened. Floating to the top step, it leaned over the duke. A menacing voice chilled everyone within earshot. "The high wizard escaped?"

Orlythe swallowed despite his resolve to remain firm in the wraith's presence. It was all he could do not to slink away from the veiny white flesh visible within the wraith's cowl. "That's what we're trying to determine. He must have had help."

The wraith held his gaze for several long, uncomfortable moments before straightening to its full height. "That is most unfortunate. We must send word to Orphic Den of these developments."

Keeper of the Jewel

Duke Orlythe frowned, his mind reeling from the mention of Bayl. "The wizard's guild? What do they have to do with Aelfwynne's escape? And what do you mean you dealt with Bayl?"

The wraith turned on the spot, as if experiencing the dimly lit chamber for the first time. Facing Orlythe again, it said. "The queen is on the move. If she suspects the amount of magic at play here at Grim Keep, she'll undoubtedly attempt to enlist the aid of Gullveig. We must prevent that from happening."

The duke was glad he had been sitting down. "My sister marches against me?"

"There can be no other explanation for the mobilization of South March's standing army."

"That's absurd. What have I done?" As ludicrous as that sounded, Khae should not have been aware that anything was amiss. He turned a dark look on Afara, infuriated that no one had informed him of these events. "A Highcliff raven must have made it through."

"Or a dragon," the wraith growled, diverting Orlythe's attention from Afara.

Orlythe shook his head. "No. I would've been informed if a dragon had flown to Orlythia."

"Regardless, I have it on good authority that three thousand swords and a thousand bows have rounded the Wizard's Sleeve. Unless they're marching on Urdanya, my guess is the queen is on her way to speak with Sagora."

Orlythe had no way to confirm the wraith's claim but he had no reason to dispute it either. If the queen *was* on the march, the only logical reason, especially since she hadn't communicated with him directly, was that she was moving on Grim Town.

Keeper of the Jewel

"But it's too soon. Odyne hasn't been dealt with. Without Urdanya's forces, we cannot hope to repel the royal army."

"Nonetheless, it's happening. We must move quickly to ensure the queen doesn't enlist the aid of Orphic Den. I will deal with the guild."

Orlythe swallowed. A bitterness churned bile in the back of his throat, warning him that his pact with the wraith would eventually lead to his downfall.

"How will you get there before Khae?"

"Call in your swiftest dragon."

Orlythe nodded and indicated for Afara to look after it.

The human wizard stared at the wraith a while longer before bowing to the duke and slipping from the throne room.

Even though several Grim Guard stood at attention around the chamber, Orlythe felt alone with the wraith. He hoped his brow didn't show the strain he was under. "Your actions have lit a fire beneath us that is quickly spreading out of control. What do you expect me to do while you're gone?"

A hideous laugh filled the chamber sending chills up Orlythe's spine as the wraith glided down the steps and drifted toward the exit.

It stopped before the lava fountain, its cowl twisting to allow the wraith's fiery orbs to stare back at him. "Why, fan the flames, Duke Orlythe. Fan the flames! You must see to it that the high wizard is made to heel if we're to survive the coming days."

The halberd bearing Grim Guard stepped back as the wraith floated by and disappeared from Orlythe's view.

Slumping in the uncomfortable embrace of the Lava Throne, Orlythe stared at the mesmerizing lava oozing its way down the tiers of the fountain. If Khae knew of

Keeper of the Jewel

Ouderling's demise, nothing short of cutting her head off would stop her from exacting her vengeance.

It was time to whet his sword.

Keeper of the Jewel

Shorn

"Tell her to get stuffed." Ouderling pulled the cover over her head and turned to face the wall.

"The princess says to get stuffed," Jyllana called through their sleeping chamber door,

Ouderling gritted her teeth, squeezing the pillow beneath her head hard. "Ouderling!"

Jyllana walked back to the bed. "What's that?"

Ouderling turned over, throwing her pillow at the door; immediately regretting it. Every muscle in her body ached. She glared at Jyllana's innocent face. "Nothing!"

Jyllana frowned and moved to where the cabinet stood at the foot of the bed. "I don't think Balewynd will be put off."

Resigned to the fact that her self-appointed trainer would remain patiently outside their door until she showed her face, Ouderling gingerly eased her legs over the edge of the bed and accepted her ivory comb from Jyllana. Worrying the knots from her thick hair proved more difficult this morning as she hadn't taken the time to comb it out before dropping unconscious in exhaustion the previous night.

"Does that elf ever sleep?" Ouderling muttered, scrunching her face as the comb tore a chunk of hair free.

"I'm sure she must." Jyllana padded back to the door and called out, "The princess will be out shortly!"

Turning to Ouderling, Jyllana looked sheepishly at the floor, avoiding her withering scowl.

Keeper of the Jewel

"How…many…times…," Ouderling accentuated each word by tugging in cadence on her hair, "must…I…tell you? Don't call…me…," she yanked, tearing an impressive knot of hair free, "princess!"

"My apologies. It's a habit."

"Then break it!" The princess tossed the comb aside and rose to her feet, only to sit right back down again, grimacing at the pain in her thighs.

Jyllana produced a stone platter from the top of the cabinet, loaded with nuts, fruit, and a goblet of wizard's tea. "Here. Get this into you."

Ouderling stared at the platter placed in her lap. Her mouth watered as she realized how hungry she was. "Where'd you get this?"

"I got up early and sweet talked the cooks. On the way back, I bumped into Xantha. When I told her about how your first day with…," she nodded toward the door, "…she made a cup of wizard's tea for you. Claims it'll take the edge off your aching muscles."

Ouderling stared hard at the offering. It was all she could do to reign in her emotions. As usual, she had been short with Jyllana. Thinking on it, she always treated her that way.

She raised her head to see Jyllana standing before her, a pleasant smile on her face, never expecting anything in return for her kindness. Ouderling inhaled a deep breath and held out an arm. "Come here."

"Your Highness?"

Ouderling let the honorific slide. "Come here."

Jyllana did as she was bidden.

Ouderling wiggled her fingers. "Closer."

Jyllana hesitantly leaned in, careful not to disturb the platter.

Keeper of the Jewel

Ouderling wrapped an arm around the back of Jyllana's neck and hugged her as tightly as she dared while balancing the food tray. "Thank you."

"You're welcome, Your...Ouderling," Jyllana whispered.

"Have you eaten?"

Jyllana shook her head.

Releasing Jyllana, Ouderling patted the bed beside her. "Sit. You can help me eat all this."

Jyllana settled in beside her and waited for Ouderling to start before she picked at the platter's contents.

Ouderling made quick work of her good fortune. True to Xantha's word, the soothing effects of the wizard's tea did wonders to reinvigorate her tired body. Using the edge of the bedsheet to wipe her mouth, she nodded at the door. "Inform little Miss Impatient Pants I'll be ready shortly."

Despite having a full stomach and the benefit of the wizard's tea, the day's training exercise was anything but enjoyable.

Balewynd had marched Ouderling along a different trail— one that descended steeply to the rocky shoreline of Crystal Lake. She dreaded the thought of having to climb it again.

The poor excuse for a path ended directly beneath the shelf of stone abutting the entrance to Highcliff. Craning her neck, the promontory didn't appear as large as it had while standing on its surface.

Sunshine bathed the Highcliff region, bringing unseasonably warm temperatures to the Dark Mountains. Ouderling's sweat stained clothing and dripping face bore testament to the fact that although Balewynd's pace had been easier than the previous day, her trainer still expected her to move at a brisk walk.

Keeper of the Jewel

Balewynd removed her boots and waded into the water to take a seat on an exposed rock; allowing the gentle roll of the lake to lap at her exposed lower legs.

Ouderling did likewise, taking up a position on a separate boulder. Swishing sore feet through the surprisingly warm water, she said, "I thought the lake would be colder than this. It's actually warm."

Balewynd indicated the mountains across from where they sat. "Constant volcanic activity keeps it pleasant."

Plumes of steam rose at several points along the distant shoreline.

"If you look closely, you can see the lava floe tumble down the mountainsides. It's more impressive at night."

Ouderling nodded. Thinking on it, she hadn't been outside of the complex after dark. She made a point of doing so if she survived the day's training with the Guardian.

Appreciative of the break in the day's exercise, Ouderling took a moment to lie across the rock and dip her face in the lake—her mass of hair spreading out around her on the water's surface. Whipping her head back, she snapped the bulk of the water from her locks before wringing out the rest with her hands. Though she had vowed at an early age to never cut her hair, the last couple of days had her thinking otherwise.

Alone with her thoughts, the high wizard's plight came to mind. "Do you really think they would kill Master Aelfwynne?"

Balewynd's faraway stare was answer enough.

"You should take me to see the duke. He's my uncle. Let me talk to him."

Balewynd regarded her. "You wish to confront the elf who wants you dead?"

Keeper of the Jewel

Goosebumps flushed Ouderling's exposed skin as a cool breeze swirled along the shoreline. "We don't know that. Besides, I'm the heir to the throne. He wouldn't dare allow anything to happen to me in the public eye."

Balewynd frowned. "How public do you think you'll be? You're not in Orlythia anymore. We're talking about Castle Grim. Your mother may be queen, but the lands south of the Rust Wash are loyal to the duke. Other than Highcliff, of course, you won't find much sympathy down here." She paused as if contemplating whether to say more.

Ouderling picked up on her hesitation. "What is it?"

"Not many elves are aware of this…" Balewynd glanced at the underside of the rock shelf abutting the Highcliff complex. Sighing, she continued, "It's rumoured that Duke Orlythe has the ear of a number of dragons."

Ouderling blinked several times, letting the import of that sink in. "I never saw evidence of dragons near the keep."

"That's because they live amongst the Highcliff dragons."

Ouderling's jaw dropped.

"Ya, no kidding. To make matters worse, not even Master Aelfwynne knows how many are loyal to the duke." Balewynd nodded. "That's what prevents us from storming the castle to discover Master Aelfwynne's fate. Xantha fears any action on our part might precipitate a dragon war—one she believes we won't win."

"That makes no sense. Why would the dragons fight each other?"

"Grimclaw."

"Grimclaw? What's he got to do with anything? He flew north when the Dragon Witch was killed."

"It's complicated. Let's just say that Grimclaw wasn't loved by every dragon. He made a number of enemies during his rise to power with dragons who are more in line with the

Keeper of the Jewel

tenets of Duke Orlythe. When your grandmother ascended the Willow Throne, there was a great push to form a dragon army to chase the human rabble from their homelands and eradicate their scourge from the land once and for all. It was labelled by those like your uncle as a pre-emptive strike. Ironically, it turned out that Duke Orlythe's fears were realized a few years later when the kingdoms of man invaded South March. As such, he has retained a devout following across the realm."

Ouderling stared at Balewynd, her mind reeling.

"It's true. On Grimclaw's advice, your grandmother decided not to attack the northern kingdoms with an army backed by dragons. The same humans who were ultimately responsible for the murder of thousands of elves, countless dragons, Grimlock, and the Dragon Witch. In the end, not even your grandparents escaped their treachery."

The Chronicler's lessons had never mentioned what had happened immediately following rise of Nyxa the War Dragon. At least not while Ouderling had been paying attention. Nor had she ever read anything into the outcome beyond the fact that the newly formed realm of South March had rallied together under Nyxa's banner, against insurmountable odds, to repel the human threat.

Balewynd rose to her feet, the shallow water between the rocks lapping at her shins, and examined the heights around Highcliff. "A rift developed between the dragons. Many of those faithful to Grimclaw followed him north to seek a land where they wouldn't be bothered by mankind again." She nodded. "When I say mankind, that includes elves."

Ouderling slipped off the boulder and respectfully waited for Balewynd to finish saying what was on her mind.

"He appointed a group of dragons to remain behind and watch over Highcliff. His way of thanking those responsible for giving him life. Unfortunately, a good number of those dragons stayed at the request of your uncle."

Ouderling followed Balewynd to the shore and struggled to pull her boots on over wet skin. "Surely my mother must know of this."

Balewynd shrugged. "One would think so, but who knows what goes on in the courts of the ruling class? They're the ones who dictate which way the wind blows. Our job at Highcliff is to stand tall in the face of that wind. We bend to the will of those in power, but we must ensure that we never break."

Ouderling puzzled over that statement but wasn't given a chance to question its meaning.

Balewynd started up the steep slope, following the perilous animal trail onto the rockfall littering the steep slope below Highcliff.

Jyllana was nowhere to be found when Ouderling limped back to their quarters with Balewynd in tow. The Highcliff Guardian had helped her carry a pile of fancy armour she claimed Xantha had gifted to her, and left her on her own.

After their trip to the shores of Crystal Lake, Balewynd had led them back to Highcliff and taken Ouderling into a section of the elaborate complex she hadn't visited before. There she had instructed Ouderling to try on a set of armour that had been set out on a stone table within a large chamber lined with racks bearing leather, chainmail, and plate.

Folded amongst the impressive assortment of black metal plate inlaid with golden filigree, was a unique pair of black leather breeks and matching leather top that appeared too short to act as a tunic. Balewynd had explained that the long-sleeved top was designed for females to protect their upper body from the inevitable chafing the heavy armour caused.

Keeper of the Jewel

The Highcliff Guardian had patiently helped her don the clothing and metal plate, the regal set complete with a matching helm bristling with two, rear-facing, dragon horns that sprouted from the face-shield's temples.

If Ouderling hadn't been exhausted, she would have marvelled at how well everything fit. Like it had been fashioned with her in mind. Thinking on it, that made sense. It had been gifted from the legendary warrior, Xantha. She would know armour and weaponry better than most. Even the two-handed greatsword, sheathed in a black and gold scabbard, accommodated her smaller hands, though Ouderling questioned whether she would ever be able to swing it effectively.

The day had been much easier physically than the day before, but she still suffered. The sleeping chambers were thankfully quiet without her protector around. She eyed the bed longingly but decided it best not to retire before supper was served. If she didn't get a good meal in her, she doubted she would survive another day of whatever Balewynd had in store.

A shiver ran up her spine in the cold chamber, her mass of hair still wet underneath. Aside from the constant need to comb it out, the biggest problem with so much hair was the time it took to completely dry. Gallivanting across the mountainside under the intense rays of the sun hadn't helped.

She located her discarded comb and sat on a stool in front of the cabinet, trying to see her reflection in a poor mirror that sat upon its top. She mocked the reflection staring back at her. Some princess she made. If her mother could see her now, she would be beside herself. Ouderling could hear Khae's voice, "You're a princess of a great, elven nation. You must look and act the part at all times."

Keeper of the Jewel

She put the comb to her hair but thoughts of her parents stayed her hand. Her mother had sent her away and her father hadn't intervened. They had banished her to the remotest part of the kingdom, supposedly to be trained as a Highcliff Guardian. Why they would do such a thing, she had no idea. She was a princess. She shouldn't have to lift a blade in defence of the realm. There were experienced fighters for that.

Holding a great clump of long tresses, a dark thought plagued her troubled mind. Wouldn't her parents be shocked if she cut it all off? Just like they had cut *her* off.

A mischievous smile lifted her cheeks as she considered the pile of armour and leather Balewynd had helped her stack in the back corner beside the head of the bed. The gleaming array was nothing more than a confused mess of metal to her. She wasn't sure she could figure out what pieces went where, let alone don the bulky armour on her own, but she located the sword belt and pulled free the greatsword's matching dagger—its edge keen to the touch.

Back in front of the mirror, she lifted a test clump of hair and contemplated what she was about to do. Although she was raised in a world of riches, she had always considered her hair her most precious asset. It represented who she was as an individual—something that hadn't been handed to her because of her station in life. Great pride had gone into each morning's long sessions of combing it out. Being a princess, there were always servants to perform such tasks, but during the last few years, she had insisted on doing it herself. Ever since she had met Marris.

Thinking of the boor, her mood darkened. The dagger sliced clean through the clump of hair with nary a tug. Holding the severed trophy in front of her, she glared at the offending locks. If this was what life at Borreraig Palace had been all about, it was high time she was rid of it.

The shorn tresses slipped through her fingers. Grabbing a thicker chunk, she thought of her ungrateful mother. The dagger sliced true.

She imagined her smiling father. He hadn't spoken against her mother's wishes. Another hunk fell into her lap.

Visions of Buddy assailed her. She would never see his beautiful face again. The dagger sliced through the better part of the length below her neckline. Tears streaked her cheeks. Buddy was better off without her.

The mat of white-blonde hair around the stool mocked her—the tresses' dampness not entirely due to her earlier foray into the waters of Crystal Lake with Balewynd.

Glaring at the severed mass of a decade's worth of growth, she couldn't still her trembling hands. A forlorn, young elf looked back at her with disgust in the imperfect reflection of the old mirror.

Her body jerked as door hinges squealed.

"Your Highness!" Jyllana rushed to her side. "What have you done?"

Ouderling dropped her gaze to her lap, shoulders shaking uncontrollably. The dagger slipped from her fingers, clattering to the floor amongst the wreckage.

"Oh, Ouderling," Jyllana wrapped her in a great hug. "You poor, poor girl."

Keeper of the Jewel

Treachery

Queen Khae rode behind the lead riders along the windy approach to Orphic Den—the eerie aerie housing the eclectic magic guild of South March a day's ride west of Gullveig at the head of the steep pass known as the Wizard's Walk. Some of the land's most powerful practitioners lived in and around the plateau in the heights of the Wizard's Sleeve; the village of Orphic Den's mystic structures permanently enshrouded in what outsiders were led to believe was a spectral mist.

Phantom shapes flitted along the periphery of her vision; not quite substantial, and yet not a figment of her imagination. Some flew while others ran, swirling the mist with their passing. She had been told on previous visits not to concern herself with whatever it was that haunted the fog. As long as she bore no ill will toward Orphic Den's inhabitants, no harm would befall her.

The spooked faces on the Home Guard around her confirmed they were as apprehensive about the spectacle as she was. They had been warned about what they would encounter, but she couldn't fault their uneasiness. To an elf, her troops would lay down their life in the course of their duty, but nothing in their training had prepared them for the otherworldly shenanigans perpetrated on behalf of the eclectic wizard's guild.

372

Keeper of the Jewel

"It never gets better, does it?" Hammas muttered. He scanned the fog obscuring everything but their immediate vicinity, and licked his lips. "The sweetness of the mist is the strangest thing ever."

Khae swallowed her reservations. The riders beyond the line in front of them were nothing more than silhouettes. She had travelled to Gullveig on two occasions in the past. Once, long before her parents died of injuries sustained in the campaign to oust the human rabble, and again shortly afterward to give homage to the wizards whose aid had been invaluable in turning the tide of the bloody war that had brought South March to its knees.

Unable to stop herself, she licked her lips. Familiar with the strange phenomenon, tasting the sickly-sweet dampness in the air was indeed a bizarre experience. The wizards claimed no harm would befall them as a result, but she couldn't help thinking there had to be more to the unnatural mist than the wizards let on.

She muttered under her breath for only Hammas to hear, "No, it doesn't. The sooner we're free of this cursed place, the better."

"Do you honestly believe Headmaster Sagora will heed your call?"

"Don't see he has much choice." A smug grin twisted her face, her eyes blinking rapidly to rid her lashes of the drizzle that began to fall. "I *am* the queen, after all."

Hammas raised his brow, his unspoken skepticism not unexpected. The dear elf didn't have a magical bone in his body. As such, the ways of wizards and their ilk were as foreign to the king as a set of wings to a fish.

The fog darkened ahead. Vine covered towers flanking the gates of the Orphic Den keep materialized out of the gloom, its haunting silhouette highlighted by a flash of lightning.

373

Keeper of the Jewel

A grim determination lifted Khae's chin. "If he doesn't, I'll be sure to convince my brother to turn his nefarious ways on Sagora's bastion of enchanters."

Thunder rumbled, echoing off the surrounding peaks, and dissipating into the distance. The oncoming weather front had the makings of a severe storm.

Four hand-picked Home Guard stood silent vigil in the small chamber just inside the brooding keep, awaiting the withered elf chamberlain who had escorted them into Orphic Den—instructing the small party to sit. The Headmaster would be down to see them at his convenience.

Good old Hammas sensed Khae's tension. He grasped her clammy hand and rubbed it in an effort to mollify her rising anger. She was the queen of South March. Patient as she was, she had no time for the arrogance of the arcane residents of Orphic Den. It was as if her presence and that of her standing army were nothing more than an annoyance to the chamberlain.

She forced a smile as the elf in question reappeared through a rear door and nodded his head ever so slightly.

Hammas jumped to his feet, his face red. "Bow to your queen! Has Sagora not taught you any kind of respect?"

The chamberlain glared at the king but yelped when the Home Guard nearest him dropped a gauntlet on his stooped shoulder and drove him to his knees.

If she hadn't been so preoccupied with the dire state of affairs gripping the realm, Khae would have been aghast with how harshly the Home Guard dealt with the chamberlain, but given the elder's attitude, she decided he deserved what he got.

Keeper of the Jewel

She stepped beside Hammas. "Has Master Sagora managed to free a little time to spare for the queen and king or shall we come back when it's more convenient?"

The chamberlain refused to meet her gaze. He spoke as an impudent elfling might after being embarrassed before his peers. "Headmaster Sagora awaits you on the east balcony."

The Home Guard squeezed the servant's shoulder.

"Your Highness." The chamberlain snarled. Shrugging free of the Home Guard's grasp, he glared at the burly man as he rose to his feet. Taking a moment to brush bits of grit from his breeks, he stormed from the chamber.

Khae raised an eyebrow. "A pleasant fellow, that one. I guess we're to follow?"

Hammas smirked and motioned to the first two Home Guard. The second pair fell dutifully in behind.

"Ah, Your Highness. What an unexpected pleasure." A portly, grey-bearded elf in dark robes straightened to his full height as he stepped away from a thick marble railing encompassing the outer perimeter of an eastern facing balcony, several stories higher than Orphic Den's western entryway. Water run-off streamed farther out; the open-air balcony protected by a large overhang.

Fork lightning jagged in the darkness beyond the railing, followed by a cringe-worthy crack of thunder.

Khae fought the urge to roll her eyes. The headmaster must surely have known of their imminent arrival long before they had entered the Wizard's Walk—the narrow pass leading up to the mountain glen high on the shoulders of the mountain spur referred to as the Wizard's Sleeve. In fact, she was positive everyone in the village of Orphic Den had been aware of their movement ever since they had stepped foot on the mystic bridge spanning the Enchanted River that flowed out of the western foothills. She didn't dismiss the notion that Sagora had probably known of her plans before she had made them. It was never wise to underestimate a wizard as powerful as the headmaster.

Nearly as wide as he was tall, Sagora was a specimen to behold as he towered over Hammas. The offspring of a sorceress, and a male giant from the kingdom of Serpens beyond the wastelands north of the dwarven realm of Sarsen Rest, Sagora's stern demeanor and obese stature were enough to instil fear into most anyone he encountered. Khae had never met anyone near as large as the headmaster of Orphic Den.

"I wish I could say the pleasure was all mine, headmaster, but I'm sure you've surmised by the amount of steel travelling with us, we're in the midst of a crisis."

Sagora intertwined plump fingers, his hands resting on his ample girth; every digit resplendent with twinkling rings bearing a variety of precious gemstones. Along with three amulets dangling below the thin point of his short beard, the wizard's baubles were enough to purchase a small kingdom.

"I would be remiss in my duties to Your Highness if I hadn't noted the force you command. Have the northern rabble emerged from their holes?"

If it were only that simple, Khae mused. "No, headmaster. I've received unsettling news out of Castle Grim."

The headmaster raised a bushy eyebrow. "Your brother? I was wondering when he would rear his ugly mug."

Hammas rolled his eyes. "You and everyone north of the Wash."

Sagora clicked his tongue. "And just what do you require of the wizard's guild? That's why you're here, of course, is it not? If I'm not mistaken, the kingdom is unravelling and

Keeper of the Jewel

the crown suddenly has an interest in the talents of Orphic Den."

Khae hoped her face didn't reveal the ire the wizard's words elicited in her. "The crown has always valued the support of Orphic Den. The guild's service to the realm is not only appreciated, but it is also its sworn duty. Don't lose sight of that, Master Sagora."

"Of course, my liege." Sagora spread his arms wide and dipped his head; stringy, grey locks falling past the front of his wide shoulders. "I meant no disrespect."

"None taken, headmaster."

Sagora snapped his fingers and a thin servant elf appeared as if out of thin air. She curtsied before the royal couple, her meek voice hard to understand. "What is your pleasure, Your Majesties?"

Khae frowned.

Sagora's impatient voice boomed, "She means, what would you and the good king like to sip on? You must be parched after a hard trip up the pass."

"Ah." Khae turned to the servant. "We'll have whatever the headmaster is drinking."

The servant nodded, not meeting Khae's gaze.

Sagora snapped his fingers, glowering, and the servant sprang into action, a hint of fear reflected on her pale complexion. His face softened as he motioned for Khae and Hammas to make themselves comfortable on one of the many couches facing the edge of the balcony.

If not for the impenetrable bank of fog swirling in the heavy downpour beyond the railing, it was said the distant waters of Ors Sea could be viewed through a gap in the mountains on a clear day. As it was, Khae could barely see the spire of the tower rising up from Orphic Den's outer wall.

Keeper of the Jewel

Sipping on a heady, red wine, Sagora's pudgy cheeks lifted. "What has the Grim Duke done this time? Something rather outlandish I assume, considering the response of such a large host. He's not entertaining ideas of a dragon army again, is he?"

Khae almost choked on her wine. Though her brother championed the use of dragons to conquer foreign lands, the dragon issue hadn't crossed her mind. Thankful the wine's effects likely kept her fair skin from paling with the significance of the insinuation, she took a deep breath to steady her nerves and sipped at her goblet to wet her dry mouth. "Not that we're aware of. I fear there may be more at play than Orlythe and Afara Maral."

Sagora's face darkened. "Ah yes. The *human* wizard. An unfortunate appointment that one. Almost as bad as…"

The headmaster's last words were drowned in his goblet but Khae wasn't naïve. She hadn't met an elven wizard yet who would venture to say a kind word about the goblin high wizard appointed by her mother. Aelfwynne had never been well received by South March's magic community. By anyone in South March if she cared to be truthful.

She found it difficult to bite back with an angry retort. Aelfwynne had done more for the realm than anyone she could think of. That included her parents—the founding queen and king of South March! It could be argued that perhaps only Grimlock, the Dragon Witch, and the mighty Grimclaw himself had been more instrumental in ensuring the preservation of the elven nation.

"I care less about the guild's view on Aelfwynne. He's a stalwart defender of our land. The fact that he's a goblin and not an elf has no bearing on the size of his heart, nor where his allegiances lie." Despite her practiced ability to speak calmly, Khae's emotions consumed her. She glared at

Keeper of the Jewel

Sagora—his insufferable attitude doing little to quell her anger. "If there were more elves like the high wizard, South March would be better for it."

Sagora returned her stare, his large jowls unmoving. Taking a long pull from his goblet he nodded. "Of course, Your Highness. I mean Aelfwynne no disrespect. Now, what is it you wish to inquire of Orphic Den?"

"Inquire?" Khae sat forward; Hammas' hand on her forearm holding her on the couch they shared. "I didn't march all this way to inquire. I've come to enlist the aid of the guild. Until I know what we're up against, I want every available resource at my command. Should it turn out I'm mistaken, I'll immediately release your wizards of their obligation."

Sagora maintained eye contact as he placed his empty goblet on the polished stone table between them. Intertwining his fingers, he adjusted a couple of the rings and licked his lips. "I need not remind Your Highness," he nodded at Hammas as well, "that the wizard's guild is an autonomous entity, not governed by the laws of the land."

The headmaster raised his voice as Khae made to interrupt, "An agreement entered into by Queen Nyxa, may the spirits treat her as she deserves. An accord signed without prejudice or duress, I might add." He raised pompous eyebrows and dipped his head toward the diminutive servant cowering in the shadows by the central doorway leading back into Orphic Den. "I can produce said agreement forthwith should you require to dispute the matter."

The four Home Guard became more attentive, their vigilance not lost on the headmaster. It was Khae's turn to hold Hammas back.

Sagora held large palms up between them. "Please. I mean the crown no disrespect. I merely point out the rules that were agreed upon by our learned elders so that my decision isn't received in the wrong light."

Hammas' purple face was on the verge of spitting. "And that is?"

"It is as you may have already concluded. Orphic Den is not in the business of choosing one royal house over another, especially where fellow wizards are involved."

"A human wizard!" Hammas tried to wrest his hand free of Khae's grip.

Khae briefly entertained releasing him on the petulant headmaster, but she doubted that even with the assistance of the seasoned Home Guard standing at the ready, hands upon the hilts of their weapons, that they had a chance of subduing the wizard. Nor was she foolish enough to believe that the troops awaiting her return by the front gates were capable of enforcing her wishes in Orphic Den.

She patted Hammas' clenched hand but her scowl remained on Sagora. "What treachery is this, headmaster? I shan't hesitate to report this slight to the high wizard. I'm sure he'll take a dim view of your action."

If the threat was supposed to rattle the headmaster, he showed no sign that it bothered him. "That is, of course, your prerogative, Your Highness. Until then, on behalf of everyone in Orphic Den, I wish you great speed and anxiously await to hear of the outcome."

Khae stared with her jaw hanging open. "That's it? That's all you have to say on the matter?"

Sagora nodded, his voice calm, "It is indeed, Your Highness."

Khae jumped to her feet and leaned halfway over the table, pointing a finger at the headmaster's nonchalant expression. "I'm the queen of South March. The Queen of the Elves! Your queen! I demand your assistance."

Keeper of the Jewel

Sagora tilted his head, as if his visitors wore on his patience. "Or what, Your Highness? What *will* you do if I refuse to cooperate?"

"Why, I'll…I'll…" Khae didn't know what she was going to do. Throwing idle threats at the headmaster of the wizard's guild was obviously not about to alter his decision. Maintaining as much dignity as possible without screaming, she said, "I demand to know what has become of the alliance between the crown and Orphic Den?"

Sagora nodded slowly. "It never ceases to amaze me that this so-called alliance is only convenient when it suits the crown. Where were you when our voices were ignored with regard to the appointment of…" Sagora's cheeks reddened deeper than the hue brought on by the wine, "the goblin pig?"

"High Wizard Aelfwynne! His appointment had nothing to do with me and you know that!"

"How about when that human scum became resident wizard of Grim Keep?"

"That was my brother's decision."

"And what about Orlythia?"

Khae frowned deep. "What about Orlythia?"

"Correct me if I'm wrong, Your Highness, but wasn't it your decision *not* to employ a resident wizard in the royal palace?"

"Yes but—"

"But nothing. The slight to Orphic Den on all three occasions cut deep. Our so-called valuable service was overlooked and ignored." Sagora hefted his bulk from the protesting couch and looked down on Khae. "How convenient that the crown crawls back to the guild now that it deems us worthy to risk our lives to achieve its ends."

Keeper of the Jewel

Hammas' hand went to his sword hilt, the action prompting the Home Guard to pull their weapons free, but a stern shake of Khae's head stayed everyone's hand.

If the apparent threat bothered Sagora he hid it well. Running his tongue between his teeth and upper lip, he said, "Now if you'll excuse me, I've important matters to attend."

The headmaster made to walk around the table but a Home Guard stepped in front of him.

Sagora cast a patient look at Khae.

After a tense moment, Khae whispered, "Let him go."

She watched the arrogant behemoth of an elf disappear through the central doorway, the servant girl on his heels. Considering her half drank wine swirling in her goblet, Khae threw it as hard as she could—the thin stone shattering as it impacted the doorframe Sagora had just passed.

Usually such an outburst would have embarrassed the queen. Not tonight. She spun and pointed a finger at Hammas. "When this is over with my brother, we'll be coming back to pay a visit to the headmaster."

Hammas said nothing.

Khae motioned for the Home Guard to lead them from the balcony and spoke to no one in particular, "That flippant wizard better be ready to accept my new terms of agreement between the crown and the guild or he'll be digging his baubles out of his ass."

A long drone of ominous thunder rumbled through the Wizard's Sleeve.

Keeper of the Jewel

Bleeding Heart

Blood dripped to the white marble floor, a growing pool of viscous liquid adding itself to the historical discoloration around the lava stone basin in Afara Maral's inner chamber. The wizard's fingers red with complicity, Afara grumbled at the crimson water as if it were the wraith itself. "Discover the staff yourself you soulless letch."

He spun to face a quivering lump of greyish-brown flesh that mocked him from atop a black marble pedestal in the centre of the small chamber. The chamberlain's lifeless heart had refused to divulge the secret of the Staff of Reckoning's hiding place.

"Curse you, Bayl Tayn." Afara spoke to the heart. "I knew there was something different about you but the duke refused to see it. How your meddling ways thwart me from beyond the grave is something the pretender will have to deal with. I'm done with all of this. Soon, a human wizard will control the Crystal Cavern. A day that will spell the end of elven privilege."

He shook his head, wiping his hands on a stained towel tucked into his belt like an apron. Closing an ancient tome that sat before the lump of meat, he absently wiped at the blood staining the carved leather cover and assumed his seat in a ratty, high-backed chair before a lone, bay window.

Moonlight glinted off distant waves, Lake Grim visible through grime-coated glass. Alone in his lofty chamber at

Keeper of the Jewel

the pinnacle of Grim Keep's wizard tower, Afara plunked the hefty tome in his lap and rifled its yellowed pages until he found the spell he had attempted to employ on the chamberlain's heart.

The ancient invocation passed his lips exactly the way he had intoned them. Satisfied he hadn't erred in his diction or enunciation, he slammed the book shut. "Blast you, Bayl. I ought to seek out a necromancer so I can have the satisfaction of killing you myself."

The darkness outside lightened considerably as the moon passed a break in the clouds, enticing Afara to put the tome aside and lean on the deep windowsill to get a better view of the greater world. A dark blot of mountains lined the distant shore.

His attention was drawn to the faint, orangey glow tinging the swirling clouds obscuring the faraway peaks—a radiance he longed to be part of. Somewhere beyond the wall of the incoming weather front, Highcliff lay nestled amongst the chain of active volcanoes that comprised the Dark Mountains.

"Soon, my friend," he said to himself. "We'll descend on the sacred community like a meteor storm."

As much as his words were meant to console him, he couldn't shake the bitterness that continued to consume his every waking thought. The wraith! How had the evil thing survived its clash with the Dragon Witch? Worse, why had it come calling now, just as he had been prepared to initiate the final part of his scheme.

Undermining the foolish duke's plans to usurp his sister's monarchy, he had planned on taking advantage of the resulting chaos. If the high wizard and his Guardians could be coaxed away from Highcliff to defend Queen Khae he might yet succeed.

Keeper of the Jewel

Afara gritted his teeth. He would be damned before he allowed the wraith to claim the Crystal Cavern in his stead.

He shuddered and stormed across the chamber, stopping to stare at Bayl's rotting heart. "If only you belonged to the wraith."

A slow smile puckered his sunken cheeks. He liked the thought of that.

He stroked his thin lips in thought. "Yes. Yes! But how?"

He spun on the discarded tome and stared. Somewhere within its pages he was sure he had read something that might serve him well.

He nodded. The timing was right. He had no idea where the high wizard had gotten off to, but he was fairly certain Aelfwynne was nowhere near Highcliff. The dragons loyal to Orlythe would have said as much if the high wizard had made it back. Perhaps he should go talk to the winged beasts and find out for himself.

If they confirmed Aelfwynne's absence, all he would need would be a diversion to pull the rest of the Guardians from their aerie.

He smiled a dark, sinister smile. Despite the duke's apprehension at the bad timing, the march of the queen might prove fortuitous after all.

If he provoked an armed response from Orlythe, he might yet acquire the coveted prize before the wraith returned.

Keeper of the Jewel

Dithreab's Slighe

Castle Grim's bulk disappeared behind the sparse tree cover beyond the field of grass abutting its dark walls. Scale jogged as fast as he dared without rattling the high wizard's brain from his skull.

In the cover of darkness, they had snuck through a seldom used, unmanned side gate—Scale's magic had made quick work of the rusted iron locks. The keep had come alive as they slipped into the night—a great clamour arising from the castle walls around the cathedral.

On Aelfwynne's direction, he loped across the bluffs lining the western shoreline of Lake Grim. The high wizard wasn't willing to risk another incident with the magical lock binding him, but he claimed to know of someone who might assist them.

They stopped as the three-quarter moon disappeared behind the western mountains, leaving the wooded terrain too difficult to safely traverse. Before the rising sun had banished the mist creeping along the forest floor, they were off again.

Scale wasn't sure if it was an animal's trail they followed, but whoever frequented these woods hadn't made it a priority to follow the most direct route into the foothills of Faelyn's Nest in the Mardeireach—the western group of peaks that abutted the volcanic ring of the Dark Mountains surrounding Crystal Lake.

Keeper of the Jewel

Stopping when the sun's rays shone directly down through the thick canopy covering the coastal heights of the second highest peak in the Mardeireach, Scale struggled to lower Aelfwynne to the ground. His arms and shoulders ached almost as much as his lower back—his thigh muscles had never felt so weak.

"How much farther, Master Aelfwynne?"

Aelfwynne didn't look any better than Scale felt. The goblin's features contorted as he stretched out his limbs as best he could given the chains securing his ankles and wrists behind his back. "We've a long way to go yet, boy. If we don't get a move on, the duke's elves will find us."

Scale swallowed, looking back the way they had come. He estimated he had put several leagues between them and Castle Grim. If not for the winding path they followed, it could have been more, but the high wizard insisted they follow the erratic course.

He pulled a piece of lint covered cheese he had pilfered before leaving the stable yards from his pocket. Picking at bits of debris, he broke off half and held it before Aelfwynne's mouth.

The goblin sniffed at it, looked questioningly at Scale for a moment, and bit down on the offering.

Scale held his hand steady until the chunk was pulled from his fingers, unconsciously wiping them on his tunic afterward. "I don't understand why you insist we stick to this animal path. We could be high on the mountainside before nightfall if I followed a straight route."

"Dithreab's Slighe is the accepted course for anyone wishing to avoid dragon detection."

Scale blinked several times. The goblin's explanation meant nothing to him. He struggled to pronounce the first two words, "Dithreab's Slighe? What's that?"

Keeper of the Jewel

"Not what? Whom. Dithreab is a recluse who has lived in the Mardeireach longer than I've been alive." Aelfwynne said, reverence in his tone. "Slighe is an ancient term for trail, a word rumoured to have originated from a language not of this world, if you choose to believe Dithreab."

Scale's brow furrowed deeper. Talking to wizards was tedious. A slow smile crept across his weary face at the irony. To think he aspired to become one.

He fumbled in his pockets, gathering loose bits of crumbled cheese, and held them between him and the wizard.

Aelfwynne turned up his nose. "I'll pass."

Scale shrugged and devoured the crumbs as he spoke, spitting out bits of fuzz. "I don't understand. We aren't running from dragons."

Aelfwynne gazed at the thick canopy. "Don't be so sure, boy. It's only a matter of time before they discover we slipped through the maintenance gate. Once Orlythe finds out we've left the castle, his dragons will search for us."

Scale's mouth froze in mid chew. "*His* dragons?"

"Aye. The duke isn't as powerless as many are led to believe. Though I doubt he would be foolish enough to instigate a dragon war, he holds sway in the south. If what I fear is about to happen, South March may be on the verge of civil war."

Scale's wide eyes stared at the high wizard. "We have to do something."

Aelfwynne nodded. "At the moment, I'm a little tied up."

If Aelfwynne thought he was being funny, Scale didn't laugh. He jumped to his feet and plucked the goblin from the ground, unceremoniously throwing the wizard over his shoulder. A quick check back the way they had come and a

Keeper of the Jewel

cursory glance at the leafy forest rooftop and he was away, running faster than before despite his protesting muscles.

Flopping helplessly on his back, the high wizard complained, "Easy, you witless northerner! You're going to rattle me senseless!"

"You passed it!" Aelfwynne craned his neck, trying to concentrate on a certain spot despite the way his head bobbed up and down with the cadence of Scale's footfalls.

Scale halted his weary jog and spun around, eyeing the darkening forest. "Where? I don't see anything."

"Neither can I, now, you big galoop. Look to the moss covered boulder."

Scale peered around the undergrowth at dozens of moss covered boulders. "Which one?"

"Spin me around so I can see."

Scale did as he was directed.

"There. That one."

Though he could feel Aelfwynne fidgeting on his back, he had no idea which rock the wizard meant. Hefting the goblin from his shoulder and holding him as if he were an infant in front of him, he asked, "Where?"

"That one, you big galoop. Beside the birch tree." Aelfwynne thrust his pointy face toward a large, white, tree trunk. "Follow the birch run."

As if the wizard's words had unlocked a secret, the hidden byway made itself visible—a line of birch trees stretched diagonally up a steep crag.

The ascent was made more difficult by thick ground cover and hidden depressions, but Scale picked his way up to a small ledge and looked around. The forest floor stretched out far below; the waters of Lake Grim shimmering through the foliage whenever a gust of wind swept through the woods.

Keeper of the Jewel

A rough stone wall rose before him, impassable to anyone without wings.

Scale took a step toward the base of the cliff. "Um, I think we hit a dead end."

A twig snapped beneath his boot and a root grabbed at his foot causing him to stumble.

"Get down!" Aelfwynne shouted from behind Scale's back.

Whether he wanted to hit the ground or not, Scale couldn't prevent his feet from catching in the undergrowth. He stumbled and fell hard.

Aelfwynne rolled from his shoulder to thump against the rock wall with an audible gasp.

The whoosh of something big cutting through the air drew Scale's attention as a large shadow passed over them. He looked up to see the sharpened back end of a tree trunk whistle by, crashing through thick pine boughs. Before he could question what had happened, the tree trunk reappeared, swinging past their position in the opposite direction, the other end of the log equally honed to a deadly point.

Aelfwynne's disconcerting, beady eyes stared at him.

Keeping low to the ground, Scale asked, "What's that?"

"That is Dithreab's hammer." Aelfwynne's gaze followed the swinging trunk as it made another pass, its arc lessening with each subsequent swing. "It seems I may have forgot about that."

Between passings of the deadly tree, Scale scrambled to lie beside Aelfwynne against the cliff. "You think?"

"Not to worry. Dithreab shall appear shortly to deal with it."

Keeper of the Jewel

An uncomfortable silence settled between them as they kept an eye on the monotonous path of the deadly tree trunk until it finally came to a stop overhead.

Aelfwynne looked around. "At least I *hope* he's still around."

Scale sat against the rock, brushing the debris from his pilfered Grim Guard uniform. "What's that supposed to mean?"

Aelfwynne shrugged. It would be dark soon. "I hope he's still alive."

Keeper of the Jewel

If Only

Ors Spill raced out of the foothills of the Steel Mountains; its banks swollen from the recent storm. Giving her backside and lower back a break from the saddle, Khae oversaw the fording of the mighty river as it spirited storm runoff along with the water that flowed down the channel from the inland sea. An old bridge had once stood where the caravan waded into the frigid waters, the river frothing around its remains. It had been swept away during a spring thaw many years ago.

Thousands of armoured elves pushed into the treacherous current, their struggle causing the queen to silently vow that whenever the crisis was over, she would commission stone masons to connect the town of Nayda to the northland.

Leading the army through the mountain pass in the Wizard's Sleeve, she had briefly entertained following the roadway at its bottom to Urdanya, but decided against it. Marching a large force through the great city might cause undue stress on the fragile relations the crown held with the governing factions of South March's largest population centre. Over half the elven nation lived in and around Urdanya; the expansive city stretched many leagues down the Ors Spill and sprawled along the ocean on either side of the river's mouth.

She shook her head at the army's struggle. She should have anticipated the swollen river.

Keeper of the Jewel

Lips rolled between her teeth, Khae pondered the real reason she had no wish to go anywhere near Urdanya. Her sister. Princess Odyne lived in the ancient castle dominating the north shore of the river mouth, ruling the vast city as if she were the anointed Queen of the Elves.

If only she and her sister got along, they might be able to convince their brother that the path he followed would someday take him to the brink. She sighed. That day might have arrived. Further to that dilemma, without Princess Odyne's blessing, an assault on Castle Grim might ignite a larger dispute. Odyne had made no qualms about her resentment of Khae being the first-born twin when their mother had died.

The fact that Khae had no control over who had come first vexed her to no end. It wasn't her fault Odyne was born second. Although they had been inseparable during the first decade of their life, something had changed in Odyne as puberty set in. She had withdrawn into a dark shell—no doubt encouraged by their brother.

Odyne openly turned up her nose with regard to Khae's natural predilection of nature's essence, asserting that she and Orlythe were the true magic-users in the family. Luckily, Odyne and Orlythe often fought like bitter enemies during their elfling years. The chances of them uniting against the crown were slim. Nevertheless, troubling thoughts concerning her siblings were always close to the surface of her mind. Orlythe ruled the south. Odyne held sway in Urdanya. If they ever conspired against the crown as a unified force, Khae doubted she could hold onto it.

"There goes another!" Hammas shouted at a knot of Home Guard waiting their turn at the foot of the knoll he and Khae stood on. "Rope them off before we lose any more!"

Keeper of the Jewel

He shook his head and turned to Khae. "Seriously. You'd think they'd never crossed a river before."

Khae stared past her husband at the overturned wagon bobbing in the fast-running current. It came to a jarring stop for a moment, pivoted on whatever had caught it, and slipped into the mainstream. The last of its spoked wheels sank beneath the brown water and was lost to sight—the river's surface ablaze with the last vestiges of the day's light. If they didn't hurry, the bulk of the troops would be forced to make the treacherous crossing in darkness.

She sighed. "It doesn't look like any horses went with it."

"We can't afford to lose the wagons." Hammas scanned the crossing, grimacing as the next team of horses were urged into the river, a large wagon tethered to their harness. "If your brother bars his gates, we'll not be lasting long without supplies."

"Let's hope it doesn't come to that."

The wagon entered the water and the team of horses immediately began to struggle.

Hammas threw his hands in the air and stormed off the bluff, yelling orders at the troops along the banks as the river threatened to sweep the wagon away.

Khae bit her lower lip. If only she had listened to Ouderling, they might not be in this position. Perhaps her daughter had been right all along. Maybe Borreraig Palace was safer than Highcliff. The wards infused in the foundation stones by the masons of Sarsen Rest had never been tested.

If only the gulf dividing the elves from the rest of mankind hadn't been torn asunder with the invasion of the north men. Since ascending the throne, she had fought hard to displace the ingrained prejudices the elves maintained against the rest of the world. As far as her people were concerned, Sarsen

Keeper of the Jewel

Rest, Serpens, Gritian, Carillon, Nordicia, Madrigail, Kraidic, Aldebaran, and all the other kingdoms on this side of the Niad Ocean weren't worthy of elven consideration.

Down at the river's edge, Hammas directed crews of male and female troops, most of whom had stripped to their small clothes and were securing the wagon and horse team with ropes. Khae shivered. An elven chain of burly Home Guard stood at various points in the cold water, passing supplies across to the far side of the river.

Troops milled along the banks on both sides—those on the far shore gearing up and re-assembling to prepare for the next leg in the journey. Behind the queen, a squad of archers and elite Home Guard watched the woods surrounding them, prepared for any eventuality.

A well-groomed elf dropped to a knee before Khae, his eyes on the ground. "Your Highness, it's time for you to cross."

Startled by the middle-aged elf's appearance, Khae blinked a couple times. The troops standing on guard around her bore two flat, wooden contraptions, each rigged with handholds.

She looked at the captain of the guard, the same elf who usually stood at her side during petitions, and wagged her finger. "No. Not happening. I'll walk like everyone else." She glanced at the two crews holding the pallets. "So will the king."

She held a hand out in front of her and nodded to the captain. "After you, Kall."

Captain Kall bowed his head respectfully and started down the embankment, barking orders for everyone to be aware that the queen was moving.

A small smile forced its way across her lips as she listened to the captain harp at the troops standing around. Kall was a good elf. Loyal to a fault. As long as he was around, she never had to fear for her safety.

She followed on the captain's heels. The sooner they were across the river, the sooner they would be on their way to pay a surprise visit on her brother. If Prince Orlythe had anything to do with the message in High Wizard Aelfwynne's missive, she would have to act swiftly and severely.

She sighed. Such was the life of a monarch.

If only Odyne had found her way into the world first, life would have been so much less complicated.

Keeper of the Jewel

Midnight Rendevous

Ouderling stared at the short-haired elf looking back at her from the poor excuse of a mirror—her gaunt features eerie in the flickering light of a lone candle that fought for life on top of the old cabinet in her sleeping chamber. She had no idea what time it was, but the fact that Balewynd hadn't come knocking meant it had to be sometime in the middle of the night. She glanced uneasily at the empty bed. Where Jyllana had gone, she had no idea. Perhaps to relieve herself.

The last thing she remembered was Jyllana tucking her in after fetching supper. Since then, the floor around the stool had been swept clean of her mass of hair. What her protector had done with it, she had no idea.

Huddled in the shadows, her discarded pile of useless armour mocked her. There was no way she was worthy enough to don the finely wrought gear. Perhaps Jyllana would appreciate them—she estimated she and her faithful protector were around the same size.

Not able to sleep any more, the princess scooped up her brown cloak and slipped from the chamber.

Sparsely illuminated, the side passageways were tomblike. Not a soul stirred. Contemplating her options, she recalled her conversation with Balewynd about viewing the lava fields on the far side of Crystal Lake at night.

Keeper of the Jewel

Once outside, she was glad she had opted to wear her cloak. Wind gusted across the shelf; its dark surface swirling with eddies of ash whenever a gap in the thin veil of clouds revealed the three-quarter moon. Walking across the promontory, she marvelled at the bite of the wind on her neck as her short locks fluttered around her cheeks. She ran fingers through the foreign sensation and swallowed. What had she done?

Across the dark expanse of water, orange ribbons of lava traced erratic paths down the distant slopes—their glow disappearing amidst plumes of roiling mist along the water's edge. Her breath caught. There were so many fiery streams. It was a wonder the lake didn't boil over.

The pervasive cold seeped through her clothing as she sat on the edge and dangled her feet over the glittering waves far below, pondering the crazy string of events that had unfolded since that chaotic morning her mother had burst into her sleeping chamber and turned her life on its head.

Bittersweet memories of Marris misted her vision. Perhaps she had been harsh with the elf she once believed she would spend the rest of her life with. She remembered fondly the day he had balked at the notion that someday he might be king. A tear traced its way down her cheek, lingering long enough to be blown away by the breeze. Those carefree days seemed so long ago.

A distant screech echoed across the lake, the sudden sound sending shivers up her spine. A high-pitched cry from the opposite direction answered.

Dragons!

Afraid to be caught out on the ledge by herself, especially in the middle of the night, she laid on her side and scanned the vast sky over Crystal Lake. It wasn't until the original screech sounded again, much closer, that she spotted a dragon's silhouette. Appearing through a thin layer of cloud, the dragon's blue scales sparkled in the moonlight.

The second dragon shrieked; its call so close Ouderling thought it must be right above her.

Without warning, a rush of wind passed overhead. Dawnbreaker rose into view, spreading her wings to land near the centre of the platform.

Ouderling barely had time to recover her breath before the larger, blue dragon dropped from the sky, landing beside Dawnbreaker.

Voices drew Ouderling's attention to the main exit tunnel. Her trainer, Balewynd, stole across the promontory with the male elf, Pecklyn, and…she squinted…Jyllana! Though hard to discern from where she lay, especially dressed all in black, she would know her protector anywhere. So that's where she had gone.

The three elves approached the dragons, stopping long enough for Pecklyn and Balewynd to exchange words Ouderling couldn't hear.

She frowned. It looked as if they were getting ready to fly somewhere.

Envious, Ouderling debated whether she should let them know she was there.

Jyllana had told her about flying on the back of Dawnbreaker with Pecklyn. Watching the blonde-haired elf hold out his hand to assist Jyllana onto Dawnbreaker's shoulders, she wondered if the twinge of jealously she experienced was because Jyllana was about to fly again or was it something deeper?

Pecklyn climbed in behind Jyllana and wrapped his arms around her, leaning in close. With a nod to Balewynd sitting high on the blue dragon, Pecklyn patted Dawnbreaker's neck. "Time to save Aelfy!"

Keeper of the Jewel

The dragons simultaneously crouched and leapt into the sky, their unfolding wings pushing great volumes of air beneath them. Dawnbreaker dropped below the level of the promontory for a couple of wingbeats before her thick body rose toward the clouds.

Ouderling climbed to her feet, watching the dragons bank far out over Crystal Lake and ascend into the night sky. Several wingbeats and they were gone, flying beyond the bulk of Highcliff's dark mountain.

"Save Aelfy?" Ouderling muttered, her gaze rivetted on where she had last seen the dragons. Her eyes grew wide. They were going to Grim Keep without her!

She swallowed her despair. Jyllana hadn't bothered mentioning anything to her. Storming across the platform, she went in search of the one person in all of Highcliff who would know what was going on.

400

Keeper of the Jewel

Hermitude

Aelfwynne gnashed his sharp teeth. Though Scale had done his best given the circumstances, the high wizard would be content if he never saw the Home Guard's backside again. Begrudgingly, he had to hand it to the fledgling wizard, his physical stamina was to be admired. He had safely escaped Castle Grim and gotten them to Dithreab's doorstep—if indeed, the old hermit still lived.

"What now, Master Aelfwynne?" Scale stood on the far side of the sprung log trap, examining the forest floor falling away below. A gentle breeze ruffled his unkempt hair.

"Now we wait."

Scale turned to regard Aelfwynne, rolled his eyes, and looked away again.

"Patience is a wizard's constant companion. You must learn to accept that if you wish to follow your heart's desire." Aelfwynne shivered, scanning the lonely woods. "To be an adept magic-user, you'll discover that patience is the key to enlightenment on a long journey of self discovery. But, know this, it can be a lonely life."

"It seems I'm cut out for it then." Scale hung his head and muttered to the wind, "The duke ordered the execution of everyone I hold dear. Even if we avoid detection from the dragons patrolling the skies and I make it back to Orlythia alive, I doubt the queen will value my position in the Home Guard. Being the lone survivor and all."

401

Keeper of the Jewel

"You forget the princess and her protector."

"How could I forget them. But they're different. My job was to protect them...To protect everyone. Yet I remained at Castle Grim."

"Not by your choice."

"No. By my actions...Or inaction, if truth be told."

A long silence settled between them. Aelfwynne wasn't one to commiserate with another, but he couldn't help feeling sorry for Scale. Through no fault of his own, albeit he had allowed Ouderling to go against Captain Gerrant's orders, he had been left behind. After the death of the princess' escort, he had been abandoned within a hostile castle. If not for his quick thinking, Scale would undoubtedly have been killed by the Grim Guard. Nor could Aelfwynne deny that without Scale's involvement, he, himself, would have suffered a horrible death at the hands of Orlythe's dark wizard.

"Fretting about the future will accomplish nothing. You can only manage what happens in the here and now. If you are to atone for your perceived inaction, stop feeling sorry for yourself and concentrate on what you *can* control. Whatever the queen has in store for your future is out of your hands."

Scale stiffened. He lifted his chin to stare at where Castle Grim would be visible in the distance if not for the leagues of forest between them, his dirty-blonde bangs lifting on the wind.

"Move and I'll slit your throat," a high-pitched voice growled with a strange accent.

Aelfwynne blinked in surprise at the sudden appearance of a brown, stick-like creature hanging suspended at the end of a gossamer thread, a tiny, curved dagger pressed against Scale's throat.

Keeper of the Jewel

"What's a Grim Guard doin' skulkin' about me woods, eh? Speak quick, else I cut ya."

Afraid to move, Scale whispered, "It's not what it looks like. I stole this uniform."

"An impersonator and a thief are ya? Even worse. Tell me why I shouldnae slit ya clean an' bleed ya?"

"Because he's with me, knot head," Aelfwynne said with a large smile. Despite the serious nature of their troubles, he hadn't felt this happy in a long time. His old friend was alive and cantankerous as always.

Twig-sized legs perched on Scale's shoulder; the stick creature turned his bark-covered face to see Aelfwynne huddled against the base of the cliff. He took his time assessing the goblin's predicament. "Yer spirit still haunts our world, I see, hmm?"

"No thanks to you, Dithreab."

"I'm savin' your hide now, am I not?"

"By threatening to kill the one who rescued me from certain death? I think not. Put down the knife and help me out for a change."

Slivers for eyebrows, Dithreab squinted at Aelfwynne as if taking measure of the situation. Nodding, the sprite twirled his little blade in front of Scale's eyes before sliding it into a sheath attached to the midsection of his tubular body.

With a jerky motion, Dithreab sprang from Scale's shoulder and landed on the ground beside the high wizard, tumbling in the high grass. Small, deep green eyes surveyed Aelfwynne. "I see your fortunes haven't changed much. Ye ain't t' be learnin' what I be teachin' ya." He indicated Scale with an outstretched, wooden thumb. "It doesnae pay t' hang around this lot."

Keeper of the Jewel

Aelfwynne sighed. It did his heart good to see his old friend. Even if Dithreab was the most obnoxious creature he had ever met. "Seems my head is more wooden than yours."

"If ye were only so lucky." Dithreab jumped sideways as Scale spun around, but his words were directed at the high wizard. "Yet ye still be throwin' yer lot in with pointy ears."

Aelfwynne glanced at Scale who stared at the forest sprite. The elf's reaction was not unexpected. Few of the mankind persuasion were privy to an audience with the likes of Dithreab. The world's intermediaries between the realm of the living and the Fae.

"Dithreab, this is Scale Wood. A member of the queen's guard."

"Nyxa's here?" Dithreab searched the small ledge.

"She's dead, remember? Her daughter, Khae, occupies the Willow Throne."

"Yes. Yes. The throne built of me ancestors' corpses." Dithreab nodded as if he were struggling to remember. "Where's Nyxa's bud? Is she close? Allow me t' inspect her."

"Easy, my wooden friend. If luck's on our side, she's on her way, but first," Aelfwynne fidgeted to expose his bound hands and feet, "perhaps you can do something about these."

Dithreab frowned and scuttled to Aelfwynne's side, the sprite no taller than the length of Aelfwynne's stubby, upper arm.

"Ah, ah!" Aelfwynne pulled the bindings away from Dithreab's probing sliver fingers. "They're magically bound."

"Of a certainty they are. Ya take me for a crazy elf? I sense things, remember?" A comical frown twisted the wood sprite's gnarly features. "Curious. They exude the stain of man."

Keeper of the Jewel

"They were secured by a human wizard."

Dithreab hissed like a feral cat and jumped back. "Afara Maral!"

Aelfwynne nodded. "Aye. Can you get them off me?"

The indignant look of the wood sprite was endearing.

Aelfwynne squirmed to keep the lock away from Dithreab. "Without blowing me up?"

"Yer doubt cuts me, it does. Ye forget who yer speaking t', dragon breath."

Aelfwynne couldn't help but laugh at the sprite's term of endearment. "You're certain?"

Dithreab placed sliver fingers on the bark of his midriff and tilted his thin head. "Ya mockin' me?"

"No. I value the use of my arms and legs. I don't relish being as short as you."

"Ye could only be so lucky." Dithreab waggled a finger for Aelfwynne to turn over. "Come, come. Let yer ol' chum come t' yer aid...Again."

Aelfwynne studied the sprite's serious face beneath a single green leaf that sprouted from the top of Dithreab's head like a cap of hair. "Don't make me hurt you," he muttered and struggled to roll onto his stomach. He cast a worried look at Scale. "Watch him. If he tries anything untoward, squish him like the bug he is."

"Ach! Please." Dithreab didn't spare Scale a sideways glance as he probed the thin keyhole of the lock securing the magically infused chains. Performing a brief inspection, Dithreab stepped back and folded his twigs over his chest. "I see the human scum has become quite powerful." He regarded Scale. "Tis a good thing ye didn't attempt it."

Scale frowned. "You know I'm a magic-user?"

"I can smell an elf wizard a league away. Yer a strong one too, if I'm not t' be mistaken, eh, dragon breath?"

Keeper of the Jewel

"Just get these off. Or are you no match for the human wizard?"

Dithreab straightened. "Better goblins have died for less."

"And better knot heads have kindled my hearth. Get these off before I pick my teeth with your carcass."

Dithreab shook his head in disgust, the leaf sprouting from his head jiggling as he did so. With a sudden extension of one of his arms he pointed at Aelfwynne's bindings.

A barely perceptible arc of white energy crackled between his fingertip and the lock, eliciting an audible click. A puff of smoke wafted from the keyhole by his wrists and the lock fell open. A second zap to the manacles binding Aelfwynne's ankles and the goblin was free.

"Nothing t' it," a smug Dithreab said, crossing his arms and nodding at the offending metal. "Now, be quick about it, we must leave here afore we become dragon fodder."

Scale cast a worried glance at the thick forest canopy.

"Don't worry, laddie. They may not see ya, but ye can bet yer last golden galleon they sensed me magic." Dithreab cocked a wooden eyebrow and scrabbled across the undergrowth away from them. "Be a good elf an' grab those fetters. Won't do t' leave 'em sittin' aboot."

Aelfwynne nodded at Scale's curious look, but frowned at the sprite's odd reference of a golden galleon.

Not far from where they stood upon the high ledge, a rotting tree stump creaked, its front half lifting off the forest floor.

"In ye get afore it closes agin." Dithreab glanced at Aelfwynne struggling to get his limbs to respond after being bound for so long in one position. He turned to Scale. "Ye best be luggin' yer burden a wee bit farther lest the old fool get left behind."

Keeper of the Jewel

Aelfwynne winced at the pain as blood returned to his extremities. The old sprite had the right of it.

The chains dangling from his hands, Scale hesitated, his focus on the sprung log trap. "What about your elf impaler?"

A squeaky chitter escaped the wood sprite. "Oh, me laddie, yer a rich one. That's meant t' deter nosy dragons from snoopin' about. I'll reset it in good time."

"You built a trap to impale dragons?"

"Bah. Look at me. All small and wooden like. I ain't exactly the type t' tangle with a fire breathin' beastie now, am I? As to anythin' else that may happen along," Dithreab shrugged, "I like t' deal with 'em meself."

With a mischievous smirk, the tiny creature loped across the undergrowth and slipped into a tunnel that had appeared beneath the stump. "Be quick about it. The duke's dragons will be along anytime now."

Musky loam turned up Scale's nostrils as he crawled into the ground, following Aelfwynne's backside. Even the goblin had to crouch low to travel the dangerous route beneath the forest floor. The small fireball he conjured was difficult to concentrate on as he pulled himself through the congested space, ducking roots and stubbing his knees on partially submerged rocks.

Ahead of them, muted by Aelfwynne's body, the wood sprite chattered to no one in particular, many of his words making no sense.

"Yer a slow lot...Ain't t' be livin' forever...Ye gonna expire afore we get there."

Scale had lost all sense of direction by the time the tunnel opened up to the point that Aelfwynne could stand straight. Dirt walls gave way to stacked stone. Two large tree roots bisected the small chamber Dithreab led them into, the thick shoots acting as decorative pillars. Around the roots, the sprite had piled several elf-sized tomes—ancient by the look of their tattered, leather covers. The books appeared too big for Dithreab to have moved them by himself, and yet, there they were.

Dithreab scrambled onto one of the tomes and sat back against the spine of a second book propped on its edge like a backrest. His fleshless slit of a mouth uttered what sounded like a chant. Light infused the small chamber, radiating from the wings of dozens of tiny butterflies.

Scale stuck out a finger to touch one of the fingernail-sized lights; mesmerized as it landed in his palm. Its glowing wings beat slowly. "Wow…"

"Faerie light." Dithreab said as if that explained it. "That one's t' be likin' ya. They all must, actually, otherwise we'd still be cast in the darkness of yer pitiful fire."

Aelfwynne sat on a chunk of stone protruding from the cavern floor and considered Dithreab. "I thought you weren't on speaking terms with the Fae."

"Thanks t' ye, I'm lucky they have anythin' t' do with me. But aye, I'm grudgingly accepted by a few of the ones I was closest t'."

"That's a good sign, no?"

Dithreab shrugged. "If'n ye mean I still have dealin's wit 'em, then aye. But it ain't like olden days. They abide me company in order t' keep tabs on current events. Ever since yer debacle at the tower, the Fae have all but washed their hands of yer world. I ain't t' be wagerin' that'll change anytime soon. In fact, if'n ya ask me…"

"The queen spoke to Rhiannon recently," Aelfwynne interrupted.

Keeper of the Jewel

Dithreab's diatribe fell away. Green, beady eyes blinked several times, his high-pitched timbre incredulous, "She spoke to the White Witch? The queen of the Fae?"

Aelfwynne nodded.

"That's highly improbable. Nobody speaks t' the White Witch and lives t' tell of it."

"Highly improbable, perhaps, but not impossible it would seem."

"I be findin' that hard t' believe. How do you know it t' be true? Were you there?"

Aelfwynne spit out a harsh laugh. "Hardly. The tower will likely fall upon me if I ever set foot in it again."

Scales' mind swirled trying to make sense of the conversation. Attempting to make sense of everything that had happened to him of late. Deep beneath the forest floor, a wood sprite stared at a goblin, transfixed by the high wizard's suggestion that someone had spoken to a faerie creature Aelfwynne had referred to as the White Witch. Now *that* was improbable.

Dithreab leaned forward, his voice a deep snarl, "Nyxa's child lies. I've warned ye about their kind afore. Mayhap, ye should listen t' yer old friend for a change, eh?"

Aelfwynne's shaking head made the wood sprite sit back and listen.

"Queen Khae is the strongest practitioner of nature's essence I've ever come across…" His voice dropped to a whisper. "Except for her son, of course, but we'll never know the extent of Ordyl's ability."

"Ya!" Dithreab scoffed. "Ye seen t' that, alright."

A hurt look twisted Aelfwynne's face.

Dithreab skittered across the tome and patted Aelfwynne's thigh. "Ye meant well, me friend. As much as I despise ye for what ya did, yer intentions were pure."

Keeper of the Jewel

Aelfwynne's eyes narrowed. "When I tell you Khae spoke with Rhiannon, I don't speak lightly. The White Witch has foreseen a dire threat facing South March and beyond."

Dithreab leaned across the gap between the book and Aelfwynne, but before he responded the high wizard held up a warning hand.

"The Soul has returned."

It was as if all of Dithreab's abounding energy and haughtiness drained from him. He lowered his shaking body to the edge of the tome to await Aelfwynne's explanation.

Aelfwynne nodded. "I saw it with my own eyes. If not for the duke lusting after my magic, I would already be dead."

Dithreab frowned.

"Afara was preparing to use the harrowing spell on me."

Dithreab's slit eyes grew wide.

"Lucky for me, fate intervened." Aelfwynne indicated Scale with a nod and proceeded to fill Dithreab in on everything that had happened since rescuing the princess from the grotdraak.

Dithreab stared hard. "If what ye say be true, an' I sense no deception, ye best be gettin' back t' Highcliff afore it's too late."

"Why don't you come with us? The defense of the Crystal Cavern would benefit from a strong magician like you. The Soul will never know what hit it."

Dithreab held his intense gaze a moment longer. Looking away he muttered, "Ye knows I cannae."

"Your oath was many years ago. Nyxa is gone. Nothing you do can change that. Stand with the Highcliff Guardians. If not for Khae, then for Nyxa's granddaughter."

Dithreab looked up.

Aelfwynne nodded. "If I'm right and the duke has thrown in his lot with the Soul, Nyxa's legacy is in jeopardy.

Keeper of the Jewel

Highcliff is strong, but Afara Maral is more accomplished than the wizard's guild gives him credit for. Add the dragons and the Soul into the mix and I'm afraid Grimclaw's Edict will come to nothing. The dragons loyal to Grimclaw will be slaughtered and a new regime will claim the Crystal Cavern."

Dithreab's jaw hung.

Aelfwynne nodded. "Aye. If the Soul gains access to the earth blood, no one, not even you, my ancient friend, will be able to prevent it from destroying the world."

Scale hung on the high wizard's words, as enrapt as the wood sprite, even though he didn't understand everything Aelfwynne said. He had no way of knowing how powerful Dithreab's magic was, but considering the respect afforded him by the cynical goblin, it must be substantial.

"Alas, I cannae. Ye know that. If'n I bridge the gap an' fight for ya mortals, it'll endanger the Fae." His high-pitch fell to a frightening timbre, "And *that* I cannae allow."

Aelfwynne glared at the sprite. He took a deep breath and exhaled audibly. "Then we must be off on our own."

The goblin got to his feet and turned to Scale, indicating the entrance tunnel. "Come. We have to return to Highcliff before it's too late."

"That route is closed t' ya now."

If looks were able to tell a story, Scale thought for sure the high wizard was on the verge of smiting the little creature.

Dithreab leapt to his feet and skittered across the tome. Jumping to the dirt floor he said, "The duke's dragons will have sensed the magic I employed. It'll be a good while afore we can return t' the woods that way." He pointed to the shadows behind the second root. "But, if'n ye be followin' me, I be showin' ye a better route."

411

Keeper of the Jewel

Aelfwynne and Scale exchanged glances. Crossing his arms over his dirty tunic, the high wizard raised his eyebrows for the wood sprite to elaborate.

"Yer own dragons ain't t' be lookin' for ya way out here. Nor is the Passage o' Dolor open after what ye have imparted about the cave beastie. But," Dithreab skittered around the second root, several faerie lights fluttering after him to reveal a separate tunnel, "if ye come this way, ye can give ol' Grim Duke the slip."

"I know I'm going to regret this. I usually do whenever I ask you anything." Aelfwynne raised a skeptical brow at Scale. "Just where, exactly, will this tunnel take us?"

"Ah, me friend. If'n there's one thing me hermitude's taught me over the years, is there's always a rub. Let's just say, Orlythe's troops won't follow ye where yer aboot to go…Not even dragons."

Aelfwynne's glower intensified, twisting his face in disbelief. "Dithreab!"

Grabbing a small rucksack from within what appeared as a secret compartment in the root directly behind the tome, Dithreab nodded—the wood sprite affording Aelfwynne a mischievous grin. "The Path of the Errant Knight."

Keeper of the Jewel

Perch

Eolande and Perch were the only creatures present in the Crystal Cavern as Ouderling strolled along its meandering path toward the centre of the enormous cave. The brown wyvern's wings beat rapidly where it hovered near the ceiling on the far side of the cavern.

Glad she hadn't bumped into anyone else along the way, she was in no mood for pleasantries. Jyllana, Balewynd, and Pecklyn had obviously deemed it better not to include her in their plans. She shook her head. Who better to talk sense into the duke than his niece?

The various coloured crystal formations lining the irregular walls took on a bluish tinge. Rounding a jut in the path, the bubbling earth blood fount dominated the centre of the wide space before her—the path meandering around its jagged brim on either side and disappearing beyond another bend. Ouderling paused to gaze at the earth blood, still unsure what it actually was.

A flutter of wings drew her attention upward. Perch dropped to the path on the far side of the fount with his ancient goblin rider, Eolande, on his shoulders.

Eolande slipped from Perch and ambled around the earth blood pool. He bowed. "Princess. I hadn't expected to see anyone in here tonight. What can I do for you?"

"Nothing, really. I'm looking for Xantha."

Keeper of the Jewel

Eolande tilted his overly large head. "Xantha isn't to be disturbed at the moment."

The goblin's answer did little to ease Ouderling's annoyance at being precluded from the happenings at Highcliff, but she kept her tone civil. "Why? What's she doing? Not sleeping, I imagine."

"That would be an accurate assessment, Your Highness. I'm not at liberty to say more." Eolande's face appeared apologetic but his voice held firm. "Is there something *I* can help you with?"

Ouderling's eyes reddened more with each subsequent breath. Why wasn't anyone confiding in her? She was the heir to the Willow Throne. They should be kneeling at her feet and asking permission to do whatever they were doing.

She sighed. This was exactly the way she had asked to be treated. Now that it was happening, it frustrated her. Being a member of the royal family had instilled in her an expectation to be obeyed. It was as difficult for her to accept that she was just another Highcliff Guardian as it was for the Highcliff Guardians to think of her as anyone but a princess.

Forcing herself to remain calm, she asked through clenched teeth, "And just when do you suppose she'll be *less indisposed*."

Eolande's fleshless lips curled at the corners. "When Xantha deems herself...*less indisposed*."

As nice as Eolande appeared on the surface, Ouderling couldn't rein in her temper. "Why is everyone hiding things from me? Where is everyone? There's barely a soul in the complex. Guardians are flying off into the night to do who knows what, and no one's bothered to mention anything to me...About anything! Why?"

"Because you're not meant to know."

Keeper of the Jewel

Eolande's straight forward response stole the heat from her tirade.

"According to Aelfwynne, your presence in Highcliff is at the bequest of the queen. If it were up to the high wizard, you would've been sent home already."

"But…But…He changed his mind. He agreed my place is here."

"Begrudgingly," Eolande raised a hairless brow. "It's true. Master Aelfwynne doesn't believe you have the mettle required to become a true Highcliff Guardian."

Ouderling cared less that her jaw hung open. She sputtered, "But—"

"But nothing, Your Highness. With all due respect, Master Aelfwynne may be a gruff character to deal with, but he has the biggest of hearts. If he claims you aren't cut out for the rigours of Guardian life, it isn't meant as a sign of disrespect. As high wizard, it's his prerogative to speak his mind. Hurtful or not, it doesn't alter the fact that your presence has compromised the safety of our tightknit community."

Ouderling swallowed hard, not sure how to respond to Eolande's no nonsense explanation. Determined not to let the threatening tears fall, she glared at Eolande a moment longer and spun to leave.

"I don't agree with Master Aelfwynne."

Ouderling stiffened, looking questioningly at Eolande.

Eolande shrugged and glanced over his shoulder to where Perch walked around the fount, his leathery skin bathed in blue luminescence.

If not for the solid jag of crystals Ouderling leaned on, she would have fallen to the floor in disbelief. Perch passed by the goblin and stretched his neck to sniff at her, nostrils flaring. She flinched and tucked her head against her shoulder as the wyvern's inspection tickled the side of her face.

"You're different than the others. Master Aelfwynne may not see it yet, but I sense in you our salvation."

The crystals dug into her back. There was no escaping the closeness of the ancient beast, but the significance of the voice sounding in her head stole away any compunction to flee. Struggling to breathe, she leaned forward, tentatively putting a hand on Perch's snout below a wide-spaced set of light brown eyes that appeared as if they were searching her soul.

The ability of the elves and other magical creatures to communicate with dragons wasn't uncommon, but experiencing it firsthand was nothing short of incredible. Swallowing her debilitating fear, she asked softly, "You're speaking to me, aren't you?"

Other than the earth blood fount's constant burble, all sound in the cavern ceased. It was like the world had stopped to witness the miracle of the thousand-year-old wyvern as he kneeled before her, laying his head at her feet. *"Indeed, fair princess. I, Perch of Highcliff, humbly vow my allegiance to you. May the earth blood grant me the years I need to keep you safe from the foreseeable dangers we shall inevitably encounter. May my oath provide me with the strength I require to deter those who come against you when you least expect it."*

Ouderling stared hard at Perch's bowed head. Out of the corner of her eye, Eolande had taken a knee as well. As if sensing her gaze, the goblin looked up with the hint of a smile. "If Perch avows his loyalty to you, Your Highness, I would be amiss not to follow his lead."

"I...I don't know what to say. This is all so...unexpected." Ouderling's voice came as little more than a croak.

416

Keeper of the Jewel

"To me, as well," Eolande agreed. His voice dropped to a whisper, "Accept our fealty."

"Um, of course." The princess looked between Eolande and Perch, the gravity of the moment sinking in. Her years of observing her parents perform their roles as heads of State came to bear. Finding her voice, she said with as much royal decorum as she could muster. "Arise, oh worthy wyvern and goblin. Your pledge is welcome comfort in these days of uncertainty. I accept your oath. As heir to the Willow Throne, I will do everything in my power to ensure the safety of you and everyone you hold dear." Nodding at Eolande, she didn't try to hide the broad smile lifting her cheeks, displacing her tears of happiness. "Including the worthy Crystal Cavern caretakers."

Perch rose to his feet, a wyvern head taller than Ouderling while on all fours. *"Thank you, Your Highness. You honour me."*

Ouderling wiped at her tears and wagged a finger at Perch. "While I'm at Highcliff, you must refrain from referring to me by my title. I'm a Guardian in training, nothing more. Is that clear?"

Perch dipped his head. *"Yes, Ouderling Wys. It will be as you wish, but know this; even when the day comes that you ascend the Willow Throne, you'll always be a princess to me."*

Anything Ouderling wanted to add was stripped from her by Perch's proclamation. She thought her tears were under control. She was mistaken.

Eolande rose to his feet and leaned in to whisper something to Perch. If the wyvern answered the goblin, his words never registered in Ouderling's head.

Keeper of the Jewel

Perch turned to Ouderling. *"Xantha has informed me that she outfitted you in Highcliff armour befitting one of your station. I need you to bring me your sword."*

Ouderling blinked, confused by the odd request, but neither Perch nor Eolande said anything more. Instead, they stared at her as if inspecting a shard of crystal.

Not knowing what else to do, Ouderling went to retrieve her sword.

Where Xantha had gotten to barely crossed Ouderling's mind as she stared at the fine armour piled in the corner of her sleeping quarters. Fine, useless armour. Her emotions had taken a tumultuous ride since Jyllana had flown into the night with Balewynd and Pecklyn.

Jyllana had mentioned how incredible it had been when Perch and Dawnbreaker had spoken to her. Jealous of her protector, Ouderling had shrugged off Jyllana's excitement, not appreciating the miracle of dragon speech. Now that she had experienced it firsthand, she could think of nothing else. The fact that Perch wanted her to bring him her newly attained sword never phased her. So enamoured with the scaly beast, she doubted there was anything he could ask that she wouldn't do.

The longsword felt lighter than usual in her hands as she pulled it free of the black leather scabbard and examined its length of unblemished steel. The blade didn't have a nick on it. It likely had never seen action.

The walk back to the Crystal Cavern was a blur. Strutting down the main corridor with sword in hand, it felt like she was off to save the world—that nobody else in South March were more important to the survival of the realm than their favoured sword, Princess Ouderling Wys of Borreraig Palace.

Keeper of the Jewel

A pair of male elves stepped from a side passage, startling her out of her dreamlike state. Fully armoured, they marched past her without giving her the time of day. She forced a smile and lowered her head as they passed. Embarrassed by her delusions of importance, the swagger left her step.

Perch and Eolande looked straight at her as she rounded a bend in the path bisecting the Crystal Cavern. It was like they were expecting her at that very moment. She didn't doubt they were aware of her presence long before she came into view.

"Ah, good. Give your sword to Eolande and climb onto my shoulders."

Conscious of how her eyes must be bulging, she blinked at the wyvern in disbelief.

Eolande stepped up to her and gently pulled the forgotten sword from her hands. In turn, he produced a sheathed dagger—its ivory handle protruding from a brown leather scabbard.

Ouderling accepted the dagger. "What's this?"

"Don't unsheathe it until Perch instructs you to," was all he said as he nodded for her to approach Perch crouched beside the earth blood fount.

"But…I've never flown a dragon before."

"Please. Wyverns are much more civilized than dragons."

Not knowing what to do, she stalled, her frightened gaze flicking between Eolande and Perch. "Won't I hurt you? I'm bigger than Eolande. Heavier too. Do you think it's safe?"

"You may be taller than Eolande, but I assure you he weighs a slight bit more than you." Perch craned his head to stare her straight in the eye. *"The only way to hurt me is to refuse."*

Eolande smiled. "It's okay. You'll be fine. You have my word."

Keeper of the Jewel

"But I thought flying dragons…," she swallowed, "I mean wyverns, was only allowed by the appointed rider?"

"That's an elven superstition, brought about by Grimclaw's Law. In most cases, that is *the way it plays out, but no law prevents me from flying anyone I want. Nor do I have to fly anyone at all. Choosing a rider is akin to someone like you selecting a lifelong mate. If I choose a rider, it's out of a desire to bond with them. That being said, dragonkind generally opt for longer-lived species such as elves. Humans are susceptible to dying early, thus we rarely expend much time on them. When we bond with a rider it's a deep connection. One that seriously affects us should anything happen to our rider."*

Ouderling stared, trying hard to process his words.

"If it helps you understand, most of dragonkind only ever chooses one rider in their lifetime if they choose at all. That doesn't prevent us from flying other riders, but when we do, you can be confident that the secondary rider is someone special as well."

Ouderling frowned. "But you don't even know me. Other than being an unwanted visitor at Highcliff, I'm nothing more to you than just another elf."

"Don't allow your limited perception of the world to misguide you. Eolande and I have shared centuries of history together. If not for your grandparents, neither one of us would be here today. Through their memory we've a good feeling about you."

The wyvern's words made a little sense. Perch was offering to fly her out of a sense of his obligation to her grandparents.

The wyvern shook his head as if hearing her thoughts. When he spoke, she wasn't certain he hadn't.

Keeper of the Jewel

"My offer to fly you is not to be taken lightly. Though grateful for Queen Nyxa and King Orlythe's intervention on behalf of dragonkind, I choose to fly you on your own merit."

"My merit? What have I done but bring death and hardship to Highcliff in the short time I've been here?"

"It's not what you've done that interests me, Ouderling Wys. As with your most honourable protector, I sense in you a future in which you are capable of accomplishing great things if given the chance to discover your true self."

She shook her head. "I don't understand."

"Nor would I expect you to at this stage in your life. You'll just have to trust the ramblings of a senile wyvern," he glanced at Eolande who watched on with a knowing smile, *"And those of my life partner, Eolande."*

Eolande nodded as he inspected the sword, turning it over in his hands, paying particular attention to the weapon's pommel. Without a word, he walked deeper into the cavern, leaving the area of the earth blood fount.

Perch waited until his rider was gone before he said, *"Come. Secure the dagger to your belt and climb on before I die of old age."*

"Where are we going?" Ouderling asked as she secured the dagger's sheath on her simple, leather belt.

"I'll tell you soon enough, but not until we're in the air."

The wyvern's skin felt cold and rough to her touch. Conscious of Perch's foreleg, she tried not to place her weight on it.

"You couldn't hurt me if you tried. Grab a scale and pull yourself up."

Unsure of how to position herself, she did as instructed and slid her legs on either side of his neck.

"Perfect. Now hold on tight. Take-off can be disconcerting to new fliers. Just don't choke me."

Keeper of the Jewel

Ouderling swallowed and ducked beneath the tips of Perch's temple horns—the foreign sensation of a dragon between her legs overshadowed by the thrill of hugging his scaly neck. She couldn't believe she actually sat on the shoulders of a creature this size.

A squeak escaped her as Perch suddenly crouched and sprung into the air; the change in momentum driving the wind from her lungs. Gasping for breath, she dared to open her eyes but immediately closed them again to avoid watching the blue-tinged crystal formations drop away at an alarming rate.

"Not so tight!"

Startled by Perch's emphatic plea, she opened her eyes, doing her best not to strangle him as she hung on for dear life.

Without warning, their upward flight levelled out. Swallowing her fear, Ouderling glanced around. Multi-coloured crystal formations jutted out from the cavern walls and projected from the ceiling like stalactites not far above her head—their polished surfaces radiating a dull light of their own. Looking down, she gasped. The earth blood fount appeared no bigger than the rim of a goblet.

"Incredible, isn't it?"

She imagined Perch meant the thousands of individual shoots of pulsing stone. Taking time to appreciate them, she said, "Wow...It's amazing. Are they all magic stones?"

"On their own, no. But, in conjunction with the earth blood, they are immensely powerful. Much like a piece of steel isn't naturally magnetic, but were the steel to come into contact with a lodestone, it would begin to become so. Given enough exposure, the magnetic properties of the steel would be enhanced until it mimicked the lodestone."

Keeper of the Jewel

History lessons spurred Ouderling's curiosity. "Is it true Grimclaw was born from the crystals?"

"That's a common misconception. More myth than reality, but still, it's not far from the truth. The earth blood's magical properties are amplified exponentially by the significant amount of naturally occurring crystals in the cavern. Harnessed by an adept magic-user, there's little that cannot be conjured within these walls."

Recent events began to make sense. "That's why my uncle covets the magic of the Crystal Cavern."

"He and many others. That is always our fear. Thus, the creation of the legion of Highcliff Guardians. Our small band is entrusted to prevent that eventuality from coming to pass."

The mention of a legion of Guardians niggled at her. During her short time at Highcliff she hadn't seen more than a handful of Guardians around the vast complex. "How many Guardians are there?"

It was strange to feel a wyvern shrug beneath her.

"I haven't counted them lately. I would say there are twenty to thirty at present. Over the years, some die, while others seek fulfillment in their lives by rejoining the rest of the realm. There's certainly less now than there used to be. Master Aelfwynne doesn't often accept new recruits, other than those born here, of course."

"Like Pecklyn and Balewynd."

"Pecklyn, yes. Balewynd, no. She was born in Grim Town and raised at Castle Grim."

It seemed as if Perch's smooth flight missed a beat at the mention of the black castle.

"She's the daughter of the duke's head chamberlain."

"Was."

Keeper of the Jewel

As soon as the word left her lips, their elevation noticeably dropped.

Perch craned his neck to eye her with concern. *"What's happened to Balewynd?"*

"Nothing. She's fine, but someone killed her father the other day."

"That's dreadful news. Balewynd holds a dear place in my heart. Come to think on it, she's the last outsider to be accepted into Highcliff in a long time."

"Really?"

"Ironic, now that I think on it. Why Master Aelfwynne allowed the daughter of Duke Orlythe's head chamberlain anywhere near Highcliff is a mystery. That being said, if there's one thing I've learned over the centuries, it's to trust Master Aelfwynne's judgement. Like I said before, if not for him, I wouldn't be enjoying the honour of flying Princess Ouderling around the Crystal Cavern."

Ouderling laughed, "Just Ouderling, remember."

"Don't worry, I'll remember if we're ever in public together, but alone, you'll always be my princess."

Warmth flushed Ouderling—a surreal sense of euphoria embracing her. Her feelings of inadequacy sloughed away. For the first time since she had been informed by her mother that Highcliff was to be part of her life for the foreseeable future, she experienced a sense of belonging. She had a long way to go, but she would show Master Aelfwynne that his reservations about her were unfounded.

Her elation waned as the reality of the current events came to mind. She may never be given the chance if the rumours out of Grim Keep were true.

A sudden, reckless thought grabbed hold of her. "Do you ever leave the cavern?"

"Of course, you silly girl. All the time. Why do you ask?"

Keeper of the Jewel

"No reason really…"

"Ouderling."

She laughed. He sounded just like her father.

Taking a deep breath, she blurted, "I need you to take me to Castle Grim."

Keeper of the Jewel

Make a Stand

Dawnbreaker banked over the rolling moors on the eastern side of Castle Grim, the twinkling lights of Grim Town sprawled around the castle's outer wall far below, shining with an ethereal glow through a roiling mist that crept across the land. Aided by an overcast sky and urged on by her rider, the muscular dragon eyed the spires of the cathedral towering over the western ramparts as she picked up speed and plummeted from the sky. Gliding low over the plains to avoid detection until the last possible moment, Pecklyn welcomed the tingling adrenaline consuming him.

He leaned into Jyllana sitting between him and Dawnbreaker's thick neck and shouted to be heard above the rushing wind tugging at his long hair. "You sure you're ready for this? We'll only get one chance at it!"

He felt Jyllana nod, but even with her assurance, he worried the Home Guard might not be up to what was required.

Close behind, Balewynd flew Mirage—the aloof Guardian's presence providing him the mental strength he needed. No matter what happened in the coming moments, he knew without a doubt that Balewynd was capable of doing whatever needed to be done.

A brief smile eased the worry from his face. Balewynd's irrefutable character was like the sun. No matter what happened. No matter how dire the ensuing hours of darkness

Keeper of the Jewel

became, the sun was sure to rise in the morning. With Balewynd watching his back, he had little to fear.

"Keep tight to the far side of Dawnbreaker's neck until I tell you otherwise. Her hide will shelter you from arrowshot."

Jyllana ducked behind Dawnbreaker's neck.

Grim Town disappeared in the wake of their rapid approach as the castle's north face loomed overhead—crenellated ramparts whipped by in a blur. Halfway along the great expanse of outer wall, shouts disturbed the still of the night, followed by the shrill of alarm bells.

Dawnbreaker's rapid flight slowed significantly, her wings tilted to drag at the air.

The hiss of an arrow cutting the air overhead made Pecklyn duck. He did his best not to squish Jyllana or displace her from where she fought to hang onto during the momentum shift. "Get ready!"

The ornate heights of the cathedral rose up on the far side of the wall as Dawnbreaker climbed level with the top of the crenellated bulwark.

"Now!" Pecklyn twisted on Dawnbreaker's shoulder, digging his outside boot into her flank. Grabbing Jyllana's tight leather vest he lifted her free of Dawnbreaker's neck and assisted her leap to the top of the wall. Following right behind her, the two of them tumbled along the stone walkway—Dawnbreaker's rapid flight quickly swallowed by the misty darkness.

Jyllana would have fallen over the inside edge if not for Pecklyn's quick hand. He grabbed onto her belt, arresting her fall—her upper body dangling over the shadowy bailey beyond the cathedral.

A loud battle cry sent shivers up Pecklyn's spine. His sword hand grasped at his hilt but his blade was stuck in its

427

scabbard, jammed beneath his prone body. If he wanted to keep Jyllana from falling to her death, he couldn't roll over to fend off the attack of the Grim Guard bearing down on where they sprawled on the edge of the walkway—the fury in the Grim Guard's eyes chilling as the black-bearded elf swung a spiked mace overhead to crush them.

The Grim Guard's eyes widened—his face transforming rapidly from rage to incredulousness to shock to agonizing pain.

A dark shape soared past the outside wall, but Pecklyn's attention was rivetted on the black death that fell on the Grim Guard like a falcon hitting its prey in midair.

Balewynd rode the surprised guard to the walkway beside Pecklyn and Jyllana, one hand clasping the elf's raised wrist, her other savagely stabbing at the guard's face and neck, piercing him three times before they hit the walkway hard. She somersaulted across the walkway and sprung to her feet, spinning in the air to face the attack of a second Grim Guard charging on the heels of his companion.

The elf hesitated momentarily to stare at the disfigured face of his fallen colleague. His hesitation cost him his life.

Balewynd sprung across the gap separating them, leading with her bloodied dagger. The blade dove between the elf's boiled leather chest armour and sword belt.

The guard's sword slipped from his fingers to clatter on top of the wall, surprise evident on his clean-shaven face at the significance of what had just happened to him.

Balewynd grabbed the Grim Guard's arm and pulled herself up to face him, thrusting her dagger deeper, twisting it as she stared him in the eye. "That's for my father!"

The Grim Guard grunted and collapsed over Balewynd's arm.

Keeper of the Jewel

Unable to support his weight, she pulled her dagger free and watched as the elf hit the ground hard, a pool of blood expanding around his midsection. Not affording her victim any more of her time, she spun to inspect the shadows along the wall in both directions before turning her attention on Pecklyn and Jyllana. "We don't have much time."

With Balewynd's assistance, Pecklyn rose to his feet, one hand pulling Jyllana back from the brink. Looking down the wall to the west, he urged Jyllana to follow Balewynd along the walkway, back toward where the cathedral was built close to the rampart, and dashed after them.

Balewynd paused beside the immense cathedral's corner tower, its façade resplendent with ornate architecture, her eyes assessing the structure. Blood dripped from her dagger as she indicated a large, stained-glass window across a narrow gap that separated the cathedral from the wall itself. "Pecklyn and I will enter the castle here." Not bothering to look at Jyllana, she added, "You stay put and guard our escape route. As soon as you hear us coming, call for the dragons."

When Jyllana didn't respond, Balewynd spun on her. "You got that?"

Jyllana nodded.

Pecklyn smiled for Jyllana's benefit and turned to watch Balewynd leap the gap with catlike agility. The bottom panel of colourful glass shattered under the weight of Balewynd's dagger hilt, and she disappeared inside.

Pecklyn jumped the gap, wavering momentarily on the broad windowsill. The gap wasn't overly wide but the long drop to the dark shadows at the base of the wall was great enough to make him leery of the ramifications of a misjudged leap.

Keeper of the Jewel

Bending to lean through the broken window, careful not to get cut by its jagged edges, it took him a moment to locate Balewynd.

Her legs stretched between a thin ledge and the top of a three-story tall statue of a robed elf riding a dragon, Balewynd tied a thin rope around the tip of the statue's carved marble polearm. She glanced at him as she tested the knot and descended into the darkness of the cathedral.

Not sure whether it was the cold of dragon flight that had given her the chills or the fact that she crouched in the shadows of Castle Grim's cathedral, expecting to be found out at any moment by the Grim Guard, Jyllana scanned the eastern and western approaches of the dark bastion's north wall. Thankful for the overcast sky, she could just make out the two bodies Balewynd had dispatched. If they were discovered, it wouldn't be long before the battlements were crawling with Grim Guard.

A long assessment of the mist shrouded western walkway gave her little assurance that no one was coming from that direction, but she had no choice, she had to act. Stepping out of the shadows, she ran hunched over to attend to the bodies. It would be easier to roll them over the inner edge of the wall but that wouldn't make them any less visible. Troops on the ground would soon discover them.

If not for the gaps provided by the crenellations along the outer edge of the wall, she doubted she could hoist the brutes' dead weight high enough to get them to the brink of the bulwark. Even so, the waist-high gaps pushed her strength to the limit. Slight of stature, she strained to lift the elves' carcasses into a gap along the wall.

The second elf Balewynd had dispatched left a gory stain on the walkway, the glaring evidence exacerbated as Jyllana dragged him to the outer edge and pushed him over the brink, but there was nothing to be done about it. With a last shove, she winced as his body thudded on the ground far below. Leaning out, she could barely make out where he ended up.

Shouts echoed off the castle's many walls. Ducking against the protective barrier of the crenellation, she scanned the walkway in both directions, relieved that nothing appeared to move.

The second Grim Guard was heavier than the first. Coupled with the fact she had overexerted herself already, she almost gave up trying to hoist his bulk into the crenellated gap. An audible grunt escaped her as the Grim Guard's corpse scraped across the stone surface and tumbled out of sight. She cringed at the squishy sound of his impact. He had landed on top of his companion.

"There!" A deep voice cried out. Two arrows thumped into the bodies at the base of the outer wall.

"I think you hit one! Have someone check the outer wall!"

Though she couldn't see the speaker, his voice had come from somewhere along the western ramparts—likely from the corner tower that rose two stories higher than the wall; its bulk shrouded by heavy mists rolling in off the moors.

Heavy footsteps sounded above the growing chaos—metal boots rang off stone from the direction of the tower.

Jyllana paused momentarily, eyes riveted on the blood-stained walkway. It was only a matter of time before the entire garrison descended upon the area. If the broken window was discovered, Balewynd and Pecklyn would be trapped.

The walkway disappeared beneath her black leather boots in a blur as she sprinted past the window in question and searched for a place farther along the wall in which to draw the Grim Guard's attention.

Keeper of the Jewel

Spotting another wall tower in the distance, she decided it would be better to jump the gap separating the outer wall and the decorative ledge lining the cathedral high above the castle grounds.

She ran hard along the mist shrouded ledge for a few moments before pausing at the corner of the cathedral wall. Chills raised the fine hair on the back of her neck—her ponytail blowing in a sudden gust of wind. The ornately carved ledge had come to a sudden end.

Daggers in hand, she spun and dropped to a knee to face the way she had come. A beam of moonlight broke through the clouds, exposing her as sure as if she basked in the midday sun.

Still unaware of her presence, a group of Grim Guard stopped to inspect the blood-stained walkway, but looked her way when an archer pointed. "There's one!"

Knocking an arrow, the archer raised his bow. "I've got her in my sights. Get her down from there!"

Notwithstanding the horrors she had witnessed in the Passage of Dolor, Jyllana had never experienced action as a member of the Home Guard. With the standing army

432

stationed in and around Orlythia, the palace guard found they had little to concern themselves with. Only a fool would dare infiltrate Borreraig Palace. Still, her training had been rigorous and her mindset had prepared her for the eventuality that someday she might have to end another elf's life. Staring at the Grim Guard closing on her location, that time was upon her.

Wind swirled amongst the angular cathedral construction, roiling the deepening fog. Facing the threat of serious harm from the archer, she had to act quickly if she was to be of any use to Balewynd or Pecklyn.

An arrow zipped by her knees, making her jump—nearly falling off the edge. Catching her balance, it was difficult to see much beyond the rooftop that angled sharply upward to where it shot high overhead, forming the bulk of the cathedral's easternmost boundary and precluding any chance of exiting the ledge.

Her mind processed the significance of that realization. Wavering on the brink of the rooftop's eave, the dark bailey far below beckoned her to a quick death as it stretched away toward the bulk of Grim Keep.

Milling on the ground far below, dozens of black clad Grim Guard inspected the cathedral's heights.

"There!" A bearded elf pointed up.

Eyes wide, she turned at the sound of several Grim Guard materializing out the mist along the castle wall behind her, weapons drawn.

Daggers held at the ready, it was time to make a stand.

Keeper of the Jewel

Summon Your Dragon

"Urdanya, my Lord." Afara held Duke Orlythe's inquisitive gaze.

Orlythe nodded. It made sense, but the wraith's timing could not have been worse. With the reports of his sister's vanguard crossing the Rust Wash before nightfall, he could have benefitted from its assistance. He only hoped that the wraith had circumvented aid from Orphic Den.

Looking beyond the wizard, he stared at the mesmerising flow of the lava fountain, his thoughts many leagues north of Castle Grim. The only good thing about the Queen's imminent arrival would be the alibi it provided him when she received the news that was sure to unsettle her further.

Snapping out of his troubled stupor, he regarded the human wizard. Obstinate and egocentric, the dark magic-user possessed the ability to stretch his patience to its limits. Not only had the man failed to perform the harrowing on the high wizard, but he had allowed himself to be duped into believing the Staff of Reckoning had been consumed by Crag's Forge. Had Afara been anyone else, his head would have already left the company of his body, but the wizard still had a vital role to play if Orlythe wished to ascend the Willow Throne.

"Are you sure the high wizard is on Faelyn's Nest?"

"As sure as the information provided by your dragon patrols."

Keeper of the Jewel

"And there's no way one of the dragons loyal to Highcliff could have spirited him to safety?"

"I'd be foolish to assume anything concerning the meddling goblin, but unless he's managed to find a way to turn himself and a dragon invisible, I'd say it's highly unlikely."

"Highly unlikely?" The duke's voice rose. "That's the best you've got?"

Unperturbed, Afara said calmly, "Yes, m'lord."

Orlythe curbed the urge to sink a dagger into Afara's heart. The satisfaction would only be temporary. To actually do so would deprive him of one of his most valuable assets.

"And what of the Staff of Reckoning?" The duke knew the answer before he asked but couldn't help himself. "Have you at least located that?"

"No m'lord."

"I thought the wraith provided you with the means to divine its hiding place?"

Afara shrugged. "The chamberlain's heart was of no use. I suspect there was more to the chamberlain than he let on."

Orlythe couldn't argue with that. News of the traitorous Bayl had cut him deeply. Of all those in the employ of Castle Grim, Bayl was the last elf he would have imagined betraying him.

He clenched his fists. He should never have agreed to allow the chamberlain's daughter to go off to Highcliff. She would have provided the collateral needed to prevent such an occurrence from happening. Nevertheless, there was still time to make good on that oversight. He imagined he would see her soon enough.

A Grim Guard rushed into the throne room. "M'lord! Invaders spotted on the north wall."

Orlythe jumped to his feet. "Dragons?"

Keeper of the Jewel

The gasping elf stopped dutifully at the base of the throne dais. "No...Well, yes, m'lord, but they've flown off."

Orlythe frowned. Images of his haughty sister came to mind. "Then what? Is the queen at the gates?"

The question gave the burly Grim Guard pause. "No, m'lord. Least not that I'm aware of. The dragons dropped off their riders, but we've only found one."

"Bring him to me at once."

"It's a female, m'lord, and we haven't captured her yet. Last I saw she was cornered on the cathedral roof."

Xantha! Immediately, Orlythe thought of the high wizard's bizarre concubine. Only she would be bold enough to infiltrate Castle Grim. He was glad the old Guardian wasn't as capable as she had been in her youth. She might have razed the castle to the ground on her own.

Putting memories of Xantha aside, he wondered briefly who the other riders might be—he had fallen out of touch with the ranks of the Highcliff Guardians. If he had to guess, the grandson of the notorious Islen Ors, a scout in Queen Nyxa's army before the formation of South March, would likely be one of them. Perhaps Bayl's daughter as well. No doubt they were attempting to rescue Aelfwynne.

A grim smile lifted the corners of his thick mustache. They were in for a big surprise. The irony of them giving their lives to save someone who wasn't in the castle made him smile.

"Shall I deal with them, m'lord?" Afara asked.

Orlythe's first reaction was to say yes but he caught himself. He had total confidence the Grim Guard were capable of handling a few, pitiful Guardians, even if Xantha had come.

"No. I've a better use for your talents." Orlythe turned his attention on the Grim Guard messenger. "Very well. Make

Keeper of the Jewel

sure Captain Drake is aware of what's happening. Capture the intruders, and if possible, bring them to me, but don't hesitate to kill them if they put up a fight."

"Yes, m'lord." The Grim Guard bowed his head and turned to leave.

Orlythe called after him, "I want them dealt with before the sun rises."

The guard turned long enough to bow his head. "Of course, m'lord. It shall be done."

"That's the last thing I need," Orlythe muttered as he returned to the unforgiving embrace of the Lava Throne. He would have a difficult time explaining the actions of the rogue Highcliff Guardians if Khae were to arrive before they were dealt with.

Afara leaned toward him. "I'm sorry?"

Orlythe shook his head. "Nothing."

Afara nodded, a mischievous grin on his sallow face. "Perhaps it's time to up the stakes. Surprise Khae's army and crush the resistance before she's fully convinced of your treason."

The duke rested his bearded chin in one hand, contemplating the unfolding events. He frowned, absently mulling Afara's suggestion as he concentrated on what he needed to do to deal with his sister. Though not ideally how he had foreseen his ascension to the Willow Throne transpiring, the more he pondered the events of the last few days, the more a semblance of a new plan formed within his scheming mind. Perhaps the sallow-faced wizard was right.

Notwithstanding how late in the night it had become— early morning if he cared to dwell on it—a sinister smile lit up his face, his black eyes twinkling in the rushlight. If he could keep the Highcliff Guardians occupied, an ambush on the queen's army might just work.

Keeper of the Jewel

"It's time my human wizard paid a visit to Highcliff. Summon your dragon."

Keeper of the Jewel

Soulbiter

Wyvern laughter was a strange thing to witness. At least that's what Ouderling believed she was hearing in response to her request for Perch to fly her to Castle Grim.

"What's so funny? If my uncle is as complicit in Master Aelfwynne's disappearance as we're being led to believe, I'm the only one who stands a chance of reasoning with him."

"You forget he tried to kill you."

"No. I don't." She knew her reluctance to accept the facts was not a smart move on her part but the notion that everything that had happened recently had been orchestrated by her uncle seemed inconceivable. "I struggle to believe he's that evil. Though, I do understand the reasoning behind such a claim. Regardless, I'm a princess of the realm. My order, however insignificant it might seem coming from a seventeen-year-old, still bears weight in any court in the land. My uncle wouldn't dare allow harm to befall me. My mother would have his head."

"You forget already what you said earlier. At Highcliff you're a trainee. Nothing more."

"I forget nothing. This is different."

"You can't change rules to suit your needs. That's no way for the echelons of leadership to be run. Were we to follow your way of thinking, High Wizard Aelfwynne's authority would mean nothing should we find ourselves questioning

Keeper of the Jewel

his orders." Perch's rapid, shallow wing beats brought them to a thin stalactite hanging from the centre of the cavern—the single shard oddly not part of a larger formation. *"Besides, Eolande has something else in store for you."*

Ouderling's next words escaped her as Perch's proclamation sunk in. She frowned, wondering what that could be. Not able to help herself, she ran a fingertip along the end of the pulsing, crimson shard.

"That particular crystal is know as the Focal Stone. If you look down, you'll notice we're directly above the earth blood pool."

She did as instructed, nearly losing her seat in the process.

Perch jerked beneath her, arresting her overbalanced body. *"Easy, princess. I wouldn't recommend diving into the pool from this height."*

Ouderling swallowed as the realization that she had almost plummeted to her death coursed through her. Regaining her composure, her eyes were drawn to the Focal Stone. "What's it do?"

"As I mentioned earlier, earth blood acts like a lodestone, infusing magic into the crystals. Storing it, if you will. The Focal Stone, however, has developed a magical property of its own. Through it, the stored magic of the entire cavern can be harnessed by those possessing the ability to channel such power."

Ouderling's head swum with Perch's ramblings. Nothing really made sense, but it was clear that the Focal Stone was an integral part of the Crystal Cavern.

"Use the dagger to cut off its tip."

Confusion forced her to blink several times, not certain she had heard Perch correctly. "You want me to do what?"

"Slice off a small piece of the Focal Stone's tip with the magical blade Eolande gave you."

Keeper of the Jewel

"Won't that ruin the crystal?"

"Perhaps, but I doubt it, else Eolande wouldn't have requested it. He'd do it himself, but he's of the belief that if it's done by your hand, the severed stone may retain its properties."

"That makes no sense. I'm no wizard."

"Don't ask me. I just fly the old caretaker around. But, if Eolande says that that's the case with the crystal, I'd be inclined to believe him. There's more to Eolande than most give him credit for. Believe it or not, the great Aelfwynne often seeks Eolande's counsel during times of need."

Unsure of herself, Ouderling grasped the ivory-tusked handle of the carved dagger and pulled it free of its nondescript sheath. Inset with tiny gemstones and inlaid with delicate ribbons of gold, the exquisitely carved blade appeared to glow of its own accord, its gleaming surfaces reflecting the multi-hued crystals pulsing all across the rooftop.

As soon as the dagger's tip cleared its sheath, a sting shot up her arm, causing her to fumble with the weapon to keep it from falling from her grasp.

"Careful you don't touch its edges. It'll sever your skin as quick as a blink."

"It shocked me."

The strange sound she had come to associate with wyvern laughter echoed throughout the cavern.

"I don't find that funny."

"I'm sorry, princess. Eolande should have warned you."

"Warned me of what?"

"Hmm? That might be hard to explain to one so young and inexperienced in the ways of magic."

An eerie silence gripped the Crystal Cavern but before Ouderling questioned Perch further, he said, *"You hold in*

Keeper of the Jewel

your hand, Soulbiter. A blade that is rumoured to have come from a different world.

Ouderling frowned deeper. "You mean like the Fae?"

"No. Someplace not connected with our world at all. From the same world as the Dragon Witch, I am told. That's all I know of its origin. Nor do I think Eolande knows anymore than that either, but that's not what's important. Now, use the blade before Eolande gets cranky. He doesn't like to be kept waiting."

Afraid to regrip Soulbiter's hilt, she studied its intricately worked surfaces. Golden filigree intertwined the dagger's guard, flowing around the ivory handle. She placed a tentative finger against the white bone expecting to be stung, but nothing happened.

The hilt felt cold but comforting in her grasp as she inspected it in the pulsing cavern glow. Steadying herself on Perch's neck, she grasped the Focal Stone with her free hand and placed Soulbiter's edge against the crystal's tip. The stone resisted its touch, just as she thought it would.

Worried she might take the edge off the blade she pulled it away.

"What's the matter? Won't it cut?"

"How can it? Am I supposed to hack at it?"

"Don't do that! You'll bring down the entire Focal Stone."

"Then I'm not sure what you expect me to do."

"Use your magic."

"I don't know how. No one ever taught me."

"You're the future heir to South March's highest seat and nobody has taken the initiative to train you yet? I find that curiously troubling."

"Tell me about it. Mother's afraid I'll follow in my brother's footsteps."

"But Ordyl was blessed with great ability."

Keeper of the Jewel

"Exactly. A lot of good it did him. He died pursuing it."

"Oh, well, that changes things."

"What do you mean?"

"When you first unsheathed Soulbiter it affected you, did it not?"

"I'll say. Stung like a bee."

"Good."

"Good?"

"The dagger's aptly named. It bites the bearer. Tries to taste their soul."

"That sounds dreadful."

"Only if you had died as a result. You see? Soulbiter is a blade of moral character. If it deems you unworthy of its touch, it'll inflict upon you a horrible fate. Were you not to die immediately, you'd wish you had."

Ouderling's first response was to drop the cursed weapon—to fling it as far away from her as possible, but something about the way it felt in her grasp stopped her. Straddling the shoulder of the wyvern, high above the cavern floor, she studied Soulbiter, turning it this way and that, appreciating its elegance. "How can anything this beautiful be so evil."

"Evil in the wrong hands."

She swallowed, wondering what it would have done to her if it had chosen otherwise. Worse, Perch had allowed her to take the chance. Highcliff was indeed a dangerous place to foreigners. Visions of her first taste of wizard's tea in Aelfwynne's chamber came to mind. It became apparent that in order to belong to Highcliff, one had to survive its deadly initiations. She wondered how many had succumbed to the mystical aerie's curse.

Swallowing her apprehension, she stared at Soulbiter's blade. "So…It's alive?"

Keeper of the Jewel

The cavern rumbled with wyvern amusement. *"No, princess. It's a length of cold steel. But the magic within is not to be trifled with. Now, remember, Eolande awaits our return. You might be able to walk away when this is done, but I have to fly him again. Place the dagger against the tip of the Focal Stone and concentrate on cutting it. Release your inhibitions and Soulbiter will do the rest."*

Daring to touch the dagger's blade, she didn't feel the cut it inflicted; the slice so fine her eyes widened at the sight of blood on its keen edge. Wounded finger in mouth, she silently berated her stupidity. What did she think was going to happen?

"Princess!" Perch urged.

"Right." Ouderling regripped the Focal Stone. Placing one of Soulbiter's edges against the glowing surface she inhaled deeply and attempted to relax.

Like her mother and grandmother before her, she also possessed nature's essence, but unlike the queen, or her brother for that matter, she had never experienced what it was like to use it. Knowing what it had done to her brother, just the thought of accessing the foreign presence had scared her as a child. However, she intrinsically knew where it lingered within her mind.

Her fear of the magic was a direct result of her parents cautioning her of the harm it could bring her should she choose to follow in her brother's footsteps. She hadn't been much older than a toddler elfling when they had ingrained the dire omen in her head. It had affected her so deeply that the nuance of her gift had sat untried for over seventeen years. She doubted it would respond now. Nor did she think it would be useful against the forces they were up against. Speaking with bits of light from an ethereal world hardly seemed like the wisest thing to be wasting her time on.

444

Keeper of the Jewel

The same edge of the blade that had cut her finger rested against the Focal Stone, unmoving. Luckily, Perch's flight was so calm that if she closed her eyes, she wouldn't know she was flying at all.

A chilling thought crossed her mind as she stared at Soulbiter pressed against the Focal Stone. What if her parents were wrong? What if the magic she perceived she had wasn't what her mother believed it to be? A darker thought came to mind and began to fester, shedding the dimmest of light on the fact that perhaps she had been too hasty to discount the power of nature's essence. Without her mother's or grandmother's ability to wield magic, how could she expect to lead South March when her time came? There were always going to be pretenders to the throne. Elves bent on the power that came with the royal seat. Her uncle not the least of which.

"Release your reservations...Flush your mind...Close your eyes...Concentrate only on what you hear...At this moment in time, nothing else matters." Perch's soothing voice seemed a long way off.

She stared at the top of his scaley head and nodded. Closing her eyes, she attempted to purge her underlying fear.

The wyvern's rapidly beating wings and the bubbling earth blood pool filled her consciousness along with her pulse that hammered throughout her body. The chill of the cavern raised gooseflesh on her exposed skin. A slight mustiness combined with a whiff of wet rock wafted heady on the air.

"Release your worldly worries...Envision the Crystal Cavern for the wonder that it is...Allow its essence to seep into you...Let its allure whisk your troubles away...Feel your connection to that which you have neglected for far too long."

Keeper of the Jewel

Perch's faraway words drifted into her mind as if in a dream—lolling her into a carefree daze.

"Now feel your connection to the Focal Stone...Hear it speak to you through Soulbiter...Embrace its magic...You are Ouderling Wys...Heir to the Willow Throne...Through you, may we yet know salvation."

Ouderling blinked at that. The strong sentiment snapped her out of the trancelike state she had fallen into. Staring hard at her hands, she couldn't believe what she saw.

"I knew you could do it," Perch's voice sounded normal once again. *"That's why you'll always be* my *princess. In time, you'll come to believe in yourself as I do."*

It came as an afterthought that tears rolled unabashedly down her cheeks. A severed piece of the Focal Stone, the length of her thumb, lay in her upturned palm—her pointer finger dripping blood where Soulbiter had bit it.

Keeper of the Jewel

Eolande's Gift

Eolande smiled at Ouderling as Perch spread his wings wide to catch their descent. Laying Ouderling's sword on the edge of the earth blood pool he rubbed at Perch's cheek and gazed knowingly into Ouderling's eyes. "How was your flight?"

Ouderling slipped from Perch's shoulder, careful to jump clear of his leg. "Incredible! I'd be content to spend the rest of my life flying around with Perch."

Eolande shot her a serious look. "Um, I'm Perch's rider."

Ouderling lowered her gaze, afraid she had upset Eolande, but laughed as a sly smile crossed his face. Remembering Soulbiter, she undid the thong tying the sheath to her belt and held it out to him.

Eolande shook his head. "Nay, that's yours to keep."

She couldn't believe her ears. "Oh no. I can't take this. Why, it's…It's…"

"A blade befitting a princess."

"Ah, yes. See? Perch knows," Eolande said. "It's been too long since Soulbiter has found someone worthy enough to wield her."

"Her?"

Eolande shrugged. "You know how it is? Everything is named after a female. Who knows why? In your hands, it can be a he."

"Oh, but I can't. This blade is special. It must be priceless."

447

Keeper of the Jewel

"Exactly why Aelfwynne would insist it be given to you."

"Me?" Ouderling spat. "I'm the last person Master Aelfwynne would bestow such a treasure on. He wants me gone. Well, he did when he was…"

"Tsk, tsk." Eolande wagged a gnarled finger and nodded at her closed fist that held the severed shard. "Trust me. When Aelfwynne hears how you became one with Soulbiter, long enough to cut the Focal Stone, he'll kneel at your feet and swear his undying fealty."

Although she appreciated the import of Eolande's words, the implication didn't sit well with her. Nor did she miss the fact that Eolande believed Aelfwynne was still alive. As encouraging as that seemed, she couldn't help but blurt, "I'm the heir to the Willow Throne. I would expect nothing less."

"Ah. You broach the heart of the matter. Fealty by privilege is but a hollow virtue. True loyalty cannot be bought. Nor can it be ordained. If you are to achieve the potential Perch and I see in you, you'll only do so by attracting devout followers. Elves and dragons, and even goblins, who're prepared to fight for what you hold dear."

Cold shivers washed over her skin as the truth of his words sunk in. She swallowed, unable to speak.

Eolande nodded. "It's still early days in the life of Ouderling Wys, but, and this I fear is a big but, if you can find a way to live through the coming darkness, your light will surely guide the way for generations to come."

Movement behind her drew her attention. Another wyvern had moved in beside Perch, one much smaller than the ancient wyrm. As one, the two wyverns lowered their chests to the cavern floor and bowed their heads.

"Princess, I present to you, my granddaughter. Allow Miragan and I to be the first to pledge our loyalty to you." Perch's voice whispered solemnly in her head. *"Not out of*

Keeper of the Jewel

fealty to the crown, but for the love we sense exuding from your soul. As long as our wings beat, we shall carry you wherever the winds may blow."

Vaguely aware that she had lowered herself to kneel on the cavern floor, Ouderling gaped, her mind reeling. She had come to the Crystal Cavern to demand that Xantha tell her what was going on. Never in her wildest dreams had she expected anything like this.

Blinking and trying to focus on the here and now, she realized that Eolande stood over her, his callused hand waiting to assist her to her feet.

"Now, if you'll provide me with the crystal shard, I've a surprise for you." Eolande smiled as he helped her up.

"I...I don't think I can take any more surprises."

He stared at her clenched hand.

"Oh, yes. Here."

Eolande's eyes bulged as he relieved her of the shard.

"Is something wrong?"

"I hadn't meant for you to take that much."

"Sorry. I had no idea. Is that bad?"

"No. Well, I hope not anyway." He rolled the thumb-length shard in his palm. "No matter. It's my fault. I should've told you."

Ouderling was afraid she had just thrown away everything that had transpired between her and the wyverns. "Can I put some back?"

"I think not," Eolande chuckled nervously, staring at the ceiling—the remains of the Focal Stone difficult to discern from where they stood. As he studied the glittering roof, he nodded, the worry on his face easing into deep thought. "Perhaps this is a good thing."

Ouderling exchanged glances with Perch and smiled for Miragan's benefit.

Keeper of the Jewel

"Yes." Eolande's voice rose, "Yes! That's exactly what I'll do."

"I'm sorry?" Ouderling asked, but Eolande had turned to approach the edge of the earth blood pool.

"Gather round, everyone," Eolande spoke, but his attention was on Ouderling's two-handed broadsword next to the bubbling pool. He placed the shard at the base of the sword's pommel and nodded some more. "I'll need you to use Soulbiter to cut the shard in half."

Ouderling approached Eolande, unsure of herself. She held the sheathed dagger out to him. "Perhaps you should do it. You know what you're doing."

"Oh no, princess. I can't do that. Soulbiter and I don't get along. She almost killed me once, long ago. But that's not important." Eolande placed the shard on the lip of the earth blood pool, his green skin awash in white-blue brilliance. "I'll hold it steady."

Ouderling couldn't suppress her apprehension. "What if I cut you?"

"I'll die a horrible death."

It was all Ouderling could do not to drop Soulbiter into the earth blood. "What?"

Eolande gave her a wry smile. "Let that be a lesson to you from an ancient being. Don't be afraid of the answer if you dare to ask the question. Soulbiter's talent is to seek out the darkness in one's spirit and attack it. If the wielder's heart isn't pure, the blade might kill them, even if the actual cutting stroke isn't lethal by nature."

"Great. That doesn't make me feel any better."

Eolande made to say something more but Ouderling cut him off. "How about you just refrain from answering any more of my questions?"

Keeper of the Jewel

She unsheathed Soulbiter, grimacing as she expected to feel its sting, but it never came. Kneeling beside Eolande, she held the blade between them, her hand trembling.

Eolande raised hairless eyebrows. "You're not instilling much confidence in me."

"Ya, me either," Ouderling croaked. Taking a deep breath, she lowered the dagger's edge to the chunk of Focal Stone. "I'm sorry if I slip."

Eolande leaned away but held the shard steady and grimaced as Soulbiter grated on its surface.

"Remember...Allow your magical essence to find its way to the surface...Don't resist."

The odd sensation of something stirring in a deep recess of her mind left her light-headed. The dagger's blade reflected the increasing crimson glow that radiated from the shard where metal met rock, dazzling her further. Barely perceptible, like everything was happening in slow-motion, Soulbiter sank into the Focal Stone without the aid of her having to employ a sawing motion.

And then it was through. Soulbiter clanged off the jagged rim of the earth blood pool.

Eolande sprang back from the pool, half the shard held in red-tinged fingers.

Ouderling gasped. "Did I cut you?"

Eolande examined his fingers, switching the shard to his other hand, and shook his head. The crimson hue was but the light exuding from the severed crystal. He took a deep breath. "Now for the hard part."

"Hard part?" Ouderling stood on trembling legs.

Putting the piece he held into a small pouch on his belt, Eolande extended his hand. "It's time to bestow your sword with a magic befitting a future queen. A queen who will traverse the winds of fate on the back of dragonkind."

Keeper of the Jewel

Perch approached the earth blood pool. *"I'm ready."*

"Ready? For what?" Ouderling's gaze flicked between them.

"To truly become the dragon queen, I must bestow upon you our magic."

"Wait a minute. I never professed a desire to be a queen of the dragons. Heck, I don't even want to be the Queen of the Elves. I just want…I just want…"

Eolande, Perch, and even young Miragan stared at her, waiting.

She threw her hands in the air. "I don't know what I want." Her shoulders slumped and she looked at the ground, afraid her audience considered her a complete disaster. Exactly what Aelfwynne had insinuated.

A scaly snout pushed against the underside of her arm. She expected to see Perch, but it was his granddaughter who nuzzled into her, Miragan's small voice sounding in her head, *"Please, pretty lady. Granddaddy says we need you. He's afraid of what will happen to me once he's gone. Who will help me grow up if Granddaddy dies?"*

A thick lump formed in Ouderling's throat, threatening to choke her. She stepped back and knelt in front of the small wyvern, holding Miragan's snout between the heels of her hands as best she could with Soulbiter in one and the remaining piece of the Focal Stone in the other. The wyvern's sad face brought tears to her eyes.

She glanced at Perch and then at Eolande, but neither bothered to say anything.

"Granddaddy said you have the heart of a dragon."

"He did, did he?" Ouderling spat out a wet laugh.

Miragan nodded in her grasp. *"Uh huh."*

Big, round, brown eyes stared intently back at Ouderling, the innocence and sincerity of the wyvernling choked her even more. A newfound sense of purpose stirred from deep within. Straining to swallow, she whispered, "Well, you tell your Granddaddy that as long as I draw breath, I'll do everything in my power to make sure you fly the Crystal Cavern with your own grandchildren some day."

"Granddaddy's afraid you won't accept who you are."

Ouderling did a double take and glared at Perch.

Perch hung his head.

Ouderling returned her attention to the wyvernling, but said so that everyone present could hear, "You tell that old, leather bird that I *am* Ouderling Wys. Princess of South March and future heir to the Willow Throne. There isn't anyone in this world, or the next, that can take that away from me." She leaned in and kissed the wyvernling between her nostrils and intent, watery eyes. "I promise you, here and now, that although I don't believe any elf should ever consider themselves queen of the dragons, I will act on your behalf long after we have found a dragon, *or wyvern*, worthy to assert such a claim."

Miragan rubbed her head against Ouderling's side.

"This old, leather bird appreciates that," Perch's voice replaced Miragan's. *"I knew I was right about you."*

His voice dropped to a whisper in her head. Whether that meant nobody else could hear him, she had no idea.

"Remember what I told you. Master Eolande awaits at your leisure. Something he isn't fond of doing."

Ouderling stepped away from Miragan and spun to face Perch. "Right. You said something about bestowing magic on me?"

"Well, not on you, *exactly. Master Eolande needs you to assist him with your sword."*

She looked at the goblin who knelt beside the earth blood pool. "Master now, is he?"

Keeper of the Jewel

Perch raised his scaly brows; an odd sight to behold.

"I haven't been called that in a long time. There aren't many left who remember those days." Eolande indicated with a nod that she should join him by the earth blood. "But no matter. All I need you to do is grasp the sword's hilt with one hand up by the guard. Leave me room to access the tang."

He adjusted how the sword lay amongst the crystals lining the pool so that its tip was immersed in the earth blood, its gleaming surface shining light blue and dripping.

Eolande motioned for her to grasp the sword's hilt. "It's okay. The earth blood won't hurt you. At least not for a bit, but I hope to be done by then. Give me the other half of the shard."

She did as he asked and knelt in front of the earth blood. The pommel felt cool in her hand as she wrapped her fingers around its girth. Beside her, Eolande inspected the metal tip of the hilt, placing each shard against it and murmuring to himself.

Ouderling had no idea what was about to happen but the goblin's apparent hesitation piqued her curiosity. "What's the matter?"

"Nothing, actually. I'm impressed, is all. You managed to cut the shard perfectly in half."

"Is that good?"

"I'll say. Beyond good if you knew what I have in mind for the future."

She waited for him to elaborate, but he said no more on the subject. "Are you ready Perch?"

"*Yes,*" the wyvern responded and moved into position behind them.

Ouderling looked over her shoulder. "What's going on?"

Keeper of the Jewel

"Shh. I need you to concentrate like you did when you used Soulbiter. Focus on this point here." Eolande pointed to the shiny metal knob that comprised the end of the tang. "Try to sense the composition of the steel. Allow your magic to flow through you and into the sword."

Not waiting for a response, he concentrated on the end of the sword's hilt and broke into a rhythmic chant.

Ouderling frowned but didn't interrupt his litany of foreign words. Not sure what language he spoke, she assumed it must be goblin.

"Ignore Master Eolande..." Perch's soothing voice startled her, but as she listened, her tension eased and her mind opened. *"You are Nyxa's granddaughter...Embrace your heritage...It's time you accepted your mother's legacy...You are the essence of nature...You are the sword."*

The sword in her hand blurred. The Crystal Cavern spun slowly around her. Eolande's invocation sounded a long way off.

A hand clamped onto her shoulder, preventing her from falling into the earth blood, steadying her.

Just like with Soulbiter, a part of her that she had been faintly aware of seeped into the forefront of her mind—a separate entity thriving on its sudden release. It gathered her reeling emotions and organized her thoughts into a clarity she had never experienced before. For the first time in her life, she had attuned herself to her nature's essence.

"Excellent...I can sense it...You're doing great, princess." The wyvern's voice threatened to lull her to sleep, so comforting was its tone. *"Pay attention to Master Eolande...Allow his magic to guide yours...Meld with the earth blood."*

Afraid she was about to lose consciousness, she concentrated for all she was worth on the goblin's hand as he positioned the Focal Stone shard against the bulk of the tang's knob. Not sure of anything anymore, it was as if the steel around the shard emitted a white aura.

"Join your essence to his...Envision the amalgamation of steel and stone."

Euphoria made her gape in disbelief as the sensation of her magic tingled down her neck and crawled along the length of her outstretched arm. She watched in awe, as if she were a spectator of her own self-discovery. Tendrils of wispy, purple mist escaped her clenched fingers and crept down the hilt to meld with Eolande's magic.

The hilt warmed in her hand. A bright light burst forth from the space between the shard and the tang, forcing her to look away. She sucked in a deep breath, the action almost severing her link with her essence.

"Concentrate!"

Runnels of earth blood flowed against the pull of gravity, rolling up the sword's blade and around its guard. Too afraid to do anything but watch through squinted eyes, the earth blood enveloped her hand momentarily and then oozed to join the melding magic Eolande commanded.

The goblin nodded at Perch.

Perch forced his muzzle between them. The tips of his upward curving, lower jaw horns brushed Ouderling's shoulder.

"It's time to welcome the elves into the dragon fold."

A green vapour escaped Perch's nostrils, swirled in front of his face momentarily, and spiralled down to comingle with the magical essences already present.

"Now hold steady...Imagine the shard as part of the sword...Embed the stone."

Had she not been so enrapt, she would have questioned the wyvern as to what he meant, but as she watched, the steel

456

Keeper of the Jewel

tang appeared to liquify for the briefest of instants. Before her very eyes, the jewel sunk into the metal, but instead of absorbing the glowing, crimson stone, the steel molded itself around it. In the blink of an eye, the Focal Stone shard had mounted itself beautifully in the tang of the sword.

And then, just as quickly as the stone had shaped and set itself, the magical auras receded.

Shocked by the sudden change, Ouderling fell back onto her rump, her magic releasing its hold. She sat dazed, blinking at the sword in Eolande's hands as he pulled the blade clear of the earth blood and placed it in her lap.

"What's this?"

"It is Eolande's gift. The sum of his life's work has gone into that very moment. Treasure it, for I doubt the world will ever witness its likeness again."

"But why me? Surely there are other more worthy elves. Guardians who I'll never be able to live up to."

"Because, My Liege," Eolande took a knee and bowed his head. "You are the keeper of the jewel."

Keeper of the Jewel

The Face of Evil

Jyllana marveled at how ruthless and clinical Balewynd had been when she dispatched the two Grim Guard upon the battlements. Now that she faced certain death in the eye, she was surprised at how odd it felt that everything around her seemed to have slowed down. As if giving her a last long look at life.

Metal clad elves charged her position high above the outer bailey of Castle Grim while an archer held her in place with an unwavering bow. Nor did the irony of the cathedral's proximity escape her surreal observations, its hallowed shell promising salvation if she could only immerse herself within its sanctity.

As the first of the guards teetered on the edge of the castle wall, working up the nerve to jump up to where she crouched, she clung to the fleeting hope that she had steered them away from where Balewynd and Pecklyn had slipped through the window.

All she had to do now was decide how she wanted to die. Fight the half dozen Grim Guard and hopefully take a couple with her? Jump to her death? Those were really her only options. Putting down her daggers and surrendering, only to be dragged in front of the duke was a fate she refused to entertain.

But, as thoughts of the massacre in the Passage of Dolor assailed her frantic thoughts, it dawned on her that perhaps she might avenge their deaths. Although she doubted she would get anywhere near enough to attempt an attack on the duke, she would die content knowing she had tried.

She laid her daggers down and lifted her chin in defiance, her palms held before her in surrender.

A deafening screech was the only warning the Grim Guard received. Bathed in a swath of flames, the troops fell writhing to the ground, crying in agony as Dawnbreaker dropped from the shadows like a ballista bolt. Her tail bashed a crenellation, the resounding crunch of shattering stone not interrupting her flight past Jyllana's position.

Much to the lone archer's horror, Dawnbreaker's left wing swiped him off his feet and hurled him screaming over the outer wall; his bow tumbling through the air to land farther along the walkway.

"Find Pecklyn and get them out of there. The entire castle is on alert."

Dawnbreaker's gruff, female voice startled Jyllana as she watched the squat dragon rise into the night sky and veer off toward the plains fronting Castle Grim. Ballistae released their charges in the distance, but whether the large bolts came anywhere near Dawnbreaker's receding silhouette, Jyllana had no way to tell.

She scanned the walkway in both directions before leaping from the cathedral's eave to the outer wall and crouched low. Confirming no one else was close by, she sprinted back the way she had come and jumped the gap to the cathedral close to the broken stained-glass window. After a cursory look around, she slipped into the holy building's dark interior.

It took a moment to realize how her companions had descended to the marble floor. Not afraid of heights, she was still astonished at Pecklyn and Balewynd's audacious behaviour. Not many elves she knew would have attempted to walk along the thin ledge circumventing the high row of windows, let alone step across to the dragon statue and rappel its uncertain surface using a thin rope attached to a dubious-looking polearm.

Left with no choice, she jumped onto the marble elf's shoulders, taking a deep intake of breath as the statue swayed beneath her. Dropping quickly to the floor, her palms burned with the friction of the rope.

The interior of the cathedral was poorly lit, its sheer size making it seem like a massive, ornate cavern. She stood halfway between a large set of double doors far to her left, and a spacious, raised altar adorned with statues and pieces of grand furniture.

Being the daughter of parents employed by the royal army, Jyllana had been in several cathedrals around South March. Though their family had never been one to regularly attend religious functions in Orlythia, Jyllana knew enough about how things worked. There were ample perfunctory rites that most people felt obliged to attend throughout the year. Her parents had made it a point that she be present as well, ostensibly to give her a chance to rub elbows with nobility with the hopes of attaining a better station in life.

Unsure how to proceed, a cold jolt of fear shot through her as the massive doors flew open, emitting a wide beam of moonlight. Faces cast in shadow, several fully-armored Grim Guard streamed across the threshold.

Jyllana snuck back to the dragon statue and hunkered down, daggers in hand. If they found her, she was finished.

"What're we doing in here?" A male voiced echoed off the heights.

"Drake believes they might've accessed the cathedral from the wall."

Keeper of the Jewel

"That's crap! The wall's forty feet off the ground. Unless they sprouted wings, how would they have gotten down?"

Heavy footfalls and voices drew closer to Jyllana's hiding spot.

"Don't ask me," the first voice sounded almost on top of Jyllana. "Take it up with the captain."

"Don't be daft. I prefer my head where it is."

"There!" a female shrieked.

The fine hairs on Jyllana's neck stood on end. The elf's voice sounded close. Weapons being drawn rang off the walls.

"Well, I'll be. A rope," the first male voice said.

"Up there," another female voice chimed in, "the window's broken."

"You. Tell the captain we found the point of entry," the first male voice ordered.

Heavy footfalls receded into the distance. A hinge squealed, followed by a door banging shut, and silence settled over the cathedral floor.

Jyllana pressed her body against the back of the statue's base, afraid to breathe.

Feet shuffled as the Grim Guard moved throughout the dimly lit interior.

"Where'd you suppose they went?" the second male voice asked. "They must still be in here or we'd have spotted them in the bailey."

"Perhaps. Spread out and search everywhere. If they're here, they'll be lying low until the furor dies down."

Jyllana swallowed, regripping her daggers in sweaty palms.

Several of the Grim Guard moved away from the statue, but it was obvious by the hushed whispers of the two female guards that they remained close by.

Keeper of the Jewel

"They must be pretty desperate to enter this way. You think they're Guardians?" The first female voice asked.

"Ain't no one else bold enough to attempt such foolery," her companion replied. "You think one of our guys would scale down a rope like this? I'm surprised it held their weight."

"We should cut it down."

"Ya, right. Be my guest." The second female's voice dropped to a whisper. "I wonder…"

The soft clink of the Grim Guard's carefully placed footfalls told Jyllana that at least one of the females was slinking around the base of the statue. She swallowed and prepared to lunge as soon as the guard rounded the back corner of the pedestal.

A dark shadow followed the pointed end of a short sword as the Grim Guard's leg came into view, followed closely by her shoulder. The layered shadows of the cathedral floor cast her with an evil silhouette—her eyes as wide as Jyllana's, wary of what she might encounter.

Trying hard to staunch her trembling, Jyllana prepared to pounce.

"This way!" A male's voice echoed from somewhere far off. "They're in the tunnels!"

Just before she turned her attention on Jyllana, the Grim Guard froze. Straightening, she glanced back across the cathedral floor.

"Come on! We've got them!" The first female fled toward the altar. Her companion gave up her inspection and ran after her.

Jyllana resisted the urge to lower her shaking body to the floor, paralyzed by fear. She wasn't sure she would have been able to attack the Grim Guard and that troubled her. Other than the Passage of Dolor, the only real stress she had

Keeper of the Jewel

experienced as a Home Guard had been keeping track of Ouderling's elusive movements at Borreraig Palace whenever the rebellious princess decided she'd had enough of her handlers.

The noise in the cathedral lessened. In no time at all, the dark interior reverted to complete silence. Legs trembling, Jyllana rose from where she cowered to examine the expansive, shiny marble floor covered with row upon row of wooden pews.

The Grim Guard had run toward the altar's far side and disappeared without a trace. Jyllana's first instinct was to flee in the opposite direction, away from danger, but she chided herself. She had entered the cathedral to warn Balewynd and Pecklyn not to come back this way. Judging from the reaction of the Grim Guard, the duke's troops had discovered where the Guardians had gone.

A deep breath did nothing to still her shaking limbs, nor help calm her pounding heart. Calling on a strength she didn't know she possessed, she light-stepped across the open floor and followed the front of the altar around to its other side.

A narrow hallway circumvented the dais' sidewall, the long passageway aglow in soft rushlight. Ahead, a dark hole gaped in the middle of the floor at the base of an open hatch.

Muted voices reached her, emanating from the tunnel below. Balewynd and Pecklyn must have had found a passageway beneath the cathedral. One that now brimmed with a squad of Grim Guard hard on their heels.

Taking a last look around, she sheathed her daggers and plucked a rushlight from the wall.

As she descended a steep flight of narrow steps into the ground, her blood ran cold. The squeal of a hinge could only mean one thing. Reinforcements had entered the cathedral.

Keeper of the Jewel

She stopped halfway down the steps and climbed back up long enough to lower the hatch, cringing as its hinges imitated the squeal of the cathedral's door.

With any luck, it would take the newcomers a while to discover where the noise had originated.

Her light footsteps were muffled further by the closeness of the musty tunnel. Not knowing where she was going, she hoped she wouldn't be faced with an intersection. Every so often, a voice reached her from up ahead, but it was the noise of the hatch opening behind her that made her cringe.

She staggered under the chilling revelation. The reinforcements had located the access door. If the ones she chased slowed or turned around, she would be trapped.

Keeper of the Jewel

The Same Mercy

"**Brimstone,**" Balewynd said matter-of-factly, noticing Pecklyn's reaction to the acrid aroma.

A soft, orange glow permeated the absolute darkness of the tunnel ahead. They had been underground for a long time, ever since Pecklyn had discerned a magical essence recently employed on a hidden hatchway in the cathedral floor. Little known to most, he possessed a rare ability to detect magic's usage.

He assured Balewynd it wasn't Aelfwynne's and added, "I doubt anyone in the duke's staff would damage Castle Grim property on purpose. Strange as this sounds, I suspect someone else has come in search of the high wizard."

Balewynd frowned. "The wraith?"

Pecklyn's face twisted in thought. "I doubt it. He's working with the duke, isn't he?"

Balewynd shrugged, not happy to contemplate someone else in the mix.

They found their way into the dungeon levels, hiding in various cells along the way to avoid detection by random guard patrols.

They had been underground for a lot longer than Balewynd cared to consider, slinking into the bedrock. She had a sinking feeling they wouldn't reach the surface again until morning.

465

Keeper of the Jewel

Peering into the darkness behind her before starting toward the light, she absently wondered how Jyllana was faring on the wall. The princess' protector seemed competent enough, but she was only one elf. Putting her concern for Jyllana's safety out of her mind, she put a finger to her lips and whispered, "Up ahead is Crag's Forge."

The flicker of the dying torch Pecklyn had scrounged from the dungeon levels provided barely enough light for them to see much beyond where they stood—its glare diminishing their dark vision ability.

Her back to the wall, Balewynd slipped up the tunnel on her own and paused to listen at the entrance. Hearing nothing but the infernal roar of the forge, she motioned for Pecklyn to join her, and peered into the chamber. A blast of warm air slammed her in the face.

It had been a long time since her last visit to the fabled wizard's forge, but she remembered it fondly. Her father had brought her here on many occasions to escape whatever festivity the duke was presiding over in the drafty halls above. Her father had relished the rare moments of peace and quiet but she had learned later that the real reason he had brought her to Crag's Forge was to protect her from the lewd, vulgar, noble letches who frequented Orlythe's galas.

She smiled grimly. She had loved visiting the forge, mesmerized by the lava endlessly passing behind the open face of the forge. Her father had delighted in pitching different objects into the flow, and together they would "ooh" and "ahh," as whatever he held in a set of long tongs was consumed by the molten rock.

On occasion, he would let her hold the tongs—always with a loving hand hanging onto her to keep her from being pulled into the fiery cascade. She couldn't recall how many sets of tongs they had ruined.

Keeper of the Jewel

Stepping across the threshold, she said louder than she had spoken since entering the castle, "Its empty!"

A quick scan of the forge area confirmed her fear. She had been wrong about where the duke was holding Aelfwynne. Her legs threatened to buckle as another thought crossed her mind. She stared at the lava cascading beyond the gap in the far wall. "What if they killed him already?"

Pecklyn brushed by her and approached the undying fires of Crag's Forge but stopped to examine the granite slab in the centre of the room—a broken length of chain dangling from its side. He inspected the chain and looked at Balewynd. "I sense the same magic I detected in the cathedral."

He let the chain drop and scanned the chamber, his attention coming to rest on a spot between two large cabinets. Kneeling, he lifted a broken piece of curved steel and sniffed at it. His nostrils curled up as if repulsed by what he smelled. "That's the stain of Maral, I'm sure of it."

Balewynd accepted the severed metal. "It's a manacle. They must have had him chained down here." Her attention returned to the forge. "You don't think they…?"

Pecklyn followed her gaze. "I wouldn't put it past them, but I don't think so." He nodded at the steel in her black gloved fingers. "The broken restraint and the cathedral hatch are telling. If I'm not mistaken, someone beat us here."

With everything that had happened recently, Balewynd wasn't sure if that was good or not. She opened the cabinet doors, the vials and contents in various sized pottery meaning nothing to her. The extent of her elven magic was little better than the average citizen of South March. "See anything worth taking?"

Keeper of the Jewel

Pecklyn didn't bother to look. He shook his head and started for the exit. "We'd better get back to the dragons before sunrise or we'll be trapped."

She took a last look around and followed Pecklyn and his torch up the tunnel. It was hard to discern how much time they had spent underground, but she doubted they would get back to the north wall to call the dragons before sunrise. With the castle on alert, being picked up would be problematic during the day. She gritted her teeth. She couldn't worry about that now. They hadn't found Aelfwynne. That meant they had to search the individual cells in the dungeon levels.

Pecklyn ran several paces ahead, the torch light bobbing up and down, its scant light revealing nuances in the tunnel walls. He slowed to navigate the narrow section. Turning sideways, he disappeared around the bulk of the granite outcropping. Just as quickly, he re-emerged, his face twisted in shock.

Her jagged-edged dagger instinctively in hand, Balewynd squinted to see beyond Pecklyn's retreat. "What is it?"

"Grim Guard! Lots of them!" He pushed her back down the tunnel.

The scrape of metal on rock followed them toward Crag's Forge as the Grim Guard squeezed their armoured bodies through the narrows.

Spinning around inside the forge chamber on the far side of the central pedestal, Balewynd faced the open entranceway.

Pecklyn searched the walls. "Is there no other way out of here?"

Balewynd shook her head, her gaze flicking to the roaring forge. "Not one I'd recommend."

Keeper of the Jewel

"That's not funny." Pecklyn took up a position on the other side of the granite slab and muttered, "You picked a fine time to find a sense of humour."

The first Grim Guard charged around the corner, stumbled twice, and hit the back wall of Crag's Forge, grabbing at his neck and gurgling as he slid to the ground—a throwing knife embedded in his throat.

The next guard into the chamber ducked instinctively, searching for the knife thrower. Locking eyes with Balewynd, the female Grim Guard never saw Pecklyn's saber whistle through the space separating them. The blade took her on the bridge of the nose, dropping her to the ground, never to see again.

Two more Grim Guard entered the fray, the first barely raising his sword in time to block Balewynd's dagger thrust as she charged at him.

Pecklyn dispatched the second elf who had begun to swing a heavy mace at Balewynd's exposed shoulder. The elf howled at the sight of his dismembered upper arm but his agony was short-lived. Pecklyn drove the end of his saber beneath the bottom of his boiled-leather chest armour, thrusting it upward with a killing stroke.

"Hold!" A deep voice called out.

Eyes rivetted on the entryway, no one else entered the forge.

Pecklyn pulled his saber free of the dying elf, stepping over him to stand beside Balewynd.

"Throw down your weapons!" the voice commanded.

"Come in here and take them from us!" Balewynd shouted back, her adrenaline surging.

"You're trapped. You can't hope to win free!"

Balewynd raised her eyebrows. If the Grim Guard believed they were strong enough to take them on, they wouldn't have stopped in the tunnel. She nodded at Pecklyn, her partner in most things, and instinctively they burst into the tunnel, working as one.

The Grim Guard who had been issuing the orders was about to respond, but his mouth hung open as he parried Pecklyn's saber. Before he could utter a sound, Balewynd's dagger punctured his throat; not once, but twice. He fell back into the startled female elf behind him, knocking the crossbow bolt from the unwieldy weapon she was arming.

The female Grim Guard cowered behind raised arms, providing little defense against Pecklyn's slashing blade.

Four burly Grim Guard remained in the cramped tunnel waiting their turn to enter Crag's Forge. Shocked by how efficiently their companions had been cut down they began to back away.

Balewynd sprung at the first elf as he turned to flee, dragging his superior weight to the tunnel floor beneath her; her serrated blade inflicting multiple stab wounds before they came to rest.

The next elf in line's mistake was to think he could take Balewynd out with a swipe of his short axe. Pecklyn's saber took the elf's wrist in mid swing. Tilting his head to avoid being hit by the dislodged axe, Pecklyn directed his recovery swing to slash the anguished elf's throat.

Balewynd pushed past Pecklyn, leaping the dying Grim Guard at his feet, and sprinted after the remaining two elves—determined not to let them sound the alarm.

Having no choice but to slow down at the narrows, the trailing Grim Guard spun to face Balewynd, short sword at the ready.

Balewynd slowed but never stopped her advance. Her bright blue eyes narrowed. "You chose the wrong girl to harass, Olf."

Keeper of the Jewel

Recognition showed in the elf's wide eyes. "Balewynd Tayn? Is that you?"

"You're one of the reasons my father sent me to Highcliff," she growled, closing on him. Anticipating.

"Wait. I was younger then. And foolish."

"And I was vulnerable. And helpless." She faked a rushed step, deftly avoided Olf's hastily swung sword, and moved inside his reach.

Olf's free hand surprised Balewynd. He caught her wrist and twisted; his brute strength far superior. A cynical sneer split his hairless lips for but the briefest of moments before he doubled over her raised leg, her knee taking him in the groin with enough force to knock him against the confines of the narrows.

"Olf! Grab her!" The last Grim Guard had stopped in the tight space, but couldn't get at Balewynd through Olf's body blocking the tunnel.

Olf twisted Balewynd's dagger, pulling her against him. He smashed his forehead into her face, mashing her nose against her skull.

A white light exploded in Balewynd's head, rendering her barely aware of the dagger slipping from her fingers.

"Perhaps you'll come around in the end, eh, you spoiled chamberlain's brat? The old fool had it coming."

White rage clenched Balewynd's muscles. She thrashed and kicked and tried to head butt Olf, but she was like a child in his grasp.

The last Grim Guard pushed Olf into the wider tunnel and pulled a dagger from his belt. "Hold her stead—"

The elf dropped limp without a sound—the fletches of a crossbow bolt protruding from the wiry hair of his mustache.

Keeper of the Jewel

"Nobody puts a hand on Balewynd," Pecklyn emerged from the dark, tossing the spent crossbow aside and drawing his saber.

Olf released her and raised his hands in defeat. "I'm unarmed. I surrender."

Pecklyn placed the tip of his saber against the elf's cheek. Intense eyes on Olf, he asked Balewynd, "You alright?"

Balewynd leaned against the tunnel wall, trying to catch her breath, blood streaming from her battered nose. She nodded.

"What should we do with this elf? You know him?"

Balewynd lifted her head to glare at Olf. "He's one of…Orlythe's preferred…noble's sons."

"One of the ones you told me about?"

She nodded, chest heaving, eyes watering.

Pecklyn increased the pressure on his saber, drawing blood.

"P-please. Spare me. I beg you." Terror visible in Olf's eyes, he shook his head ever so slightly in denial.

Pecklyn's saber pierced Olf's cheek, ground past his upper teeth, and slid into his brain.

Olf's body spasmed and went limp, sliding to the ground, dead.

Pecklyn spat on Olf's corpse. Pulling his sword free of the gory wound, he wiped it against Olf's blank stare. "I give to you the same mercy you gave those who begged *you* to stop."

Keeper of the Jewel

Belonging

Miragan nuzzled Ouderling between the shoulder blades, knocking the princess forward a couple of steps, almost causing her to lose her grip on the wondrous sword in her hands.

"Miragan," Perch chided.

"It's okay." Ouderling inspected the hilt of her sword, her fingers lingering on the crimson gemstone imbedded in the tang, and turned to face the wyvernling. "You're a strong little girl, aren't you?"

Miragan nodded.

It was hard to tell with wyverns, but Ouderling was sure Miragan blushed. "Someday you'll make a Guardian very happy..." She trailed off, noting Eolande shaking his head. "What?"

"Wyverns only fly goblins."

Ouderling frowned. "Why's that?"

"Grimclaw's Law." Eolande said as if that were common knowledge. He shrugged. "Apparently only elves are worthy enough to fly a dragon."

"But Master Aelfwynne flew to Castle Grim on dragonback."

"True, but he's the high wizard."

Faced with the brutal reality of the goblin's statement, Ouderling saw the underlying truth. She doubted Grimclaw was the only one behind the prejudicial tenets. Likely a high-

Keeper of the Jewel

ranking elf or two had something to do with the discriminating laws. "Well, that's not right."

Eolande raised a skeptical brow. "Right or not, that's the way of the world."

"*Was* the way of the world." Ouderling lifted a haughty chin in defiance. "When I become queen, many injustices will be abolished."

She smiled at Miragan but Perch's voice startled her senses.

"That's a fine thing to say, princess. I only wish I could live long enough to see it."

"Don't say that. You're not dying." Ouderling stepped beside Perch and stared him in the eye. "Are you?"

The pleasant sound of his laugh filled Ouderling with a peace she hadn't known in a long time but his words cut that sensation short.

"We all must die. Eolande and I near the end of our flight. Without the crystals and the proximity of the earth blood we would've passed long ago, so don't be sad for us. Neither wyvern nor goblin are long lived like dragons—or elves, for that matter."

"But look at you. You both look healthy to me."

Perch hung his head. Miragan shuffled in beside him, her sad voice pulling at Ouderling's heart.

"You can't die, grandpappy. You're my bestest friend."

A somber quiet enveloped the cavern.

Ouderling listened to the gurgle of the earth blood, not knowing what to say.

Eolande broke the silence. "Perch and I are tired. We've experienced many things in our lifetime. Suffered much hardship and pain over the last ten centuries. *But,* we've also known great joy. We were fortunate enough to witness the

Keeper of the Jewel

formation of South March and have even spoken with the Dragon Witch. Not many alive can attest to that."

"No, but…" Ouderling was at a loss.

"There are no buts. Perch and I have flown our course. Soon we must succumb to the inevitable rest calling for us." The ancient goblin stepped up to Miragan and hugged her head in his short arms. "It's up to you, young Miragan, to carry on our tradition. Do you think you're up to tending the Crystal Cavern when we're gone?"

The wyvernling nodded in his grasp, but the underlying sadness in her eyes brought tears to Ouderling.

"Don't cry for us." Eolande's gaze included Ouderling as well as Miragan. "The knowledge that you two will lead the way into the future gladdens our heart. We shall leave this world content that our lives have been blessed by the presence of Miragan and Ouderling. Thus, the cycle completes itself."

The bed chamber Ouderling shared with Jyllana felt ever so empty without the presence of her long-time protector. As dim as the small area was in the glow of a single candle wavering on top of the cabinet, it seemed blacker than a moonless night without the radiance of the green-eyed, red-haired gem.

Ouderling had barely stopped her heart from breaking after leaving the Crystal Cavern to get some much-needed rest, but her chest grew tight again. If something were to happen to Jyllana by her uncle's hand, she vowed she would march through the Passage of Dolor, grotdraak or not, swim Lake Grim, and tear the elf's throat out with her bare hands.

She plunked herself on the little stool in front of the dresser and considered her reflection in the mirror. Red, puffy eyes, surrounded by black rings, peered through the mess of her hacked tresses. The sight did little to cheer her up.

The mystical dagger, Soulbiter, made its presence known—its hilt jabbing into her ribs. Adjusting it, she had an idea. Soulbiter's edge was keener than any blade around. She pulled it free of its sheath, recalling her vow to Miragan. It was time to take control of her life before it spiralled beyond her reach.

Soulbiter made clean, quick work of straightening the mess she had made of her hair. When she laid the beautifully crafted blade on the bureau, she smiled. Content for the first time in a long time with the reflection that stared back at her.

That done, it felt as if her eyes had filled with sand, but there was still one more thing she wanted to do before succumbing to sleep.

Piece by painstaking piece, she laid out the fancy armour Xantha had provided for her on the pallet and proceeded to don the suit. The tight, leather breeks and matching chest covering fit snuggly over her bare skin. She took a moment to appreciate the surprising comfort and warmth the long-sleeved undergarment provided.

It took a while to remember how everything went on, but with a dogged perseverance she hadn't known she was capable of, she outfitted herself—marvelling as each segment fit into place, and how well the armour conformed to her slight frame. From the toes of her metal boots to the detailed craftmanship of the black metal cuirass, the fancy suit of armour allowed her to move freely.

Pulling on the forearm-length gauntlets, she unsheathed her sword and stood before the bureau to examine herself in the mirror, pleasantly shocked by the transformation.

Keeper of the Jewel

Staring back at her was the vision of a warrior of the highest calibre. Tired as she was, the sight of her new self exorcised the lingering doubts in her mind.

Princess Ouderling of South March smiled. A sense of belonging flushed her with a maturity she had never known before.

She pulled the last piece over her head—the open-faced helm sporting two ivory horns. Holding her sword in a mock battle stance, she was prepared in that moment to put aside her nay-sayers. She *was* a Highcliff Guardian.

The newly acquired gemstone, seeming to shine of its own accord, glinted in the mirror.

She held her chin high, rivetted by the reflection admiring her. Just like Eolande had said. She was the keeper of the jewel.

Keeper of the Jewel

Too Late

Pecklyn grabbed Balewynd by the arm, preventing her from charging up the tunnel toward the lower dungeon level. "You're hurt."

In typical Balewynd style, she ripped free of his grasp. He feared she might take a swing at him.

"You're bleeding."

Balewynd located her dagger and wiped at the blood oozing from her broken nose. She spat a wad of crimson on top of Olf's head. "It'll heal."

With that, she was off. Stepping over the elf with the crossbow bolt buried in his face, she disappeared through the cleft, not waiting for the light of Pecklyn's torch.

Balewynd's bare shoulders were covered with blood where she had wiped her damaged face, but nothing Pecklyn said would slow her down. He knew better than to argue. All he could do was try to keep pace as she burst through a simple wooden door and entered the lower dungeons.

The dimly lit honeycomb of short passageways smelled of urine, rust, and rot, mixed with a heady aroma of burnt pitch and damp loam. Methodically, they examined each cell. Even though they all appeared empty on the lower level, they checked them all.

Time slowed to a crawl. Pecklyn couldn't believe how many cells comprised the dungeon labyrinth. Climbing a curving ramp, they ascended to the middle level and began

478

their search anew—this time encountering the wreckage of prisoners—some so far gone that any resemblance to an elf had deserted them a long time ago. The smell of human waste was enough to make them gag.

Upon reaching the top level, they looked at each other in despair. Neither believed Aelfwynne would be housed amongst the common rabble serving shorter sentences.

A cursory inspection of the main corridor showed them that most cell doors sat ajar. They had no sooner passed the first set of empty cells when a distant creak and loud clang told them they weren't alone. Pecklyn grabbed Balewynd's forearm and held her back to prevent her from running headlong into whoever had joined them beneath the keep. Ducking into an open cell, Pecklyn didn't have to guess who it might be. It wouldn't be long before the entire Grim Guard garrison flooded the tunnels.

As much as that thought sobered him, his mind drifted to the one person he didn't relish crossing paths with. The duke's human wizard. Afara Maral was sure to enter the fray at some point. When that happened, he held no illusion that he and Balewynd would be shown little mercy.

He studied Balewynd's battered face, bruising already, darkening the skin around her eyes. Depending on how bad the brute had hurt her, it might not be long before her eyes swelled shut.

He put his hands on her bare shoulders, her skin sticky with blood, and stared her in the eye. "Okay. Let's do this. We don't have much time. If we don't win free soon, we're as good as dead."

She swallowed noticeably, the fire in her pained eyes intense.

"I know I don't have to say this, but don't hold back."

Keeper of the Jewel

She shook her head and tried to leave the cell but he held on a moment longer, forcing her to look back at him.

"No matter what happens, always know this. I love you, Bale."

Her features narrowed as if she resented his words. Pulling free of his grasp, she exited the cell without waiting for him, and charged toward the oncoming noise.

Pecklyn smiled as he ran in her wake, pitying the first few Grim Guard she encountered.

It didn't take her long to outdistance him. One moment she was several strides ahead and the next she had disappeared around a corner. Pecklyn feared her bloodlust would lead her into making a fatal mistake. He ran faster than he ever had as chaos erupted ahead.

Rounding a corner, he slowed to allow his brain time to digest what was happening. Elves were shouting. Some in pain, others in outrage.

Crouched on the back of a large, unmoving, female Grim Guard, Balewynd hissed at half a dozen heavily armoured troops who had been taken by surprise by the ferocious Highcliff Guardian in black leather, her upper body splattered with dried blood.

"There's another!" The biggest Grim Guard pointed at Pecklyn. "Get them, you fools, there's only two!"

An ear-piercing screech lifted the hair on Pecklyn's neck. "Threeee!"

From beyond the light of the last Grim Guard's torch, the high ponytail of Ouderling Wys' protector bobbed into view, the black clad Home Guard a blur of movement as she leapt at the Grim Guard closest to her through an open cell door. The elf went down in an agonized heap before he knew what had hit him, his torch hissing and sputtering as it bounced off the wall and tumbled to the ground amongst the startled Grim Guard huddled in a knot of confusion.

Jyllana's distraction was all the invitation Balewynd and Pecklyn required. Lumped together in the narrow passageway between cells, the Grim Guard fell quickly to a frenzy of slashes and stabs.

The battle was over almost before it had started. Two highly trained Highcliff Guardians and a member of the queen's elite Royal Guard had dispatched their targets with ruthless efficiency.

Pecklyn smiled wide as he hugged Jyllana and spun her slight frame around in the tunnel. "Are we glad to see you."

Jyllana's spooked eyes held his for but a moment before she removed herself from his embrace and started back the way she had come. "Don't thank me so fast. There's more coming. Lots of them. They're swarming the tunnels."

Pecklyn exchanged a concerned glance with Balewynd. Their escape route was cut off.

Jyllana had no sooner spoken than the distant sound of squealing hinges got their attention, followed by the commotion of marching feet.

Pecklyn ran beyond Jyllana and listened, holding his hand up for his companions to wait, but Balewynd pushed by him. "Bale! There are too many."

"Follow me," his Guardian companion whispered harshly and darted toward the coming troops.

Pecklyn allowed Jyllana to go ahead. Looking back, he half expected to see a squad of Grim Guard coming at them from behind.

Balewynd stopped at an intersection and motioned for them to take the left tunnel. It led between several cells, turned a corner to the left, and ended at a solid wall.

Keeper of the Jewel

Pecklyn considered the space. They could all fit behind the wall but doubted it would do them any good. The Grim Guard were sure to search the side passages.

He was about to creep back down the tunnel to check on their advance but stopped and looked around in alarm as the ground rumbled beneath his feet. "What the…?"

Balewynd leaned out of a gap that had opened in the end wall, raising her eyebrows twice before disappearing into the fissure.

Pecklyn frowned and ran back. A hidden passageway, barely tall enough to accommodate an average-sized elf, gaped where solid stone had stood moments before.

Jyllana was nowhere to be seen, but Balewynd waited on the threshold, her discoloured face swollen and raw. "We could really use that torch."

Pecklyn smiled and handed it to her. Taking a last look up the cell tunnel, he followed her into the darkness. "How'd you know this was here?"

She leered. "Really?"

"Right. Right. The daughter of the head chamberlain." His last word was clipped, rising in volume as the ground trembled beneath the weight of a slab of rock grating into place to seal off the wall.

"Not many know of these byways," Balewynd's voice sounded different in the close confines of the narrow tunnel—Jyllana's sweating complexion visible just beyond her as the Home Guard walked back to them. "You don't expect the duke or his wizard to walk past those he imprisoned whenever he feels the need to attend Crag's Forge, do you? There are several of these byways throughout the dungeon levels."

Pecklyn ducked to keep from scuffing the top of his head. "They could've made them bigger."

Keeper of the Jewel

Balewynd handed Jyllana the torch and motioned for her to proceed. "Not to worry. It's not long."

What the term 'long' meant to Balewynd differed appreciably from what it meant to Pecklyn, but eventually the tunnel opened onto a larger one. Before long, they were confronted by a steep flight of flagstone steps at the end of the reinforced, earthen passageway.

"Where's it go?" Pecklyn asked, pausing to listen for pursuit.

"It empties into an antechamber next to the throne room."

The way Balewynd casually threw that out there sounded like they were about to exit in the middle of a distant field, far from harm's way. His eyes widened. "It does what?"

"You heard me." She shrugged. "Don't have much choice. With everyone flooding the lower levels looking for us, the castle will probably be empty."

"Probably? The duke's elite guard won't be looking for us. They'll stay with him."

Balewynd shrugged again as if it mattered little. She started to climb. "Then we'd better hope the pretender is elsewhere."

Pecklyn looked at Jyllana for help, but the princess' protector said nothing. Sighing, he ascended the steps, checking to ensure his saber sat properly in its sheath and his daggers were easily accessible.

An iron-bound door blocked their progress, but it opened quietly under Balewynd's touch. "Thankfully, it's only locked from the outside," she whispered and stuck her head out. "Clear."

They entered a small storeroom lined with shelves bearing supplies for sconces and rushlights. Balewynd carefully opened the exit door to inspect the illuminated hallway beyond. After a moment she pulled the door open long enough to allow Jyllana and Pecklyn to tip-toe into the corridor.

Pecklyn tossed the torch down the steps, not caring that it was still burning. Though he had been in Grim Keep on many occasions, he had no idea where they were. He waited for Balewynd to softly push the door shut.

"That leads to the throne room's main entrance," Balewynd tipped her head. "Stay close."

She led them in the opposite direction, climbing a set of narrow steps only to descend another flight shortly afterward. They hurried down a side corridor that emptied onto the long approach to the throne room near the keep's main entrance.

Pecklyn appreciated Balewynd's knowledge of the castle. She had led them in a round-a-bout fashion to the same place they would have ended up had they tried to sneak past the throne room, but this way, they were able to avoid detection by the duke's elite guard if the duke sat on the Lava Throne.

Balewynd motioned them against the inside wall of the corridor as footfalls echoed in the cavernous foyer fronting ornate, black doors.

Three Grim Guard stormed across the open space and left the keep, the tall doors yawning open long enough for them to notice sunshine glinting off the marble floor.

"Great," Balewynd muttered.

Jyllana's head swung back and forth as if expecting more troops. "What?"

"Its daylight," Pecklyn answered. "At least midafternoon judging by the way the light refracted off the floor."

Jyllana frowned.

Worried, Pecklyn stared at Balewynd as he elaborated for Jyllana's sake, "It means we're too late. We'll never escape the castle during the day."

Keeper of the Jewel

Path of the Errant Knight

Scale stretched his back, relieved to finally stand straight again. He had lost all track of time wandering through the tight confines of Dithreab's warrens, but by the cast of the shadows beneath thick cloud cover, he estimated it was somewhere in the middle of the night.

The air was cooler in the upper foothills of the Mardeireach as the semblance of a path beneath their feet led them along the slopes of the second tallest mountain in the vast, coastal chain. Though not snow-capped like its neighbours to the south—their distant peaks catching the moonlight—Faelyn's Nest was reputedly the gateway to the mystic lands west of the Niad Ocean.

Scale scratched at his scalp. How he and Aelfwynne were ever going to make it back to Highcliff while travelling in the wrong direction was troubling. If the rumours of the trail they sought were to be believed, their remains were likely to become part of the local history of the fabled area.

Dithreab scrabbled along the pathway and leaped onto a small rock. Wooden hands on where his hips should be, the wood sprite shook his head. "The time fer haste is at hand. Ain't about t' be getting' where yer needin' t' be, standin' around."

Aelfwynne muttered low enough for only Scale to hear, "You best listen to the imp, but beware. Who knows what trickery he has planned?"

Keeper of the Jewel

Scale did a double take, but the high wizard said no more.

"Remember. Stick to me slighe an' dinnae stray else ye rue the day ya didnae listen t' Dithreab. Ye hears me, ol' friend?"

"Aye. Don't have much choice the way you blather on." Aelfwynne strode past Scale and stared down at Dithreab, clearly unhappy about their circumstance.

Appearing crestfallen, Dithreab's peculiar features dropped into what could only be construed as a pout.

Aelfwynne rolled his eyes and took a knee, looking Dithreab in the eye. "Thank you."

"Again?" Dithreab met his gaze with a smirk.

The high wizard took a deep breath. Scale had seen it before in the little time he had known Aelfwynne. It was the goblin's way of reigning in his impatience.

"Again." Aelfwynne nodded. "Though I'm not happy about our present course, I'm thankful that you unbound me and have spirited us away from Orlythe's probing dragons."

"Bah. Tis nothin'. Yer real test lies ahead."

"You sure you can't join us? Scale and I would be appreciative of your...counsel."

Dithreab shook his head. "Ye knows I cannae. But yer not t' be worryin'. At least about Orlythe's beasties. Ol' Dithreab'll keep 'em occupied, of that ye can be certain."

At the mention of dragons, Scale scanned the night sky. Unless one was flying low, they would be hard to spot against the brooding clouds.

"Och, aye, I almost forgot." Dithreab grinned at Aelfwynne as he shrugged free of his rucksack and held it between them. "Take this."

"What's this?" Aelfwynne accepted the small sack and worried at the taught drawstring.

"It's me gift to ye, dragon breath. A wee token of me friendship."

Keeper of the Jewel

Aelfwynne frowned at the wood sprite's words. Using his pointed fingernails, he pulled the sack open and upended its contents into his palm. A dark crimson gemstone glinted in the faint light. He cast a quizzical look at Dithreab.

"Pretty, eh? Had it for as long as I can remember. Never had the opportunity to use it. Do ye recognize it?"

The high wizard turned the gem over in his palm, inspecting the multi-faceted stone and nodding. "Mmm, I remember the stone. What's it do?"

To Scale, Dithreab's answering grin appeared more malicious than pleasant.

"Let's just say, it'll pull ye out of an irrevocable position. Lucky for me, there ain't been a time that me magic ain't been enough t' save me."

The wood sprite's voice dropped in timbre as his beady eyes took in Scale, causing the elf to shiver.

"Where yer goin', I'm t' be thinkin' yer gonna have use of it. But, be warned. The magic of the stone can only be used once, so use it wisely."

"Always a riddle with you, knot head," Aelfwynne complained. "If you're not willing to tell me what it does, how'll I know how to activate it?"

Scale gasped as Dithreab's mouth revealed pointed teeth he hadn't noticed before.

"Oh, ye'll know alright. Ye just need t' think o' me an' the stone'll do the rest."

Aelfwynne stared hard at his ancient friend. Shaking his head, he held out his free hand, a sad look on his face. "I guess this is good-bye then."

"Dinnae be sad. The way the two of ye are goin', yer like t' be joinin' me shortly."

Keeper of the Jewel

Scale swallowed his discomfort at Dithreab's ominous words. The wood sprite's hand looked tiny in Aelfwynne's small claws as they dispensed with their good-byes.

After Aelfwynne backed away, Scale approached the stone Dithreab stood on and gazed down at the little creature, wondering if he would ever witness such a sight again. "Good-bye, Master Dithreab. It was an honour to meet you."

A broad smile lit up the sprite's face. "Of course it was laddie. Ain't often one such as ye is blessed by one of me kind. Remember me well."

Scale laughed despite himself—a warmth infusing him with a happiness he hadn't experienced in many a long day. Dithreab was a character he wasn't likely to soon forget. He wanted to say more to the magical creature, something profound, but the words wouldn't come. Noting Aelfwynne trudging up the steep path ahead, he forced a smile. "Well, I guess I'd better get going."

Dithreab cocked a knowing look. "Ye best be watchin' what ye say in his company. Be sure of yerself laddie. That be the way into his confidence."

Scale frowned. Nothing the sprite said made much sense.

"Go! Shoo! Look after him fer me, would ya? He's the only friend I've got. He may be gruff and insufferable on the outside, but dinnae let him fool ya. He's got the heart of Rhiannon, that one. Just don't be tellin' him I said so, ye hear?"

Scale laughed louder. "I won't."

Setting off after the goblin's green hide, Scale was afraid to pinch himself in case he was dreaming. He put his mind to keeping pace with the surprisingly fast-moving high wizard. The meandering slighe ascended the heights of Faelyn's Nest, an onerous climb at the best of times, but if they wished to evade the duke's aerial searchers, they needed to get as deep into the mountains as possible before the sun crested the peaks unseen in the east.

"You sure this is the right path?" Scale stopped to take a pull from a small waterskin the wood sprite had found for them. It wasn't any bigger than the palm of his hand, which meant it would have been massive on Dithreab's back, but it was better than having nothing at all. Fortunately, fresh running streams were plentiful on the lower slopes of Faelyn's Nest.

Aelfwynne waited for his turn at the waterskin, the wisp of fine hair on his head blowing in the strong winds of the higher elevation. "You seen any other paths in this forsaken forest?"

"No, but—"

"Then it's the right path!" Aelfwynne snatched the suede bladder from Scale's hand and squeezed it dry. Wiping his fleshless lips, he said, "Sun's about to rise. Judging by our altitude, we're getting close to the Path of the Errant Knight."

Just the mention of the fabled trail raised an alarm in Scale's head. Fascinated by everything there was to know about the history of South March and the fiefdoms that had held sway before the rise of the elven nation, he had paid great attention to the Chroniclers back in Orlythia while growing up in the shadow of his father. Part of that had been due to his father's overbearing attitude. If Scale had returned home after a session with the royal teachers and wasn't able to provide a comprehensive account of what he'd learned that day, his father would assign him back-breaking chores around the homestead that no normal elfling his age should have to endure. As much as he had detested his father at the time, he had learned to appreciate how helpful the hard-nosed tactics had been when he joined the Home Guard.

The thick forest canopy made it impossible to see where they were in conjunction with the mountainside, but just like Dithreab's Slighe south of the wood sprite's home, if that was indeed where the creature lived, the impenetrable leafy ceiling prevented searching eyes from spotting them from the sky.

Watching his companion's receding backside, it seemed as if the goblin was in a nastier mood than he had been in before they had encountered Dithreab. He raised his eyebrows and muttered, "Great."

It was a miracle they were able to follow the faint path in the early morning twilight, but by midafternoon Aelfwynne stopped at its terminus and studied a well-trodden trail. Judging by the high wizard's perceptible trepidation, Scale couldn't help but wonder if they would have been better off getting lost.

A wide roadway, for it was much grander than any trail Scale had envisioned when they set out from Dithreab's warren, meandered along the barren terrain above the treeline. It disappeared over a high ridge to the north, but he knew their course lay south, around the western shores of Lake Grim—the lake's icy waters partially visible through a layer of grey cloud below where they trekked.

"I fear I'm going to miss my staff shortly," Aelfwynne said to the bitter wind blowing in from the unseen ocean many leagues to the west. Without explanation, he trudged down the roadway into a deep defile that joined Faelyn's Nest to a series of rugged tors.

Plumes of smoke wafted on the breeze in the distance, marking the volatile peaks that formed the backdrop of the

Keeper of the Jewel

southern reaches of the Steel Mountains as the chain swept in from the east to surround Crystal Lake. Recalling the lessons of the Chroniclers, Scale envisioned approximately how far they still had to travel to reach Highcliff. If the high wizard's fears were justified, there was a good chance they would arrive long after the perceived threat befell the dragon hold.

Scrambling to keep up, he shouted after Aelfwynne, "How is it this path is so well-kept? From what I understand, no one in their right mind would venture this way."

Aelfwynne stiffened and spun on him, beady, red eyes glaring. "That would explain our presence."

"But look at it. Other than Urdanya's Walk along the upper banks of Ors Spill, there isn't a roadway in all of South March that can compare to this one."

The high wizard studied the wide pathway north. "This may be hard for an elf to understand, but more than just your kind exist in the world."

Scale followed his gaze, expecting to see someone coming down from the heights. "Obviously, but—"

"But what? You think elves are the only creatures capable of rational thought?"

"No, but—"

"But nothing! The world doesn't revolve around this tiny kingdom. Nor do pointed ears mean you're all that important in the grand scheme of things. Like it or not, many intelligent creatures roam the lands, creatures who would love to knock your kind off their high pedestal. Dragon, man, dwarf, giant, sprite, fae, you name it." He looked up at Scale and nodded. "Aye. Even lowly goblins like me deserve to be counted in with those capable of doing great things."

Scale frowned, wondering where that had come from. He put his hands up between them in surrender. "I never meant anything by commenting on the road. It just appears, to me anyway, out of place up here in the middle of nowhere."

Aelfwynne held his stare for a moment before turning and starting down the Path of the Errant Night. "The middle of nowhere to you."

Scale swallowed and searched the roadway in both directions, making sure he stayed close to the high wizard as they trudged on.

The descent became steeper as the afternoon wore on, the angle taxing Scale's weary legs. "I meant no offense, Master Aelfwynne. Of course elves aren't the only intelligent creatures in the world. In fact, there are days I think we're anything but...Especially recently."

Aelfwynne hopped over a small rivulet and found a suitable pool of water in which to slake his thirst.

Late day sunshine filtered through thickening clouds drifting past the obscured peak of Faelyn's Nest—the moisture laden ceiling almost low enough to touch. Apart from an orangey glow to the south, the bleak landscape consisted of nothing but dull brown and black—dirt and rock, with little vegetation.

Waiting his turn at the water hole, Scale sighed. "I'm not sure how to say it without provoking another lecture, but it seems strange to me that the Path of the Errant Knight, notorious in folklore for its many dangers, appears this well travelled. I mean, without trying to repeat myself, who in their right mind would willingly venture this way if it places their life in constant danger?"

Aelfwynne finished lapping at the water and stood to regard him across the sluice. "I'll tell you who. The very creatures your folklore speaks of. The ones who'll tear you to shreds as soon as look at you. Not necessarily for your meat, mind, but to rid the world of one more creature who has played a part in unbalancing nature." He nodded to where the sun fell beyond the clouds. "Fear not. You'll soon discover the answer to your questions. The advent of nightfall will unveil those responsible for the Path of the Errant Knight. Pray we live to see the dawn."

Keeper of the Jewel

There Comes a Time

There comes a time in everyone's life, if one is patient enough to allow their scheming plans time to reach fruition, that even the most unreal of dreams will come to pass within their reach. Afara Maral, a human wizard in a prestigious elven court, one that answered only to Odyne's mismanaged seat on the Sea Throne in Urdanya, and of course, the undeserving incumbent who occupied the Willow Throne in Orlythia, found himself on the cusp of a coup to rock the ages.

Straddling his aptly named red dragon, Demonic, the two sat on a high bluff northeast of Grim Town, squinting in the dying light to observe the disciplined march of the royal army as it emerged from the forest land south of the Rust Wash and cut a wide swath across the expansive plains that would take them to Duke Orlythe's seat of power. One the surly tyrant was surely about to lose, one way or another.

"Should I release them while the queen is in the open?" Demonic growled, smoke escaping his fanged maw.

"Patience my friend. Wait until they're against the castle walls and then we'll smash them."

"And the duke will respond?"

"He'll have no choice. Queen Khae's commanders will assume the dragon attack is his doing. No one else controls your kind except the high wizard. The queen will react with

Keeper of the Jewel

a vengeance the land hasn't seen since Nyxa drove the north men scurrying back to their barbaric kingdoms."

"Are we to engage both sides?"

"Raze them all."

Demonic shifted under him, the upstart dragon barely more than a dragonling, but Afara had seen his potential from the day of his hatching five years prior. A natural born leader with the tenacity and strength required to win over the loyalty of Duke Grim's dragon allies.

As caretaker of the ferocious beasts, Afara Maral was grudgingly respected by most dragons not keen on being subjugated by Grimclaw's Law.

"At their present rate, it'll be well into the night before they reach the castle."

"So much the better. The cover of darkness will disguise the attack until it is too late. Once engaged, the rival forces will embroil themselves in a fierce and bloody battle."

"What of the Highcliff dragons?"

"They will respond, of course. They're committed to the high wizard, who in turn, is committed to Queen Khae. They wouldn't dare sit idle while their sovereign is threatened."

Demonic craned his scaly, horned head to stare at Afara. *"Do you think it wise to provoke a dragon war."*

"It's the only way."

Blood-red eyes narrowed and a lick of flame escaped one of Demonic's nostrils. *"They will blame me."*

Afara raised his brows twice in quick succession. "You won't be there."

Demonic growled and shifted, but Afara's pale-skinned face showed no concern. "By the order of the duke, you and I are supposed to be paying a visit to Highcliff."

"So, we're to fly to Highcliff? Are we going to finish what the duke could not?"

495

Keeper of the Jewel

Afara frowned at the back of Demonic's multi-horned head. "What do you mean by that?"

"Kill the princess."

A jolt of fear stiffened Afara's slumped form. "The princess is still alive?"

"She and one other from the palace."

"Why wasn't I informed of this?"

"You never asked."

"I never asked?" Afara was incredulous. "Did you not think that an important bit of information to divulge?"

"The affairs of the duke are no concern to us."

Afara wanted to inflict pain on the arrogant beast. "Has anyone informed the duke?"

"No."

Afara swallowed, staring into the distance. Digesting the startling revelation, he nodded slowly. Perhaps this development wasn't so bad after all.

"What do you want me to do? I can have Eldron speak with Ryedyn. Your apprentice can inform the duke."

"No!" Afara said more emphatically than he ever had in his life. "No. The less the duke knows, the better it will be for your dragons."

"Very well. Should we go and kill the princess now?"

Afara noted the anticipation in Demonic's voice. He smiled. "Patience, my scaly friend. All in due time. Soon, the Guardians will abandon their post. When they do, you and I will seize control of the Crystal Cavern. If the princess is there, we'll deal with her ourselves."

Keeper of the Jewel

More than Coincidence

Ouderling slept most of the day away, waking a couple of times, but too tired to do anything besides roll over and drift off again until a distant noise jarred her awake. She looked around, expecting to see Jyllana, but no one looked back.

At first, she put her lethargy down to how late she had stayed up with Eolande, Perch, and Miragan. A magical night she would never forget. But as she lay on her pallet, wrapped in a thin blanket to ward off the ever-present chill, she realized it was more than that. Accessing the magic that had sat latent within her since the day she was born had taken its toll.

A knock sounded at her door, and then the muffled words of someone she wasn't familiar with, "I'll just leave your food by your door then."

It took her a few moments to realize it had been the caller's original knock that had woken her. She yawned and stared at the pile of armour carefully arrayed in the corner. She couldn't wait for the day she actually got to train in it.

The main passageway lay quiet. Whoever had been kind enough to drop off a board of steaming food was nowhere to be seen.

She tore into the fare like a ravenous beast; she hadn't eaten since yesterday. Placing the empty tray aside, she dressed in her usual dun-coloured attire and ventured into the

497

complex, unsure of what to do with herself. Usually, Balewynd or Xantha dictated her schedule, but the younger Guardian was away and the older one was…

She stopped in the main tunnel and searched for the small side tunnel that led into Aelfwynne's chamber.

"I wonder?" she said to the empty corridor and made her way to the entrance of the high wizard's chamber.

She paused outside, debating what to do. Knock? There was no door, just a short tunnel. She glanced around, hoping to inquire about the etiquette expected when one sought to inquire if the Master of Highcliff was in residence, but the hallway was empty.

An eerie sensation feathered its way up her back. Something didn't feel right. The high wizard had been supposedly captured by her uncle, likely dead if she believed the gossip. Balewynd and Pecklyn, two of the more notable younger Guardians, had gone to investigate. It felt like they had been gone forever, but in all actuality, it hadn't been a day yet.

It dawned on her that she hadn't spoken to, or even seen, Xantha since Balewynd had related the death of her father.

Something big was about to happen. She sensed it in her bones. She sensed it with…Her eyes grew wide. She sensed the disturbance with her nature's essence!

Fear tingled deep inside her. She had no idea what her newly awakened magic was telling her.

The cramped tunnel was cold against the palms of her hands and felt through the knees of her breeks as she made up her mind and crawled into Aelfwynne's chamber.

Upon reaching the small grotto she was greeted by a pair of sad, purple eyes glinting in the faint glow of smoldering embers.

"Xantha?"

Keeper of the Jewel

The old elf didn't answer. She looked away from Ouderling as if she didn't want company.

Ouderling assumed her usual place on the opposite side of the firepit. "I'm worried about you. I came to see if you—"

"Save it!"

Ouderling tilted her head with a curious frown. "I don't understand. Have I done something to upset you?"

The elder's haggard face lifted to meet her gaze from across the smoky pit. The venom in Xantha's glare would have made Ouderling shrivel when she had first come to Highcliff. Not anymore.

She offered Xantha as much compassion as she could squeeze into her face. "We must maintain hope, Elder Guardian." The honorific felt strange passing her lips, but Ouderling owed Xantha nothing less. "Balewynd and Pecklyn..." she swallowed, trying to keep her voice steady, "and even Jyllana will bring him back. You'll see."

"They should've returned by now," Xantha growled. "They'll all be dead."

"You don't know that."

"I know Orlythe Wys and his evil wizard. More importantly, I have dealt with the Soul."

"The Soul?"

"The Dragon Witch Wraith! It has returned to South March. It seeks to subvert the Crystal Cavern. With Aelfwynne gone, it won't be long until it comes for us. When that happens, South March will fall."

Xantha's earlier words echoed in Ouderling's mind, *Aelfwynne feared this might come to pass. The soulless creature the Dragon Witch gave her life to defeat has returned...From the dead, apparently.*

Ouderling tried to appreciate the seriousness of that proclamation. Not for the first time, she found herself wishing she had paid more attention to the Chronicler while growing up. She made a silent pact with herself. Should she survive the imminent darkness everyone foresaw, she vowed to learn everything there was to know about the history of South March and whatever there was to discern about the elves before then.

"You would've been better off if you'd left when Aelfwynne wanted you to."

Ouderling swallowed. She hung her head, fighting back tears, and whispered, "I'm sorry."

A lengthy silence ensued. Long after the embers had ceased to provide warmth, Ouderling muttered, "I should go."

"Sit!"

Xantha's stern order shocked her. She looked up, expecting to stare into the Guardian's angry eyes, but was confused as the corner of Xantha's lips turned up in the meekest of smiles.

"I'm the one who should apologize. You aren't to blame for what has happened. It's not your fault you were born to the queen."

Ouderling didn't know what to say, but she didn't feel any less responsible.

"Your mother did what she thought was right given the circumstances. As Queen of the Elves, it is her place. As it is ours to obey her rule. That's why Highcliff was established. To protect the Crystal Cavern from all enemies. Queen Nyxa entrusted the Highcliff Guardians with this obligation. The fact that the Soul has threatened Queen Khae's *only* living daughter should be reason enough for Highcliff to open its doors to you, princess."

Keeper of the Jewel

Xantha lifted her chin. "I'm glad you came to me. I've languished in self-pity for days. Aelfwynne's spirit will be thoroughly disgusted, I assure you of that."

Ouderling tried to interject—to allay Xantha's fears of her mate's demise, but Xantha spoke louder, "Come morning, I will call on the dragons. It's high time we unified our forces and performed the duty entrusted to us long ago. It's time we honoured our pledge to Queen Nyxa."

Ouderling gaped.

Xantha nodded. "Aye. Your uncle will either come clean or we'll burn Castle Grim to the ground."

"But I thought…Doesn't my…?" Ouderling wrestled with Xantha's proclamation. "I'm told my uncle has dragons of his own. Won't that precipitate a dragon war?"

"So be it. It's high time their true allegiances were accounted for. I've been on Aelfwynne about this for years. He was afraid to act without you mother's consent but I fear we're left with no choice. The dragons' loyalties must be ascertained before it's too late."

Ouderling hadn't thought about her parents role in all of this. "Have you even thought about including my mother in this conversation. I'm sure she'll have something to say about it...What?"

Xantha's troubled mien held Ouderling's stare.

"We've been cut off from the rest of the kingdom. Nothing is getting through to Orlythia. We even tried to send word to your aunt in Urdanya but have received no response. The duke's forces must be intercepting our missives."

"But…But that's absurd."

"Absurd or not, that's what we're faced with. Without Aelfwynne, Highcliff's in a tenuous position. I refuse to allow everything we've endured over the last few centuries to have been in vain. If the duke wants a dragon war, then so shall he have one."

Ouderling swallowed. She wasn't the wisest when it came to worldly events, but neither was she naïve. If her uncle gained control of the dragons, Orlythia would be hard-pressed to defend against them. Everything her grandparents had fought so hard to build would crumble down around her parents. It wasn't much of a leap to think that if Orlythe *had* been prepared to kill her, he wouldn't think twice about murdering his sister to lay claim to the highest house in the land. Perhaps in all the lands.

"Elder Xantha!" A muted voice came from beyond the exit tunnel of Aelfwynne's chamber, the male's voice urgent.

Xantha shouted back, "In here!"

"I must speak with you at once."

The elder exchanged a concerned glance with Ouderling. "Coming!"

The black-haired elf, Cynder, awaited them in the main passageway. He stood straighter as Xantha exited the high wizard's tunnel. "The queen marches on Castle Grim."

Not quite clear of the tunnel, Ouderling looked up in alarm and bumped her head.

"Are you certain of this?"

"Aye. Ashe is with one of the Watchmen on the platform."

It was hard to match Xantha's long strides as she hurried toward the complex's main exit.

Xantha mumbled for Ouderling's benefit, "A Watchman is a dragon scout. Most are stationed along the southwest coast but ever since Aelfwynne went missing I have instructed them to fly patrols over the Mardeireach."

Ouderling was surprised how dark it was as they burst onto the platform and spotted a large yellow dragon and Ashe—

the rock shelf bathed in dull light as the moon struggled to peer through the cloud cover.

"Elder Xantha!" Ashe regarded their approach from beside the dragon. "Atsila reports the sighting of thousands of Queen Khae's troops upon the plains north of Grim Town."

"Good work." Xantha stepped beside Atsila and patted her flank. "Was the queen with them?"

If the dragon answered, Ouderling never heard.

"But you're sure it's the Royal Army?" Xantha asked and nodded as if she had received a reply. "And where are they now?"

Xantha listened before turning to Ouderling. "Perhaps all is not lost. The Royal Army is at the gates of Castle Grim. Your mother is sure to be with them. She'll set her brother straight."

"What's my mother doing there?"

"She must've gotten wind that something was amiss." Xantha shrugged. "If anyone was able to get word past the duke's blockade, I'm sure Aelfwynne did before he..." She trailed off, her features hardening.

Atsila tilted her head, her focus on Xantha.

Xantha nodded several times.

"What's she saying?" Ouderling asked, curiosity getting the better of her.

"Atsila, it's okay." Xantha nodded at Ouderling. "This is the princess. Allow her to hear you."

"As you wish, elder. I was saying, there's something odd happening in the warrens. Extra activity amongst those we suspect are loyal to the duke."

Although Ouderling had heard dragonspeak, especially last night with Perch and Miragan, the foreign voice in her head was disconcerting even if Atsila was soft spoken for someone her size.

503

Keeper of the Jewel

Xantha scratched at her head in thought. "You think it has something to do with queen's arrival?"

"It's hard to say what the motivation is, but several Watchmen are leaning that way. A difference of opinion has divided us ever since Grimclaw left the elves. It was only a matter of time before that disparity came to a head. Many of us share a bleak view regarding the Duke of Grim's underlying intentions."

"It strikes me as more than just a coincidence that the uprising corresponds with the arrival of the queen." Xantha turned her attention on Cynder and Ashe. "Assemble the riders and have them call their dragons. As soon as you're ready to fly, join me at Castle Grim."

Cynder and Ashe nodded, their faces grave, and bolted into Highcliff.

The elder Guardian waited until they disappeared into the entrance tunnel. Searching the shadows of the platform as if expecting an assassin to leap out of the darkness, she mounted Atsila like it was something she did everyday and said, "Fly me to the queen. I must get to her before the duke."

Keeper of the Jewel

The Chazgul

"**Mardeireach**. Inhospitable at the best of times. Deadly at the worst."

Aelfwynne's idea of a pleasant conversation as they trekked through the ominous range was not something Scale wished to participate in. His mind was troubled by enough worst-case scenarios his imagination dreamt up involving creatures he was loath to encounter. He didn't need the high wizard evoking any more. If he allowed himself to believe half the tales Aelfwynne related as they braved the cold night, there was little chance they would live to see the sunrise.

Several times the astute goblin had spotted dragons high in the evening sky. Each time, they had sought shelter behind a boulder or beneath one of the scarce firs. The ancient master claimed their aerial visitors could quite easily be members of the Watchmen—a curious name, Scale thought, for a group of creatures who reportedly abhorred man. Even so, the high wizard couldn't be entirely certain where the distant dragons' allegiances lay, as the Watchmen usually patrolled the coast.

Not versed in the ways of dragonkind, nor the southland for that matter, Scale accepted Aelfwynne's counsel. The fact that he really had no choice disturbed Scale's sense of always needing to be in control.

Keeper of the Jewel

They stopped several times to listen and scan the darkness. Each time, Scale noted the painstakingly slow course of the moon as it passed overhead, partially hidden beyond a thin layer of listless clouds.

Grateful for small mercies, he appreciated the fact they weren't buffeted by the strong winds that had assailed them earlier in the day. Though he had no way to ascertain where they were, judging by their perpetual uphill climb, they had to be thousands of feet above the mainland. Nor was he unthankful for the fact that they hadn't been beset by the nightmarish creatures rumoured to prowl the region.

Whatever the high wizard feared, they must be hardy to eke out a living this far above the treeline. Aside from the odd fir and low scrub, only dull, grey rock stretched into the cloud shrouded slopes ahead.

Aelfwynne's dark mood wasn't lost on Scale. The peculiar goblin grumbled to himself as he led the way, cast in a small cocoon of wizard's fire burning above his upturned palm.

"I should've sent her home…Crazy knot head…What good is that?…Bizarre dragon movement…Should have known…Intercepted by Orlythe's dragons…Gerrant Wood…"

"What's that?" Scale asked, hearing his father's name.

"Nothing," Aelfwynne grumbled.

The wizard's mumblings troubled him. "You mentioned my father. What should you have known?"

"Huh?"

Not put off by Aelfwynne's cranky disposition, Scale persisted, "You said something about my father and bizarre dragon movement."

"Doesn't concern you."

"I beg your pardon, Master Aelfwynne. Like it or not, I'm in this as deep as you are." His voice dropped to a whisper.

Keeper of the Jewel

"The duke had my companions murdered in case you've forgotten. Seeing that I'm the one who rescued you and am now walking the Path of the Errant Knight, I believe it concerns me greatly."

The look the high wizard shot him made him flinch but he didn't back down.

Aelfwynne studied him a moment longer before he started to walk again. "Very well. You may have a point."

Damn right I have a point, Scale thought but wasn't brave enough to say it aloud as he fell into step.

"Life in Highcliff is much different than the posh existence you're used to at Orlythia. Out here in the wild, we live and die by the whim of a being higher than us."

"Like a god?"

"Hardly. A god wouldn't trouble himself with this place. I'm talking about dragons, you witless northerner!"

"Right." Scale felt foolish, as if he should have known that. He was glad for the poor light. It wouldn't do to blush in front of the high wizard.

"For lack of a better way to describe it, there've been tremors within the dragon community of late."

"Since the princess arrived, you mean?"

Aelfwynne stopped and frowned. Shaking his head, he started walking again. "I had thought that too, but now that you mention it, no. It started before her arrival. Shortly before I received a letter from the queen begging me to watch over her."

"The princess?"

"Of course, the princess, you imbecile. Who else do you think has caused me so much angst?" Aelfwynne spat, and stopped to point a crooked finger up at him. "And don't you dare call her by her title while she's at Highcliff. From what I understand, she'll chew your face off."

507

Keeper of the Jewel

Scale had no idea what that was supposed to mean but the high wizard said no more.

Doing his best to conjure his own fireball, Scale's meagre light was barely enough to see by; the tiny flames flickering in and out of existence. Much to Aelfwynne's consternation, Scale tripped several times as he focused on his spell-casting and neglected to watch where he was going.

Well into the night, Scale turned his ankle in a rut. He stumbled into the high wizard, nearly pushing the goblin down a steep slope.

Aelfwynne's fire went out as he arrested what could have resulted in a fatal fall. "What *are* you doing? You almost killed me!"

"Sorry, Master. I tripped." Scale's fire had gone out as well, leaving them in darkness—the shadows so thick that had he not known where Aelfwynne stood, he doubted he would have been able to spot him.

He concentrated on bringing another fireball to life, attempting to do so quickly to impress the high wizard, but Aelfwynne's harsh words brought him up short.

"Extinguish that and listen!"

Scale did as he was told, expecting the high wizard to berate him for some reason or another, but Aelfwynne cupped an ear and leaned in the direction they had come. "You hear that?"

Scale imitated the high wizard. Other than the wind and the goblin's raspy breathing, nothing made itself apparent. He whispered, "No. What is it?"

"Some Home Guard you are. You're supposed to protect those you travel with."

Admonished, Scale could do nothing but gape.

"Listen harder. Clear your mind. Let nothing else matter but the here and now."

Keeper of the Jewel

Scale did as instructed. He stretched his neck, took a deep breath, and concentrated on the wind, listening for anything that seemed out of the ordinary.

"Well?"

"Nothing, Master."

"Your father would have sensed it long ago. You sure you're a Wood?"

Feeling his anger rise, Scale glared, but he left it at that.

"Something stalks us. It's still a long way off but distances are inconsequential in the mountains. Whatever it is, it'll be on us in its own time," Aelfwynne said, a small fireball coalescing above his palm. He started up the path at a leisurely walk.

"Shouldn't we run?"

"This far away from Highcliff or shelter of any kind? What's the use? I'd rather be rested when whatever it is attacks."

Even though he hadn't heard anything, Scale struggled to keep from bolting up the roadway and leaving the high wizard on his own. If not for a profound dread of what might be awaiting them farther along, he just might have.

He made a point to stay beside Aelfwynne, and stumbled along, looking over his shoulder as much as trying to see where they were going. Any thought of conjuring his own fireball had been eradicated by the inexplicable, but very real fear gripping him.

The moonlight lessened as night deepened toward dawn; the all but hidden celestial orb dropped behind the western peaks. It seemed as if time slowed to a crawl.

Hoping beyond hope for the ensuing morn to banish the darkness and hopefully deter whatever pursued them, Scale almost squeaked when Aelfwynne's magical fire extinguished and the goblin whispered, "Easy. They're all around us."

Calm was the last ability Scale had the capacity to possess at the moment. His head whipped around, but whatever Aelfwynne sensed, Scale couldn't see. "Where?"

"Shh!"

Scale flinched; Aelfwynne's shushing noise louder than his question.

And then he heard it. Or rather, heard *them*. An odd growl stirred somewhere in the darkness up the slope to their left, followed by another predatory rumble from beyond a low cluster of scrub on their right.

Long dagger in hand, he crouched and turned one way and then another. A third rumble from behind made him jump, but try as he might, he couldn't see what assailed them.

"Remain still," Aelfwynne hissed. "Any sudden movement will bring them down on us like an avalanche."

"What are they?"

"Chazgul."

"Chaz-what?"

"Chaz-*gul*. Predators known to haunt the higher reaches of the Mardeireach. Extremely dangerous if cornered. Lethal when hunting in packs."

Scale gulped. "That's not good."

"That would be a fair assessment," Aelfwynne agreed. "I count at least six of the demon beasts close by, but there's bound to be more. Now, put away your blade...slowly. Steel will be little deterrent against these things. You'll only provoke them further. Magic is what's required."

Scale turned an incredulous look on the high wizard. "I don't know how to use my magic."

Keeper of the Jewel

"Then you'd better prepare yourself to meet whichever god you pray to. I'd sooner fight a dragon than a pack of slavering chazgul."

Keeper of the Jewel

Castle Walls

Commander Keel's intimidating size astride his warhorse provided Khae little comfort as she plodded her dirty white mare in his wake. The royal army commander's purple plumed helm bobbed in cadence with his broad shoulders; silhouetted in the faint moonlight bathing the Bascule Plains.

She had been this way on many occasions during the course of her lifetime. With each subsequent return, she enjoyed laying eyes on the black walls of Castle Grim less and less. Nor was this visit likely to bolster her enjoyment of the daunting keep.

All the way from the Wizard's Sleeve had she brooded about the blatant denial of support from Orphic Den. The very notion made her set her jaw and glare. When this business with her brother was over, she promised to pay a return visit to Headmaster Sagora and lay down the law— the *queen's* law. One that would demand compliance should there ever come a need of the magic guild's services in the future. To think that the wizard society operated on South March soil with impunity, only to ignore a request from the crown, infuriated her to no end. Sagora's refusal was not in the spirit of the accord drawn up between her mother and the old warlock, Gullveig.

Weary of the forced march, her mind wandered. What had happened to Gullveig? Superstition had him living deep

Keeper of the Jewel

within the bowels of Grim Watch Tower but she thought otherwise. Though she couldn't deny the plausibility that the warlock had infused an essence of his soul into the very bedrock supporting the mysterious edifice, she was fairly confident the old conjurer had left the world of the living long ago. Likely around the same time the Dragon Witch had perished.

The monotonous, thunderous clip-clop of thousands of hooves, the-ever-present jangle of harnesses, and the ominous squeak of leather armour melded into a cacophony that thundered inside her bleary mind. How the foot soldiers maintained such a rigorous pace was a glowing testament to Commander Keel's strict training regimen.

Captain Kall, a slightly smaller, but no less intimidating elf than the commander, rode in front of Hammas. He leaned in to speak quietly with the commander of the royal army.

Khae couldn't make out what they said, but she knew it could only be about the preparations for when they reached their destination. Professional to a fault, neither elf did much else other than live their role of service to the elves of South March.

She smiled at that. She wasn't aware of elves existing anywhere else in the world, but little was known of the mystic lands rumoured to exist beyond the Niad Ocean. Other than the fact that the original Dragon Witch had emerged from over the waves bearing Grimclaw's seed.

It wasn't obvious at first, but as a strange rumble rose above the noise of the rank and file, those around her sat higher in the saddle.

"Hammas," Khae whispered, standing tall in her stirrups, but all she saw were the armoured shoulders and helmeted heads of those closest to them, their armour gleaming under the glare of multiple torches.

Keeper of the Jewel

She slumped in her saddle and urged Faelnyr to step closer to Hammas' black charger. She kicked out a foot to nudge the king's shin—the elf miraculously asleep on horseback.

Hammas snorted and opened his eyes, clearly disoriented. "Wh-what is it? Are we there yet?"

Khae rolled her eyes. "Aye. You missed it. We're on our way back to Orlythia."

Hammas frowned, blinking rapidly, and looked around. He gave her a condescending glare.

"Seriously. How can you sleep in the saddle?"

Hammas shrugged. "I don't know. Tired, I guess."

She shook her head. The elf would sleep standing up if someone held onto him. "Well listen. Something's happening. Can't you hear it?"

It took her a moment to sense it again, but as she concentrated, the distant thunder had grown louder. The skies, though overcast, didn't appear threatening. "What do you suppose it is?"

Hammas listened, his face indicating he heard it too. Ignoring her question, he raised his voice, "Keel. What's happening. Are the duke's troops marching on us?"

"No, Your Majesty. I just received a report that the Herd of Bascule is surrounding us."

The commander had no sooner finished speaking when the entire procession came to a stop.

Faelnyr postured nervously beneath Khae, matching Shadow's unease as Hammas worked to steady him; the animals perceiving things neither of them could see.

"Did you say they're surrounding us?" Queen Khae's voice squeaked. She couldn't imagine how many horses it would take to circumvent a host four-thousand strong.

"That's the word, Your Majesty. With your leave, I'll endeavour to discover more."

Keeper of the Jewel

"Of course, commander."

Keel nodded, glanced at Captain Kall, and urged his armour-plated warhorse through the ranks, quickly swallowed by the masses.

Captain Kall immediately began dispatching orders to set up a protective ring around her and Hammas—a perfunctory measure her personal guard were trained to employ. Until the unknown threat had been cleared, it was Captain Kall's duty to see to the protection of the royal couple.

"Is this really necessary?" Khae asked, resignation taking the edge from her words.

"Yes, Your Highness. I'm sure it's nothing, but—"

A solitary cry rose above the din of the countless horses encircling the royal army. "Dragon!"

The shout had no sooner registered, when dozens of similar warnings sounded all around their sheltered spot in the middle of the vanguard.

In the dim light afforded by the obscured moon, it took Khae several moments to pick out the black speck in the sky; far east of where she assumed Castle Grim to lie. To her astonishment, it was coming straight at them.

"Shields!" Captain Kall ordered. "Nothing gets through!"

Queen Khae and King Hammas were physically pulled from their horses with little regard to their dignity. Held between Faelnyr and Shadow, they were ordered to kneel on the ground. Tower shields clanged overtop of their position, severing their view of the sky beneath a metal ceiling.

Khae exchanged a worried glance with Hammas. Surely her brother hadn't gone mad and attacked them with dragons.

She swallowed. She had let Orlythe carry on for far too long as the disgruntled Duke of Grim. Hunkering down in the king's embrace, she was reminded of a conversation they had recently in which she had flippantly declared, *'We should just lay siege to his castle and be done with it.'* Hammas, of course, had been all too receptive.

The irony of that sentiment rung loud in her head. Perhaps Hammas had been right all along. In the king's estimation, Orlythe should have been exiled long ago for his role in the current dragon dissension rumoured to be plaguing Highcliff.

"Archers, draw!"

Though she couldn't see them, Khae imagined what an impressive sight a thousand archers acting in unison would look like from the air. She couldn't deny she was more than a little afraid, but she was confident her troops could handle whatever came against them. Three hundred and fifty to four hundred archers along each flank, and another hundred to hundred and fifty warding the front and rear of the royal host, would deal with anything that dared to fly into their midst.

"What now, Xantha?"

The elder Guardian saw it too. Spread far below, rank upon endless rank bearing the queen's green, fully-armoured troops stared up at their approach; not the least of which were a formidable number of archers. But it was the riderless horses galloping around the royal army that gave her pause.

"Reach out to Queen Khae. Let her know who's coming."

"I won't be able to hear her from this far away."

"That's okay. We'll just have to hope she understands and calls the archers off. Fly over the Herd of Bascule, but remain out of bowshot."

"Okay, but I don't know where she is. If she's in the middle, the distance involved may be problematic."

Xantha's eyes weren't what they used to be. In her youth, her dragon friends had been jealous of her acute vision, but time had taken its toll. Hidden in the glare of hundreds of torches, individual troops were difficult to make out.

Atsila redirected her flight to circle the army, allowing Xantha time to study the masses in the poor light. At first, she reckoned Hammas would demand that he ride at the forefront of the army as its leader, but as they passed over the lead riders, there didn't appear to be enough officious-looking elves to signify a contingent of the queen's retainers.

She had known Khae for the queen's entire life, but as a Highcliff Guardian, Xantha rarely had the occasion to visit with the queen as anything more than a member of Aelfwynne's entourage. Though they had always been pleasant with each other, Xantha wasn't sure South March's leader would recognize her anymore.

"Any luck?"

"I can't honestly say if she can hear me or not. There's too many elves down there. You sure she's travelling with them?"

Xantha considered the back of Atsila's head. The dragon had a good point. But the more she thought on it, the more she was convinced. "The Queen Khae I know would never allow her troops to go into battle without her leading them."

"How do you know there's to be a battle?"

"I don't. But an army that big can't be anything else but a show of force. The palace must've gotten wind that something isn't right down here. If Khae has learned of Orlythe's plot to kill the princess, she will tear Castle Grim to the ground. Besides, if the duke is as stupid as he is stubborn, blood will be shed."

Xantha leaned to her left, examining the eastern flank. Her gaze drifted toward the middle. "There! The shield wall in the centre. That's where she'll be."

Keeper of the Jewel

"I doubt my voice can carry that far. If she were my rider, maybe."

"Fly closer."

"We'll take arrow shot."

"Fly evasively!"

Atsila's smooth flapping missed a beat.

"Okay, okay." Xantha sighed in frustration. "Put down on the field outside of the rampaging horses. I'll have to walk in."

Hammas stood up, having to crouch to avoid smacking his head off of the interlocked shields protecting them.

The Home Guard in charge of the shield bearers opened his mouth, ostensibly to tell Hammas to get back down, but the king's angered glare stopped him.

"I'm the king, dammit! If you value your position in our house, you'll order the shields lowered."

Khae wasn't certain Captain Hondrick would capitulate; the elf in charge of the brigade known as the Queen's Shield took his role seriously.

Normally, Khae liked to err on the side of caution. Hammas was the loose cannon in their marriage, but whenever he flexed his muscle, it usually wasn't done without justification. Cowering on the Bascule Plains, afraid of her brother's wrath, didn't sit well with her either. When Captain Hondrick's gaze of indecision fell on her, she gave him a subtle nod.

"Shields! Stand at the ready!"

A dozen tower shields as tall as the king, and half as wide, parted to reveal the dark sky overhead.

Searching the skies, it was apparent by where the troops' attention around them was focused that the dragon was somewhere to the east.

Keeper of the Jewel

King Hammas stepped beside Hondrick and followed his gaze. "Do you see it?"

"No, Your Highness."

They remained that way for many moments, the continual pounding of the Herd of Bascule raising a cloud of dust around the army.

Khae's voice noticeably startled Hammas as she spoke into his ear, "You think the horses are my brother's doing?"

The king stiffened. Facing her, he opened his mouth but didn't answer, his face twisted in thought. Finally, he said, "No. I don't think so. The Herd of Bascule owes its allegiance to no one. I can't see Orlythe controlling them."

"Magic, perhaps?"

Hammas raised his eyebrows. "Possibly, but I doubt it. To what end?"

"To pin us down while the dragons he's subverted char our bones."

Hammas frowned. Casting his gaze skyward, he raised his voice, "Have you seen any more dragons, captain?"

"No, Your Highness."

Khae shrugged as he looked back at her.

A clamor arose from the eastern flank. The body of footmen and accompanying horses split long enough to allow a runner through. Clearly out of breath, the messenger dropped to a knee in front of Khae, his head bowed.

"Arise, good elf. What news?" Khae asked.

The short-haired messenger rose, but kept his eyes cast down. "The dragon has landed, Your Majesty."

Khae exchanged a puzzled look with Hammas.

"A lone rider has dismounted and awaits, Your Majesty."

"Then bring them forward."

The messenger swallowed. "We can't, Your Majesty."

"Why not?"

519

Keeper of the Jewel

"The Herd of Bascule prevents anyone from crossing between them, Your Majesty."

Khae took a deep breath to calm her frustration. "Very well. Instruct the flank officer closest to where the rider awaits to bring them forward as soon as conditions change."

"Aye, Your Majesty. It shall be done." Not waiting to be dismissed, the messenger was gone before Khae had time to blink, his slight form swallowed by the rank and file.

How long Xantha stood on the far side of the stampeding Herd of Bascule, she didn't know, but it wasn't until early morning twilight lifted the deepest of shadows from the land that the horses finally tired of their blockade and disappeared into the east, making a wide detour around Atsila who patiently sat many paces away.

As soon as it was safe to approach, half a dozen large elves surrounded her, while a seventh elf, obviously the one in charge, demanded, "State your business, rider."

Xantha recognized the towering elf's insignia. "I have come from Highcliff, Commander, with an urgent message for the queen."

As soon as Commander Keel heard the word, 'Highcliff,' the apprehension on his face softened. "And you are?"

"Elder Guardian Xantha. Mate of High Wizard Aelfwynne."

Commander Keel scrutinized her.

Nor could she blame him. It was a lofty claim. She hadn't attended the royal palace in years, preferring to leave the pomp and ceremony to the high wizard. A secret smile passed her lips. Pomp and ceremony were the last things Aelfwynne wished to deal with either, but out of a sense of duty, he had always made it a point to show his colours when called upon. Nor could she blame the commander for doubting her claim to be a goblin's mate.

"Your weapons." Commander Keel ordered.

Xantha unbuckled her belt and handed it to a pair of waiting hands. She raised her arms to allow for a thorough frisking.

"Bind her hands behind her back."

Two sets of callused hands didn't wait for permission.

Restrained like a common criminal, Xantha was paraded through hundreds of curious onlookers. Had she been centuries younger, she would have been outraged at the treatment. It would've taken a violent struggle to subdue her, one that would have left more than one of her handlers with lasting marks. But not anymore. Especially knowing what she did about the recent events involving the duke and Aelfwynne. She couldn't blame the Home Guard.

The closer she got to the middle of the stationary army, the more some of the older, higher-ranking officials recognized her. She nodded to them in turn, doing her best to smile through her humiliation.

The entire event was over almost as soon as it began. All of the rough handling and perceived disrespect was worth the fallen look on the commander's face as Queen Khae stepped forward.

"Xantha! What have they done to you?" The queen turned on Commander Keel. "Release her at once, you fool. Do you realize who this is?"

Commander Keel's face darkened at the admonishment. He motioned for the handlers to remove Xantha's restraints, and dipped his head. "She claims to be a Highcliff Guardian, Your Majesty."

Khae gaped. "*A* Highcliff Guardian? She's one of the original Guardians."

Keeper of the Jewel

"Yes, Your Highness." Keel's voice remained impassive; the elf well trained. He nodded at a Home Guard carrying Xantha's sword belt. "What of her weapons?"

"I'll have you know, commander, there was a time not too long ago that this warrior would have whipped half this army with her bare hands and not broken a sweat." The queen appeared livid enough to spit. "Give her back her weapons at once."

"Yes, Your Highness." Commander Keel indicated for that to happen.

Xantha did her best to keep from smiling until she had secured her sword belt around the top of her hips and was led away by the queen who had wrapped an arm around her thick back.

"My apologies, Xantha. I wish I had known it was you. What news do you have from Highcliff? How does Master Aelfwynne fare?"

Xantha stopped walking and stared grimly at the queen.

The happiness drained from Khae's face. "What's happened?"

Xantha stared at the ground, trying hard to keep her emotions in check. "It's a long story, my queen."

Khae lifted Xantha's chin to look her in the eye. "I am Khae, to you. No matter whose company we're in, do you hear me?"

Xantha didn't acknowledge the queen at first, but Khae's grip increased and she nodded into the queen's hand.

"It is I who should be kneeling before you, Elder Guardian. Your service to our realm is legendary. Should I ever be afforded the chance to achieve half the accolades you are credited with, I shall die a happy elf."

Xantha nodded again. She appreciated the queen's reverence. If nothing else, it spoke to the monarch's virtue.

Keeper of the Jewel

That her old friend Nyxa lived on through her daughter was no longer in question. Queen Khae possessed the strength and guile South March needed to pull the realm through the darkness hanging over the land like an evil pall.

"Is Aelfwynne alright?"

Xantha hesitated. The queen had enough to chew on at the moment. Less than a league away, the castle walls of the Duke of Grim stood before the royal army. Unless she was dreadfully wrong, a trait that was foreign to her, the future of South March was about to be contested. An irretrievable confrontation between Khae and her brother that would spell the deaths of thousands of elves. Should the dragons become involved, a scenario she didn't think could be avoided the more she thought on Orlythe's complicity in recent events, there would be a good deal more death than that.

And yet, how could she not burden the queen? Aelfwynne's fate was an important piece of information she needed to hear. Khae's brother had not only detained, and in all likelihood, murdered the highest wizard in the land, but had conspired to have the princess killed as well.

She pulled her chin free of Khae's grasp, heaved a deep breath, and put her large hands on Khae's shoulders; conscious of the fact that the king listened beside her. "I have grave news, my queen. News that you must hear before you face your brother."

Khae's face fell. Wrapping her arms around Xantha, she held the ancient elf, staring in concern at Hammas.

Hammas patted Xantha on the back and waited until they separated, their cheeks glistening. "Walk with us and tell us everything that has gone on since our daughter arrived at Highcliff," he said, his attention on the ever-observant Commander Keel.

Keeper of the Jewel

With a nod, the commander broke into action, issuing the order to march toward the daunting, black castle walls that were being revealed in the dawn's early light.

Keeper of the Jewel

Eternal Forest

Dithreab sighed. He knew one day it would come to this. Centuries of servitude to a cause not his own had finally conspired against him, leaving him with no other choice. It was time to go.

Standing before the large tome he had sat on while entertaining his old friend, Aelfwynne—the thick cover propped open against one of the root pillars—he gazed at a hidden scrying bowl sunk into the yellowed pages.

Having lost his tenuous hold on the Herd of Bascule, he resigned himself to watch them disappear into the east. At least they had provided a temporary reprieve to the queen's forced march. With any luck, the dragon rider would warn the queen that not everything was what it seemed.

As he watched, the royal forces assembled before the gates of Castle Grim. An impressive show of force to those not in the know, Dithreab could tell by the size of the caravan that the queen had only brought the troops from Orlythia and its surrounding area.

Had this unforeseen occurrence happened months ago, he wouldn't have fretted overly much, but being a wood sprite had its advantages…or disadvantages, depending on how he chose to look at them. His link with the Fae had kept him well informed of the subtle nuances pervading the land. As such, he had been acutely aware of a stirring in the dragon community over the last few weeks. One that could no longer be ignored.

Coupled with the disturbing news related by his old friend about the attempted assassination of the heir to the Willow Throne, he despaired that everything he had devoted his life to was unravelling at an astonishing rate. He only hoped his aid would be utilized in time.

"Now, dragon breath!" He muttered through clenched teeth. "What're you waiting for?"

The scene in the small vessel set into the tome became murky, transforming from early twilight over the Bascule Plains to the misty heights of the Mardeireach. The image wavered. For a moment, Dithreab believed he had lost his otherworldly connection, but with deeper concentration, the murky liquid clarified.

The sun hadn't risen over the eastern reaches of the Steel Mountains but its dawn feelers had lifted the deepest shadows basking a section of the Path of the Errant Knight.

As if viewed from a distance, he could barely make out the two figures he sought—their size difference giving their identities away.

At once, he knew they were in trouble. Threatened by a peril not even the formidable high wizard would be strong enough to repel.

"Come on. Use it." Dithreab shook a wooden fist at the bowl. He wanted to reach through the vision and shake Aelfwynne. Neither he nor the elf named Scale were strong enough to defeat an entire pack of ravenous chazgul.

Even though the fledgling elf wizard had exuded an air of profound power, Dithreab knew it would not save them this day. Scale had yet to tap into his unrealized proficiency. Someday, perhaps, with the right teaching, the young elf had the potential to make a difference, but not today. Today, he

Keeper of the Jewel

was but another hapless prey to the creatures closing in around them.

Dithreab had hoped beyond hope that Aelfwynne might have found a way to survive the arduous trek along the dastardly roadway and made it back to Highcliff in the next couple of weeks on his own, but the queen's arrival, and indeed that of the chazgul, had expedited a dire need for the wood sprite's intervention. If only the goblin wasn't so thick headed.

A shade of darkness lifted from the scene in the scrying bowl, revealing the desperate straits Aelfwynne and his companion were in. Unless Aelfwynne remembered the gemstone, it would only be a matter of time before it became a wasted gift.

Concentrating for all he was worth, he willed Aelfwynne to think about his options—to recall their parting words. He cringed as the chazgul closed their trap. Of all the creatures to come across, the high wizard and his companion had found a way to be set upon by the chazgul.

Fire burst from Aelfwynne's outstretched fingers, blasting one of the hairless, grey-skinned beasts off the side of the mountain—its hideous, burning form made Dithreab shudder as it fell out of view.

Undeterred, the demon creatures advanced. Resembling massive, humanoid creatures that crawled on all fours, their long taloned hands and feet supported arched backs that bristled with thin spikes running the length of their enhanced spine.

A ball of fire sparked to life in Scale's palms but when he attempted to throw it, the poorly conjured spell arced ineffectually through the air and fizzled out short of its intended target.

Keeper of the Jewel

Aelfwynne discharged another killing blast but no matter how many his old friend dispatched, Dithreab could see there were too many.

"The bauble, you old fool!" Dithreab screamed at the image.

His mounting apprehension caused him to lose control of the scrying spell. Weakened by its deployment, Dithreab rested his hands against the edges of the book and hung his head. He was too old for this. The liquid turned opaque and the image was gone. His stick-like body slid down the pages of the front of the tome until he sat on the earthen floor of his lair defeated.

It was deathly quiet where he lived. Where he had lived for countless years on end. Always tending to the needs of a land that had no idea he existed. As odd as that seemed if he were to allow himself to think about it, he had never done so in hopes of garnering recognition. He cared little if anyone ever thought to thank him. He did it for the Fae. For a particular Faerie creature who had given her life long ago to preserve the life of another. She had been his life. When she had gone, the only way past his grief was by devoting his life to carrying on in a way she would approve. Either that or stop living.

He fingered a tiny leaf he kept safely tucked in an interior pocket of his tiny, gossamer surcoat. She had bound her hair with it that very afternoon she had left him.

A single tear dripped off his tubular face, landing on the tiny leaf. It quivered for the briefest of moments, as if it tried to communicate with him, before falling to the ground to be absorbed by the soil.

He shuddered in grief. He couldn't picture her face anymore.

Keeper of the Jewel

Time slipped by him as he sat alone, wondering how life might have been different had she not died that day. How beautiful and fulfilling his days might have been.

He blinked several times, the interior of his shabby lair coming into focus. If he wasn't mistaken, dawn would be breaking over the land.

Closing his eyes tight, he took a deep breath and concentrated one last time, willing everything he had into one last attempt to do her memory proud.

His body spasmed with a knowing jolt, the sensation informing him his days were over.

Releasing his breath, a rueful smile parted his bark face. It was time to go. Time to visit the eternal forest.

The tiny leaf slipped from his dead fingers—fluttering once in the air before landing on top of the dampness his tear had left behind.

Keeper of the Jewel

Unleash the Beasts

Familial responsibility had always been a thorn in Orlythe's side. Complying with the unjust laws of the land, he had suffered an unfair fate—cloistered in the remote southlands while his sister and aunt prospered in the north and west. Though elves had little in common with the barbarians north of the border, he envied their practice regarding succession. The kingdoms of man demanded a male inherit the throne. The first-born male.

Orlythe was both of those things. Although elven law differed with regard to gender, he was still first-born and that should account for something.

Conscious of the reports that had filtered in throughout the night, he gave Captain Drake, who stood in the shadows at the base of the dais, a subtle nod. The captain's humourless eyes met his. Without a word, the loyal elf departed the throne room.

Orlythe drummed impatient fingernails on the arm of the Lava Throne. It wouldn't be long before his sister hammered on the gate. It was time to put an end to the backward culture of the elves. It was time to assert his claim to the throne.

Waiting for the signal to act, he pondered the untimely disappearance of the wraith. Judging by reports out of Orphic Den, he could only assume the despicable creature had convinced Sagora to deny the guild's participation in the queen's march. Even so, he was troubled by the fact he had no idea where the wraith had gone to since. Urdanya, if he believed his wizard, but lately, he wondered if trusting the human spellcaster was as wise as he had once thought it would be.

Their plans hadn't involved an open skirmish with his sister this soon, but the more he thought on it, the more her untimely arrival played into his hands. Perhaps Afara had the right of it after all. Vanquish the queen and the core of the South March army in one fell swoop and the road to the throne would open up before him. He smirked at his cleverness. All it would take would be one fell swoop of a horde of dragons.

Had an open call to arms been raised in Orlythia, Khae would have responded with the full might of the kingdom's forces and sacked Castle Grim, dragons or not. But, taking advantage of her lapse of strategic planning, destroying the few thousand troops that marched across the plains was a manageable proposition. Especially with the assistance of the fire breathing beasts that were supposedly aligned with the Highcliff Guardians. Fortified behind the impregnable black walls of Castle Grim that separated him from those seeking to condemn him, his victory was pretty much assured.

Nor did he fear the repercussions of such an action in the eyes of the rest of the realm. The queen's march could only be perceived as an open act of aggression. The sight of four thousand troops tromping across the heartland wasn't one to be lost on the population of South March. The host had made an ill-fated stop in Gullveig; their passage close enough to the cities of Brysis, Rhysa, and Nayda to have made an impression. When word got out that he had only been defending himself from a queen who had gone mad and attacked him for no reason, the population would have little choice but to turn their favour his way.

Distant drumbeats reached the throne room. He swallowed as the relevance hammered itself home. It was time.

Rising from the Lava Throne, Duke Orlythe straightened his flowing black surcoat, adjusting how it fell around his obsidian sword of state.

The elite Grim Guard in and around the throne room came to attention, assembling to escort him to the wall.

He snapped his fingers to get the attention of a wiry elf standing by himself in front of the lava fountain.

Seldom seen in the castle proper, Afara's apprentice, Ryedyn, fell into step as he passed across the threshold and advanced down the long passageway toward the main gate. Crossing the wide foyer, the Grim Guard led him into the first light of the day, hurrying toward the stairs that climbed the watchtowers on either side of the main gate.

The shores of Lake Grim were strangely still. Absent was the ever-present wind sweeping out of the Mardeireach to buffet the steely waves and snap the black pennants of Castle Grim. Also missing was the constant birdsong dominating the spires and towers of the dark keep at their back.

As the plains came into view in the light of the new dawn, Orlythe's breath caught in his throat. Four thousand, well-drilled troops stared back at him—their armour gleaming in the rising sun as it attempted to disperse the swirling mist clinging to the ramparts. Regardless of his confidence, his sister's host was impressive to behold.

It took him a moment to locate her and the fool king. The royal couple sat astride their horses near the front of the procession—the sight lifting an ironic smirk on the duke's face. Khae wasn't their mother. She lacked the strategical prowess of the War Dragon. Penned in on all sides, the queen

Keeper of the Jewel

and king were susceptible to the unknown fate that conspired to claim them.

His eyes were drawn to a yellow dragon standing behind the queen. He squinted; a sneer lifting his mustache. The high wizard's detested concubine rode the dragon. The old hag had dared to come against him.

So be it. Turning to Ryedyn, Orlythe growled, "Unleash the beasts."

Keeper of the Jewel

War Drums of Destiny

Demonic shuffled under Afara, the red dragon sensing the imminent confrontation.

"Patience, my friend. It won't be long now."

The queen's forces had assembled before the gates of Castle Grim. As expected, the imposing, black barbican remained down, barring the leader of South March access to one of her many castles. That fact alone was surely to be perceived as a slight of the utmost significance—Duke Orlythe's involvement in the unrest that had gripped the southern duchy made glaringly apparent. There could be no doubt in the queen's mind that the rumours that had reached her were substantiated.

The atmosphere in the royal army would be taut; ripe to erupt in irrevocable violence once provoked. All it needed was a little push.

As if on cue, the staccato of drums reached Afara and Demonic on the still air.

The queen's army straightened, a collective ripple of anticipation; their synchronized movement seemingly choreographed.

The taper had been lit.

Afara's gaze drifted above the dark blot of Castle Grim to the black peaks shrouded in perpetual mist beyond the wide expanse of Grim Lake.

"What of Atsila?"

Keeper of the Jewel

"The yellow dragon? You needn't worry about her. Soon, the field will be rife with confusion as to who initiated the first blow and the sides will clash. With any luck, they'll destroy each other. Atsila will become an unfortunate victim."

"What of the duke?"

Afara frowned at the back of Demonic's head. Perhaps he had misjudged the young dragon. He would have to keep an eye on him going forward. It wouldn't do to have a rogue dragon turn on him.

"What *of* the duke? He'll either live or he'll die. Whatever the case, once we seize control of the Crystal Cavern, his existence will become a moot point. If he dies, so be it. If he lives, I will have need of someone to lead my forces and crush the rest of the resistance we are sure to incur. After that," he shrugged, "you can eat him."

Demonic emitted a throaty laugh, the gesture easing Afara's doubts regarding the dragon's allegiance.

Movement on the western horizon drew his attention. A knowing smirk crossed his face. His faithful apprentice had summoned the dragons.

A cry arose from those assembled on the field far below. Arms pointed and horses shied.

Afara grinned wider than he had in a long time as it dawned on four thousand elves how precarious their regimented formation had left them. Four thousand lives poised to suffer a horrific end.

He inhaled deeply, appreciating the cool morning air filling his lungs. Four thousand elves who didn't believe he had a right to be considered a wizard in their court were about to discover what happened to those who held true to that belief.

Keeper of the Jewel

Looking to the south, he anticipated the inevitable response from Highcliff. His only regret was that he wouldn't be around to enjoy the slaughter.

Keeper of the Jewel

Leap of Faith

"I don't like this," Jyllana said as a regular cadence rumbled from somewhere beyond the small anteroom Balewynd had found for them to hide in.

"We have no choice. Attempting to call the dragons in broad daylight will result in their deaths," Balewynd mumbled from where she lay amongst a pile of stores she had put together as a resting place. "It's not like we can march through the gates."

Exhausted from their ordeal, they had fallen asleep and slept right through the night. By the time they woke again, a quick inspection had informed them the sun was about to rise again. Deflated, they had resigned themselves to another day in hiding.

Pecklyn got up from his chosen corner and joined Jyllana at the door. "What do you think's happening?"

Jyllana put her ear to the wooden barrier. "It definitely sounds like drums."

"Drums? Like war drums?"

Jyllana held up a hand so that she could listen. After a while she nodded. "Yep. That's gotta be what that is."

Balewynd jumped to her feet and joined them, pressing her ear against the wood—her eyes swollen and purple around the edges, but she could see. She pulled back and located the door handle. "We've got to get out of here."

Keeper of the Jewel

Pecklyn grabbed her hand, preventing her from springing the latch. "Whoa. Wait a moment. You just said we can't march through the gates."

Balewynd wrenched her hand free and glared. "We have no choice. Who do you think the duke is going to war against? Xantha must've roused Highcliff."

Pecklyn frowned. "That can't be possible. If she did, they would attack on dragonback. War drums wouldn't be sounding. The Grim Guard would be too busy running for cover."

Jyllana listened to the back-and-forth conversation. She knew little of how Highcliff worked, especially in times of threat, but she agreed with Pecklyn. War drums could only mean that Castle Grim was under siege and the duke was about to launch an offensive.

"Pecklyn's right," Jyllana said. Balewynd's hard stare made her take a step back, but she added with conviction, "I don't know who's attacking the castle, but war drums are usually beaten when an army is on the offensive. There must be troops at the gate."

"That makes no sense. In order for a foreign army to reach this far into South March..." Balewynd's eyes grew wide. She swallowed, her voice incredulous. "The queen!"

Pecklyn threw the latch and pulled the door open wide enough to peer out. At once, the percussive beat intensified. He pulled his head back in. "Hall's clear."

The regular cadence of many drums sent shivers along Jyllana's skin, but it was a distant shriek that took her breath away.

"Dragons!" Pecklyn stormed into the hallway, looking both ways.

538

Keeper of the Jewel

Balewynd charged out behind him and started toward the main entrance. Jyllana and Pecklyn followed on her heels, their weapons in hand.

Balewynd slid to a halt on the edge of the great foyer, barely able to keep herself from tipping forward into the path of a troop of Grim Guard who approached from the direction of the throne room. She urged Jyllana and Pecklyn to hide against the inside wall of the corridor as twenty fierce Grim Guard marched across the open space and pushed through the exit doors.

Balewynd wasted no time leaning into the intersection. She nodded to let them know the way was clear and started after the recently departed Grim Guard.

Pecklyn and Jyllana had started toward the far corridor but hesitated as Balewynd neared the exit.

"Bale!" Pecklyn's harsh whisper stopped her hand. "What're you doing. You can't go out that way, you'll be seen."

Balewynd's eyes were intense. "It's the quickest way back to the cathedral."

"But—" Pecklyn started to say.

Balewynd cut him off. "If there's an army outside the gate, the Grim Guard's attention will lie outward." Without waiting for a response, she slipped through the massive doors and was gone.

Pecklyn shook his head and sighed. "Come on. Once her mind's made up, there's no changing it."

Jyllana nodded and followed, slipping into the early morning light as Pecklyn held the door for her.

The colossal gatehouse towered above the shadowy grounds on the far side of the bailey. Crenellated walls emerged from either side of the twin gatehouse towers, lined with elves in black leather armour—their attention on the Bascule Plains.

Movement to their left exposed Balewynd's furtive form slinking along the base of the keep. She looked over her shoulder and motioned for them to follow.

Jyllana struggled to keep pace with Pecklyn, but a series of screeches from somewhere beyond the walls helped to pick up her pace.

The screeches echoed off the castle walls; an ear-piercing cacophony enough to make an elf shiver. But it was the next noise that caused Jyllana to stop and stare. Although she couldn't see what was happening beyond the black stone ramparts, she knew enough to recognize the sound of dragon fire being disgorged.

She had originally thought the dragons must have come from Highcliff and were about to attack Castle Grim, but the distant cry of elves screaming in agony confirmed that the dragon attack had been against whoever stood outside the gates. Her jaw dropped. If Balewynd's suspicions about the duke were correct, dragons were attacking the queen!

"Jyllana!"

Pecklyn's shout reached through her stupor. He had stopped at the base of the corner tower of the keep and was frantically motioning for her to hurry up.

Whether it was chance or Pecklyn's shout that alerted the Grim Guard on the wall to their presence didn't matter much. The fact that archers were nocking arrows and aiming at them did.

Three arrows thwapped into the keep's wall and shattered where Jyllana had stood a moment before.

Not wanting to slow her run, Jyllana didn't look to the wall to see the troops taking aim at her. She kept her eyes focused on Pecklyn darting across the wide area between the keep

Keeper of the Jewel

and the cathedral. In the distance, Balewynd's black form entered the shadows of the great building.

Booted feet clattered down the many stairwells emptying off the ramparts as dozens of Grim Guard came for them.

A javelin whistled past Jyllana's face as she bolted across the open space, causing her to stumble but she never fell. Catching her step, she entered the deeper shadows and bolted up the grand steps fronting the cathedral two at a time.

Thankful the large, double doors were ajar, she turned sideways and jumped through the narrow gap ahead of two arrows clattering off the top of the steps. A third missile imbedded itself into the thick door where her face had passed a heartbeat before.

She stumbled and slowed her headlong dash, allowing her eyes to adjust to the darkness. Noise on the right side of the pew-filled chamber drew her attention to the statue of the dragon and its rider along the outer wall.

In the faint light streaming through the bank of stained-glass windows running the length of the apse three stories off the floor, she could make out Balewynd three-quarters of the way up the rope.

"Come on!" Pecklyn urged from the base of the statue. He started up after Balewynd; not as fast as the female Guardian, but with a dogged determination that would see him to the top in no time.

Jyllana weaved her way through the wooden benches. All she had to do was make it to the statue and climb the rope.

Her heart skipped a beat. The cathedral doors banged open, followed by a chorus of angry shouts.

"There! Don't let them escape! Inform the wall!"

An arrow thumped into the pew beside Jyllana. She yelped and latched onto the rope. Looking up, Pecklyn was already halfway to the top. Of Balewynd, she saw no sign.

541

Keeper of the Jewel

The interior of the cathedral erupted with the sound of heavy boots and jangling armour.

Jyllana attacked the rope but cried out in dismay as her sweaty hands slipped on the thin cord. A sinking feeling gripped her. There was no way she was going to be able to ascend the rope.

"Climb!" Pecklyn ordered.

"I can't!" She cried out in anguish. "Go without me!"

"Wrap your legs in the rope and hang on!"

"We got one!" A deep voice proclaimed as he rounded the end of the last pew and reached out to grab her.

A sudden tug lifted her off the floor. Followed closely by another, and then another. Her body started to spin on the end of the rope.

The Grim Guard grasped her trailing leg. "Not so fast."

Kicking him under the chin with the toe of her soft-soled boot, the Grim Guard released her.

"Grab her!" the kicked elf shouted, holding his face, but his companions' jumps fell short.

Trying hard to control her spinning, Jyllana steadied herself against the underside of the dragon's wing and assisted her ascent by relieving some of her weight as her feet found purchase on different parts of the three-story tall statue.

An arrow shot straight up, missing her nose by a hair. Another arrow splintered on the underside of the statue's arm where Pecklyn stood, the Guardian seemingly unconcerned—his sole attention on his next pull of the rope.

He reached a hand down, clasped her wrist, and with a grunt, hoisted her onto the shoulders of the statue. Not wasting time, he cupped his hands, waited for her foot, and assisted her to the thin ledge running along the base of stained-glass windows.

Keeper of the Jewel

Jyllana paused momentarily to calm her erratic breathing.

"You waiting for an invitation?" Balewynd looked over her shoulder and yelled at them from where she crouched on the windowsill. "They'll be here anytime now."

Throat dry as sand, Jyllana dug deep and offered Pecklyn a helping hand. When she looked back to the window, Balewynd was gone.

Careful not to cut herself on the jagged edges of the broken glass, Jyllana ducked through the window and stood on the outside ledge—the sight beyond the castle walls almost causing her to fall to her death between the cathedral and the outer wall.

Assembled on the plains in front of Castle Grim, thousands of elves clad in the queen's colours were scrambling to get under the cover of raised tower shields as dragon after dragon dropped out of the sky to rain fire and terror onto the vulnerable troops.

Pecklyn pushed past her, his visible dismay matching hers. He found Balewynd on the castle wall, leaning through a gap in the crenellated parapet. With a nod to Jyllana, he leapt the gap and asked his Guardian partner, "Is that the queen's army?"

Balewynd regarded him with tears tracing streaks down her filthy cheeks. Her voiced cracked as she looked down the wall to where a group of Grim Guard advanced on their position. "The dragons have turned."

"Not all of them! No way!" Pecklyn fumed. "Dawnbreaker!"

Jyllana considered their peril. She thought about running toward the western corner tower but her breath caught in her throat. A group of black clad troops bearing swords and axes exited the lofty structure. They were trapped.

Keeper of the Jewel

"I called them, already," Balewynd said as she faced the nearer of the two groups closing in on them from the direction of the main gate; a throwing knife in each of her hands.

"There!" Pecklyn shouted, pointing at distant specks descending from out of the clouds far over Lake Grim—the steely waters lost to sight behind the cathedral.

"Are you ready?" Pecklyn grabbed Jyllana and shook her. "We're only going to get one shot at this."

Jyllana couldn't take her eyes from the advancing Grim Guard, her jaw hanging open as she tried to concentrate on what Pecklyn was saying. Screams of agony and dragon shrieks coming from the battlefield added to the chaos on the ramparts.

"You remember when you first arrived at Highcliff and you saw me jump off the edge of the promontory?"

His voice sounded strange. It was as if he spoke to her in a dream. Her head bobbed back and forth as he shook her harder.

"Jyllana! Listen. Its easy if you allow yourself to trust in the dragons. It's known as a leap of faith. You can do it."

She nodded. At least, she thought she did. She couldn't be sure. Everything blurred together. Her hands trembled violently. Absently, she realized she was in shock. She heard Pecklyn screaming at her but all she could do was stare blankly back at him.

"I'm here." Dawnbreaker's voice exploded in her head.

"Okay, take my hand. We'll do this together." Pecklyn gave her no choice.

Hauling her into a gap along the crenellated bulwark, he searched the sky. "Get ready Bale! We'll see you above."

Elves shouted. Arrows were loosed. The Grim Guard were on them. Balewynd stood defiant in the middle of the wall.

Keeper of the Jewel

A male and female elf in the duke's livery dropped to the rampart floor, the male elf tumbling over the inside brink, clutching at a throwing knife protruding from his neck.

"Now!" Dawnbreaker cried.

It was the oddest of sensations being pulled off the top of a high castle wall to plummet to your death, only to have the wind driven from your lungs as your prone body impacted the unforgiving, scaley hide of a dragon.

"Now!" The muted voice of Mirage echoed through Jyllana's disoriented thoughts.

The shriek of countless dragons and the screams of those dying on the plains below were but part of a dislocated consciousness as the ground dropped away at an alarming rate.

The last thing that went through Jyllana's muddled thoughts were the chaotic voices of dragons entering her head.

Keeper of the Jewel

Dithreab's Bauble

Chazgul. Of all the ways over the centuries that Aelfwynne thought he might die, being eaten by a pack of chazgul was, admittedly, far down on that list. Nor was the irony of the sun glinting off the peaks that stretched into the distance lost on him. Chazgul detested sunlight. But, unlike trolls, once engaged, they were relentless. To make matters worse, had he listened to Scale and hurried along the Path of the Errant Knight, they might have avoided their horrific fate. He shook his head in dismay. He was getting old.

The warmth of the fireball roiling in his claw-tipped palms provided him little comfort. There were too many. Summoning fireball after fireball had drained his stamina to a dangerous level. Soon he would falter. When that happened, they were finished.

Despite his warning not to use a physical weapon, Scale shuffled around uselessly beside him, pointing his dagger at the snarling beasts as they closed in. Not that he blamed the young elf. The chazgul's grotesquely twisted faces hunkered low to the ground, baring meat-rending fangs, were enough to terrify a seasoned fighter. Aelfwynne didn't have to check to see if his own knees were knocking together.

A chazgul launched itself at Scale. The elf cried out and ducked, cowering as he awaited a gory end.

Aelfwynne turned and blasted the creature, his fireball taking the chazgul full in the face and knocking it aside. It

Keeper of the Jewel

landed next to Scale, writhing and eerily screaming through the flames—its hideous cries echoing off the heights.

Scale jumped. Consumed by the wizard's fire, the beast still managed to snap at his legs. A burning paw reached out, grasped Scale by the ankle, and held on tight, dragging its fiery body toward him.

No matter how he tried, Scale couldn't pull his foot free. With a flurry of dagger strikes to the creature's extended arm, he shouted at the beast and kicked at its flaming head.

Aelfwynne had no choice but to let Scale battle for his life on his own as three chazgul crept toward him from the opposite direction. It was only a matter of time now.

Aelfwynne considered throwing himself off the side of the mountain, sparing him the inevitable agony of having his body ripped apart. He cringed at how painful a death at the claws of a chazgul would be, especially knowing they weren't likely to kill him outright. The beasts were renowned to play with their food before devouring it.

Scale's scream spun him around. Desperately attempting to pull the dead chazgul's claws from his ankle, he stared into the feral eyes of another beast closing in on him.

Aelfwynne discharged a hastily summoned fireball that struck the chazgul on the shoulder, knocking it off track, but it wasn't about to relent. Coarse hair singed, it shook off the blast and started for Scale again, its charred flesh smoking.

Unable to help the elf any further, Aelfwynne spun to face several chazgul that were almost on top of him, expecting their attack at any moment. If only he had the Staff of Reckoning. But he knew in his heart that even with its added strength, he wouldn't be strong enough to defeat the number of creatures attacking them.

In all of his centuries, there had never been a time that his magic hadn't been strong enough to make a difference…

Keeper of the Jewel

His jaw dropped. Staring death in the eye, Dithreab's condescending voice grated in his head, *'The bauble, you old fool!'*

As if in a dream, the scene of their parting slammed home.

'What's this?' He saw himself ask as Dithreab gave him a small sack containing the tiny, crimson gemstone.

The mischievous imp had smiled. *'It's me gift to ya, dragon breath. A wee token of me friendship...Where yer goin', I'm t' be thinkin' yer gonna have use of it. But, be warned. The magic of the stone can only be used once, so use it wisely.'*

The memory flashed through his mind in a moment, but its import was timeless. Reaching into his vest pocket he located the tiny stone and held it before him between two claws.

A series of deep, threatening growls returned his mind to the present. To his imminent demise.

The chazguls' muscles tensed, on the verge of leaping at him, but instead of conjuring a defensive spell, he remembered his ancient friend's words. *'Ye just need t' think o' me an' the stone'll do the rest.'*

Having been an adept magic-user for several hundred years, the sensation of experiencing the invocation of a powerful spell wasn't unfamiliar. The gemstone flared bright, casting the killing ground in a blood-red glow.

In that moment, it was as if everything around him on the Path of the Errant Knight had drawn to a standstill. The chazgul emitted a mournful, high-pitched squeal, halting their advance, and searching the sky.

The creatures' senses were more in tune with the natural elements around them than that of the wizard or the Home Guard. Aelfwynne followed their lead, scanning the sky, not sure what he was looking for.

Keeper of the Jewel

"Master! There!" Scale hobbled up beside him, pointing with his bloody dagger.

A sudden wind swirled the clouds. A bright light exploded overhead. Everyone covered their eyes lest they go blind. Even the chazgul.

Aelfwynne blinked several times in the unnatural brilliance and squinted, unsure of what he was witnessing.

A thunderous shriek reverberated off the mountainside and a dragon descended into their midst.

Scale pulled Aelfwynne out of the path of the white wyrm, throwing the high wizard to the ground to cover him with his body as a swath of deadly dragon fire purged the Path of the Errant Knight.

Keeper of the Jewel

Dragon Insurgence

Dawnbreaker rose high above the fiery fields of the Bascule Plains, her thick body pressing into Pecklyn's thighs due to the speed at which she climbed. It was hard to keep his eyes focused on the raging battle below, but it was even harder to understand how the dragon insurgence had been allowed to happen. Holding the stiff body of the princess' protector in his arms to keep her from falling to her death, he closed his eyes in despair.

Without having to put much thought into it, he knew the answer. He had been aware of the division in the factions loyal to Highcliff and those dragons who had, until moments earlier, hidden their allegiance to the Duke of Grim. Everyone at Highcliff was responsible for the senseless death being meted out before the black gates of the castle. Each and every Guardian had a role to play in the insurrection. Having only briefly observed the fiery carnage, Pecklyn knew with a certainty that he would take the guilt of not dealing with the festering rift to the grave.

Jyllana's head lolled to one side, rogue wisps of her bound hair tickling his cheek. Suddenly her eyes opened wide and her upper body shuddered with a great intake of breath.

It was all Pecklyn could do to hang onto her lest she slip from Dawnbreaker's shoulders. "It's okay! I got you!" he shouted, but the wind shredded his voice to oblivion.

Keeper of the Jewel

The chaotic scene of the fiery battlefield disappeared, lost to a hazy film of cloud that dampened their skin and left goosebumps in their wake.

Dawnbreaker burst through the top of the clouds, her wings glistening in the blinding sunshine.

"Level off," Pecklyn instructed. "Find Balewynd."

Their hair-raising ascent slowed well above the clouds; Dawnbreaker's wings angling to soar horizontally.

Jyllana's frightened gaze studied the empty sky above, but Pecklyn knew her unease had nothing to do with flying on the back of a dragon. He nodded grimly, "Dragons loyal to the duke have attacked Queen Khae's forces."

"We…" Jyllana swallowed, obviously struggling with the gravity of the situation. "We have to help."

Pecklyn's grim smile and slight nod was his answer. As desperate as the queen's plight had appeared in the brief glimpse he had of the battleground, he needed to discover whether Balewynd and Mirage had escaped the battering from the hostile troops stationed along the castle walls.

Many arrows had followed Dawnbreaker's hasty ascent. Though he didn't know for sure, he suspected the Grim Guard had loosed dragon killers after them as well. Thankfully, ballista bolts were rarely effective against a solitary dragon.

Although Mirage and Dawnbreaker had presented two point-blank targets, they had dropped from the sky with such speed, Pecklyn doubted the ballista crews had time to get their bearings. Even knowing that, he sighed with relief when Mirage's bulk materialized through the top of the clouds not far from where they flew.

A brief smile lit up Pecklyn's face. "You made it!"

Mirage craned his neck and slowed until Dawnbreaker flew alongside him.

Keeper of the Jewel

Pecklyn's elation faded. Balewynd's face had swollen to the point that he wondered how she could even see, but the pain and discomfort she must be experiencing didn't lessen the intensity of her glare.

He dipped his head in understanding and asked Jyllana, "You ready?"

Jyllana nodded. Pulling her daggers free, she hugged Dawnbreaker's neck as best she could.

Pecklyn wrapped an arm around her waist, withdrew his sword with his other, and held it above his head. "Defend the queen at all costs!"

Balewynd dropped his gaze, set her sights forward, and leaned into the side of Mirage's neck. The big blue tucked in his wings and disappeared like a javelin thrown into the clouds.

Even knowing what to expect, Pecklyn's breath caught as they followed, bursting through the underside of the clouds to observe the widespread carnage littering the plains fronting the dark fortress. Fearing the worst, he was gladdened to see a yellow dragon ferociously protecting the airspace above the queen's position.

"Who defends the queen?"

"Atsila."

"What's a Watchman doing out here?"

Dawnbreaker didn't respond, her great head turning to the flight of a green dragon descending on Atsila's position.

He followed her gaze. "We have to help her!"

Before the words had passed his lips, he knew they couldn't reach the yellow dragon in time. The treachery of the green dragon, Eldron, filled him with a deep sense of dismay. At the last moment, Atsila recognized her peril and turned to face the oncoming threat.

Keeper of the Jewel

Pecklyn gaped. Sitting astride the Watchman's neck was none other than Elder Guardian Xantha; a great spear poised to strike in her aged hand.

The ensuing collision and gouts of exchanged dragon fire happened so quickly it was difficult to ascertain the outcome, but as the dragons passed each other, fighting to maintain their flight, Pecklyn's heart sank. Atsila's back was empty—the scales along the side of her face and down her neck and wing blackened and smoldering.

"After Eldron!" Pecklyn fought to speak past his terror, his gaze following the flight of the green dragon as it back-flapped and drew up to come at Atsila again.

Atsila imitated her foe, spinning in the air above a field of interlocked tower shields.

Somewhere beneath all that metal, Pecklyn hoped the queen still lived. He glanced briefly at Atsila as she came about and did a double take.

Clinging to the side of Atsila's thick neck with one hand, Xantha righted herself on the dragon's shoulder and hefted her spear, ready for Eldron's next attack.

Dawnbreaker closed in from the side but her flight slowed and her angle of descent levelled off. *"Sunfire's moving to intercept."*

Pecklyn spotted the orange dragon Dawnbreaker had indicated. His morale slipped further, appalled by how many dragons had thrown in their lot with the duke. "We have to save Xantha!"

The words had no sooner left his mouth than a blue blur dropped from the sky like a boulder, slamming into the top of Eldron with such force that people otherwise engaged on the battlefield stopped to take notice.

Pecklyn's stomach sank.

Keeper of the Jewel

Balewynd had flown Mirage like a battering ram. The blue and green dragon plummeted from the sky in a tangle of wings and claws—Pecklyn's closest friend swallowed in the cataclysmic collision.

Dawnbreaker's shriek was the only warning Sunfire had before being doused in a firestorm as they collided in midair, Sunfire's closest wing crumpling against her side. Bones snapped—the noise similar to a tree limb being torn from its trunk.

Had Pecklyn not have been such an astute rider, he and Jyllana would have been thrown to their deaths. Even so, it took everything he had to keep the two of them on Dawnbreaker's shoulders as their forward momentum came to a crashing halt.

For the briefest of moments, Pecklyn feared the impact had seriously injured Dawnbreaker, but after falling momentarily, the hardy dragon extended her wings, lifting them above the fiery plains.

Arrows peppered the air from every direction, a few whistling close to Dawnbreaker's flight.

Pecklyn spun on her shoulders, frantically trying to discover where Mirage and Balewynd had fallen.

"There!" Jyllana pointed with one of her daggers.

He followed the extended blade. Between the queen's front line and the gatehouse towers of Castle Grim, Mirage's prone body lay broken, draped over the unmoving form of Eldron.

Balewynd's blue raised his head, his body flinching as arrow after arrow thudded against his tough hide—loosed from the Grim Guard archers stationed along the ramparts. Most of the thin missiles shattered or bounced harmlessly off his scaly hide, yet Pecklyn could see where a few had found their mark between his protective scales.

Keeper of the Jewel

He shouted in despair, "Torch the gatehouse! Draw their fire!"

Dawnbreaker altered her course, drifting low over the heads of the queen's troops. Several arrows impacted her underside; the royal army having no idea whether they were friend or foe. If Dawnbreaker incurred any damage, she didn't let on.

Approaching the twin black towers comprising the gatehouse, Pecklyn's blood ran cold. "Ballistae! Two of them!"

Mounted on top of each tower, crews ratcheted tree-sized bolts into place while Grim Guard lancers positioned behind the dragon-slayers aimed the deadly machines at Mirage who was struggling to regain his feet in front of the gates.

Dawnbreaker adjusted her flight to incorporate both killing machines, but as she spread a gout of deadly fire across the first ballista, bathing everyone in killing flames, a ballista bolt fired from somewhere else along the castle wall, thumped into her side and fell away, not hitting her flush.

His dragon knocked off course and faltering, Pecklyn watched on in horror. Unconcerned with his own pending fate, he watched helplessly as the ratchets of the second ballista clanked home. An elf stepped back and raised his arm to signal it was ready to fire.

The lancer responsible for deploying the bolt nodded and leaned over his aiming mechanism.

Pecklyn's face crunched together in anticipation of the shot that never came.

The lancer abruptly stood up straight, his pained glare staring at Dawnbreaker before he fell backward—a familiar dagger handle sticking out of his face.

Pecklyn blinked several times in bewilderment until he caught Jyllana's wide grin.

Keeper of the Jewel

A sudden cheer from the battlefield lifted the hair on Pecklyn's arms.

Hovering above Queen Khae's position, Xantha pointed her spear, directing everyone's attention toward the castle.

High above Castle Grim's haunting towers, a wing of dragons flew toward the battlefield with riders visible upon their backs.

The Highcliff Guardians were coming.

Keeper of the Jewel

Zorain

Scale had come to accept his fate. He was to die alongside a goblin in a remote part of South March. In one instant he had been defending himself against creatures so hideous he shuddered just looking at them, and in the next he lay atop the goblin, shielding the high wizard from a dragon who had materialized out of thin air to rain fire down on them.

The searing heat felt like it was melting the pilfered Grim Guard leather into his skin—the sheer noise of the swath of fire causing him to whimper. But, for some reason, the full strength of the dragon attack missed them.

Afraid to move, he searched their immediate area. The chazgul that had escaped the dragon assault skittered into rock formations or bid a hasty retreat down the Path of the Errant Knight, their prey forgotten.

"Get off me, you fool. What's happening?" Aelfwynne growled beneath him.

Scale rose to his knees and helped Aelfwynne stand, his eyes never leaving the white dragon who had landed not far from where they cowered—its orange eyes watching them.

Aelfwynne frowned and hobbled to the dragon's side. "Zorain? What're you doing here?"

After a moment, Aelfwynne's frown deepened. "What do you mean you don't know how you got here?"

The white dragon searched their surroundings, his blue spikes reminding Scale of long crystals. When the beast turned its attention back to them, it stared at Scale with narrowed eyes, flames licking between exposed teeth.

Scale swallowed.

"Oh, him? He's alright," Aelfwynne said as if he were responding to a question and added, "The uniform? He stole it from the castle. It's okay, you can let him hear you."

"We thought you were dead."

Scale jumped as a deep male voice resonated in his head. It took him a moment to realize it belonged to the dragon Aelfwynne referred to as Zorain. Scale had heard years ago that dragons spoke inside one's head, but he never thought it possible that one day he might experience it. As incredible as it was, it was terrifying knowing someone was able to do that to him so easily.

"Ya, well, so did I. But here I am."

Scale was amazed by how casually the goblin spoke to the dragon.

"Did you cast a spell on me?"

"Me? No, why...?" A look of wonder gripped Aelfwynne. He searched his pockets and the ground around him, finally locating what he sought. Holding the gemstone Dithreab had given him in his open palm he extended it toward Zorain. "What do you make of this?"

The dragon sniffed at it.

Scale swallowed, mesmerized by how the diminutive high wizard stood calmly before an enormous, fire-breathing creature with nary a care in the world.

"I sense an immensely powerful magic. One beyond the scope of mankind. Or even that of dragonkind if I have the right of it. I'm inclined to think it has connections to the Fae."

Aelfwynne nodded and pulled the stone away from Zorain, turning it in his palm.

Keeper of the Jewel

"If I'm not mistaken, the magic conjured was a one-time use. Linked to the caster. In order to summon that much magic—to summon a creature as large as me, I'm thinking it cost the caster dearly."

Stricken, Aelfwynne gazed up at Zorain.

The dragon closed his eyes as if confirming his assessment. *"The stone is nothing but a bauble now."*

Scale put a consoling hand on Aelfwynne's shoulder.

Zorain lowered his chest to the ground. *"Come. Allow me to transport you. Your presence is sorely needed."*

"You'll be flying me *and* Scale, correct?"

"If I must."

"You must. Scale has proven himself worthy of a dragon's trust," Aelfwynne said as he struggled to climb onto Zorain's shoulders.

Despite his misgivings about getting too close to the dragon, Scale assisted the high wizard, but paused and stared at the goblin's backside as Aelfwynne muttered, "Even if he is a bumbling fool."

Unsure of how to go about it, Scale clumsily made his way up Zorain's side and settled in behind Aelfwynne, anxiety overwhelming him. He was about to fly on the back of a— "Whoa!"

Zorain leapt into the air, the sudden jump and subsequent drop before his wings thrust enough air to keep them aloft, jarred Scale's sensibilities. Heart in throat, Scale feared they would plummet thousands of feet into the shale valley that paralleled the Path of the Errant Knight, but in a matter of heartbeats, the mountainside dropped away to meld with the dizzying peaks of the Mardeireach.

A sadness pervaded Aelfwynne's voice as he looked back at the mountain. "We were fortunate the chazgul hunted us."

Keeper of the Jewel

Scale frowned. The old wizard was daft. "You think it lucky we were hunted by those…those things?"

"Oh, aye," Aelfwynne muttered, barely audible over the rushing wind of dragon flight. "If not for the chazgul, we would've fallen victim long ago. Their presence scared off all of the other deadly creatures that stalk the Path of the Errant Knight."

Scale struggled to comprehend the apparent danger they had been in since leaving the company of the wood sprite. If this is what being a wizard entailed, perhaps he should stick to parlour tricks. Plying his trade on the streets of Urdanya, he would only have to deal with cutthroats and thieves.

It took Scale a while before the tension eased from his muscles. Once acclimatized, the cold wind in his hair and the breathtaking vista of the endless chain of jagged tors passing far below filled him with a wonder he had never known. If not for his sensible fear of the fire breathing beasts, he thought it quite possible to develop a love for flying the skies.

Sitting in front of him, the high wizard mumbled to himself, much like he had done all through the night—as if it helped him to better deal with his problems by speaking his thoughts aloud. Most of the goblin's words were consumed by the wind, but Scale heard odd snatches.

"I knew they would be intercepted…Orlythe's dragons…Traitors…Decoys…Send one south…What a waste of valuable birds…"

Tiring of the nonsensical chatter, Scale bent to speak into Aelfwynne's ear. "What's that?"

Aelfwynne stiffened and glared over his shoulder. "Nothing."

Turning his attention back to where they were flying, the high wizard asked, "Where are you taking us?"

Keeper of the Jewel

"I was flying over Faelyn's Nest on my way to..." Zorain craned his neck to stare at them, his eyes widening.

The look of shock on a dragon's face was one of the strangest things Scale had ever witnessed.

"You don't know what's happening, do you?"

Aelfwynne returned the dragon's surprised look. "What do you mean?"

"Queen Khae's forces are being annihilated before the gates of Castle Grim."

Scale imagined the high wizard's face fell as surely as did his own.

"The queen is here? At Grim Town?" Aelfwynne blurted.

"Aye. A bloody battle has been joined. Several dragons have sided with the duke and are defending his walls."

"His walls? He's the queen's emissary. Those are her walls!" Aelfwynne shouted.

"I agree, but all is not lost, Master Aelfwynne. Atsila flew to warn Highcliff. With any luck the Guardians will respond in time."

"This is worse than I thought," Aelfwynne muttered, his voice dropping into one of introspection.

In his short time with the high wizard, Scale had gotten used to the wizard's abrupt mood changes. More importantly, he had learned it best to leave the goblin to his broodings. No good would come out of questioning the high wizard when he was in one of his moods.

Aelfwynne's head perked up, a knowing look upon his face. He slapped the side of Zorain's neck. "We have to hurry if we're to make a difference."

561

Keeper of the Jewel

The Keeper of the Jewel

𝕬𝖇𝖆𝖓𝖉𝖔𝖓𝖊𝖉. That was how Ouderling felt watching Cynder and Ashe, and several older Guardians she had seen around the complex but had never met, fly away on the backs of their dragons. Everyone of importance had left Highcliff to deal with the rapidly unfolding crisis at Castle Grim. Everyone except the second highest ranking authority in all the land.

She gazed for a long while at the last place she had seen the dragons in the western sky above the rock shelf abutting Highcliff. The sight of eight winged beasts and their riders, flying in the semblance of a formation had been nothing short of breathtaking.

Far to the west, a snow-capped peak glinted in the rays of the rising sun. A curious stirring conjured an odd image in her mind. As if a dragon had emerged from where the sunshine had refracted off a distant mountain tor. The surreal sensation lasted for but a moment and then it was gone.

A sudden gust of bitter wind buffeted her short locks around her face. She pulled her brown cloak tight and returned to the empty complex. Scuffing the bottom of her soft-soled boots as she went, she wondered what she was doing there.

Nobody took her seriously. Sure, an old wyvern and his ancient rider had filled her head with nice thoughts, but it was the opinion of the one who really mattered, the one who

562

Keeper of the Jewel

had detested her presence in the south ever since she had met him in the Passage of Dolor, that mattered. Aelfwynne, the high wizard appointed by her grandmother, had made it plain she was not welcome.

The entrance tunnel gaped empty before her. Though not busy with traffic at the best of times, the cold tunnel was noticeably bereft of the hardy elves who had pledged their lives to the preservation of the Crystal Cavern. If she wasn't mistaken, only the handful of goblin caretakers and their respective wyverns had remained behind.

A wry smile and a stronger scuff of her boot accompanied the image of the high wizard. His malicious grim would haunt her dreams for years to come, but not as much as his ill-founded opinion of her. The senile, old goblin had based his entire opinion of her on the mention of the word, 'guess.' She shook her head. What a stupid way to judge someone.

She wandered through the quiet tunnels and paused outside the door of her temporary chambers—one they still required her to share with Jyllana even though there were many empty chambers throughout the expansive complex. The tunnel systems of Highcliff were so convoluted she doubted she had seen half of them yet. The distances required to get from one place to another reminded her of Borreraig Palace.

A faint yearning tugged at her heart. Marris' face conjured itself in her mind as if he stood in the cold tunnel before her. She sighed, catching herself reaching out to run loving fingers along his chiselled features. If only they had run away together. But no. Marris had decided it was better to betray her to her father.

Her chamber door banged open beneath her sudden push. It slammed closed behind her just as hard.

The empty room and pile of exquisite armour stacked neatly in the corner mocked her, as if the silent chamber and the unused gear confirmed how unimportant her place in the world really was. Princess or not, her role in South March was inconsequential.

She slumped onto her pallet and held her head in her hands, remaining that way until she heard a clatter pass by her door; the loud noise jolting her out of her misery.

Looking up, the special armour given to her by Xantha glinted in the flickering candlelight. Armour that felt so empowering to wear. Armour that fit so well it had to have been designed with her in mind. Armour that was wasted.

She sighed and decided to don the exquisitely wrought suit one last time before she abandoned it. If for no other reason than to prove to herself how preposterous it was of her to consider that she could ever become a true Highcliff Guardian.

Another clamour arose beyond her closed door. She paused to stare at the old, wooden barrier but the sound died away.

Struggling to pull off her suede boots, she grunted in disgust. Some fighter she made. She could barely remove her footwear.

Accompanied by a frustrated grunt, the first boot finally came off. It had no sooner come loose in her hands than it bounced off the door with a loud thump. The second boot joined it shortly afterward.

Vigourously stripping out of her clothes, she yanked the decorative, skin-tight breeks belonging to the suit up her thin legs and pulled the tight, long-sleeved tunic over her head.

Her angered thoughts, coupled with the effort required to don the snug leather, left her bathed in a sheen of sweat. Picking up the first metal boot of the vaunted armour, she barely restrained herself from tossing it after her original footwear.

Keeper of the Jewel

Thankfully, the richly detailed boots went on without much difficulty, but she struggled to remember how to fit the fancy greaves over her shins and secure them in place.

Once the greaves were on, she plodded around the small chamber to ensure the boots meshed with the shin armour before she hefted the largest piece of the daunting suit. The cuirass felt cold on her damp skin as it slid over her head and its weight settled onto her shoulders.

Staring at herself in the mirror she grimaced, unsure what came next. The thigh armour, abdomen protection, or hip guards? Even though she had equipped herself the other day, for the life of her, she couldn't recall what went on after the cuirass. Placing the remaining equipment on the pallet, she debated whether it mattered what order they went on.

Frustrated by the whole process, she decided that all she wanted to do was slip on the elbow-length gauntlets one last time. Of the entire ensemble, the knee-high greaves and the beautifully designed metal and leather gauntlets were her favourite parts of the suit.

Flexing her fingers, she was awed by how perfectly the gloves fit. If not for their weight, she doubted she'd know she was wearing them if someone snuck them on her while she slept.

A sudden bang at the door made her jump. Before she had a chance to draw her next breath the door flew open, barely missing her.

"There you are! Come quick! Eolande's hurt!"

The wrinkled face of an old female goblin stared at her, grave concern in her beady eyes.

Ouderling didn't know her name, but she had seen the caretaker in the Crystal Cavern tending to the stones. It took Ouderling a moment to comprehend what had been said. A twinge of fear startled her senses. She wasn't a healer. How was she supposed to know what to do?

"What happened?"

The old goblin grabbed her by the gauntlet and pulled her from the room—the little creature's strength impressive. Dragging Ouderling in the direction of the main exit tunnel, the caretaker said, "A wizard is trying to enter Highcliff. He's hurting everyone!"

Ouderling dug in her metal boots and yanked the goblin to a halt. "A wizard? Who?"

"The human wizard from Duke Orlythe's court, Your Majesty." She tugged on Ouderling's hand. "Come quick!"

Ouderling's eyes searched around as she tried to comprehend what was happening. There were only two wizards at her uncle's castle that she knew of, but the inference of a human wizard could only mean…

"Hang on. I need to get a weapon." Not waiting for a response, Ouderling charged back into her room. If what the goblin said was true, she shuddered to think about what it meant for Highcliff.

Not bothering to take the sword belt, she pulled the two-handed broadsword Eolande had embedded with a piece of the Focal Stone free of its scabbard and ran from the chamber.

The goblin hadn't bothered to wait. By the time she saw her again, the caretaker was approaching the distant light of the exit onto the stone shelf.

A muted screech reached her; its piercing cry so loud it could only be the sound a dragon or wyvern might make.

Her boots rang off the stone floor of the tunnel; the fact that they might be slippery on the smooth surface absently went through her troubled thoughts. What was the duke's wizard doing at Highcliff? Especially with reports of

Keeper of the Jewel

something big happening at Castle Grim. Perhaps more importantly, how had he gotten here?

A gout of fire greeted the unfortunate goblin as she exited the tunnel; tongues of flame licking at the threshold of Highcliff. Her little body ablaze, the caretaker dropped to the shelf, squirmed momentarily, and went still.

Ouderling skidded to a halt, unable to breathe as she stared dumbfoundedly at the horror of the gruesome sight. Everything seemed so surreal. Like a nightmare she would soon wake from.

Creeping to the edge of the tunnel, her nostrils turned up with the acrid aroma of burnt flesh. Try as she might, she could not take her eyes off the grisly remains of the caretaker. She gagged, fighting the urge to wretch.

"Afara Maral! Enough! Have you lost your mind? This is Highcliff!"

Ouderling recognized Eolande's voice. Swallowing the building terror threatening to incapacitate her, she stepped past the charred body, her jaw dropping open in disbelief.

Three more withered bodies littered the promontory between where she stood and where a tall, thin man in black robes faced off with Eolande. If she wasn't mistaken, several, small bodies lay unmoving beyond them.

Confirmation that the wizard was Afara Maral paled in comparison to the sight of one of the fiercest dragons she had ever seen. Locking eyes with the red beast, it took a step toward her, flames dripping from the sides of its fanged maw.

"Demonic, no!" Eolande cried. "That's Princess Ouderling!"

Afara Maral squinted, his look of confusion softening as he nodded in recognition. "Ahhhh, princess. So, you *are* alive. I see you've cut your hair. How quaint."

Keeper of the Jewel

The human wizard gave her a mock bow, his malevolent smirk sending shivers up her spine. He raised his hands; long, bony fingers pointed her way. "It's time to correct Orlythe's mistake."

"Princess! Run!"

A brown shape dropped from the sky. Baring rows of meat-rending fangs, Perch fell toward the wizard, but his killing blow never happened.

A red blur, faster than Ouderling could follow, leapt from the platform and intercepted the wyvern. The dragon called Demonic took Perch's throat in his gaping maw and drove the wyvern over the brink of the rock shelf—disappearing from view with a tumultuous roar and gnashing of teeth.

"Perch!" Ouderling ran to the edge of the promontory, climbing a raised irregularity in the grey stone in time to see the intertwined beasts splash into the lake far below.

Miragan cried out from above. She too had witnessed the fall of her grandfather. She plummeted from the sky and hovered above where Perch and Demonic had disappeared beneath the lake's surface.

A wyvern larger than Perch scuttled from the exit tunnel, attracting the attention of everyone left alive on the shelf. The way the wyvern searched for and located Afara, Ouderling could only assume it knew where the threat lay.

A blue orb materialized in Afara's palms.

Before the wyvern had time to fly half the distance separating it from the wizard, a ball of ice blasted one of its wings, knocking it back to the platform. A smaller ice blast exploded against the wyvern's head, stunning it long enough to be consumed by a fireball that followed in its wake. The wizard's fire dropped the wyvern to the shelf. Emitting a shrilling cry, its wings crumpled in the intense heat. It tried to stand but fell to the ground and stopped moving.

Keeper of the Jewel

"No!" Ouderling cried. Her eyes found the remains of two more wyverns beyond the wizard—both shredded and bleeding profusely. Though hard to tell in the heavy mist shrouding the platform, one of the downed wyverns appeared to be alive, fighting a painful battle to survive—its laboured breathing short and ragged.

"Yes, princess. The reign of the Highcliff Guardians, and indeed, that of your parents and the elves of South March in general, is about to come to an inglorious end." Afara hissed, a sly smirk twisting one side of his sallow face.

"But you're my uncle's wizard. You pledged your service to the crown."

"Your uncle is a fool. Your mother will see him dead." Afara shrugged. "Or he will kill her. Either way is fine by me. When the battle at the gate is done, there will be little left of your mother's elite troops to make a difference. Or of the Grim Guard, for that matter. While they embroil themselves in a dragon war, they have left the most important treasure in all the world unguarded."

"My mother won't stand for this."

A maniacal laugh escaped the dark wizard. He gazed at the charred corpses and mangled bodies sprawled across the rock shelf. "Your mother will be dead. The same as these pitiful creatures who thought to stand against me."

Ouderling shook her head, refusing to believe what the scrawny man implied. Her limbs trembled uncontrollably, but her morbid fear was pushed aside by her rising anger.

The knowledge of her inability to do anything enraged her. She feared her teenage hostility would amount to nothing more than one of her usual temper tantrums. An all-consuming fury that would muddle her mind and leave her bereft of rational thought.

Keeper of the Jewel

Breathing heavily, she was powerless in the face of such evil. Aelfwynne had been right all along. She didn't have what it took to become a Highcliff Guardian. She lacked the skill. In fact, if she allowed herself to admit it, neither did she possess the mental toughness. She was nothing more than a figurehead. The heir to the Willow Throne. She wasn't a fighter.

She could tell by how her eyes burned as she glared at Afara Maral that they had turned blood-red. An intimidating sight to behold for a normal elf, but the human wizard was neither.

Out of the corner of her eye she noticed her gauntlets and the fancy sword Eolande had embedded with the Focal Stone shard, and recalled the incredulous feelings her image in the mirror had evoked in her.

Raising the sword above her head, a subtle energy trickled through the gauntlets, infusing her skin. The sensation stirred her dormant nature's essence, the combined magic soothing her unease. Her eyes cooled to ice-blue.

The crimson gemstone glowed of its own accord.

In a detached voice she heard herself say, "Come no closer, Afara Maral."

Again, the maniacal laugh. Afara started forward, unconcerned. "And who's going to stop me?"

Eolande stepped toward Afara, a dagger held high.

Afara threw a casual palm the goblin's way, hitting him with a minor fireball that suddenly flared to life.

Eolande's dagger fell to the ground, clanging as it bounced on the shelf. He staggered backward clutching his chest and collapsed dangerously close to the brink.

Ouderling swallowed, trying to curb the building terror battling against her newly found magical presence. If she couldn't get a handle on it, the fear would incapacitate her.

570

Keeper of the Jewel

She lifted her chin. "I will!"

As if on cue, the cliffside exploded with the flight of hundreds of birds, their raucous cries adding to the pandemonium.

Keeper of the Jewel

Momentarily distracted by the strange phenomenon, Afara raised his hands, flames licking at his fingers. "You? You're nothing but a foolish elfling. A parasite that needs to be stomped on. It's time to reunite you with your brother."

The mention of Ordyl shook her to the core but she refused to allow the wizard to frighten her. "I am Ouderling Wys. A Highcliff Guardian."

She maintained her battle stance, unconcerned that it was likely not the smartest way to stand in the face of danger. The trembling in her arms stilled. Her muscles flexed, warmed by the presence exuding from the Focal Stone shard as it comingled with her stirring essence.

Fire coalesced in the wizard's hands—a smirk twisting his angular face.

Glaring in defiance at the human wizard who was about to end her life, she remembered fondly how Eolande had knelt before her beside the earth blood pool. She glanced at the ancient goblin's unmoving body, the heartbreaking sight fueling her determination to avenge him.

Drawing strength from the old caretaker's memory, she declared, "I am the keeper of the jewel!"

Keeper of the Jewel

Dragon Mage

As much as Scale thought he had gotten used to the euphoria of flying high above the land, marvelling as each crag and tor passed beneath them, he wasn't prepared for the dizzying sensation that gripped him when the heights abruptly gave way, exposing the steely waves of a vast lake situated amidst a ring of smoking volcanoes.

"Hurry!" Aelfwynne shouted.

Zorain's wings undulated rapidly several times—the incredible thrust disconcerting—and angled his outstretched membranes to cut through the mist shrouded heights.

The abrupt increase in speed left Scale breathless, their reckless descent aimed at a distant jag of black rock protruding from a mountainside on the north shore of the lake. Though hard to see from such a distance, there appeared to be something happening on the ledge.

"I knew it!" Aelfwynne's voice cracked. "The figure in black! Kill it!"

If Scale thought their flight was wild before, it was all he could do not to scream as Zorain tucked in his wings and plummeted from the sky.

An ear-piercing shriek escaped the dragon's mouth, followed by a recoil of his head before he extended his neck and spewed forth a breath of dragon fire—the deadly swath engulfing the black-cloaked figure Aelfwynne had indicated.

Keeper of the Jewel

Scale struggled to keep from squishing Aelfwynne against Zorain's neck as the dragon's wings shot out wide and back-flapped, arresting their flight. Looking back, Scale was shocked to discover Afara Maral staring at them, a spell of protection fizzling out in the air around him. The duke's human wizard had repulsed Zorain's attack.

Instead of being irritated by the arrival of a dragon and the high wizard, Afara's face lit up with an evil smirk.

"Aelfwynne. What a pleasant surprise," Afara hissed. "You're just in time to witness the beginning of the end of elven rule."

"High Wizard Aelfwynne to you, Maral." Aelfwynne growled. Not waiting for Zorain to land, he leapt to the ground, rolled once, and stood upright at the base of the cliff, facing the wizard. Scanning the rock shelf, his attention lingered momentarily on the destruction Afara had wrought. "Your treachery ends here."

The fireball poised in Afara's hands crackled, flames dripping to the stone at his feet. He looked to the clouds and laughed.

Claw-tipped hands limned with flames, Aelfwynne snarled, "Where's Orlythe? Is the coward afraid to show his face?"

Afara's shrewd gaze locked on Aelfwynne. "Dead for all I know. If not yet, I'm sure your Guardians will see to it soon enough."

Aelfwynne frowned, his gaze darting around the platform, as if expecting an ambush.

"Oh, you won't find him here. He's cowering behind his walls, hoping to avoid the fallout of the dragon war." Afara started toward Aelfwynne, but stopped to glance at Scale who had slipped from Zorain and had pulled his dagger free.

Keeper of the Jewel

Afara stared hard at Scale, as if trying to recognize him. Shaking his head, he rolled his eyes. "So, that's how you escaped. You had help from one of Orlythe's troops. How ironic."

Scale bristled and started toward Afara. "I'm no Grim Guard."

"Scale, no!" Aelfwynne held up a fiery hand and jutted his chin to indicate Eolande's motionless form on the edge of the platform behind Afara. "See to that goblin over there. Pull him away from the brink."

Zorain growled, smoke billowing from flared nostrils.

Aelfwynne's gaze took in the downed wyverns. He nodded toward a young elf half-clad in fancy armour, the sight of her shorn tresses throwing him momentarily. "Hold, Zorain. Let me deal with Afara. You must guard the princess."

The princess? Scale looked closer at the distraught, short-haired elf half-clad in fancy armour and holding a sword over her head. How the slight girl even lifted the large weapon was surprising, but not as much as the relevance of who Aelfwynne claimed her to be.

He squinted and was stunned by what he knew to be true. In the heat of the moment, he hadn't taken the time to wonder who the elf might be. Those intense, blue eyes could belong to none other than Princess Ouderling.

He swallowed, berating himself for not realizing it sooner. She looked so different. So much more mature than the spoiled brat they had escorted from Orlythia a short while ago. She looked...deadly.

"You're too late to save the princess," Afara said calmly, but his rapid action took everyone by surprise.

A fireball soared across the intervening distance; its trajectory aimed at Ouderling's head.

575

Keeper of the Jewel

Scale stumbled, his dumbstruck attention on the irregular jag of raised rock and the fireball sizzling across the shelf, as his momentum carried him toward the fallen goblin many steps behind Afara.

Afara's fireball struck and exploded—long fingers of flame arcing away from the point of impact—the immediate area blossoming in a crimson glow.

"No!" Aelfwynne shouted, discharging a small fireball at Afara.

Zorain roared and lurched forward, spewing fire of his own at the human wizard.

Afara's maniacal laugh rose above the chaos, a hastily raised, magical shield absorbing the onslaught.

As Afara's fireball fizzled out, Ouderling stared back at him, her sword held before her unblemished face, but her attention was on a red dragon who fell from the sky and slammed into Zorain.

The promontory shook under the impact.

The most horrific of sounds lifted the hair on the back of Scale's neck as the beasts snarled and snapped, entangled in a writhing mass of horns, claws, and fangs.

The battling dragons rolled between Ouderling and Afara, their path taking them over the brink and out of sight.

Afara lifted his hands, a blue ball of ice crystals roiling between bony fingers. "And then there were two."

Faster than the eye could see, the human wizard launched the iceball at Aelfwynne.

Aelfwynne's hands moved in a flurry of action but the bulk of his magical shield didn't materialize in time. The impact lifted him from his feet and dashed him against the cliff face. He dropped to the ground in a heap and didn't move.

Afara grinned. "That has been a long time coming, Dragon Mage."

Keeper of the Jewel

Looking to Ouderling, Afara raised his eyebrows, his thin frame straightening from its usual slump. Ice crystals formed between his hands. Nodding in satisfaction, he hissed, "And now there is one."

Ouderling held his stare, a slow smile lifting her cheeks.

Afara tilted his head in question, opening his mouth to say something. His eyes grew wide with shock and a disbelieving gurgle escaped his thin lips as he crumpled to the shelf dead.

"You mean, two," Scale growled, staring down at the expanding pool of blood around Afara's neck. Holding his dagger over the fallen wizard, he watched the human blood drip from its edges. "The princess is never alone."

A moan from the base of the cliff near the entrance to Highcliff drew Scale's attention. He turned to watch Aelfwynne sit up, holding his chest, but the high wizard appeared uninjured by the icy blast.

Scale held up his dagger and winked. "Sometimes steel is the better option, Master Aelfwynne."

Aelfwynne returned a conciliatory nod, but his gaze followed the princess as Ouderling jumped down to the promontory and rushed to where Eolande's body lay on the edge of the rock shelf.

Scale stepped up beside her. Whether the old goblin was dead or not, he didn't have the heart to ask.

The clouds opened up, drenching the promontory with a heavy downpour. Pulling his Grim Guard tunic tightly around him, Scale gazed out over the lake.

Movement far below drew his attention.

Though hard to discern through the misty downpour, it looked as though a small wyvern tugged at the wing of a larger one, dragging its lifeless body to shore.

577

Keeper of the Jewel

Encroaching Darkness

"**Your** father would have been proud." Aelfwynne held Scale's gaze.

The high wizard's jagged-toothed grin had been disconcerting the first time Scale had seen it in the bowels of the earth below Grim Keep, but he had learned to accept it. He smiled. Who was he kidding? The goblin's face would always instil fear in him. Especially now that it bore the scars of Afara's wizard's ice.

Caught off guard by the kind sentiment, the noise of conversation filling the platform fronting Highcliff was but a distant hum.

"Do you intend on taking my hand with you?"

Aelfwynne's claws protruded from Scale's firm grip. "Huh? Um, no. Sorry."

Again, that scary grin. "That's good. I don't think Zorain would appreciate flying me again anytime soon."

The white dragon in question waited patiently on the edge of the rock shelf, the injuries he had sustained in his battle with Demonic thankfully not severe enough to inhibit his flight. When Afara had died, the red dragon had disengaged with Zorain and flown off, as if it had sensed the wizard's demise. "You sure you don't want to come with me?"

Aelfwynne shook his head. "The pain is still too great."

Scale respected that. He followed Aelfwynne's gaze to where Zorain patiently sat; separated by dozens of Home

Keeper of the Jewel

Guard, and the queen herself, who entertained an admiring group of Guardians.

"Are you sure *you* want to do this?" Aelfwynne asked as Scale's attention fell on the blonde-haired monarch and the king.

Scale was but a minor player in the Home Guard. One who hadn't enjoyed the privilege of speaking to the royal couple. From the accolades and reverence his father had heaped upon them, Scale wasn't sure he would ever be comfortable if the occasion presented itself. "I feel we owe it to him."

"Very well." Aelfwynne patted his hand. "Be careful. His kind are tricksters at the best of times."

"I will."

"It's an honour, you know."

Scale frowned. "Huh?"

"To be chosen by an adult dragon. Most riders are paired with the beasts when they are but dragonlings. It's rare for an adult dragon to choose a rider. Zorain must sense what I have suspected all along."

"And what's that, Master?"

Aelfwynne shook his head as he rescued his crushed hand, massaging it in his other. "If I have to tell you, perhaps I'm mistaken."

"You? Mistaken?" Scale's laugh prompted the high wizard to roll his eyes.

"Now go. Before Zorain changes his mind."

"Yes, Master." Scale stepped away, but stopped. "Oh yes. I almost forgot."

He reached into his freshly laundered Grim Guard uniform, fond of how well the duke's leather fit him, and pulled out a battered, spun gold tiara.

Aelfwynne accepted it. "What's this?"

Keeper of the Jewel

"It belongs to the princess. I found it out on the plains that day I was left behind to tend the horses."

"What did you do to it?" Aelfwynne examined the bent wire crown. "Step on it?"

Scale shrugged. "More or less. Will you see she gets it?"

Aelfwynne raised questioning eyebrows. "Give it to her yourself. She's standing right there."

Scale followed his gaze to the knot of elves around the queen. "Nah. I couldn't."

Aelfwynne nodded.

"One last thing, Master."

Aelfwynne raised impatient, hairless eyebrows.

"I thought white dragons were old females?"

The wizard frowned at that but answered, "Most are, but once in a while a white dragon is born. It's supposed to be a lucky omen. Consider yourself blessed. Now go, before I have you tossed into Crag's Forge."

Scale laughed and slipped through the crowd.

Seeing his approach, Zorain knelt.

Scale clambered aboard the dragon's shoulders and righted himself. He had flown Zorain several times in the intervening days since what was being hailed as, 'The Battle at the Gate,' both upon the Bascule Plains and before the main entrance to Highcliff. Even so, his anxiety rose as he readied himself for flight.

A hush settled over the platform; most eyes turned his way to see him off.

Embarrassed, he patted Zorain on the side of the neck. "Let's get out of here, buddy. Crowds give me the heebies."

"I don't blame you," Zorain agreed. Without warning, he crouched and jumped into the air, his weight dropping him below the ledge before his wings generated enough thrust to lift them into the sky.

Keeper of the Jewel

As they winged away from Highcliff, Scale noticed the wildly waving arms of a tall, short-haired, young elf standing on an irregular jag of rock.

A warmth flushed him. Detaching herself from the knot of elves surrounding the queen, the princess had run up the small ramp and was jumping up and down, her mangled tiara clasped in a waving hand.

The pain in Pecklyn's back was one he would gladly endure for as long as he drew breath if it meant that he could be of assistance to his closest friend.

Balewynd hung off his arm, struggling to keep her ruined body upright in the company of the royal couple. She had adamantly refused being lugged around in a litter, or even a chair, for that matter. Proud, even through a twisted face that bespoke to the extent that she suffered, Balewynd insisted on facing the queen under her own power.

He had found Balewynd shortly after the dragons loyal to Duke Orlythe had surrendered to the Highcliff contingent. Though the Battle at the Gate had been short lived, the rogue dragons had inflicted serious harm on Queen Khae's forces. Many days had been spent caring for the injured and burying the dead. Of which, Pecklyn was sure Balewynd would be counted, but he found her clinging to life trapped beneath the dead body of the green dragon, Eldron.

He had flown her back to Highcliff, certain her time was at hand, but with the surprise return of Aelfwynne, the high wizard had managed to save her.

His eyes moistened seeing the goblin in question walk up to the princess. The old Master's actions had affirmed why every Guardian would lay down their life for him.

"Your Majesty." Aelfwynne grabbed Ouderling's hand and kissed it, bowing as he did so. "My sincerest apologies.

Keeper of the Jewel

I want you to know officially that you have proven yourself worthy to be a Highcliff Guardian."

Ouderling grimaced, looking regal and imposing at the same time in her full suit of armour. She patted the hilt of her sword, the crimson gemstone glinting in the rare sunshine basking the promontory. "I did nothing, Master Aelfwynne. It was my sword. The one," she pulled another goblin into view who had been hidden on her far side, "fashioned by our mutual friend."

Eolande bowed his head, his green cheeks reddening. Visible scars on his left cheek and neck showed where Afara's spell had hit him.

Ouderling didn't miss the sadness behind the ancient goblin's eyes. Forced as she knew it was, his beautiful smile couldn't hide the pain Eolande felt for the loss of Perch. She couldn't begin to imagine what kind of bond the two had formed over a millennium. She was surprised he hadn't just given up on life altogether.

She dropped to a knee and hugged Eolande, pulling his large head against her own. "Oh, Eolande. I miss him too. I wish I could have done something to save him."

Eolande nodded into her shoulder, tears sliding down his rough cheeks. "He was so proud that he got to meet you."

The people around her blurred as she teared up.

"The sword may have saved you in the end, Your Majesty," Aelfwynne said when Ouderling stood again. "But it was you who stood up to wield it in the face of the evil that threatened the Crystal Cavern. Knowing you were about to die, you held your ground. We can expect nothing more. From this day forth, you will be known as a Highcliff Guardian."

His proclamation helped push aside the grief she shared with Eolande. Pride swelled her chest. Lifting her chin in a regal manner, she unabashedly allowed herself to be seen with tears dripping off her chin.

Her sad face transformed into one of awe as Aelfwynne handed her the tiara. She gaped at the twisted golden wire. "Where did you find this?"

Pointed teeth exposed themselves with Aelfwynne's broad smile. "I had nothing to do with it." He nodded toward the white dragon who was accepting Scale on his back.

"I must thank him!" Ouderling pushed past them and ran toward Zorain, but she was too late. The Watchman had already leapt into the sky.

"Excuse me...Excuse me." Dressed in the snug black leather outfit she had pilfered from Castle Grim, Jyllana forced her way through the crowd from where she had been hovering inconspicuously. She paused long enough to shake her head at Aelfwynne. "Seriously. How does anyone expect me to keep up with her?"

With that said, Jyllana followed the princess across the platform.

Khae allowed the high wizard to kiss her hand, before she bent at the knees and hugged him tightly, the act causing him noticeable discomfort with all the eyes watching them.

She spoke with heartfelt emotion, not caring who heard. "South March will forever be in your debt. Thank you for saving our future. I wish I could hold you in my arms forever to prove how grateful I am. If you ever have need of anything, I promise I'll move a mountain to get it for you."

"You could start by letting me breathe again," Aelfwynne strained to speak.

Khae laughed. She hugged him tighter for but a moment, eliciting a grunt from the goblin, before releasing him.

Keeper of the Jewel

He followed the flight of Zorain and Scale and nodded after them. "The son of Gerrant Wood deserves the credit, Your Majesty."

Those around them followed his gaze.

"Watch him closely, for he will surely become the next Dragon Mage," Aelfwynne said solemnly.

Khae returned her attention to the high wizard. "That's good news indeed. I'm sure his training is in good hands. You truly are the gem my mother spoke of."

Aelfwynne glanced at the ground between them with humility for a moment, but when he looked back, she was caught off guard by his serious demeanour.

"What is to happen with the duke?"

Khae swallowed. She and Hammas had spent many sleepless nights since the Battle at the Gate discussing this very question.

Conscious of all the listening ears, she said as calmly as she could, "My brother blames Afara Maral, as you know."

Aelfwynne held her stare. "And you believe him?"

"Not for a moment, but something bigger must be responsible for what happened," Khae said as patiently as she could. She thought of the warning written on the note Head Chamberlain Bayl had given to his daughter and swallowed the unease its message instilled.

She took a deep breath. Today was supposed to be a day of amicable parting. A day when she returned to what remained of her troops camped upon the Bascule Plains to begin the long trek home. She would have to find a way to deal with her brother, but not today. She needed to get back to Orlythia.

Aelfwynne had offered to have her and Hammas flown to Borreraig Palace on dragonback, but she had refused, insisting her place was with her troops.

584

Keeper of the Jewel

"Yes, Your Majesty." The high wizard dipped his head. "Be careful. We can't lose sight of the fact that the Soul has returned to South March. That is concerning indeed."

"And that's why I must pray for peace between Orlythia and the duchy of Grim. As much as I despise my brother's involvement in all of this, I fear South March will soon have need of his banners."

"Of course, Your Majesty. You know best."

Khae wasn't sure if Aelfwynne meant that out of respect or whether it was a barb directed at how poorly things had turned out as a result of her allowing her brother to carry on as he did.

She found Hammas' hand and squeezed hard. She needed his strength now more than ever.

Dithreab's Slighe was impossible to find on dragonback. Zorain put down in the deep forest clinging to the foothills of Faelyn's Nest and Scale went the rest of the way in on foot. It took him a while to discover the wood sprite's trail, but once found, it wasn't long before he came upon the side trail leading up to the ledge that fronted his lair.

The log trap hung unattended. The fact that it hadn't been reset warned Scale that Aelfwynne's fear for his old friend's fate was well founded.

Without having to concentrate too hard, he invoked his magic to lift the front half of the rotting tree stump on the edge of the ledge to expose the tunnel beyond. A tight squeeze and long crawl into the earth confirmed what the high wizard had suspected. The summoning spell released on the Path of the Errant Knight had claimed the wood sprite's life.

Scale stared long and hard at the little creature, uncaring of the tears that fell from his cheeks. Twigs for feet, Dithreab sat slumped against an open tome. His wee, tubular head hung forward. His sticklike shoulders slumped.

As carefully as he could, Scale scooped the sprite's fragile body into one hand and crawled from the lair.

The setting sun cast long shadows through the forest; the dying rays of the day bringing with it a permeating cold.

As the forest gave in to nighttime's approach, Scale patted the newly turned mound of earth in front of the entrance log.

"Rest well, Dithreab. Your battle has been fought. Enjoy the rewards of wherever your heart has taken you."

A bough snapped in the woodland below the ridge, making him jump.

Just visible through the trees, a white dragon stared up at him.

Taking a last look at Dithreab's resting place, Scale sighed. He hoped his father could see him now and know that he had truly blessed his son's life.

A cold shiver wracked Aelfwynne's body. A sensation that had plagued him frequently of late. Too often to be just a normal bodily reaction.

Today had been bittersweet. He had said good-bye to his dear friend's daughter as she flew back to be with her troops. As much as he respected the queen's strength, he worried about where her priorities lay when it came to dealing with the Duke of Grim. The pretender to the Willow Throne had cost South March dearly. Had cost the world a beautiful soul.

Sighing, his mind drifted many centuries into the past to a bright spring morning on the shoulders of Faelyn's Nest. Trees resplendent with new growth bid farewell to a harsh southland winter while birdsong and chattering insects formed the chorus over a backdrop of the newly arrived warm breezes heralding the rebirth. Amongst all the beauty,

Keeper of the Jewel

the quirky face of his old friend, Dithreab, materialized from the heather. The faerie creature's impish grin had banished the high wizard's melancholy that day.

If only he had had the courage to oversee the wood sprite's burial, but he dared not leave Highcliff this soon after the Battle at the Gate. The foundation of South March had been shaken hard. He had to remain vigilant to ensure no more cracks undermined Queen Khae's rule.

Someday perhaps, when the kingdom's ills were laid to rest, he would visit his friend's last resting place. It would do him good to revisit the mountain glen and deliver a private eulogy—a telling of the tall tales that had haunted his sleep ever since the ancient creature had given his life to save him and Scale on the Path of the Errant Knight. His deepest regret was the uncertainty nagging at him as to whether Dithreab's death had been in vain. Only time would answer that question.

"Whatcha thinking?" Xantha's large hand squeezed his little one as they sat alone before the sparkling earth blood pool—their faces glowing blue.

He shrugged. Tears were not a usual companion to his old, pragmatic nature, but memories of Dithreab had him on the cusp. "Nothing, really. Just concerned about where we go from here. I was sad to see Khae leave so soon."

Xantha squeezed harder. "She has to get back to her palace to begin mending the rift her brother has created. Something you must set your mind to as well when the time is right. Until then, I have something I need to tell you."

He looked up, startled; afraid to bear witness to yet another heartbreak. The angelic smile on his soul mate's wrinkled complexion allayed his apprehension. Considering everything they had gone through, he struggled to imagine how someone as special as the legendary warrior had come

Keeper of the Jewel

to love one as vile as him—a goblin, no less. He appreciated how fortunate he had been all those years ago. Someone like Xantha only came along once in a lifetime. With uncharacteristic patience, he awaited her next words.

A sheepish grin lit up her face. "You ready for this?"

"Oh, oh. What did you do?"

"Ha! What did *we* do, more like."

He frowned. "Alright, my pet. What did *we* do?"

"We made a baby!"

Someone whacking his head with the side of a battle-axe would have come as less of a shock. Speechless, he blinked rapidly, her proclamation seeping into the turmoil that constantly besieged his troubled mind.

Attempting to come to terms with what she had imparted, his fleshless lips opened, but no sound came forth.

Had he not been sitting down, he would surely have fallen to the ground as the blurred vision of the most beautiful creature in the whole world smiled back at him, wiping at the tears on his cheeks.

From beside the burnt wreckage of a ballista atop the western gate tower, Orlythe watched grimly on as dragons from Highcliff flew his sister and her people back from the mountain aerie.

A small part of him longed to go out there and meet her. To apologize again for everything that had happened, but the more he stared, the more his revulsion of the high and mighty queen grew. He had come so close to achieving his goal, but in the end, he had lost so much.

His treacherous wizard had seen to that. Him and that dark wraith.

Keeper of the Jewel

His eyes narrowed. What a fool he had been. Led astray by a human wizard and an evil being who obviously didn't have his best interest at heart.

Perhaps the biggest setback, however, had been the withdrawal of those dragons who had once sworn him loyalty. Led by Demonic, the surviving rogue dragons had been banished from Highcliff. Wanting nothing further to do with mankind, they had deserted the region and flew north to only the wind knew where.

Bonfires sparked to life on the Bascule Plains as the evening drew on. Unconcerned about the encroaching cold, he stared well into the night, wondering where to go from here.

The moon had climbed over the eastern mountains by the time heavy footsteps clattered up to him.

"A raven came in at sunset, m'lord."

Orlythe gazed wearily into the humourless eyes of Captain Drake and accepted a tiny scroll from the elf's hand.

Not wishing to be bothered by whatever was written on the parchment, he crumpled it in his fist and returned his attention to the activity beyond the walls.

"You should read it, m'lord."

Duke Orlythe wanted to scream at the elf to leave him alone. He drew a deep breath and glared at Captain Drake.

"I believe its from the wraith, m'lord."

The simple word, 'wraith,' jolted Orlythe's sensibilities. Instantly his mind was on alert. With trembling hands, only partially due to the deepening cold, he uncrumpled the missive.

In the light of the captain's torch, he read the simple words,

Odyne has been dealt with.

Keeper of the Jewel

He swallowed, his black eyes searching the night sky as the relevance hit home.

Staring out over the Bascule Plains to where his sister had retired to her pavilion for the night, a grim smile twisted his pepper-grey mustache.

A fiery glow limned the skies across the vast expanse of Crystal Lake, its unusually still waters reflecting the starlit sky. According to the inhabitants of Highcliff, only on the rarest of occasions was a cloudless sky enjoyed above the notorious ring of volcanoes.

Ouderling's feet dangled over the edge of the promontory abutting the entrance to the Highcliff complex. It had been a busy day at Highcliff. Her parents had finally departed for their long trip north, leaving her in the Guardians' capable hands.

Incessant cricket chirps filled the still air; the serenity of the moment reminding her of her secret oasis on the outskirts of Orlythia. The place where she had shared spirit and body with Marris. She sighed sadly, wondering how he was coping now that she was no longer there, curious as to whether they would ever rekindle the love they once shared. The one she had mercilessly sabotaged.

Life had been so much simpler back then.

She chuckled. It had only been what? A few weeks since she had embarked on this crazy journey.

"What's so funny?"

Ouderling blinked several times, turning her head to look into the prettiest eyes she had ever seen. She hadn't realized she had laughed out loud, but Jyllana was giving her a questioning look.

"Huh? Oh, nothing. I was just thinking."

"Of?"

Keeper of the Jewel

It was astounding to discover what a difference a few weeks of hardship had on one's life. Weeks fraught with peril and death. Had Jyllana questioned her like this back at Borreraig Palace, Ouderling would have berated her for being an insolent servant and reported her to her superior.

Her smile faded. Jyllana's superior had died so that they might live.

She patted Jyllana's thigh and gazed out to where a bank of clouds drifted across the eerie light above the distant peaks. "It doesn't matter now. I'm thinking our lives will never be the same again."

A long silence settled over the flat jut of rock protruding over Crystal Lake. Wind swept down from the heights, tussling their hair, intermingling the princess' snow-white locks with the loose strands of her protector's red hair.

The imagery gave Ouderling pause. The stark difference in colours equally as profound as their stations in life. And yet, here they were, side-by-side, doing their best to survive in a hostile world. A world drastically different than the safety and innocence of Borreraig Palace under the watchful eye of her parents.

It wasn't until that moment that Ouderling realized how much she missed their love. She had always been an ornery child. Unappreciative and spiteful. Not worthy of their endless devotion.

A great sadness gripped her. Even after living through everything that had happened since that fateful morning her mother had crashed unannounced into her bed chambers, she still struggled to understand the why's of the decisions that were made. The passage of time had helped soften the hurt of her parents' rash decision, but the pain was still raw. And yet, she knew they had acted out of love for her.

Keeper of the Jewel

Jyllana, to her credit, remained quiet. Always the faithful one, her protector knew when to respect her silence.

She stole a sideways glance, admiring Jyllana's profile. Appreciating how much the elf's steadying presence had come to mean to her. Just the thought of the close bond they had formed raised gooseflesh on her skin.

She placed an arm around Jyllana's slight shoulders and leaned her head toward the one person whose unexpected friendship meant more to her than any she had ever known.

Staring at the bank of thick clouds moving in to mask the fiery glow across the lake, extinguishing the faint light, she muttered, "Thank you for being the constant in my life. I'd be lost without you by my side."

Jyllana leaned her head against Ouderling's and wrapped her arm around the princess and squeezed. Alone together, they faced the encroaching darkness.

Keeper of the Jewel

To Grim Watch Tower

It was the best part of the day. Waking early and sneaking through the empty palace halls to enjoy the brief solitude of pre-dawn with Hammas by her side. How Khae enjoyed their daily ritual. Greeting each new day with the one person who really mattered—appreciating each other as the rising sun banished the lingering shadows of the long night.

Of course, there were always Home Guard watching their every move, but they were well-trained and made themselves as inconspicuous as their duty allowed while she and Hammas basked in the sanctuary offered by the palace gardens. Other than their bedchamber, it was the only place Khae truly felt removed from the public eye.

Her head in Hammas' lap, she hugged his thighs and craned her neck to accept his gentle kiss. They had just arrived back at Borreraig Palace late last night, relieved to be home after their harrowing ordeal on the plains fronting Castle Grim. She dropped her head back onto his thighs and sighed.

"She's in good hands, Khae," Hammas whispered,

Khae forced a meek smile. He knew her too well.

He ran loving fingers through her thick hair, gently massaging her scalp.

Not wishing to spoil the moment, she said anyway, "Do you think I did the right thing?"

Keeper of the Jewel

She felt Hammas sigh, the gesture answer enough, but true to the wonderful husband he was, he replied, "You did what you had to do."

"But was it the *right* thing to do?"

Again, the shrug. "He's your brother. I understand your reluctance to deal with him. Time will tell."

"I have to believe he was misled by Afara. It would bother me to no end to think otherwise. Surely he must see the error of his ways."

The serenity of the gardens was slowly being replaced by the hustle and bustle of the palace coming to life. It wouldn't be long before they were forced to abandon their refuge and meet the trials of the new day.

Khae sat up and stretched, saddened their brief respite had drawn to a close. It always happened so fast. She considered the king's serious demeanour. "Do you honestly believe he'll give us grief in the future?"

Hammas refused to meet her gaze. She knew that meant his answer wouldn't be what she wanted to hear.

He swallowed and said to the hydrangeas lining the walkway, "You can't change a dragon's scales."

The Queen of the Elves nodded. Deep down, she knew he was right.

Lifting her chin to face the day, she realized what she had to do. Something that would not amuse her husband.

It was time she dared a return visit to Grim Watch Tower.

The End...

...of the innocence.

I hope you enjoyed Keeper of the Jewel.

If you would be kind enough to leave a review on Amazon or wherever you purchased the book, it would help make a big difference to how this book is represented in the Algorithms. Thanking you in advance.

Coming November 2021

Dragon Sect, book 2 in the Highcliff Guardians.

The much-anticipated sequel to *Keeper of the Jewel*, *Dragon Sect* delves into the clandestine society of Windwalkers.

I offer personalized, signed, paperback copies, complete with bling!

A discount is offered on the purchase of a trilogy.

If you wish to order, please follow this link:
https://forms.gle/FAbJ1iMCGa7R792Z9

To keep up with everything going on in the Soul Forge Universe, please visit my website at:
https://www.richardhstephens.com/

All books are written within the Soul Forge Universe.

Books by Richard H. Stephens
in Chronological Reading Order

Highcliff Guardians
Keeper of the Jewel –Book 1

The Queen of the Elves is bothered by a disturbance in nature's essence. One she believes will lead to the death of her only living child.

Daring to visit the haunted tower on Grim Ward Island, Queen Khae's worst nightmare is revealed.

In a desperate attempt to save the heir to the Willow Throne, the princess is exiled to the only place capable of protecting her. Highcliff. The home of the coveted Crystal Cavern and the dragons that watch over it.

Legends of the Lurker Series

Reecah's Flight –Book 1

Everyone knows dragons are dangerous, but to hunt them is insane.

There is something strange about the woman living on top of the hill and the people of Fishmonger Bay leave her alone. At least until the day she visits the village witch.

Her life spinning out of control, Reecah must decide whether to slay the dragon or risk becoming a victim of her people.

Can Reecah find the key to unlock her family heritage or will she fall prey to the secret so many have died to protect?

Reecah's Gift – Book 2

The appalling mannerisms of those entrusted to protect the kingdom are shocking.

Braving the perils of a cutthroat city isn't what Reecah envisioned when she sought out a better place.

Can a ruthless giant equip her with the skills she needs to confront the king, or will his unorthodox ways end up being the death of her dreams?

Is an alliance with a murderous elf and a sly dwarf the best way to avert the plight of the dragons? And what is this *Gift* everyone seems to know about? Everyone, except Reecah.

Find out how the machinations of the evil prince and a traitorous wizard turn Reecah's quest on its head in this epic, second installment of the Legends of the Lurker.

Reecah's Legacy – Book 3

The culmination of the Legends of the Lurker trilogy.

Reecah Windwalker comes into her own as she finds peace with her past and bravely sets out to fulfill her legacy.

Keeping a promise to a dead witch, Reecah seeks those who can help her learn the ways of her dragon magic as she embarks on a desperate journey to save the last of the dragons from the dark heir.

The races come together, but their combined strength may not be enough to prevent the high king's dragon slayers from eradicating the beauty from the land.

Of Trolls and Evil Things

The (standalone) prequel to the Soul Forge Saga series!

Travel down an ever-darkening path where two orphans battle to survive a perilous mountainside, evading predators and prowlers that prey upon its slopes, and within its catacombs.

When danger forces them from their mountain home, they wander the cutthroat streets of Cliff Face in an effort to survive.

Strange circumstances spin their lives out of control, forcing them onto the nefarious slopes of Mt. Gloom to escape the unpleasant reality looming over them—only to discover their worst nightmare awaits them with open arms.

The Royal Tournament

(A standalone story from the Soul Forge Universe)

The Royal Tournament has at long last come to the village of Millsford.

For Javen Milford, a local farm boy, the news couldn't be better. Finally, Javen can perform his chores on the homestead and partake in the biggest military games in the Kingdom, hoping that just maybe, he might catch the eye of the king.

Javen enters the kingdom's flagship tournament only to discover that in order to win, one must be prepared to die.

The Banebridge Companion Novels
Larina – Book 1

Growing up on the streets of Storms End, Larina knows the only way to survive is to take matters into her own hands.

Skulking about the seedy alleyways and taverns of a great city fallen from grace, survival has become a game of steal and lie, or die.

Larina uses her ill-begotten abilities to help the vulnerable, less fortunate souls abandoned by life. An act that fills her with a sense of purpose and pride.

That all changes when the man with the black warhammer comes to town. Now the Storms End Lightning Bolt must decide whether those she has fought so hard to protect will be better off if she ends up dead.

Sadyra – Book 2

Living in the shadows to avoid the brutality of parents harbouring a dark secret, Sadyra must force a violent confrontation if she is to keep her younger sisters from harm's way.

Begrudgingly accepted to work alongside a hardened group of sailors, Sadyra learns how to survive in a ruthless world.

To save her sisters from a fate worse than death, Sadyra goes against everything she feels is right, and life as she knows it will never be the same.

Pollard – Book 3

Called together to prepare for the defense of the kingdom's most sacred resource, the son of Thoril Half-Hand sets out to train the realm's most promising fighters.

To keep the recruits performing as a cohesive unit, Pollard is unprepared to deal with the eclectic personalities of those entrusted to oversee the future defence of Zephyr.

A dark secret assails the band of warriors and their very existence is threatened by creatures they are sworn to protect.

Soul Forge Saga
Soul Forge – Book 1

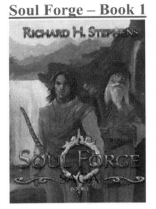

Haunted by the murder of his family, a forgotten hero embarks upon a perilous quest fraught with demons both real and imagined.

Silurian Mintaka only wants another drink, but when the people of Zephyr need someone to save them from an evil sorcerer, he agrees to put aside his bitterness and wreak his revenge.

Deception, betrayal, and fantastic beasts stand in his way. With the fate of the kingdom in the hands of a homicidal lunatic, the only thing left to do is pray.

Wizard of the North –Book 2

What do you get when you disturb a 500-year-old spirit who is in charge of protecting an ancient magic? A death-defying flight to the heart of a serpent's nest.

If pulling a man through the flames wasn't enough, the highest wizard in the land detonates a thousand years of magical lore.

Not sure whether the king survived the firestorm, the people are left with little choice but to place their trust in a corrupt bishop.

A beast is unleashed and the kingdom's future lies in the hands of an eclectic band of companions who have lost their way.

Can an upstart mage, who isn't what they appear, stand against the evil sweeping the realm?

Into the Madness – Book 3

The epic conclusion of the Soul Forge Saga.

How do you survive a confrontation with a wyrm bent on destroying the world? Walk into its gaping maw and fight it from within.

A ragtag group of assassins set out to end the land's suffering only to discover death awaiting them with open arms.

A carefully hidden truth is revealed—the key to the kingdom's salvation if the Wizard of the North and her unstable companion can live long enough to unlock its secret.

Waylaid by an eccentric necromancer, and suffering a tragic loss that threatens to ruin their poorly laid plan, the companions stagger toward a fate no one ever envisioned.

An obsidian nightmare is summoned and Zephyr will never be the same.

Born in Simcoe, Ontario, in 1965, I began writing circa 1974; a bored child looking for something to while away the long, summertime days. My penchant for reading The Hardy Boys led to an inspiration one sweltering summer afternoon when my best friend and I thought, 'We could write one of those.' And so, I did.

As my reading horizons broadened, so did my writing. Star Wars inspired a 600-page novel about outer space that caught the attention of a special teacher who encouraged me to keep writing.

A trip to a local bookstore saw the proprietor introduce me to Stephen R. Donaldson and Terry Brooks. My writing life was forever changed.

At 17, I left high school to join the working world to support my first son. For the next twenty-two years I worked as a shipper at a local bakery. At the age of 36, I went back to high school to complete my education. After graduating with honours at the age of thirty-nine, I became a member of our local Police Service, and worked for 12 years in the provincial court system.

In early 2017, I retired from the Police Service to pursue my love of writing full-time. With the help and support of my lovely wife Caroline and our five children, I have now realized my boyhood dream.

If you wish to keep up to date on new releases, promotions and giveaways, please subscribe to my newsletter by checking out the contact tab on my website.

www.richardhstephens.com

Facebook:	**@richardhughstephens**
Twitter:	**@RHStephens1**
Instagram:	**@richard_h_stephens**
YouTube:	**https://bit.ly/2NKpOhn**

www.amazon.com/author/richardhstephens

Made in the USA
Monee, IL
16 August 2021

75834852R00343